HARD LANDING

The Echo Platoon Series
Book Two

Marliss Melton

Blackhawk photo by Matt Hintsa.
Cover and Book design by eBook Prep
www.ebookprep.com

April, 2015
ISBN: 978-1-61417-725-8

ePublishing Works!
www.epublishingworks.com

DEDICATION

I dedicate this story to the eleven servicemen who died in the Black Hawk helicopter crash that took place on Friday, March 13, 2015. Among those who perished were Marines from the 2nd Special Operations Battalion of the Marine Corps' Special Operations Command at Camp Lejeune. And among those seven Marines was a very special man—Master Sgt. Thomas Saunders, whom I knew when he was just a toddler. As his teenaged neighbor, I babysat Thomas and his sweet younger sister. Even then, I recognized that he was destined to be a remarkable young man and a blessing to his amazing parents. He could not have asked for a finer family. At three, he could recite the names dinosaurs I had never heard of. Last year, the Marine Corps Association and Foundation named him the "critical skills operator of the year." Our country will be forever grateful for his service, but we will never get over his loss and the loss of his brave comrades. Surely God's legions are invincible now.

ACKNOWLEDGMENTS

Most people have heard the famous African saying that it takes a village to raise a child. I have the same opinion about the process of book writing. It takes a group effort to create a story that lives up to its fullest potential. I am so fortunate to have collected a special group of friends and devoted readers who make up my village. My assistant, Wendie Grogan, has seen this story from its infant stages through completion, offering feedback that has shaped its evolution. My editor and best friend Sydney Jane Baily, an author in her own right, also contributed to its maturation. Then there was my cadre of amazing Beta readers—Teresa Jensen, Suzanne Gochenouer, Susan Whitney, Susan Mitchell, Penny Doyle, Pam Orndorff, Kelli Jo Calvert, Kathy Kemp, Joyce McCoig, Graziella Burnie, Jacqueline Jacobs, Susan Fowler, Carey Sullivan, Donna Zenter, and Don Klein, who all contributed in making this story as clean and consistent as possible. My final proofreader Stephanie Pope put the icing on the cake.

I'd be remiss not to thank my area experts—Rachel Fontana who helped me with craft; my son Conrad and sister Loren for contributing to the plot; Carmen who assisted with legal aspects; my father who advised me on military law; and my surgeon, Dr. Harry Kraus (also an author!), for his input on medical treatment and procedure.

Even with this long list of names, I am sure I have overlooked someone else who influenced the growth of this story. To them and to all the members of my village, please accept my sincerest gratitude for your help in raising "my child."

THE
ECHO PLATOON SERIES

Danger Close
Hard Landing
Friendly Fire

ALSO BY MARLISS MELTON

The Taskforce Series
The Protector
The Guardian
The Enforcer

CHAPTER 1

Brantley Adams stepped out of his 1986 Ford Bronco, clutching his contribution to the party—a case of his favorite bottled beer. Checking that he'd cracked the windows of his vintage truck to counteract the sweltering Virginia Beach heat, he locked it up and marched toward the sprawling white brick ranch-style house where his commander lived.

Lieutenant Commander Max McDougal—the Team-guys called him Mad Max whenever he was out of earshot—headed up Brant's task unit. He didn't command all of SEAL Team 12, just Brant's task unit, but he carried a great deal of influence and enjoyed throwing his weight around. Hosting parties on every national holiday was only one of the strategies he used to exercise his power. Brant grumbled under his breath. Here he was, forced to make an appearance at another of his CO's parties when he would rather have been enjoying his day off.

Approaching the man's whitewashed house, he had to admit Max owned a lovely piece of property, about an acre in size and situated on Rudee Lake. The ranch-style home looked humble in comparison to the elaborate homes on either side. The pool in the backyard was one of its nicest features, as was the private pier and the dry dock for Max's boat. A three-car garage housed his Tahoe and his kit car. Max loved his toys. He also laid claim to the prettiest, most pleasant wife on planet Earth, who happened to be Brant's good friend. Unfortunately, the way he saw it, the CO treated his wife as another of his ego-enhancing possessions.

As he traversed the paving stones bisecting the lush lawn, the option of playing hooky slowed his step. These social functions weren't mandatory, but if he wanted to stay on Max's good side—and no one wanted to get on the CO's bad side—he should probably show his face. Not that he needed to kiss the CO's butt, as he had zero desire to be promoted to senior chief—too much responsibility. He was happy to remain a chief for as long as he stayed on the Teams.

Then why am I here? he asked himself. The answer occurred to him at once: He wanted to visit with Rebecca, Max's wife.

As usual, he'd have to be careful not to spend too much time alone with her. He rolled his eyes with annoyance. Max watched Rebecca jealously—not that he needed to. She seemed as true blue as apple pie, and Brant had no intention of making any moves on his commander's wife. Who would be that stupid? He merely wanted to hang out with her—period, the end. Was that asking too much? With a shake of his head, he ascended the front stoop, artfully graced with potted geraniums that were indicative of Rebecca's nurturing touch.

He didn't bother knocking. Everyone knew just to

come on in. Once inside the foyer, he could see straight through the great room and out the wall of rear windows to the throng gathered around the shell-shaped pool. The house itself looked deserted, with the exception of the one dark-haired woman he was hoping to see—*Rebecca.* She entered the eating area via the French doors, and his outlook suddenly improved.

Stepping inside, he cut right through the formal parlor and dining room, keeping out of sight of those out back. Arriving at the rear of the kitchen, he leaned against the opening to watch her slice additional celery for the veggie plate.

What was it about Rebecca McDougal that made him smile inside? He wasn't attracted to her sexually—not much anyway. She wasn't his type, which tended to be blondes with big knockers. Rebecca projected femininity, but she didn't ooze it the way some women did. She represented everything that was honest, considerate, and classy.

He liked the way her glossy brown hair—today caught up in a ponytail—brushed her shoulders when she moved. The length of her neck, the dainty cleft in her chin, and the slight scoop of her nose created a profile he never tired of looking at.

"Hey," he said, cluing her in to his presence.

To his astonishment, she jumped like a startled cat. The knife in her hand came close to slicing her cheek open as she whirled to face him, lifting up her hands simultaneously as if to ward him off.

Whoa, sister.

"Bronco," she breathed, her gaze softening and her hands lowering. "God, you scared me."

"Sorry." He stepped closer, taking in her strained smile and the way she broke eye contact almost right away. Hosting these enormous parties couldn't be easy. The skin of her face, usually soft and incandescent, looked like it was pulled taut over her forehead and especially around her mouth. "How are you doing?" he asked her.

"Good." She glanced at him again, her dimples flashing momentarily, but they promptly disappeared as she took in the box of beer hanging from his left hand. "The cooler's out back, if you want to stick those in there." Turning her back to him, she went back to slicing celery.

Brant didn't move. Everything about her greeting struck him as off. She hadn't asked him how he was doing, for one thing, and she'd never *not* shown an interest in what was going on in his life. An awkward silence ensued, but then she broke it, asking, "Where's your date?"

"Couldn't find one," he replied. Truth was he was dating two women at once, both of them SEAL groupies. The probability of one finding out about the other if he brought either to the party wasn't worth the inevitable drama. Besides, he'd come here to see Rebecca, which neither of his playmates would understand.

"Oh, please," she scoffed. The blade of her knife struck the cutting board at regular intervals. *Thwack. Thwack. Thwack.*

"All right. You got me. I didn't know which one to bring." He hoisted the beer onto the countertop so he could lean a hip against it and watch her work. "In fact, I'm tired of juggling females. I think I'm going to try celibacy for a while." The inspiration simply came to him.

She snorted at what she clearly perceived was a falsehood. "Sure you are."

"You don't believe me?" Her lack of faith wounded him. "You think I can't handle celibacy?"

"Maybe for a day, but I bet you couldn't last a week."

"Really?" Now he wanted to prove her wrong.

She set her knife down, turned her head and contemplated him. Chestnut-brown eyes trekked over his chest, then back up to his face, sparking an unexpected thrill in him. He tamped down his response at once, blaming it on her flowered sundress with its plunging neckline, which showed a surprising amount of cleavage—not that he was looking. He liked and respected Rebecca too much to think of her as anything more than a friend.

"Try it," she suggested, her face hardening in a way that he didn't understand. "Let's see how long you last."

Wow, something had her riled up. Now that he realized as much, he could see a storm brewing behind her pleasant façade.

He sent her a searching look. "What's my sex life got to do with anything?"

She went still, blinked, and looked away. "Nothing." Her sweet mouth twisted into a semblance of a smile. "I'm sorry. I didn't mean to go there." She started to turn away, but he reached for her elbow and drew her back around.

"Hey." It might have been the first time they'd ever touched with the exception of that Christmas Eve, almost three years ago, when the CO introduced his new bride to him. The skin on her forearm was even smoother and softer than her palm had been that day. He squashed the urge to rub his thumb over it. "Something's bothering you, Becca. You want to talk about it?"

Eyes wide, she swallowed visibly. "I'm fine," she said in a tight voice.

When women said that, it meant they were anything

but fine. A weight of concern dropped into the pit of Brant's stomach. He searched her gaze, wishing he could read her mind. "You know you can tell me anything," he murmured.

They had touched on a multitude of topics over the last three years, carrying on conversations so interesting and stimulating that he hadn't wanted them to end. But their conversations had never become too intimate, for obvious reasons.

Her eyelashes, long and curved, swept downward, as she regarded his tanned hand still on her forearm, though she made no move to pull away.

A rush of air and the sudden onslaught of voices warned him that guests were entering the house. With a reluctance he didn't care to question, he released her, picked up the case of beer, and turned away. He hadn't taken two steps before he ran into her husband, followed immediately by Master Chief Kuzinsky, who inspired fear just like Max, but also respect.

The CO's gray eyes glinted as he divided a suspicious look between his chief and his wife.

Seriously? Was the man that possessive that he didn't like seeing his wife alone with his chief? Or was it Brant's reputation with the ladies that bothered him?

"You're late," the man growled. Standing two inches above Brant's six feet, he filled the kitchen with his larger-than-life aura. Nearly as broad as he was tall, with a crop of ash-brown hair and a walrus-like mustache, he reminded Brant of a nor'easter—full of bluster and potential destruction.

Best not to point out that his attendance was supposed to be voluntary.

Behind the CO, Rusty Kuzinsky, who stood a full head shorter than his commander, but was still considered the biggest badass SEAL in history for the number of firefights he'd survived, gave a subtle jerk of his auburn head, indicating Brant should get outside and join the others. Muttering his excuse, Brant sidestepped the two men and slipped out back into the humidity of a late summer's evening.

The scent of barbecued ribs, chlorine, and citronella hit him along with the warm air as he headed for the cooler. Transferring his beer offering into the giant tub of ice, he kept one for himself, twisted off the cap, and looked around as he took his first swallow. His good friend, Bullfrog, floated in the pool atop an inflatable lounge chair. Brant toasted him with his bottle and received a salute from Bullfrog's red, plastic cup. On the other side of the pool, Lt. Sam Sasseville, who went by no other name than Sam, and his pretty wife, Maddy, sat in the shade of the gazebo with their newborn sleeping in a carrier between them. Spying an empty spot next to them, Brant worked his way through the gathering, passing several more members of his unit along the way.

Haiku, the Japanese American communications specialist who often spoke in abstract riddles, was chatting up a gorgeous young woman with a puzzled look on her face.

Brant laughed to himself as he traipsed past them. He made a note to give Haiku a little advice. If you want to impress a girl with a bra size bigger than her IQ, you'd better speak plainly, and maybe just in one-word compliments.

Corey Cooper, leader of Charlie Platoon, gesticulated wildly and weaved on his feet at the edge of the pool while telling a story to a handful of listeners. His audience included Hack, their new techno-geek, Carl Wolfe, the breacher who knew more about explosives than any man alive, Halliday, a former NASCAR driver, and Bamm-Bamm, their linguist, who could speak seven languages when he wasn't yet twenty-one years old.

Brant didn't intentionally push Corey Cooper into the pool. But he did brush a little too closely, and the junior lieutenant, who'd yet to prove that he could replace his injured and retired predecessor, flailed and lost his balance, splashing everyone who'd been listening to him as he toppled backwards into the water.

"Bronco!" Maddy scolded, shaking her golden mane in exasperation.

Brant didn't bother defending his innocence. Sam's wife wouldn't believe him anyway, since she considered him the bad boy of Echo Platoon. His nickname, Bronco, didn't come from the fact that he drove an old truck by that name, but from his pre-Navy experience as a bronc rider. It was true he'd been around the arena a time or two.

Once upon a time, he'd gotten his thrills competing in rodeos in his home state of Montana. But then he'd given up trying to follow in his famous father's footsteps and fought hard to join the ranks of the U.S. Navy SEALs. Now he got his kicks descending on the enemy in the middle of the night and scaring them to death—quite literally. As rigorous and uncomfortable as platoon life got, he'd had more fun in the past eight years than he could have ever imagined.

Sam clasped his extended hand. "I was about to give up on you, brother," he chided with a cadence in his voice that betrayed his Cuban heritage.

Brant dropped into the chair beside him, while sweeping his gaze over the assemblage by habit, looking for unseen dangers. Of course, there weren't any, unless you considered the possibility that a drunken Corey Cooper appeared to be drowning in the shallow end. On closer inspection, he was only showing off his impressive lung capacity. Cooper held the team record for holding his breath underwater—anything to win the approbation of his teammates.

Brant looked over at Sam, relieved that his own platoon leader was a man he could look up to. "I had decided not to come," he admitted. Of their own accord, his eyes swung toward the sliding glass door where he could see into the kitchen. There, he noticed his commander wore the same hard expression that he wore at work when giving orders, only now he was talking to Rebecca.

"She asked about you," Sam muttered, following his gaze.

Intrigued, he looked curiously back at Sam. "What'd she say?"

Sam shrugged. "Just asked if you were coming."

They both turned their gazes toward Rebecca as she exited the sliding glass door bearing the freshly loaded veggie tray. The corners of her mouth turned up in a smile that failed to tease out her dimples. Concern tugged at Brant for a second time, and he wondered again what might be wrong. Watching her fuss over the food display then pick up discarded paper plates, he realized she wasn't mingling with the guests the way she usually did.

"Dude, you'd better stop staring at her," Sam warned out of the corner of his mouth.

He jerked his gaze away, encountering Max's glacial stare as their CO stepped outside to rejoin the party. As Brant watched, he turned with a counterfeit grin toward a knot of officers of equal and senior ranking to himself. When it came to brownnosing with the upper brass, no one could outshine Max.

Brant drained his beer in one long swallow and stood up. "Looks like I'd better rescue Cooper," he observed. He whipped off his T-shirt and kicked off his flip-flops, leaving him in only his swim trunks, which he'd worn in lieu of shorts.

Taking three long steps, he dropped feetfirst into the five-foot depth, letting the cool, clear water encapsulate him. He emptied his lungs of air so that his lean body mass carried him to the bottom of the pool. There, he quietly observed the world from a different perspective.

Bullfrog's red lounge chair floated quietly overhead, with his long, narrow feet paddling him leisurely about. Those feet, matched with Bullfrog's lean length, made him a fast and tireless swimmer—hence the nickname Bullfrog, which was especially fitting since his first name was Jeremiah, the amphibian hero of the famed song.

A trio of women sat in the water on the steps, their shapely thighs and calves visible for Brant's viewing pleasure. Right beside him, also at the bottom of the pool, Corey Cooper had turned his head to regard him warily. The grin Brant sent him had Cooper jackknifing toward the surface for a much-needed breath.

Brant waited for the lieutenant to refill his lungs before he jerked Cooper's feet out from under him. And then the roughhousing began.

Cooper's lankiness gave him a slight advantage, allowing him to sip in quick gulps of air by pushing off the bottom of the pool to crest the surface. Brant didn't always have that luxury. Nor could he hold his breath for five minutes like Cooper could, but what he lacked in length and lung capacity, he made up for in agility, honed reflexes, and eight years of experience compared to Cooper's three. In an impressively short amount of time—and to the accompanying cheers of his teammates—he twisted Cooper into a hold the Charlie Platoon leader couldn't break and made him cry uncle.

Huffing from the effort it had taken to trounce the younger man, Brant ruffled Cooper's hair good-naturedly. Out the corner of his eye, he spied Rebecca smiling at him wryly, and he checked the urge to send her a victor's grin. Every eye at the party was trained on him, making that unwise, so he grinned at Sam instead.

Then he heaved himself out of the water to drip dry. Only then did he allow himself to glance back at Rebecca, who was staring at his torso. She jerked her gaze away at once, but it was too late. He'd seen that stunned and hungry look on other women's faces. The gratification that slammed through him was as satisfying as it was inappropriate.

Water dripped off his hair and slid down his back. *No!* he told himself sternly, in the voice of the grandfather who'd helped his single mother raise him. *That woman is off-limits.*

Not because she was married—hell, he'd had affairs with plenty of married women. Not even because she was his CO's wife and hitting on her was tantamount to committing suicide. But, oddly enough, because he really liked her. Respected her. The code he'd established from the age that he'd become sexually active was inviolable. He *never* had sex with a woman that he truly liked. That way he'd never make the mistake his father made.

He'd been told by other guys that his code made no sense. To him it made perfect sense. He could be exactly like the man his father was—charismatic, athletic, and fun to be with, but with one big difference. He'd never break a woman's heart like his father had broken his mother's when he'd made her believe in a future together.

The trick was never to do that. Never spend quality

time with any one of them; that way they never got ideas that led them to heartbreak.

His approach to relationships had worked beautifully for twelve years. He saw no reason to alter it. But what if Rebecca was right? What if he'd become such a player that he couldn't go without sex for a week?

Nah, he'd done that plenty of times. Every time he went on an operation, in fact, where access to women was impossible, and he had no choice. *But that's different*, his conscience argued, *from voluntarily going without*.

Unsettled by his potential character flaw, he leaped to his feet to fetch something to eat.

An hour later, thoroughly air-dried, satiated with beer and bratwurst, he sat in the shadows of the trellis holding Maddy and Sam's baby so the couple could enjoy a moment in the pool. Baby Melinda lay in the crook of his arm, wearing a tiny pink cotton jumper. Her cheeks had gotten plump in the two weeks since she'd been born. She might look just like a doll with her dark hair and feathery eyelashes, but Brant mused that the critical way she inspected him betrayed burgeoning intelligence and her mother's discriminating taste.

He made a face at the baby to gauge her reaction. Her intense stare resembled a frown of disapproval. Wondering what she'd do if he crossed his eyes and stuck out his tongue simultaneously, he tried it. The reaction he got wasn't one that he expected as she eliminated suddenly and powerfully into her diaper. Then, to his consternation, her face crumpled, and she loosed a whimper of discomfort that grew into a plaintive wail.

Oh, crap—literally.

Alarmed, he sought to catch Maddy's or Sam's eye,

but they were soaking in the far end of the pool, totally engrossed in each other. Someone had cranked up the stereo, and the music drowned out the baby's cry, which would normally have brought Maddy flying to the rescue.

Bullfrog, still floating on the lounge chair, took note of his predicament and raised his cup to toast him. Brant cast his gaze around for a pacifier or a bottle—anything to stop the baby's crying. Hell if he was going to change her diaper. He was about to get up and carry Melinda over to her parents when a shadow fell over him, cast by the sinking sun and Rebecca's petite but toned frame.

"Need help?" she drawled. Amusement sparkled in her eyes.

"Uh, yeah. I think she soiled herself."

He came out of his chair to pass off the baby, and his knuckles accidently brushed the curve of her breast. The sudden appearance of her nipples against the fabric of her sundress was as instantaneous as it was unmistakable. Keeping her gaze locked on the baby, she pretended not to notice, but the telltale pulse fluttering in the hollow between her delicate collar bones betrayed her heightened awareness, while the sight of her erect nipples kept him tongue-tied.

Damn it, Adams. Are you really such a horny bastard?

The baby fell immediately quiet. Of course she did. Rebecca worked as a nurse in the ER, and her sweet face was a reflection of her nurturing nature.

"Don't worry, we'll get you changed," she crooned, rocking Melinda with instinctive skill and making Brant wonder why she had no children of her own yet.

"Why don't you and Max have a kid yet?" He blurted his thoughts out loud without meaning to.

She visibly stiffened. "It just hasn't happened," she

answered vaguely.

Low blow, Adams. "I'm sorry—" He started to apologize, but she waved him off and turned away to pick up Melinda's diaper bag.

"You sure Maddy wants you to do that?" he asked as she spread a cloth on a lounge chair nearby and laid the baby down on it, clearly intending to change her diaper.

"I babysat Melinda just the other day." Just the same, she checked over her shoulder. "See, Maddy's fine with it."

Brant followed her gaze and found the new mother observing them with a grateful smile.

He then watched Rebecca whisk away the soiled diaper, wipe down the area with competent thoroughness, and gird the baby in a fresh diaper, and he couldn't help but admire her gracefulness.

The sinking sun put a luster in her dark hair. A light layer of perspiration shone on her forehead and on the smooth skin of her breasts which her gaping neckline revealed to him. Strange how he knew her well enough to sense that she couldn't wait to have children of her own. What an incredible mother she would make, too. Maybe it was Max who wasn't ready.

"There, all done," she declared, putting the diaper bag away and lifting the baby in her arms again. Meeting Brant's gaze, she sent him a rueful smile. "That wasn't so hard, was it?"

Ignoring her question, he put one of his own to her. "You want to tell me what's eating you tonight?"

Her rueful smile promptly fled. Catching her lower lip between her teeth, she glanced over her shoulder at Max before turning back to him with a crease between her eyebrows. "You have to promise not to tell anyone else," she murmured earnestly.

He sensed her nervousness spiking. "Of course."

She looked down at the baby, fiddling with her bib. "I saw something last night that I don't think I was supposed to see." Her confession was so quiet he had to lean forward to catch every softly spoken word.

"What do you mean? What'd you see exactly?"

"Max was using our home computer because his laptop is in the shop. He walked away from it, and that's when I saw it."

Brant found himself glancing across the expansive patio, over the glistening surface of the shell-shaped pool and Bullfrog's long body splayed upon the floating lounge chair, to Max's rectangular frame at one end of an outdoor table. He was talking animatedly with Joe Montgomery, the HQ commander of Team 12.

"What did you see?" He figured she must have caught Max communicating with a woman.

"An investment account under Max's name with over fifty thousand dollars in it."

His eyebrows shot up. "That's a nice chunk of change."

"Right. Only, I've never heard of this investment company."

"You mean he's hiding money from you?"

She gave a slow nod. "Not only that, but we used to be in debt, and now we're not. Max has a tendency to buy things we can't afford, like the boat and the kit car. He took out a home equity line of credit on the house to pay for them and our monthly payments were huge. I thought we might lose the house to foreclosure, which would have embarrassed him to no end. Suddenly, the equity line is all paid off and he has money to spare."

Her confession piqued Brant's interest. "Does he know you saw the account?"

"Yes, he caught me looking at it." Her voice was grim, and he sensed it might have been a little scary to be caught by the CO. She took a deep breath and added, "He said that the money belonged to the task unit."

"What?" He scoffed at the falsehood. "That's impossible. Our expenditures go through the Naval Special Warfare Group. What was the name of the investment firm?"

"Emile Victor DuPonte," she murmured, looking more torn by the moment for having told him.

Brant didn't need to say what she had to be thinking. If Max was hiding a sum that large from her, what else was he hiding?

"I'm so sorry, Becca." He wished he had the right to give her the hug she clearly needed.

She looked up from the baby, her eyes full of concern. "Please don't tell anyone."

"I swear, I won't," he promised.

She nodded, glanced over her shoulder, and saw that Maddy and Sam were climbing out of the pool, headed in their direction.

Looking back at Brant she added, "Remember, you promised."

She ought to know by now that she could trust him. "Not a word," he swore.

CHAPTER 2

Parking in their three-car garage, Rebecca exited her car and promptly disabled the home security system. The absence of Max's black Tahoe suggested he was still at work, but she wasn't naïve enough to just assume that was the case. It was just like him to mislead her into thinking he wasn't home, when, in fact, he was there studying her in secret. With the system disarmed, she entered the house, moving quietly through the laundry room and into the kitchen, listening for him.

Mental games. Max played them with his SEALs to keep them on their toes; he inflicted them on his wife, too—sick bastard. She wished she had known before she married him that he would begin treating her like one of his underlings before the first year was out.

As good as Max was at leading his men, he was lousy at inspiring tenderness within the marriage. Simple trips to the grocery store became tests she inevitably failed if she forgot an item, no matter how insignificant. A mistake in pairing up his socks gave rise to harsh lectures on the importance of paying attention to detail.

If she were a fledgling Navy SEAL training for battle, she might appreciate Max's attempts to mold her into the perfect warrior. But she wasn't a warrior. She was a woman, and she would never be a perfect wife, though not for lack of trying. God knew, she had tried! But the more effort she put into pleasing him, the more faults he seemed to find. It had dawned on her, slowly at first, then more frequently and with increasing bitterness, that she would never be able to please him sufficiently. Never measure up to some ideal he had in his head. Lately, he had begun to extract retribution for her failures—no staying after work for yoga for a week; no trip to Hawaii to visit her mother; forcing her to wash and wax the car when she forgot to fill the tank on her way home from work.

She'd bought self-help books. She tried to read parts of them out loud to him, to no avail. He'd made it clear *he* wasn't the one with the problems. She'd started visiting a counselor religiously. And she had prayed. She'd thought that with patience, she could teach Max how to be a loving, tender husband. But after two years, she was ready to admit that her commander wasn't going to change. Leaving him had become the only option. It was that or live a life of loneliness punctuated by fear of failure and his peculiar punishments.

Stumbling across a secret bank account full of money and in his name had seemed a blessing. If only she could see it again, she could take a picture and prove that he was hiding money from her. That, in turn, could lead to grounds for divorce, or so she hoped. Where had it come from anyway?

This was the first night all week that she had beat him home, giving her the perfect opportunity to search online. Leaving her nursing shoes by the dryer, she tiptoed through the kitchen in her socks. With the alarm turned off, she didn't worry that the motion-sensing cameras were filming her trek across the great room. They were meant to be a deterrent to thieves, but Rebecca was convinced Max used them more to keep an eye on her, taking her to task, for instance, if she dared to take a nap after work rather than starting on his supper.

Apart from her own stealthy footfalls and the ticking of the clock in the parlor, the rooms stood still and quiet, suggesting that she was, in fact, alone—at least for a short while. She let out the breath she was holding.

Slipping into his office, she dropped into the leather desk chair. Her heartbeat drowned out the humming of the computer as she waited for the CPU to boot up and for their network to connect with the internet. Max's laptop had contracted a virus and been sent to the repair shop, forcing him to use their home PC. If not for that circumstance, she might never have known that he was hoarding money she didn't know about.

Opening her Facebook profile, just in case Max sprang out of nowhere, she accessed the browser's history, hoping to find a direct link to his account.

There were two obstacles to leaving Max. The first was Virginia's old-fashioned policy that she had to have grounds for leaving him—either adultery, abusive behavior, desertion, or the fact that he'd been convicted of a crime. While Max's mental games were mildly abusive, it would be her word against his regarding the way he chose to punish her. She couldn't rely on a judge to view Max's controlling tactics as abusive. As far as she knew he wasn't cheating on her. He hadn't deserted her. That left his being convicted of a crime, which wasn't likely ever to happen unless she caught him doing something illegal.

The second obstacle was that if she packed her bags and moved out to avoid more of Max's retaliation, he could accuse her of deserting *him*, which would likely result in her losing her half of their marital assets, plus any right to spousal support.

In other words, she was stuck in her present hellhole unless she caught Max having an affair or committing criminal actions.

One day she had dared to express her marital discontent in the hopes that Max would settle for a no-fault divorce. He had replied that she would "rue the day" she ever mentioned a divorce again.

His vague but dire threat had sent her imagination running amuck. Intuition whispered that he would harm her somehow if she dared to defy his wishes. One thing she had discovered about Max was the *no one* defied him and got away with it.

Leaning toward the monitor, she realized that the page she had viewed the other night with his account number on it had been deleted. Max had deleted the pages from the browser's history! If that didn't suggest he had something serious to hide, then nothing did. Disappointed, she leaned back into the heavy chair, thinking.

Perhaps there were other secrets Max was keeping from her, other than those necessitated by his job. Closing the browser, she got up and left the office.

Curiosity carried her to their master suite, the last of four bedrooms situated off an L-shaped hallway. Light and airy, the room provided her sanctuary after long days in the ER. She had decorated it in lovely browns and teals in deference to her husband, whose only comment had been criticism that the curtains were too sheer.

Approaching Max's dresser, she peeked into the

elaborately carved teak box he'd brought back from his excursion to Malaysia. Brimming with business cards, pens, and loose change, she doubted it would yield any mysteries, as Max was careful to leave his work at the Spec Ops building on base, where he worked. Riffling through the contents, she found nothing suspicious.

Still musing, she strode into their beige and burgundy bathroom to use the facilities. As she washed her hands, her gaze settled on Max's bottle of Viagra pills, hidden behind a row of vitamin bottles. She picked it up, surprised to see only a handful of pills remaining out of an original supply of thirty.

The walls of the room shifted closer. Her heart beat a little faster. There were more pills missing than the number of times they'd had sex in the last year. Had he spilled them into the toilet by mistake? Or was Max having sex with other women?

Oddly enough, the thought of him cheating inspired less dismay than the realization that the missing pills didn't constitute proof of adultery. She would have to hire a detective who would then have to catch Max in the act before she could claim infidelity on his part.

She put the bottle back and left the bathroom.

The framed photograph of the two of them on their wedding day drew her toward the dresser on which it sat. Max, wearing his dress-white uniform with its array of medals and ribbons, had looked so formidable next to his much younger wife. Twelve years her senior, it had never occurred to her until just then that she may have been looking for a father figure, someone with an excellent work ethic and proven track record. Someone who wouldn't leave his family and shirk his responsibilities the way her father had.

My mistake, she conceded. She had clearly married Max for the wrong reasons, never once guessing how difficult her marriage would become. If only she could simply breathe and smile and enjoy life without constantly worrying about his ridiculous expectations. And worse, his demeaning punishments intended to teach her to do better.

Why not just leave him and let him accuse her of abandoning him? Did she really need half the marital assets and spousal support? No, but she had emptied her own savings account the year before to keep their house out of foreclosure. She would never get that money back if she up and left. Plus, there was Max's threat to consider. *You will rue the day that you mention a divorce to me again.* What had he meant, exactly? She shivered at the pictures that flashed through her mind.

I'm stuck, she thought.

A vision of Bronco's smiling face pushed aside the frightening images and gave rise to inexplicable sorrow.

Don't be stupid. You don't want him.

No, of course not. She only wanted to be more like him—carefree and unencumbered. And, on days like this one, it didn't seem like that would ever be the case.

Digging his heels into the carpet, Brant resisted Bethany's attempt to tug him down the short hallway toward his bedroom. Their take-out dinner was consumed, the movie was over, and Bethany wanted what she'd come over for—a satisfying booty call.

Ordinarily, he'd have been happy to oblige. Activity in the bedroom didn't involve talking any more than watching a movie did. And bringing women to orgasm as many times as was humanly feasible was a challenge he never tired of pursuing. In fact, he'd acquired unparalleled skills in that area, and Bethany was clearly angling for the action he could give her, except he didn't feel like obliging her tonight.

"What's wrong with you?" She thrust her lower lip out in a pout that would normally have caused him to cave but which he now found rather annoying. She gave up tugging and threw herself at him instead, rubbing her oversized breasts against his chest.

Feeling her hardened nipples begging for his attention did make his libido stir. But then he remembered Rebecca's taunt—*I bet you couldn't last a week,* and immediately his ardor dwindled. He peeled Bethany's hands from the back of his neck and set her at arm's length. "I have to get up early tomorrow."

"So?"

Getting up early was standard operating procedure, and he'd never let that fact get in the way of a good romp before. "I need to catch up on my sleep," he insisted. "I'm sorry."

Her jaw dropped in astonishment. "Are you serious?"

"Yeah." He sent her an apologetic grimace, even as he grabbed her hand and led her toward the front door, snatching her purse off the back of the couch and looping the strap over her shoulder. "I'll be in touch," he promised.

"Oh, and I'm supposed to be grateful for that?" she mocked.

Her evident distress made him feel bad. "I guess not. Sorry." He reached for the doorknob, but she blocked his attempt to turn it.

"Someone else is coming over here," she guessed, her eyes snapping with suspicion. "It's that mixed-race chick, Christiana, isn't it?"

In spite of his efforts to live a double life, his sex partners had apparently still caught wind of each other. "No, Bethany," he assured her. "No one else is coming over. I just want to be alone, I promise."

"Liar!" In the next instant her purse clocked him hard across the face.

Damn, that hurt, but he supposed he deserved it—if not for his actions tonight, then in general.

Realizing what she'd done and looking suddenly fearful of reprisal, she reached for the door herself and scuttled through it.

He stuck his head out to watch her flee toward the stairs in the breezeway separating his apartment from the others on this level.

"Careful in those heels," he called out as she started down them in her stilettos.

"Fuck you!" she yelled back at him, turning just enough to flip him the bird, her face contorted with anger and pain.

Figuring he'd seen the last of Bethany, he was only mildly surprised to realize there was nothing about her he would miss. Still, he cringed at the pain he'd caused—even if it was only because she wanted good sex. But if it was because she'd pinned hopes on him or let her heart get involved, then he felt even worse. Despite his very best efforts to keep from hurting any woman, he was apparently just like his father, after all.

"Not anymore," he murmured, though he wasn't sure what he meant by his own words. All he knew was when he pictured himself through Rebecca's eyes, he couldn't see why she'd ever befriended him. He closed his apartment door and leaned against it.

Thinking of Rebecca led to wondering what Max was up to, keeping such a large sum of money secret from his wife. Who or what was Emile Victor DuPonte, anyway?

He glanced at his charging cell phone and

contemplated calling Rebecca to check up on her. She worked twelve-hour days in the ER—a job that required nerves of steel, in his opinion. By this time of night, she was undoubtedly at home, but then so was Max. Even if he had her number, calling his commander's wife would find him transferred to a West Coast Team inside of a week. Dumb idea.

He plucked up his phone wanting to call someone, anyone. He thought about Hack, the new techno geek, and wondered if that man could figure out who Emile Victor DuPonte was. Brant had already Googled the name to no avail. Accessing his contacts, he dialed his new teammate.

Stuart "Hack" Rudolph answered after only one ring. "Chief?"

"Yeah, it's me." Brant turned to survey his messy living room. Take-out boxes still littered the coffee table. The couch cushions were all topsy-turvy. He went to tidy up while talking. "Are you busy right now? I could use a personal favor." He carried the boxes and plastic utensils to the trash and dumped them.

"Nah, just messing with some code, nothing too important. What d' you need?"

Hack's peculiar accent took getting used to. Northwest Vermont, he'd explained the day they'd met when Brant had listened to him and blurted, "What the fuck, dude?"

"This is going to sound strange," Brant prepped him, straightening the pillows on the couch, "but can you tell me more about the name Emile Victor DuPonte? I think it's an investment company, but I can't find it on Google. I want to know where it's located and what it invests in." Mentioning that Max owned the account was out of the question.

"Sure thing, Bronco," Hack said, with no question

in his voice. "I'll see what I can do."

"Thanks. I owe you a six-pack."

"Bottle of red wine," Hack corrected him. "Penfolds Bin 2 Shiraz. It'll cost you twenty-seven bucks."

"Don't sell yourself short," Brant protested.

Hack chuckled and hung up.

Brant carried his phone to the sliding glass door and stepped out onto his balcony. From his apartment, situated three blocks from the beach front, south of the congested boardwalk, he could smell and hear the ocean, even if he couldn't see it. A neighborhood of overpriced homes blocked his view. With a prick of envy, he thought about Max's waterfront property and how he could never buy anything like that—not on a chief's salary. Did that make him less of a man in Rebecca's eyes?

Lowering himself into a deck chair, he pondered what to do. Since cavorting with playmates evidently took up most of his free time, he'd forgotten how to amuse himself.

He could invite Bullfrog over. The first class petty officer was probably reading one of his philosophy books with Brazilian guitar music playing softly in the background. Bullfrog didn't waste his free time on women; he spent it broadening his consciousness. It was a wonder he and Brant were even friends, considering what polar opposites they were.

Brant hesitated, recalling his promise to Rebecca not to tell a soul about her secret. He hadn't revealed too much to Hack, had he? And talking to Bullfrog was like consulting with his conscience. His friend didn't gossip—ever. Therefore, her secret would still be safe, his promise still intact—in the spirit in which it was given, if not technically.

The tinny ringing coming from his phone made him realize he'd dialed Bullfrog without making a conscious decision. His friend's distracted greeting confirmed what he was up to.

"Hey, I want to talk to you," Brant said. "Can you pop over?"

Conveniently, Bullfrog lived in the same apartment complex, same floor, on the opposite side of the breezeway, leaving him with few excuses not to comply.

"Are you alone?" his friend inquired warily.

Brant had made the mistake of inviting him over once when he'd brought home a pair of twins. That was before he realized his friend didn't do one-night stands.

"I *will* be alone if you don't come over," he pointed out.

He heard Bullfrog heave a sigh. Brant pictured him shutting a paperback. The man refused to get an e-reader. "Be there shortly."

Hours later, Brant's vibrating phone woke him from a deep sleep. He cracked an eye and glanced at the time—fifteen minutes before his alarm was due to go off.

Was this a call to action? Conditions were ripe for a hurricane to pop up in the Atlantic, and if one should ever head to Cuba, the SEALs would respond to execute a mission they'd been planning for a year. But it took days for a hurricane to move across the ocean, so that couldn't be the reason for the call.

Brant groaned. He and Bullfrog had stayed up way into the night, brainstorming all the possible reasons for Max to have a secret stash of money. He plucked his phone off the charger and peered at the caller ID. This wasn't a call to go wheels up. It was only Hack getting back to him.

"Yeah." He sat up hoping to clear the cobwebs from his brain.

"I think I found what you're looking for," Hack said without preamble.

Brant rubbed his bleary eyes. "Dude, I didn't mean for you to stay up all night working on it."

"No worries, Chief. I woke up ten minutes early and found what you're looking for. So get this: Emile Victor DuPonte is the name of a Swiss investment company."

Holy shit. Max had opened an overseas account? Well, well, that was a big no-no for members in the Spec Ops community.

"But that's not all," Hack added, bringing Brant more fully awake. "It looks like the company's not even authentic."

"What do you mean?"

"It's not recognized by FINMA, the Swiss Financial Market Supervisory Authority, as a legitimate asset management company. So maybe it's dirty, or something."

Jesus. Brant's thoughts raced in several directions at once. Could he take what he'd learned straight to the Naval Criminal Investigative Service? "Looks like I owe you that bottle of wine," he said.

"Lucky for you it's on sale right now at the Oceana NEX. Pendfolds Bin 2 Shiraz," Hack reminded him. "It'll only cost you seventeen, if you hurry."

"I'll buy you a bottle tonight," Brant promised. Heck, he'd surprise the geek and buy him two. "Thanks for the research. Please don't mention this subject with anyone else."

"No problem." Hack's voice took on a serious tone. "Hey, if you need me again, don't hesitate to call any time, Chief."

How cool to have a techno genius in his corner, but Brant hoped he wouldn't need to take him up on his offer. What he ought to do was go straight to NCIS and let them delve into Max's business. But what evidence did he have besides hearsay?

Max wasn't stupid. NCIS had absolutely no jurisdiction overseas except on Navy bases, which was probably why Max had opened a foreign account in the first place. But why would he even need one unless he was up to something illegal?

That certainly put Rebecca in an awkward spot. Max had to be worried that she would tell someone what she'd seen. Imagine how he'd react if he knew she'd told Brant already.

Disturbing visions propelled him out of bed and into the shower. Maybe there was an innocent explanation for all this, but what if there wasn't? What if Max was involved in something like arms dealing, for instance? Who would protect Rebecca from being dragged down with him?

She'd told him that her father had died when she was a teen. Her widowed mother had recently married a Coast Guard officer who'd been promptly transferred to Hawaii. Rebecca had no siblings. She was bound to have friends at the hospital where she worked, but none of them knew the real Max well enough to empathize with her situation.

She needs me. The realization had him standing taller as he soaped his chest. Maybe he couldn't provide the kind of life her affluent husband gave her, but he could lend her a listening ear when she needed one and offer her support and protection, if it came to that.

Rebecca prayed beneath her breath as the ER doctor gritted his teeth and applied the pads of the defibrillator one last time to the patient sprawled across the gurney.

"Come on!" Dr. Jack Edmonds bellowed. Sweat slid

from his temple to his clenched jaw at the exertion he'd expended trying to revive the patient's heart.

She harbored little hope that one more shock would bring the patient back to life. Given his emaciated body and the needle marks tracking the insides of his arms, this particular male wasn't in any shape to recover from the overdose that had stopped his heart, notwithstanding the fact that he couldn't be a day over thirty.

How sad. Here, in the ER, she saw it all the time. Drugs ranging from acid to crack to heroin had ruined the lives of so many people.

"He's gone." The young doctor's shoulders slouched with defeat as he turned off the heart monitor. "Time of death—11:58 A.M."

Rebecca pulled up the sheet from the gurney and draped it gingerly over the man's half-naked body. His tanned, weathered skin and sun-bleached hair suggested he'd spent a great deal of time combing the waterfront for leftover food, perhaps stealing or begging for money to get his next fix.

"Do we have any ID on him?" Dr. Edmonds asked, frowning down at the wrist band with the name John Doe typed on it and no date of birth.

"The paramedics said they searched his pockets and couldn't find any," the nurse's aide stammered. This was only her second day in the ER, and she looked distinctly green around the gills.

Rebecca regretfully covered the man's face. He had to have family somewhere who would want to know what had happened to him.

"Damn waste," the doctor swore, turning to push the defibrillator back into the corner.

Tears filmed the aide's eyes as she turned away to sterilize the defibrillator's components.

"You did your best, Jack," Rebecca assured the

young doctor. "Looks like he's been trying to escape this world for some time," she added, picking up the arm that hung off the gurney and tucking the sheet around it.

Jack Edmonds nodded his agreement. "Have him taken to the morgue, would you?" he requested in a gruff voice. "Maybe his fingerprints will tell us who he is."

"Yes, sir," she replied, wheeling the heavy gurney down the hall in search of the orderly. Discovering that the orderly had just gone on break, she opted to take the dead man to the morgue herself. Under normal circumstances, she would have stayed out of the morgue at any cost. It was one area of the hospital that she steadfastly avoided. However, her desire to reunite the dead man with his loved ones prompted her to overcome her squeamishness and push the gurney into the elevator.

Arriving in the basement seconds later, she delivered him into the hands of an affable young tech named TJ, who gave his word to let her know if someone should come to claim the body. Wondering how TJ managed to keep a smile on his face while working in such a morbid place, Rebecca fled upstairs in search of her composure.

The fate of the homeless man was still on her mind as she departed the hospital at the end of her workday. How did families become so estranged that fathers, sons, and brothers simply cut off all ties and disappeared?

The event brought back a day she would rather forget. On a spring morning during her senior year of high school, her mother had received a phone call that had sent them both into shock. Turning to Rebecca, she had clasped her hands and explained that a man going by the name Harold Rivers had died in a hospital in Minneapolis. Given his description, he was possibly Rebecca's father.

Braking at a busy intersection, Rebecca closed her eyes while waiting for the light to turn green. She could still feel the strength in her mother's fingers as they prayed together that the Harold Rivers in Minneapolis wasn't her father—that he was still out there somewhere searching for himself, working out his demons. They'd driven all the way to Minneapolis to see the body for themselves and, alas, they had found him.

The car behind her honked, startling Rebecca's eyes open. She sped forward, telling herself she only needed to get home. It wasn't always easy to shake off the trauma that took place in the ER. In this case, the homeless man's death had dredged up painful memories, making events that had happened a decade ago feel as achingly fresh as if they had taken place yesterday. She knew she would feel better after she made her way to the end of their pier and let the gentle lap of the inlet waves soothe her.

But when she turned into her driveway, a black BMW blocked her entrance to the garage. Who could this be? She pushed the remote control to open the garage and waited. Max's Tahoe was already parked inside. He'd beat her home today.

She immediately thought of his dwindling Viagra supply. *What if there's a woman inside?*

But then she realized he wouldn't be so stupid as to invite a woman over, not when his wife was due home from work at any moment. With a sigh, she killed her car's engine, intending to find out for herself who their visitor was.

She had just put one foot on the driveway when the front door opened and a dark-haired, swarthy skinned man stumbled out at an accelerated rate. Catching himself before knocking one of her geranium pots off the porch, he drew himself to his full height, directed a smirk over his shoulder, and smoothed his rumpled suit jacket. The door slammed shut behind him.

Max had tossed someone out of their home!

Startled and uncertain what to do, Rebecca froze with her car door open. The stranger started off the stoop, his stride faltering when he observed her staring at him. One corner of his mouth kicked up, growing into an oily smile as he visibly pulled himself together and sauntered in her direction.

"Good evening, madam." He tipped her a nod as he drew up next to her partially open door.

"Hello. I'll move over so you can pull out," she offered, pulling her foot back into the car.

"There's no hurry." His dialect came straight off the streets of northern New York City. Dark eyes fastened on her face and glittered with private thoughts. He jutted out a hand comprised of sausage-like fingers. "You must be Max's wife."

Rebecca ignored the hand. "Yes, I am. And you are?" Curiosity alone prompted her to ask since every instinct warned her to distance herself immediately.

"You can call me Tony." He dropped his hand with a slight sneer. "We'll meet again," he predicted, sending her a wink.

She rather hoped not. Shutting the car door between them, she prevented him from saying anymore as she started her engine.

In the same instant, Max emerged from the house like an enraged bull. He'd finally realized his visitor was still trespassing. Tony sprinted to his car, jumped into the driver's seat, and locked his door before Max could wrench it open.

Terrified that her husband would smash out the driver's side window and beat the man to a pulp,

Rebecca swung out of the way, clearing the path for the BMW to reverse out of their driveway. It exited at top speed before screeching to a halt. Its tires spun as it gained purchase on the smooth asphalt and zipped away. As leery as Tony had been of her husband, he sent him a saucy salute as he drove away.

Sitting stunned in her Jetta, Rebecca flinched as Max transferred his incredulous gaze from the retreating BMW to her watchful expression. He raised an arm and gestured for her to park her car in the garage, *now*. She complied, nosing into the quiet garage and cutting off the motor. Max immediately yanked her car door open and demanded, "What did he say to you?"

"Nothing much." Her heart beat fast and thready. Intuition whispered that the odd visitor had something to do with Max's secret money. "He said his name was Tony and that we'd meet again."

"The hell you will." A thundercloud settled over Max's scowling face. "Forget about him," he ordered, reaching into the car and pulling her out of it.

At this point, he usually asked her about work that day. She had learned that, while he asked, he didn't really listen to her reply. He only wanted to get to the part where he talked about himself. But not today.

Today, he armed the security system located in the garage, tugged her into the house, and shut the door. Then he stood over her, scowling heavily, clearly deciding what to say. "I don't know who that man was," he finally declared.

It was so obviously a lie.

"If you see him again, I want you to call me, ASAP."

Not the police, though. Of course not.

"Is he dangerous?" she asked.

"He might be. He says he knows I'm a SEAL and

that he resents the military actions taken in the Middle East."

"So, he's a terrorist." Off the top of her head, she couldn't think of any terrorists with Italian names.

"Perhaps. Just swear that you'll tell me if you see him again."

"Okay," she agreed, if only to dissipate his ire.

"I mean it." He caught her upper arms in a crushing grip and gave her a shake. "You see anything suspicious, you let me know. Got it?"

She was looking at something suspicious right now.

"Got it." She sent him a forced smile that resulted in her release. As he spun away and stalked across the living areas to the office, she rubbed her abused arms and knew without a doubt that her happily-ever-after was over—if it had ever existed at all.

But then, deep within the darkness of her heart, one bright hope flared to life. If Max was convicted of criminal behavior—and it was starting to look that way—then she would have grounds for divorce.

CHAPTER 3

———◆———

Brant browsed the wine selection in the back of the Exchange on Oceana Naval Air Station. There didn't seem to be any rhyme or reason to the display. Nor had he thought to look up what the bottle looked like before heading off to the Exchange. Kicking himself for his lack of foresight, he turned and raked the store for a sales associate.

The familiar sight of his commander's square head incited a prick of resentment. Here it was twenty hundred hours on a Friday night and he was still subjected to Max's presence. It didn't matter that the man was standing clear on the other side of the open shopping space, in the electronics section. Brant could feel him sucking the energy out of the room, like a tornado sweeping up everything in its path.

He was about to walk out of the Exchange and come back the next day when he spied the top of Rebecca's head. Her lustrous hair reflected the sheen of the halogen lights as she coursed the next aisle over from Max, a disinterested look on her sweet face.

Brant's pulse immediately accelerated. His desire to leave the store evaporated as he watched her distance herself from her husband. Maybe it was wishful thinking on Brant's part, but from all the previous conversations they had ever had, she didn't seem to enjoy her husband's company.

He thought of what he'd learned about Emile Victor DuPonte. Should he tell Rebecca what he'd discovered so she could protect herself? Definitely not here. But the desire to speak with her overruled his common sense, which was warning him to keep his distance. He found himself moving stealthily in her direction, trying to catch her eye without Max seeing him.

Max waved a hand in the air, summoning over a sales person, and Brant seized the opportunity to step into her line of sight. The pleasure that lit up her face when she noticed him made his stomach cartwheel. She was so pretty with those dimples in her cheeks.

Tipping his head toward the racks of greeting cards, he signified she should try to get away. Then he backed toward that area himself and waited on pins and needles for her to join him.

Rebecca racked her brain for a reason to browse the card aisle. Her mother's upcoming birthday provided her an instant excuse. "Um, Max," she called, wresting his attention from the sales person. "I'll be over there picking out a card for my mother."

Preoccupied with choosing a new laptop, Max waved her away.

Rebecca cruised with outward calm toward the greeting cards, aware that butterflies flitted inside her as she hunted for Bronco's sun-kissed head. Like most SEALs, he wore his hair on the long side, letting it curl against his muscle-corded neck and the tops of his ears. Sometimes, he let his facial hair grow out into a burnished goatee that made him devastatingly attractive—not that she would ever tell him that, as there were plenty of women who already did.

She found him behind the magazine section, at the very end of the card aisle where he could dart around a corner if he needed to. His eyes—as blue as the Montana sky's he'd described from his childhood—swung in her direction, and the smile that bloomed from the region of her heart found its way to her face. What was it about this man that lifted the stress right off her shoulders?

"Hey," she said, her voice made breathy by the intrigue. "What brings you here?"

He gestured toward the liquor at the back of the store. "Buying a bottle of wine for a friend."

"Ah." *A female friend, no doubt.* She fought to keep her smile in place but knew that it wavered.

"You met Hack at the party—the new guy? The wine's for him. He did me a favor."

"Oh, nice." She pictured the dark-eyed addition to the Teams and her happiness returned. "I've heard he's a genius with computers. Max should have asked him to fix his Dell. It's been in the shop with a virus for a week now and he's given up ever getting it back, so we're shopping for a replacement."

The words tumbled out of her mouth like a rushing river. She snapped her teeth together to stem the flow. There was simply so much that she wanted to tell Bronco, and their encounters were inevitably few and far between. She didn't want to wait until Veteran's Day, when Max would throw his next party.

"Has, uh, has anything new happened regarding the subject you brought up the other day?" he asked, regarding her closely.

She glanced over her shoulder to make sure Max wasn't about to pounce on them. "Well, something strange did happen yesterday," she relayed in a hushed voice. "I had just gotten home from work, and Max was tossing a stranger out of the house—some guy with a thick New York accent who introduced himself as Tony. But then Max came outside and chased him off. He told me he didn't know the guy but suspected he was a terrorist."

Bronco's expression turned quizzical. "A terrorist with a New York accent?"

She shrugged.

"Do you think this incident is related to Max's secret account?" Bronco asked.

"I don't know." She breathed the words. "But I know I wasn't supposed to see the man, any more than I should have seen the money. And he looked more like a mob boss than a terrorist."

Bronco looked past her shoulder, his jaw tightening.

"Am I imagining all this bizarre stuff?" She searched his gaze, longing for a reassuring word.

To her surprise, he consoled her with a touch, but his hand landed right on the spot that Max had bruised the previous day, and she flinched involuntarily.

Bronco's eyes flashed. With lightning-quick reflexes, he whipped back her sleeve, exposing the pale bruises. His lips immediately firmed.

"I bumped into a doorframe," she rushed to assure him.

He seemed to grow before her eyes as he searched her face. "Please tell me he doesn't hit you," he pleaded on a furious note.

"Oh, no. He doesn't," she rushed to assure him. "It's nothing. I promise."

Searching her face with skeptical concern, he gently lowered her sleeve. Pleasure trickled warmly through her as his fingertips skimmed lightly down her arm. Leaning closer, he assailed her with a woodsy scent that she'd appreciated before. "Please be careful," he pleaded. "If you see this Tony guy again, call the police and then call me."

She was about to mention that she didn't have his phone number when a gruff voice made her jump from her skin.

"There you are."

Max bore down on them, his approach so stealthy in spite of his breadth that even Bronco had been caught off guard. Neither of them spoke as Max stepped between them, dropped a heavy hand on Rebecca's shoulder, and said to her with his gray eyes fixed on Bronco, "I'm going to have to keep you on a shorter leash. Stealing my wife from me, Chief?"

"Not at all, sir." Bronco's easy grin aroused Rebecca's admiration. "Just getting her advice on which card to get for my new girlfriend." He gestured to the display of romantic cards next to them.

Max grunted. His gaze swung toward Rebecca's flushed face. "I need your opinion on two laptops," he told her in a manner that insisted his needs came first.

"I haven't found a card for my mother yet," she protested.

"Later." Pulling her around, he marched her back to the electronics section.

Sneaking a backward glance, Rebecca caught Bronco looking engrossed in selecting a card. Grateful for his quick-thinking, she relived the startling pleasure of his gentle touch and wondered if his kiss would be as warm and wonderful.

Stop it!

She and Bronco were friends, nothing more. Despite her intent not to involve him further in her troubles, she'd confided in him again. Clearly she relied on him more than she'd realized. But, for the time being, she was still married to Max. She had no business even imagining Bronco as her lover.

* * *

Max listened to the salesman list the specs for both laptops but he wasn't hearing him. He'd decided that Rebecca ought to make the final decision as to which laptop he should buy. That would reinforce the lesson she still needed to learn—that it was her job to assist him in every way she could.

"Neither one of these has the memory your old Dell had," she pointed. "Why don't you just use the home computer until your Dell is repaired?"

And there it was: that look in her eyes that made him suspect that she was manipulating him. Her brown eyes used to shine with admiration. That was what had drawn him to her in the first place, besides the fact that she seemed to have it all together. She'd admired and respected him. But now? He wasn't so sure.

How did he know that he could trust her? She'd been talking to Chief Adams a moment ago, the same way they'd been talking at his Labor Day party, like they really knew each other. Until then, he hadn't realized how chummy they'd become.

Max drew a finger along the hard, plastic edge of the laptop closest to him. Did she want him using the home PC in the hopes of getting another glimpse of his Swiss bank account? Had she told Chief Adams what she'd seen the night he'd left his browser open when he went to take a leak? What if she'd been telling him, just then, about the incident with Tony Scarpa? What would the chief make of that?

Tony had some gall dropping by his house to discuss business. Max had informed the Scarpas via Google chat that he'd had enough. Instead of releasing him, they'd buttered him up with fifty grand and the promise of another fifty if he agreed to keep working for them. Tony's visit had been meant to get a point across—they knew where he lived. He couldn't get rid of them as easily as he wanted to.

He wished he'd never gotten involved with the family in the first place. But he'd needed money to keep his house from going into foreclosure, which would have been frowned upon by his superiors. Plus, the jobs had proved to be a cinch to execute. Both victims had been dirt bags, former members of the mob. He had no regrets about killing them.

Now that he was flush, he didn't need the Scarpas the way they needed him. Still, fifty thousand surplus dollars sitting in his foreign account inspired thoughts of how he could spend it. He'd always wanted a vacation home in Bermuda. Wouldn't that make him the envy of his colleagues?

"Fine," he said, deciding that her input made sense. He would save money using the home PC and just wait for his laptop to be repaired. "We're not buying either one," he told the sales associate, waving him away.

Stammering an apology, the young man scuttled off. Max glanced at his wife and found her biting her lower lip and staring at his chest.

"What?" he challenged.

She glared up at him. "Do you have to treat everyone like dirt?" Her cheeks turned pink. "You could have apologized for wasting the boy's time instead of sending him off like that."

"Forget about him. What were you saying to Chief Adams just now?" he demanded.

"What do you mean? He asked me about a card, that's all."

"You certainly looked to be enjoying your little talk," he pointed out.

She rolled her eyes and looked away. Max fought to keep his hands from balling into fists. Tearing his gaze from her profile, he glanced uncomfortably around the open space. Luckily, the Navy Exchange was practically empty an hour before closing, decreasing the odds that someone important might see him at odds with his wife.

Inclining his mouth toward her ear, he added, "I wouldn't *enjoy* his company anymore if I were you," he told her. "Something bad might just happen to him."

She blinked up at him. "Did you just threaten one of your men?"

Satisfied that she got the picture, he simply shrugged his shoulders and walked away.

The brunette gyrating on the dance floor in front of Brant reminded him of Rebecca. Her sable hair appeared to be a shade darker, but it had that lustrous quality that Brant liked so much, and her eyes were dark, too. She had Rebecca's body type: a little on the short side, neat and understated, with breasts that promised to be a perfect handful.

But she barely spoke English, which came as a disappointment because if he *wasn't* going to have sex with her, then that left dancing and talking—or miming, as the case turned out.

The techno music reverberated in his eardrums, dictating the movements of his body which required no conscious thought on his part. He was free to let his mind wander while he did his thing and Marina spun and wriggled all around him, her white T-shirt glowing under the ultraviolet lights, and a teasing smile on her face.

Yeah, she thought she was going to get some action from a SEAL tonight.

His cock gave a throb of anticipation at the prospect of ending his streak of celibacy. No one but Rebecca even knew he'd decided to deprive himself—and he didn't have to tell her the truth, so it would cost him absolutely nothing to conveniently forget his resolution.

Viewed through an alcoholic haze induced by a shot of tequila chased by a tall mug of beer, Marina resembled Rebecca enough that he could envision what it would be like possessing her.

The music came to a frenzied climax then transitioned to a slow, sultry beat that encouraged intimacy. Marina pressed her body to his, coiled her tanned arms around his neck and, with a suggestive smile, invited him to get to know her better.

Seeing her face up close jarred him. *Not Rebecca.*

He pulled her head to his chest to avoid looking at her face. But with close proximity came a fragrance that didn't smell like Rebecca, whose scent reminded him of sugar cookies and peppermint sticks, probably because he'd first met her at Max's Christmas party. Marina smelled more like the perfume counter at Macy's. She was brushing her thighs against his, making her intentions perfectly plain. Half of the female population called men dogs for being so promiscuous, yet the other half invited promiscuity. What was a man to do?

"You like me?" Marina asked with her sultry Eastern European accent.

He pulled back to consider his reply. Her pronounced cheekbones and thin lips looked nothing like Rebecca's. He stopped dancing. Her expression vacillated between quizzical and hopeful.

"Fuck," he muttered to himself, rubbing his eyes which ached from the flashing lights. "Come with me," he offered, drawing her off the dance floor and over to the bar where the youngest member of Echo Platoon, Austin Collins, sat nursing a glass of tonic water. Nicknamed Bamm-Bamm for his obsession with The Flintstones, Collins wore a dour expression as he watched his friend Haiku order two Long Island ice teas, one for him and one for another SEAL named Halliday.

At twenty years of age, Collins was old enough to die for his country but not old enough to legally drink in this state, as the wristband on his arm informed the bartender.

"Hey, Bamm-Bamm." Brant positioned the brunette in front of the young language expert. "This is Marina. I think she's Bulgarian or something."

"Ukrainian," the girl corrected with a flash of annoyance. She'd clearly said this more than once to him already.

The kid's gloomy expression vanished. He jumped off the bar stool, offering it gallantly to Marina while spouting off something in a language that made her face light up. She took the offered seat, asking a question in return.

"I speak Russian," Collins explained to Brant, "so she can sort of understand me and vice-versa. Like Spanish and Italian."

"Great." He clapped the kid on the back. "Y'all have fun."

Chuckling inwardly at the linguist's stunned expression, he turned and walked away, scanning the crowded club for Bullfrog. Standing half a head taller than anyone else and normally off to one side, his friend was always easy to spot. Brant found him close to the door, leaning against the wall with his arms across his chest, looking bored. He hadn't wanted to come here in the first place, citing his desire to finish reading *Anna Karenina*.

Read a book on a Saturday night? Brant had scoffed. *Hell, no. We're going out dancing.*

But now he wished he *had* stayed home because his buzz was fading fast, and the ache behind his eyeballs was building, thanks to the lights and the cheap tequila. He couldn't take a woman home, so what was the point of even coming to this meat market?

"Ready to go?" he asked, shouting over the music that had quickened into another mind-numbing beat.

Bullfrog didn't budge. "Is *she* coming with us?" He nodded toward Marina, who looked to be deep in conversation with Collins.

"No. Come on, let's go." He turned and bolted for the door, counting on his teammate to follow. SEALs operated in pairs, which was the only reason why Bullfrog had ventured out in the first place.

A minute later, they sped from the parking lot in his friend's silver soft-top Jeep, with Bullfrog driving. Brant ignored his sidelong, curious stares. It was obvious that their early departure puzzled his teammate, but he didn't comment, which was an attribute that Brant utterly appreciated. Bullfrog knew when to keep quiet and drive.

It was Brant who finally broke the silence, raising his voice to be heard over the hum of the tires. "Remind me why I live this kind of lifestyle," he requested.

"To pick up chicks," Bullfrog answered flatly.

"Right. So if I was to stop doing that, there wouldn't be any point in subjecting myself to the shock-and-awe environment or the hangover the next day, would there?"

That gained him an astonished glance and the answer he'd already guessed. "Nope."

In the hush that followed, Brant accustomed himself to the oddly liberating sensation of returning home companionless. He'd thought he would feel like he was missing out on something, but the only thing he hankered for at the moment was Rebecca's company, which was never going to happen. Apart from that dissatisfaction, he felt strangely pleased with himself—cleaner, somehow.

"So, what's so special about *Anna Karenina*, anyway?" he heard himself ask.

Bullfrog's grin flashed in the Jeep's dark interior. "It's about a woman stuck in a loveless marriage. She meets someone else and falls desperately in love with him, but they can't be together. You should read it," he advised.

Brant scowled at the insinuation. "What are you saying?"

"Nothing." Bullfrog shrugged. "It's a classic. Classics convey truths about the human experience."

His friend was probably warning him about the pitfalls of befriending the CO's wife. He pretended to go along with the idea. "How many pages long is it?"

"Like twelve hundred."

"Hah." He couldn't hold still long enough to read that many pages. "I'll rent the movie. We can watch it tonight if you want." What the hell else was there to do?

Bullfrog chuckled. "Sure, why not?"

CHAPTER 4

Rebecca wiped the granite counters with isopropyl alcohol and a dry paper towel. She'd already scrubbed and disinfected the entire kitchen from the tiled floor to the top of the refrigerator, but a final wipe down left a nice glossy sheen that usually engendered satisfaction.

But not today. Her stomach continued to twist and roil.

Clearly Max was worried that she would tell Bronco about his secret account. Why else would he have made that blatant threat? *Something bad might just happen to him.* She had gone straight into her bathroom when they got home, turned on the shower and placed a surreptitious call to her friend, Maddy, in order to procure Bronco's cell phone number.

I need to warn him today, she decided. Do it now, or wait until later?

The roar of the lawnmower drew her gaze out the sliding glass doors. Max was out back, cutting the long expanse of grass between the pool and the pier, something he preferred to do himself because their gardener never cut it the way he wanted.

Swiveling her head, she assessed the camera on the ceiling. No red light. The security system wasn't armed. Max usually kept it off in the daytime, at least while he was home. She could call Bronco right now on her cell phone and Max would never know—or would he? After all, he was the one who owned their cellular phone plan, which meant he could probably research any calls she made.

She gnawed on a hangnail while considering her husband through the window.

In spite of her urgency, it would be wiser for Bronco's sake if she called him from a pay phone. If Max found out she was still talking to him, he'd make his chief's life a living hell at work.

I should never have told Bronco Max's secret.

Heaving a troubled sigh, she plodded to the trashcan to throw away the paper towel. Then again, if she hadn't told him, would she dare to even think of leaving Max? It was Bronco's moral support that made her feel brave. Still, she ought to have relied on her girlfriends for support. If only they could grasp what life with Max was like. She had been told more than once by her colleagues that she was lucky to be married to a high-ranking SEAL.

Don't you talk bad about your husband, girl, one of them had scolded her. *Think about what he's gone through for our country. Didn't he earn a Bronze Star?*

The wives of other SEALs weren't quite so adamant. Maddy had merely suggested she was approaching the four year itch, one year early. *It'll pass,* she'd promised.

Only Bronco really understood that life with Max was often scary. Like her, he seemed to recognize the potential menace lying latent in his commander. And unlike her friends, he encouraged her to think for herself, to trust her intuition.

Seeing Max's key ring on the counter instead of hanging on the hook where it belonged, she scooped it in her palm, weighing its heaviness as she went to hang it up. The set of keys struck her as a symbol of her captivity. As she slid it on the hook mounted by the door, the smallest key on the end caught her eye. The number 2850, etched into the bronze head, identified it at once.

It was the key to her old post office box. She frowned down at it.

Before marrying Max, in the absence of a permanent address, she had kept a mailbox at the Princess Ann Post Office. But she hadn't used it since their marriage. So what was Max doing carrying it around?

With a shrug, she decided she would ask him later and proceeded into the laundry room to move their clothes from the washer to the dryer. Max didn't like his clothes being left to wrinkle.

Half an hour later, she was folding the white load on their bed when he hurried into the room, stripping off his sweaty T-shirt.

"Damn it—I've got a golf game with Admiral Johansen in half an hour. Can't be late for the admiral."

He shucked off the rest of his clothes and stalked naked into their *en suite* to shower. Rebecca tore her gaze off his broad back. Max was getting fat.

Minutes later, he emerged with his hair damp, still toweling off his mat of chest hair. Grateful for his haste, which would keep him from making any sexual advances, she remained quiet while he pawed irritably through his drawers, hunting for his golfing socks. This was not the best time to ask him why he carried around her old mailbox key.

Dressing in record time, he came over to drop a kiss on her dry lips before heading to the door. "I'll be back in three hours."

"Play well," she called, feeling a distinct pressure ease off her shoulders as he walked away.

A moment later, the door between the laundry room and the garage slammed shut. She listened to the automated garage door rumble open and then close again. At last she was alone and free to take action.

But Max would have armed the security system before leaving, the way he always did under the premise of keeping her "safe" inside. He would know if she left the house because, of course, the system would send a message to his phone when she opened the garage to let herself out. He would also know how long she'd been gone when she opened it again upon her return.

First, she had to think of an excuse. Because sure as Max would throw the game to keep the admiral happy, he would interrogate her when he got back—where had she gone and what had she done? With her heart already beating faster, she abandoned the clothes she had yet to put away and hurried to the other side of the house to the laundry room. The camera in the kitchen couldn't film her behind the laundry room door where she opened the half-full bottle of detergent and poured the contents down the drain.

Oh dear, it seems I'd better run out and get some more.

Hastening to the garage, she let her mind catalogue the local shops and restaurants, trying to recollect where she'd seen a pay phone. As much as she regretted having to cut ties with Bronco, it was for the best. She'd had no right to involve him in her marital woes in the first place. For his sake, she hoped that telling him about Max's warning would quell his suspicions and keep him safe from his commander's certain retribution.

Brant pushed out of the Exchange with a Subway combo meal dangling from one hand and a large cup of iced tea in the other. Sweat still moistened his hairline from the game of rec-league basketball, in which his team had lost 51 to 23. Both teams had walked over to the Exchange afterward for a well-deserved meal, but to avoid the smug stares of the victors who now lounged in the food court making jokes and boasting, he'd left the building to eat outside.

A temperate ocean breeze dried the last traces of moisture from his brow as he turned toward the wooden bench at the far side of the building. He wasn't at all surprised to see that Bullfrog had beaten him to it, his face buried in the last pages of *Anna Karenina*. Brant thought about the movie they'd watched the previous night and shuddered. Considering the fact that the heroine jumped in front of a moving train at the very end, he couldn't fathom why Bullfrog would want to finish the book when he knew how the story ended.

His ringing cell phone interrupted his trek to the bench. Juggling his lunch to free a hand, he noted the unfamiliar number. "Hello?"

"Hey, it's Rebecca."

He jerked to a stop. The clouds above seemed to part, and a ray of sunshine streamed down, warming his shoulders.

"Well, hi." But then he wondered if creepy Tony had made another appearance and concern edged aside his pleasure. "Is everything okay?"

"Uh, sure. Everything's great."

That sounded a bit forced. "Well, that's good." Why

the hell would she risk calling him, then? He continued forward.

"I'm using a pay phone," she said, putting his mind at ease. "You have no idea how hard it was to find one. Listen, I need to tell you something," she added on an anxious note.

Bullfrog glanced up at him as he neared the bench and sat down. "Go ahead."

"Well, first off—" She hesitated, and he could picture her biting her lower lip. "Max kind of mumbled a threat against you the other day. I just thought you should know."

He lowered his lunch onto his lap and balanced his drink on the arm of the bench. "What kind of threat?"

Bullfrog paused in his reading, lowering his book to his lap.

"More of an implied threat, really. He said, 'I wouldn't enjoy his company anymore if I were you. Something bad might just happen to him.'—him being you, of course. I'm so sorry, Bronco. It's my fault for talking to you in the first place."

Frustration heated Brant all over again. "Christ, we were only talking!"

"I know," she said, with lament. "But I should never have involved you in our issues."

"I didn't leave you much choice, remember?" He deliberated telling her then what he'd learned about Max's secret account.

"Yes, but now I've drawn unnecessary attention to you, and I'm truly sorry. I probably shouldn't talk to you anymore, even at a party."

The regret that laced her voice tugged at his heartstrings. "That's bullshit. You've got to talk to somebody. Besides—" He caught himself from relaying his discovery.

"Besides, what?" she pressed.

"Becca, you deserve better than him." He winced. Shoot, he'd made it sound like he was offering himself up in Max's stead. His heart thudded as he waited for her answer.

"I know that. I've pretty much decided that I'm going to leave him."

"You—you what?" He almost dropped the phone on top of his lunch.

"I've decided to leave him. But I can't just leave, or he could claim that I deserted him. What I really need is proof that he's involved in something criminal."

Shock radiated through Brant's body. *Rebecca wants to leave Max.* It was like the universe and all of its stars and planets had shifted their alignment. When his brain started working again, he thought of a way that he could help her out. "What if I said I might have proof?" he answered slowly.

Bullfrog's head swiveled as he gave up all pretext of reading and looked at him directly.

"Like what?" Her hopeful tone plucked at him the same way her despondency had earlier.

Avoiding Bullfrog's wary stare, Brant cast an eye around to make certain no one else was near enough to overhear him. "Remember the account you told me about?"

"Yes."

"Well, I had Hack look into it for me," he murmured, just loud enough for Bullfrog to overhear. "It's a foreign account, Becca. We're not supposed to have any foreign accounts."

"Oh, my God," she breathed. "You weren't supposed to tell anyone else!"

He winced. "I didn't say it was Max's," he promised. "Hack just checked out the company for me."

"Oh. Okay." Her voice sounded a little shaky. "So

having a foreign account means he's doing something wrong, right?"

"I don't know. Probably. He could get in trouble with the Navy. And what's he doing to make all that money? Do you have any idea?"

"No." He pictured her shaking her head. "Maybe that guy Tony has something to do with it."

"Has he shown up again?"

"I haven't seen him." She fell thoughtfully silent. "Thank you for checking on that for me, Bronco, but I really need to handle this on my own from now on."

"Are you sure you're up to it?" Not that he doubted her inner strength, but he'd seen her kowtow to Max's demands, and it was hard to picture her defying him.

"I don't know. I feel like I'm walking on eggshells," she admitted.

Her words sparked an immediate visceral response in him. Now he wanted to protect her, damn it. "Listen, I'm here for you," he said on a low note. Beside him, Bullfrog dropped his face into his hands and moaned.

"Thank you. I just...I can't involve you any more than I already have."

"It's okay," he assured her. "I don't mind. Call me whenever you feel like it."

"Thanks." But he could tell by her tone that she had no intention of calling him for anything. "I'll see you."

"Bye." There was the briefest pause, and then the line went dead. Hanging up, he looked over to find his friend slowly dragging his hands from his eyes.

Bullfrog's mouth formed a straight line. "Are you sure you should have told her?" he demanded.

Brant ignored him, pulling his sandwich out of the bag to unwrap it. The ocean breeze threatened to snatch away the wax paper.

"Do you really want to get the CO in trouble? He'll ruin your career if he finds out you encouraged her."

Brant took a huge bite of his sandwich as he considered his reply. "I have to help her," he said finally. "She's a friend."

"She's the CO's wife."

"No shit, really?" He took another huge bite. "Anyway, she's planning to leave him," he added few chews later.

He refrained from mentioning how much her announcement rattled him. On the one hand, he was delighted to hear that she'd decided to move on. Max wasn't worth the dirt on the soles of her dainty little shoes. On the other hand, her being single would complicate their friendship. Without Max between them, there'd be no clear boundaries, no reason for him to deny himself the pleasure of her company. So he could spend time with her—yay. But time together would inevitably deepen their affection on both sides, and Brant didn't do deep—*ever*. Sticking to superficial connections meant less risk of anyone getting hurt. Of all the women on earth whom Brant didn't want to hurt, Rebecca was *numero uno*.

Bullfrog folded his arms over his chest and leaned back reflectively. "Max is never going to let her leave him," he predicted.

The words shook the bars of Brant's complacency. "What the hell choice does he have? If she wants to leave him, she can leave him," he insisted, taking a vicious bite out of his sandwich.

His friend turned his head and stared straight into Brant's eyes. "We're talking about Mad Max, Bronco. He only cares about what *he* wants, not the other way around. I'm telling you, from what I know of the man, he's going to make it impossible for her to leave."

Brant forced himself to swallow. "How is it

impossible?" he quietly raged. "She goes to a lawyer, tells him about Max's foreign account, and she moves out."

"She can't prove Max has a foreign account. Does she even have an account number?" Bullfrog raised his eyebrows.

Brant took a quick sip of lemonade to clear the lump now stuck in his throat. "Christ, you're right." It was suddenly, horrifyingly apparent to him. "Max is going to make her life a living hell if she tries to leave him." With no more appetite to finish his sandwich, he wrapped up the rest and dropped it back in the bag. "I have to help her find the proof she needs."

Bullfrog groaned as he shook his head. "I have a

"Don't do that." Brant pointed a warning finger at him. Bullfrog's intuitions never failed him. They were always right on target.

"I'm not doing anything. You're the one wanting to help her out."

"Yeah, except she doesn't want my help," he recalled, though he guessed that wasn't exactly the case. She was merely trying to keep his CO off his back. The truth was she was scared and rightly so. Considering the resistance she was bound to face in the form of Max's overwhelming resolve, he didn't envy her situation one bit. "I still need to help her," he insisted.

"Why? Do you plan on taking Max's place?"

The quiet question drew Brant's incredulous gaze. He glared at his friend. "Hell, no. I'm the last man she needs in her life. She deserves to be happy—don't you agree?"

"I agree," Bullfrog admitted with reluctance.

"Can you even think of a nicer, sweeter, more decent woman than Rebecca McDougal?"

A faraway look splintered his friend's hazel gaze.

"Just one," he said, so softly Brant wasn't certain he had heard him right.

"I have to help her," he repeated.

"You know you said that three times," Bullfrog pointed out. His mouth quirked at one corner. "That's like a magical number. Now you're committed to it."

"I guess I am," Brant agreed with a tremor of excitement. He'd never walked away from a challenge in his life. As long as Rebecca ended up happy, he didn't care if Max hated him so much that he transferred him to the West Coast. This wasn't about his future; it was about hers.

Rebecca topped off her gas tank, enjoying the gusty breeze that penetrated the weave of her linen dress and invigorated her spirits. *I can do this,* she assured herself.

The reading at church that morning, taken from the Book of Jeremiah, had tipped the scales regarding her decision to leave Max. *For I know the plans I have for you, plans to prosper you and not to harm you, plans to give you hope and a future.*

She had decided in that inspired moment that she would leave Max soon—as soon as she could prove he was breaking the law. His foreign investment account would be her ticket to freedom. She would pass it by the lawyer she had arranged to meet on her day off.

Screwing the gas cap back on, she gazed over the top of her car just as Max's Tahoe roared past the station. Tension whipped through her, drawing tight the muscles along her back.

Where is he headed on a Sunday at noon? she wondered. He had avoided attending church with her, citing the need to prepare for the coming work week, but Dam Neck Naval Base and the Special Ops building where he worked lay in the opposite direction.

Intuition whispered that he was up to something. Slipping into her car, Rebecca eased onto the road to follow him, keeping his SUV within sight while hanging back a quarter mile. Unlike his lumbering Tahoe, her silver Jetta blended easily into the sparse traffic.

A curve in the road took them north on Princess Anne Boulevard, in the direction of the hospital, but then Max's left turn signal blinked on. Bemused, Rebecca let him veer into the Virginia Beach Municipal Center without following him. She continued straight another block, turned left on Nimmo Drive, and backtracked toward the courthouse. But the parking lot stood empty. Where could Max have gone?

The fear of being seen by him had her gripping the steering wheel with damp hands as she drove deeper into the municipal center. At last, her gaze lit upon his Tahoe, parked in the deserted post office lot. And there was Max, hastening for the front doors. She quickly turned the other way to avoid being seen by him.

Why would Max make a trip to the post office on a Sunday, when the service desk was closed? Only the lobby with the automated teller and all the private mail boxes could be accessed on a Sunday. *Oh.* A sudden suspicion popped into her head.

Was it possible he was using her old mailbox key?

Her thoughts flew in a dozen different directions at once. She hadn't remembered to ask him about it the previous night. Had he renewed her rental without her even knowing? Why would he need another mailbox when he had a permanent address—unless, of course, he got mail he didn't want her knowing about…Just like he didn't want her knowing about his account with Emile Victor DuPonte.

A chill settled over her at the realization that she'd stumbled on yet another secret.

The urge to share it with Bronco rose up in her immediately. She tamped it down as she drove toward her home. Bronco didn't need to be told everything his commander was up to. It would only corrode the fabric of the Team's working relationship, which needed to stay strong in order for the task unit to function optimally.

I'm not going to involve him, she swore to herself. She could investigate this matter personally. If she was lucky, she would find proof that Max was breaking the law, and then she'd be able to leave her marriage in the hopes that he would be convicted.

Max could feel his designer-label polo shirt sticking to his back as he darted into the post office. Even on a Sunday, when the place was deserted, coming here elevated his pulse, especially since he had started working for the mob. At first, he had kept Rebecca's old post office box in order to monitor her correspondence, making certain she didn't have any old flames he needed to be aware of. Later, it offered a convenient way for him to receive his subscription of *Hustler* magazine. Now the Scarpas used it to send him information.

They'd identified his first two targets this way. The first time, they'd sent him a copy of a wedding invitation for a wedding taking place at Town Point Park on the Norfolk waterfront the evening of May 23, along with photos of the man they claimed was a snitch. Max had shot him during the outdoor reception, from the vantage of his boat, anchored half a mile off shore, in the Elizabeth River.

For his second victim, they'd sent him a photo of a fat, balding man sunning on the deck of a sailboat. Max had recognized the marina where the sailboat was moored. By water, it wasn't all that far from where he lived. Since his getaway had been so clean the first time, he'd opted to kill his second target the same way, though it had made him nervous to repeat the same strategy.

This time, if he went through with the job, he'd change up his *modus operandi*. Problem was he might get stuck working for the mob indefinitely. He was beginning to see how they would make it difficult for him to stop, dangling increasingly larger rewards before him. He had caught himself envisioning his second home in Bermuda lately.

Crossing the empty lobby, Max inserted the key at #2850, pulled the little door open and stared in disappointment. The box stood empty. *Damn it.* Now he would have to return on a weekday and risk running into someone he knew.

Slamming the box shut, he locked it back up and skulked out of the post office.

CHAPTER 5

Rebecca eyed her old post office box with trepidation. She had left work early on a Monday to arrive at the post office before closing. The clerk hadn't so much as blinked at her story that she'd lost her key and needed another. Now a copy of the key was in her hand, and she stood at the verge of discovering something else Max might be hiding from her.

It's going to be empty, she told herself. After all, Max would have emptied it on his visit here the day before. Sliding the key into the lock, she opened it with bated breath. Upon seeing an envelope inside, her heart started to pound. With a nervous glance behind her at the patrons rushing to beat the clock, she pulled out the letter, eyes widening to discover that the envelope was addressed to her.

With a sense of unreality, she stared at it. Not only was Max keeping secrets, but he was hiding his dirty deeds under *her* name. The address had been typed on a label and affixed to the envelope. There was no return address, just an origination stamp next to the postage indicating that the letter had been sorted in

Bronx, New York, two days earlier.

Curious to know what lay inside, she slipped it into her purse, closed the box, and left the building, greatly relieved not to run into anyone she knew, particularly Max.

Within the safety of her car, she took the letter out and studied it. *Do I open it?* How else would she discover what was inside? She could always stick the contents into another envelope, affix an identical label and re-mail it tomorrow. As long as Max paid no heed to where the letter had originated, he might never know the difference.

Checking her peripheral vision to make certain no one watched, she slid her finger under the flap and tore it slowly open. Her heart suspended its beat as she withdrew the contents with a frown. *A newspaper clipping?* She angled it toward the waning sunlight and read the title.

Sniper with Military Background Kills for the Mob.

Intrigued, she waded through an article summarizing an FBI special agent's hypothesis that two homicides attributed to the organized crime family, the Scarpas, had been perpetrated by an assassin who could only have been trained as a sniper in the U.S. Special Forces. Both victims had been shot from a watercraft anchored half a mile away. The special agent was quoted as saying, *"Only an ace sniper could mark a victim from that distance."*

A chill ascended Rebecca's spine. Why had someone sent this article to Max? Was it simply an item of interest? Max was in the Special Forces. Plus, he'd been a SEAL sniper for ten years before rising so high in rank that he no longer went into the field to fight. Someone just wanted him to read this story and know the facts.

That had to be it. It couldn't possibly be that *he* was the sniper that the FBI was looking for. That would be ludicrous.

With stiff fingers, she put the article back inside the envelope, the envelope back into her purse.

For several seconds, all she could do was stare at the brick exterior of the post office. Max's foreign account—all the money in it; where had it come from? Maybe it wasn't so farfetched to think that Max might be working for an organized crime family.

Her chest rose and fell as she thought it through. *What do I do?* She could show the article to her lawyer at their upcoming appointment. But she didn't want to wait that long. She needed to talk to someone about this *now*, someone who knew Max, who could tell her if she was out of her mind for thinking such treacherous thoughts about him.

I need to talk to Bronco.

"No," she grated, grinding a palm against her closed eye. Just the other day she had promised she wouldn't involve him any further in her problems. But he had assured her that he didn't mind and that she could call him any time.

Breathing deeply, she sought to slow her rapid heartbeat. The pay phone she had used the other day stood right up the road at the 7-11 near the hospital where she worked. The temptation proved to be too much. Starting up her car, she exited the parking lot and drove in a state of distraction straight to it.

Brant hadn't expected to see the same number pop up on his cell phone any time soon. Concerned, he reached for the volume on his truck radio and turned it down. Luckily, he'd just exited the gate of the naval annex, freeing him to talk on his phone. "Becca?"

"I'm sorry," she began. "I said I wouldn't bother you again, and here I am calling you already."

Her shaken tone had him checking his rearview mirror automatically. "What's wrong?"

He heard her inhale and exhale. "I need to show you something. Can I get you to meet me somewhere soon?"

Possibilities swarmed his thoughts like a flock of blackbirds. "You mean like right now?" He was headed to the special Jujitsu class Bullfrog was teaching every night that week.

"No, I can't right now. I need to get home." She sounded antsy, like she ought to be home already and expected to get into trouble for being late. "What about tomorrow evening? Can you meet me after work?"

"What time do you get off?"

"Right around 4 P.M."

"That's pretty early, but I can probably get away. Where do you want to meet?" The bass on someone's car radio vibrated the windows of his old Bronco as he stopped at an intersection.

He pictured her wetting her rose-tinted lips in a familiar, nervous gesture. "Do you know the park right next to the hospital where I work?"

"Uh, yeah. Gateway Park, right?"

"Yes, but the sign says Princess Anne Commons. Let's meet under the pavilion at, say, 4:15?"

Her nervousness made his blood flow faster. "You going to tell me what this is about?"

"I need to go. I'll show you tomorrow, okay? You'll be there?"

"I'll be there," he promised. "Hey," he added before she could hang up.

"What?"

"Take a deep breath, hon." The endearment popped out of his mouth without his intending to say it. "It's going to be okay. I'm glad you called me. I'm right here."

He thought he heard her breath catch, but then she said with commendable poise, "Thank you." With a click, she was gone. He lowered his cell phone onto the console next to his seat and pondered what she could have come across to rattle her so badly.

Max was probably having an affair. Brant had heard a rumor the first time they were TDY in Malaysia that the CO had hooked up with their female CIA liaison.

"Bastard," he muttered, hating the man for inciting fear in his own wife.

It wasn't until he neared his apartment complex that he realized what a hypocrite he was. He'd hooked up with a lady-of-the-night himself while in Malaysia, and at the time, he'd been dating two women back in Virginia Beach. He wasn't any more honorable of a man than his commander was. Poor Rebecca deserved better than either one of them.

In the little restroom inside of the pavilion at Gateway Park, Rebecca checked her reflection in the mirror. *Oh, for heaven's sake. It doesn't matter what I look like.*

After a sleepless night in which she'd fought to drown out Max's abrasive snores, she had worked a grueling twelve-hour day. Dark circles ringed her eyes. Her trust in her husband, along with her marriage, was falling to ruin. Yet here she was, trying to look pretty for Bronco, who had half-a-dozen women at his beck and call and thought of her only as a friend—the same way she thought of him.

All the same, she slicked pink lip gloss on her lips

and tugged her hair out of its ponytail before stepping out of the restroom to wait for him under the covered picnic area.

Situated adjacent to the hospital, the park offered the perfect retreat during warmer months for her to eat her packed lunch in the middle of her workday. Her feet gave a throb of relief as she lowered herself onto a picnic bench and shaded her eyes against the low sun to watch several children clamber on the playground equipment.

A soft footfall followed by a shift in the air announced Bronco's arrival a split second before he sat down next to her.

"Boo," he said, grinning at the way she clapped a hand to her heart.

"Where'd you come from?" she marveled.

"Thin air." He paused to examine her face, no doubt seeing all the signs of strain she had failed to erase. "Want to walk with me?"

The last thing her aching feet wanted to do was to take a walk, but his suggestion eased her concern that someone would see them sitting together. "Sure."

Side by side, they started down the path that curved away from the common area to wind among the trees and all around the periphery of the park. The leaves had thinned, allowing sunlight to slant through the green canopy and dapple the tar strip under their feet.

Rebecca looked down at her practical nursing shoes, wishing she'd taken the time to change. While Bronco, in his BDUs, resembled a poster model advertising the glamorous life of a Navy SEAL, she looked nothing short of frumpy in her light blue scrubs. Then again, this wasn't a date. The article she wanted to show him was tucked inside her scrub's front pocket.

To her gratification, he didn't bring it up right away.

"How was work?" he asked, slanting her an admiring glance.

"Rough," she admitted, considering her long day. "We had several car-accident victims, including a five-year-old girl who should've been in a booster seat but wasn't. Her collarbone was broken, but luckily not her neck. The mother, who was driving intoxicated, broke her pelvis. We had no choice but to report the incident to social services."

His burnished eyebrows came together. "You think they'll take the girl from her mother?"

"No, I think they'll assess the home situation first. The mother could probably use some counseling— she's all of twenty-one years old, so she's still learning herself."

Brant's mouth twisted into a cynical-looking smile. "Where's the father?" he asked.

"Not in the picture as far as I know. Some men aren't cut out to be fathers." She thought about her own dad.

"True. Doesn't mean they have the right to disappear, though."

Their footfalls sounded in tandem, making hers indistinguishable from his.

"That's what my father did," she heard herself confess.

He shot her a startled look. "I'm sorry. I thought he just died young."

"He did that, too, but first he left—just disappeared one day, when I was thirteen years old." She shrugged. "The next time my mom and I saw him was when we claimed his body, five years later. Turned out, he'd been living in Minneapolis all that time."

His jaw muscles jumped. "That must have sucked."

"It's fine. I don't mind talking about it. I think he did his best to be the domestic type, and he just wasn't cut out for it." She smiled to convey her acceptance of the situation. "At least his body found its way back to us. There's an unclaimed body here at this hospital." She nodded in the direction of the building where she worked. "A homeless man who looks a bit like you, as a matter of fact."

"Like me?" He sounded perturbed to hear it.

"Same age, same hair color, that kind of thing. I keep hoping someone's going to claim him, but no one has, yet."

He made a thoughtful sound in his throat. A heavy but not uncomfortable silence enveloped them as they followed the path. She was certain he would ask what she'd discovered about Max. Instead, he surprised her by saying, "My dad left, too, before I was born. He's still alive, though. Quinn Farley—maybe you've heard of him?"

She frowned. "No, should I have?"

"Maybe. He used to be a champion bull rider. Now he's a commentator for the Professional Bull-Riding Network."

She slowed to a stop, forcing him to turn around to face her.

Noting that his father's last name was different than his, she longed to pull more details out of him, but the fact that she was only now learning about this meant that he kept it a guarded secret. A yellow leaf floated to the ground between them. "Thanks for telling me," she said, simply.

He sent her a small smile. For a moment, they regarded each other with silent understanding. Then, knowing the time had come, Rebecca reached into her pocket and pulled out the folded envelope.

"Max has been using my old post office box without me knowing. I saw him swing by there on Sunday, so yesterday I got a copy of the key and checked the box for myself. I think he was looking for this."

Curiosity flashed in Brant's eyes as he took her offering, pulled out the article and perused it. She studied his expression with a held breath. A crease appeared between his eyebrows, and her stomach started to churn. She saw him arrive at the end and return to the beginning to read it a second time. He then examined the envelope, noting the lack of return address, her name in the center, and the origination stamp next to the postage. When he finally looked up at her, his eyes appeared darker.

"Well," she prompted. "Do you think Max could be working for the Scarpas?"

He gave a short laugh. "No way." He put the article back inside the envelope and shook his head. "That's absurd. He would never do that."

Now that she'd had a night to think about it, she wasn't so sure. "Not even to get out of debt? We owed forty-five thousand dollars on top of our regular mortgage, and suddenly that's all paid off. How did that happen?"

"Have you asked him that?"

She nodded. "Right after the Labor Day party. He told me some great uncle he'd never heard of died and left him fifty thousand dollars, and he immediately used that sum to pay off the equity line."

"How convenient," Bronco drawled.

"Isn't it, though? I then asked Max if he had any paperwork showing that the sum was an inheritance so we didn't get taxed on it, and he said he already gave it to our accountant."

"It's not even close to tax time," Bronco observed.

"Exactly."

His troubled gaze fell to the clipping. "You mind if I make a copy of this?" he asked.

She wondered what for, if he didn't think Max was

the shooter. "Go ahead," she agreed. "I've already made myself a copy."

"If you want, I'll put the original in a new envelope and stick it in the mail tonight. That way, Max will get it by tomorrow. Hopefully he won't notice that it was sorted in Virginia Beach and not the Bronx."

"Okay, thank you," she agreed, more than happy to hand off the task. "Should I show my copy to my lawyer on Monday?"

He started to shake his head. "This is heavy stuff, Becca. Let me pass it by Bullfrog first—you know, Jeremiah?—and maybe Master Chief Kuzinsky to get their opinions. Do you mind if I do that?"

Nervousness fizzed in her as she considered the series of events she would be setting into motion if she agreed. She hadn't wanted anyone but Bronco knowing about Max's secrets, but they were looking bigger than either one of them had suspected. And what choice did she have it she wanted Max to get ultimately convicted?

She nodded slowly. "Okay, then."

They stood for several seconds contemplating each other. Her senses felt curiously heightened, so much so that she could hear a cricket rubbing its legs together in the grass nearby and smell the faint, sweet fragrance of the leaves sloughing overhead.

"What if we get Max into trouble and he has nothing to do with what's in the article?" she asked, articulating her biggest fear.

"It would be nice to know one way or the other wouldn't it, though?" he countered.

"I guess so."

His eyes suddenly narrowed. "Hey, didn't you say his laptop got a virus and it's in the shop?"

"Yes."

"Is it still there?"

She wondered where he was going with this. "As far as I know."

"Think you could get a hold of it?"

Her stomach lurched at the request. "Why?"

"Maybe there's something incriminating on it that would give us an answer. I bet, even with a virus, Hack could search the hard drive and find out what kinds of websites Max was visiting."

She pictured the repair shop situated near her neighborhood. It wouldn't be all that hard to march in and ask to have Max's laptop back. But how long before he did the same thing and found out that she'd taken it? Plus, Hack would have to be brought into their small circle which was growing to the size of a jury.

"I don't know, Bronco." She wrung her hands as she thought it through.

"It's up to you," he assured her, but his blue gaze urged her to be brave.

She couldn't prove that Max was guilty of criminal behavior without evidence. "Fine," she agreed, swallowing her nervousness.

Some distance away, a stick snapped drawing their attention. Bronco reached for her elbow and pulled her into motion again, and a tingle of pleasure skated up her arm. To her disappointment, he promptly released her.

Side by side, they continued following the trail which curved back toward the pavilion.

"I guess you're pretty scared," he guessed, after they'd walked fifty yards or more. "I can imagine what it's like living with Max."

Glancing over, she found him studying her profile. She nodded and considered her quandary. "How will the task unit function if his own men suspect that he's a crook? I don't want to undermine the team's effectiveness."

"I promise we'll still consider him our leader unless we find something really incriminating," he assured her. "Just take care of yourself, okay?" Throwing an arm over her shoulders, he caught her off guard as he pulled her into a quick embrace.

Delight shot to every extremity of Rebecca's body. She found herself embracing him back, while marveling out how neatly she fit beneath his arm and against his side. The warmth and camaraderie sparked a sudden longing for his touch. But then he released her, and she had to avert her face to hide her disappointment. "Thank you," she managed.

They broke from the tree line at the same time that a fit brunette stepped out from under the gazebo and into the mellow sunlight. Her gaze spanned the open space and recognition lit her sculpted face. Her eyes flickered at once to Brant.

"It's Susan," Rebecca muttered, dismay slowing her step.

Bronco kept quiet as they continued their casual progress, intercepting the woman's path. Dressed in spandex running shorts and a halter top, it was apparent Susan was about to go for a jog. She took a detailed inventory of the man in uniform as she approached them.

"Hello, Rebecca." She came to full stop. "Enjoying a walk after work?"

"Just catching up with an old friend." With little ability to lie, Rebecca opted for the truth.

Susan's expectant smile forced her to make an introduction. She gestured to Bronco. "This is Chief Adams, who works with Max." She paused and turned. "My neighbor, Susan."

"Such a pleasure." Susan clung to the hand Bronco politely offered. "Well." She widened her eyes at

Rebecca as she finally let it drop. "Better get in my run. See you." With a waggle of her fingers, she stepped around them and took off down the path.

"Bye," Rebecca called. She glanced up at Brant's shadowed gaze. "I am so sorry." Her stomach had begun to knot.

"Not your fault," he assured her, but his tone sounded grim. "Is she a gossip?"

"The worst," she admitted.

"Guess we shouldn't meet for a while."

She nodded, staring anywhere but at him. The thought of not seeing him sat heavy on her heart. Either way, Max was bound to get word of their encounter.

"Call me when you've got the laptop," he added gently. He chucked her under the chin, surprising her and forcing her head up so she was forced to look him in the eye. "I'm still here," he added and sent her a reassuring wink.

And then he walked away, vanishing behind a hedge.

A weak smile lifted the drooping edges of her mouth as she beheld his quick disappearance. How sweet of him to encourage her. But their run-in with Susan had wrecked her afternoon, if not her whole week. The woman thrived on gossip and never bothered to hide her admiration for the Navy SEAL commander. It wouldn't take Susan long to inform Max about his wife's tryst in the park with the handsome chief. If Max had been serious about his threat—and there was no doubt in Rebecca's mind that he was—then Bronco was now in danger.

After everything else that had happened this past week, Rebecca might be better off packing up and moving out, giving up her quest to find grounds for divorce. Perhaps if she left him, Max would forget about threatening Bronco and come after her instead.

Brant pounded out pushups in the corner of the gym. He'd arrived too late to participate in Bullfrog's Jujitsu class; furthermore, the concentration he needed for the class had been shattered by the article Rebecca had given him. He had dismissed himself from class with a wave and worked on his own routine in the corner.

Sweat dripped off his forehead into his right eye. He scarcely felt it over the fire raging in his imagination. What, if anything, did the two homicides attributed to the mob have to do with Max? Why had someone sent him that article in the first place? Was it merely a matter of professional interest, or was someone trying to send Max a message?

Down, up. Down, up.

He pushed himself to complete fifty Hindu pushups while keeping one eye trained on the television in the lobby. On the Weather Channel, the forecaster predicted the likeliest paths for the hurricane barreling across the Atlantic, headed toward Central America. The favored path showed it passing over Cuba. If that happened, Brant's task force would go wheels up in a day or two to execute a mission for which they'd been training the better part of a year.

And wouldn't that suck? he thought with a weight in his chest. Not only would he have to leave Rebecca behind, but he'd be working more closely with Max than ever.

Conversation on the other side of the room signaled the end of Bullfrog's class. Several students lingered, as usual, to ask their sensei questions and to socialize. With a worried glance in Brant's direction, Bullfrog managed to excuse himself and break away. Approaching Brant in his bare feet, he crouched next to him.

Brant's arms gave out without warning. Collapsing onto his stomach, he turned his head to meet his friend's intent gaze. "Take a look in the side pocket of my gym bag," he requested. "Go ahead and read what's in the envelope."

He rolled to a seated position, wiping his dripping face with a towel as Bullfrog followed his directions and perused the article. He only read it once, with swiftness that engendered Brant's envy since he already knew his friend hadn't missed a single detail.

"What *is* this?" Bullfrog demanded with a quizzical look.

Brant glanced around. Apart from one remaining student, the dojo stood empty. "Max has been using Rebecca's old post office box without her knowledge. Clearly, someone sent it to him, while addressing it to her. So, what do you think? Why would anyone send that to him in the first place?"

Trouble brewed in Bullfrog's hazel eyes as he skimmed the article a second time. "Does he know she has this?"

"Hell, no. I'm going to make a copy tonight and remail the original. But tell me what you think. Why would someone send that to Max?"

Bullfrog cut Brant a censorial look. "You don't actually think Max is working for the mob," he said, but his statement sounded more like a question.

"I don't know," Brant replied. "Why does Max own a Swiss investment account with fifty thousand dollars in it?"

Bullfrog stared back at him, not answering.

"Why is some creep named Tony paying him unwanted visits at his house? And why is Mad Max using Rebecca's old mailbox, getting anonymous mail that originated in Bronx, New York?"

Bullfrog examined the envelope more closely, his nostrils flaring. "The CO would have to betray everything we stand for if he's involved in this." He shook his head and looked up. "Max would never risk his reputation."

That was true. Max's status as a SEAL commander meant everything to him. "Yeah, but we all know he lives above his means. Maybe his debts got so big that they threatened his image as a guy who has it all together, and he compromised his integrity for the sake of the almighty dollar."

Bullfrog dropped the envelope back in Brant's bag and pushed to his feet. "I know what's wrong with you," he declared suddenly.

Brant raised his eyebrows inquiringly.

"You're suffering from a severe case of lackanookie, and it's affecting your reasoning." He held out a dinner-plate-sized hand, helping Brant up alongside him.

The made-up malady made Brant laugh. Surprisingly, he felt good about the fact that he'd deprived himself, first with Bethany, then with Rebecca's lookalike. "Honestly, I haven't even thought about sex," he retorted, except in his dreams of Rebecca, which were increasing in frequency and had taken on decidedly sexual overtones.

Bullfrog issued a skeptical grunt. His gaze went past Brant's shoulder to the meteorologist predicting Cuba's utter devastation at the hands of Hurricane Ishmael. "My intuition says we're going wheels up this weekend," he predicted.

Brant groaned his annoyance. "Fuck your intuition, man."

CHAPTER 6

Butterflies swarmed Rebecca's stomach as she edged into the computer repair shop. It had taken all day yesterday to work up the courage to retrieve Max's old lap top. Peeking into her own post office box was one thing. Giving Max's laptop to Bronco so that Hack could probe its history was tantamount to sabotaging the team's cohesiveness.

She should never have agreed to this, except she needed to know if her suspicions about Max were completely unfounded. What if, in her desperation to find grounds to leave him, she was just imagining he was up to something illegal?

Calling the ER to arrange for a late arrival, she had dawdled at home that morning waiting for the shop to open. At 8:05, she stepped into the cluttered space, setting off a chime that announced her as the day's first visitor. There wasn't a soul in sight. But then a shuffling came from the back room, and a man stepped around a heavy curtain to approach the counter while wiping the traces of a greasy breakfast off his chin.

"Can I help you?"

In less than five minutes and with only a modicum of stammering, she left the shop with Max's laptop tucked under her arm. Her nervousness ticked upward as she darted across the bustling parking lot. But no one waylaid her, and soon she was speeding toward the hospital with a sense of accomplishment.

That wasn't so hard. But would she regret it in the long run? There wasn't any guarantee that Hack could get into the hard drive, let alone find something incriminating on it. And if Max went to collect his laptop and discovered that his wife had confiscated it—my God, she'd have hell to pay!

On a positive note, she had an excuse to contact Bronco again. Deciding she could call him from work this time and forego the pay phone, she hurried to the hospital, only to discover her services in the ER were urgently required. The day wore on, but the number of emergency patients did not abate until long after her lunch hour. It was two fifteen in the afternoon when she finally collapsed in the break room, swallowed down her anticipation, and tapped out his number on the land line.

He answered on the second ring. "Chief Adams."

"Hey, it's Rebecca, calling from a hospital phone."

"Oh, hey." The rich pleasure in his voice made her stomach perform a slow cartwheel.

"Hi," she said, stupidly.

"You sound out of breath."

"I got the laptop," she declared, presenting the circumstances as the reason for her breathlessness. In fact, it was the simple act of talking to him that had galvanized her cardio-pulmonary system. "It's in my car, hopefully not frying in the heat."

"Nah, it's barely seventy degrees today," he assured her. "Beautiful day," he added with gusto that invited her to notice.

She glanced hopefully at the window. "Good day to meet in the park?"

His silence tempered her enthusiasm. "We shouldn't be seen together," he reminded her.

"No, of course not." Her spirits floundered. "Then how do I get it to you? I have to work late because I came in late."

"Go unlock your car," he recommended. "I'll swing by after work and pick it up."

She wouldn't even get to see his face. "Okay." She forced her agreement through a tight throat. "Did you show the article to anyone?"

"Just to Bullfrog. He doesn't think Max is involved."

"I see." She didn't know whether to be relieved or devastated.

"But he could be wrong," Bronco added, causing her breath to hitch. "You know we're headed out of town on Friday, right?"

She hadn't known. Dismay pegged her to her seat. "The whole task unit?"

"Just Echo Platoon. We'll be gone for a week or so."

"Max didn't tell me." He tended to keep her in the dark about the task unit's activities.

"Listen," he said, then paused. "I think you should move out while he's gone."

Her brain short-circuited at the unexpected advice. "But I don't have any grounds for moving out. He'll claim that I deserted him, and I won't get a cent back that I put into that house."

"That's not what matters, Becca." She scarcely recognized his serious tone. "Forget my suspicions and forget finding grounds for divorce. Just leave him this weekend. You need to do it for your safety's sake."

A chill blew through her as she thought of the stranger named Tony and his promise that they'd meet again. Her gut had been telling her exactly what Bronco seemed to be saying—that she wasn't safe staying with Max any longer. "I'll think about it," she promised.

He released a frustrated breath. "Listen, I'll have some cellular reception while I'm gone. Maybe you can get a new cell phone and text me? I'd sure like to hear that you've made steps in breaking away. Think you could do that? For me?"

When he begged like that, it was hard to refuse him. If Max would be gone for a week, that would give her plenty of time to find a place to live and to move her belongings, but could she actually go through with it? He hadn't browbeaten her recently or assigned her with tasks that were meant to teach her a lesson. In fact, he'd been the epitome of politeness, perhaps sensing her dissatisfaction.

"If I leave him, will you—?" She floundered for words, grateful that he couldn't see the blush searing her cheeks.

"Will I what?"

"Hang out with me sometime? As…as a friend, of course," she tacked on. Her pulse beat against her eardrums as she waited for an answer.

"Yeah, sure," he said, but the thread of reservation in his tone left her doubting his word. He was probably thinking it would kill his career to be friends with his CO's ex-wife. She couldn't blame him for being cautious.

An awkward lull fell between them.

She harkened to the reason for her call. "I'll go unlock my car now. It's parked right outside the ER. You'll let me know if Hack finds anything suspicious?"

"I doubt he'll have time before we leave but, yeah, I'll let you know."

"Be safe on the mission," she begged him.

"You be safe, too, Becca." His voice was low, its rasp seeming to resonate inside her.

"Bye." She hung up the phone slowly, warmed by his apparent concern and the way he'd said her name.

Since when had Echo Platoon's playboy become so important to her? The thought of harm befalling him filled her with panic. If not for his friendship and his support, she would be feeling totally lost. And yet Bronco, being a chief who was active in the field, participating in missions so terrifying it would curl her hair to learn the details, could so easily come to harm.

An image of him lying still and cold flashed through her mind. She blinked back tears of terror, then felt silly for letting her emotions run away with her. The mental image brought to mind the homeless man who had looked so much like him. Curious to know if that man's body had been claimed yet, she picked up the receiver once more and dialed down to the basement.

"Hi, this is Rebecca from the ER. I brought you a drug overdose victim over a week ago. Late twenties, with no name. Has anybody claimed him?"

"No, he's still here," said the young tech named TJ.

"I see." She already knew that the body could stay for up to thirty days. Then, if the next of kin still couldn't be found, the state medical examiner would either donate the body to science or hand him over to a funeral home for cremation and a proper burial service. "Don't forget to let me know if someone comes looking for him."

"I won't."

"Thanks." Hanging up, she swallowed the sour taste in her mouth.

Bronco isn't going to die, she assured herself. SEALs trained long and hard to ensure their own safety in spite of the dangers they faced. He would make it back safe and sound. Question was, when she finally saw him again would she still be living like a prisoner in Max's house? Or would she be free to spend time with him the way she so badly wanted to?

And would he be willing to see her as long as Max was his commander? In any case, nothing could happen until she moved out of her home.

You will rue the day that you mention a divorce to me again.

Max's old threat echoed in her head. What did it mean exactly? Was he capable of inflicting more pain and punishment than he'd ever shown her up to now? All of her life, she'd gone out of her way to avoid conflict—to soothe and help people in distress. By contrast, Max took pleasure in crushing his opponents, in coming out the victor. How far would he go to keep her from leaving him?

And did that matter? After all that Max had put her through and with Bronco cheering her on, she would seem so spineless if she didn't finally defy her husband. All she needed now was a little push.

Max drew the letter out of his post office box, wondering what the hell had taken it so long to get there. Like the other envelopes from the Scarpas, it was addressed to Rebecca, with no return address. He narrowed his gaze on the circular origination stamp. Virginia Beach, Virginia? The other two letters had come from Bronx, New York. But, then again, Tony Scarpa was probably still in the area, and he'd probably been the one to mail the letter, so that in itself was not suspicious.

The *click-clack* of high heels drew his distracted

gaze toward the dark-haired woman walking in from the dusky outdoors. With the service desk closed, she crossed straight to the automated teller. Max would rather have come here on a Sunday, but since he was leaving the country at dawn on Friday, he didn't have much choice. The Scarpas were eager for him to get their next job done. Too bad they would have to wait for him to come back from Cuba. His first allegiance was to Uncle Sam. They had to realize that.

Tucking the letter under his armpit, he secured the box and turned briskly toward the doors, aware that the woman standing in front of the automated teller had glanced his way.

"Max? Is that you?"

He was tempted to ignore the greeting, except that he recognized the voice, and ignoring his neighbor would make their next encounter rather awkward.

He stopped in his tracks and turned to face her. "Susan." He inclined his head briefly.

Dressed in her professional attire—a red silk shirt, black skirt, and four-inch heels—the successful real estate agent exuded sex appeal, especially when she leveled her cat-like gaze on him and smiled a slow, seductive smile.

"How are you?" she purred. The machine beside her spat out a book of stamps, and she leaned way over, thrusting her lush ass behind her while letting her blouse gape.

Max caught a glimpse of her black, satin bra and his blood heated. "Fine," he clipped. While he would love taking her up on her unspoken offer, he wasn't stupid. Fucking his single neighbor wasn't exactly discreet. And it could ruin the reputation he'd fought long and hard to secure. "You?"

"Excellent. You know, it's funny that I should run into you," she mused, fanning herself with the stamps as she sashayed closer. "I ran into Rebecca the other day at Gateway Park. She was there with a man who works for you." She pretended to recollect the name. "Chief Adams, I think it was."

Her announcement hit him squarely in the solar plexus. "You saw them together?"

"Yes," she said with a hard smile. "Good looking man, too, but I wouldn't worry." She laid a consoling hand on his forearm and squeezed it in a silent invitation to take advantage of her consolation. "No one holds a candle to you, Max."

"Thank you. I'll tell her you said hi." Too shaken by her news to manage more small talk, he tugged his arm free and marched out of the post office ahead of her.

Seconds later, he shut himself into his Tahoe, so inflamed by Susan's announcement that he scarcely gave a thought to the letter tucked under his arm. Now that he considered it, Rebecca had come home late from work on both Monday *and* Tuesday evening this past week. She'd told him she'd stayed after for yoga, but was that even true? Or had she been rendezvousing at the park with his chief both evenings?

His blood heated to a simmer, then a rolling boil. My God, was she cheating on him with that cocky playboy? Surely she had more sense than that! He was certain she did, but why had she flagrantly ignored her husband's warning and connected with the chief anyway? She must think herself in love with the man!

That thought engendered an even more awful suspicion—what if she'd relayed her glimpse into Max's Swiss account to Adams? Granted, he'd immediately closed that account, opening a new one with the same company, on the off chance that she'd made a note of his account number. But the thought of his chief even suspecting that he was hoarding money offshore made him queasy. And what if Rebecca mentioned something about their visitor, Tony? Would Adams put two and two together?

Of course not. How could he know who Tony was? Even so, Adams becoming this friendly with his wife was intolerable. He was the CO, God damn it! It had to stop, and it had to stop *now,* before word of Max's erectile dysfunction became common knowledge, making him the laughing stock of the entire team!

He shuddered in dread. Whatever it took, he needed to get that message across to Rebecca, tonight, unequivocally. Her affair with Chief Adams, or whatever the hell she wanted to call it, was *over.*

Reining in his temper, he shifted his thoughts to the letter as he pulled it out from under his arm. A glance through his driver's door showed Susan driving off in her Town Car. Drawing a deep breath, he slit open the envelope. A small newspaper article fluttered into his palm. Somewhere in this article he would learn the identity of his next target. Switching on the interior light, so he could better see it, he read the article with a gathering frown.

By the time he arrived at the end, his skin felt like it had shrunk two sizes.

It was apparent that the homicides being referred to in the article were the two that he had perpetrated. It was also apparent that FBI Special Agent Doug Castle, who'd been pursuing the Scarpas for a decade, suspected they'd hired a sniper with Special Forces training to kill for them. There was no question in Max's mind who his next mark was going to be.

Oh, hell, no. He shook his head vehemently. He drew the line at killing a fellow peace keeper—an FBI agent, of all people!

Feeling short of breath, Max tugged loose the collar

of his BDU jacket. Taking out a government employee wasn't the same as killing a couple of lowlife criminals. Hell, the special agent was probably a man like himself, with true grit and a flawless service record. Besides, even if Max killed him, another agent would take his place. Special agents were like SEALs in that regard. They avenged the deaths of their colleagues, and they didn't know the meaning of the word *quit.*

"Fuck that," Max declared, tossing the article onto the seat next to him and starting up the engine.

Tonight on Google chat, he would let the Scarpas know that he'd be returning their down payment. He wasn't their puppet, and he wasn't scared of them. They could go to fucking hell for all he cared.

With moist palms and a heavy heart, Rebecca nosed her car into her garage. Bronco had retrieved Max's laptop from her car sometime that day, but it would likely be a while before Hack even got a look at it. The longer the Dell was out of the shop, the higher the odds that Max would find out she'd taken it. And then what? She'd have to answer for herself, which wasn't exactly fair, since Max was the one cheating the system, not her.

You won't have to answer for it if you're not here, she reminded herself.

Reluctant to face her husband, she slowly got out of her car. As his Tahoe indicated, he was already home. She entered the house through the laundry room, hung her purse on the hook next to Max's keys, and listened. The house stood ominously silent.

She waded cautiously deeper, her footsteps audible as she crossed the tiled kitchen and forded the great room. Not a sound suggested Max was here, though she knew he was. A quick glance through the windows showed the back yard deserted, lights shining in the shell-shaped pool.

Her nerves pulled taut as she headed down the back hallway toward the light shining through the partly open door of their bedroom. Pushing it farther open, she drew up short to see Max standing between her and the *en suite*. His commanding breadth and intimidating scowl chased the air back into her lungs.

"Hi," she said.

He folded his arms across his chest. "Where've you been?"

The hostile question dumped adrenaline into her bloodstream. "I had to work late because I felt sick this morning and went to work at nine."

He sent her an ugly little smile. "You sure you weren't meeting Chief Adams at the park?"

The reason for his hostility became instantly apparent. Susan must have approached him with her news. Anger leached into Rebecca's bones, lending her courage. "Positive," she replied, toeing off her shoes as she always did at the end of the day. "And you can call the hospital to check my hours," she added, hoping to God he didn't take her up on that.

Max stalked her slowly. She had to lock her knees to keep from backing away from him. "And yet you met him there on Monday and Tuesday, didn't you? You weren't at yoga. You were cavorting with him at the park."

In actuality, she'd gone to the post office on Monday, but he didn't need to know that. Biting her tongue to abstain from correcting him, she bent to collect her shoes. Before she had the chance, he seized her jaw between his thumb and fingers and wrenched her gaze up to meet his fulminating glare.

"Answer me!" he raged.

"I ran into Chief Adams at the park on Tuesday,"

she admitted through her teeth. "We talked for a little while, that's all."

"Is it, now? I'm surprised you would even say a word to him. I'm pretty sure I made it clear you were never to talk to him again." He kept hold of her, lowering his face until it was scant inches from hers. Onion-laced breath assaulted her nostrils. "You're *my* wife," he continued. "I will not have you ruining my good name by consorting with that playboy."

Fury and fear competed for control of her tongue. "I doubt you need any help ruining your good name."

Rage exploded in his eyes. He released her jaw only to raise his hand as though to strike her. She flinched, but the blow never came. Instead, he grabbed her arm and hurled her toward the bed. She sprawled across the mattress, tried to scramble to the other side, but collapsed onto her stomach as a heavy hand descended on the small of her back and kept her pinned.

"Do I need to remind you who your husband is?" Max grated, crawling over her.

Grabbing the elastic waist of her scrubs, he hauled them down, using both hands to pull them nearly to her knees, panties and all.

Horrified, Rebecca thrashed to free herself. "Stop it!"

But he sat on her hamstrings, pinning her legs as he fumbled to release the fly at the front of his BDUs.

"Don't do this, Max. What's wrong with you?"

"Nothing is wrong with me, damn you!" he growled. "I'm asserting my marital rights to prove a point." He shifted, wedging a knee between her thighs.

"You have no right to force me!" Rebecca railed. She managed to twist onto one elbow, but her legs were still caught beneath his haunches. "Get off me," she commanded, shoving ineffectually at his shoulder as he leaned over her, pumping his flaccid member and breathing hard. She was never more grateful for his performance issues.

This taunting went on for another half a minute as he worked on himself and kept his other hand on her naked bottom. At last, he seemed to give up.

"Fine," he relented, lifting his weight off her and letting her wriggle away. He pointed a thick finger in her direction. "But you'd better remember where your loyalty lies or, by God, you'll regret ever betraying me."

The cruelty in his slate gray eyes stunned her. Over the past year she had become increasingly aware of this ugly side of him. Lately, it was becoming the only side that she could see.

He threw himself off the bed as if the very sight of her disgusted him. With a final, scathing glare, he stalked out of their bedroom, buttoning up his pants as he went. Slamming the door shut behind him, he knocked the tiny wooden cross hanging over the lintel off its nail. It fell to the floor, landing silently on the plush carpet.

Rebecca stared at the fallen cross. It had been a wedding gift from Joe and Penny Montgomery, SEAL Team 12's commander and his sweet-natured wife. Its plunge to the floor struck her as symbolic. Her marriage was over.

She sat up slowly, blinking back the tears that pressured her eyes. To hell with finding grounds for divorcing Max. Bronco was right. He was dangerous. He couldn't make her life any more of a living hell after she left him than he was making it now.

If she was ever going to respect herself, she needed to leave. Luckily, his upcoming assignment offered the perfect opportunity for her to get away.

CHAPTER 7

Brant ducked out of the hatch of the C-17 Globemaster military transport plane and jumped onto the tarmac in Vieques, Puerto Rico. Hot, humid air buffeted his woodland-camo BDUs as he trudged with the rest of Echo Platoon to the back of the plane to collect his gear. His boots felt heavy. He had trouble finding his smile. Only half of the task unit was needed for this mission, and Charlie Platoon had been left behind. He wished it had been the other way around.

Get your head in the game, man, he scolded himself. It was his job to motivate the others, and normally a mission like this had his blood thrumming and his testosterone revved up. But not this time. *What the hell's wrong with you?*

He drew a deep breath and attempted to center himself the way Bullfrog had taught him in his Jujitsu class. Sultry air, redolent with scent of the Caribbean and of wild-growing hibiscus, reminded him that he loved Puerto Rico. The sun, the turquoise waters, the stunning sunsets—who could ask for more?

But as he glanced at his phone, it was his proximity

to the U.S. and his uninterrupted cellular service that he cared about most. And—check it out—Becca had finally texted him!

His first smile of the day tugged at the edges of his mouth as he read her message.

Hey, this is my new cell phone number. I'm looking for an apartment this weekend—R.

"Awesome." Pride rolled through him at the realization that she was actually doing it—she was leaving Mad Max! Regret caught up to him, however, keeping him from doing a happy dance. This wasn't all good news.

Sure, she'd be safer now, especially if his hunch was right and Max had gotten involved with an organized crime family. And true, they could now spend time together without Max breathing down their necks. But, as he'd already reasoned, spending time with Rebecca would only deepen their feelings of affection for each other. It violated his relationship guidelines, which meant he was going to have to end their relationship eventually.

But not any time soon, he decided. She needed his encouragement right now. And what were friends for but to be there for each other, in spirit, if not physically?

Cool, he texted back. Almost immediately, he sensed that he was being watched. Glancing up, he encountered Max's narrow-eyed stare, and an icy sensation climbed his spine. He swallowed against a dry mouth and put his phone away. Imagine how Max would react if he knew his wife was texting his chief. Turning to collect his pack, Brant slung it over his shoulder and transitioned to the transport vehicles.

Forty minutes later, he sat with his platoon members in the abandoned administration building, which was now their temporary operations command, or TOC. Several of the windows had been broken since the regular military had ceased using Vieques as a training facility. Only Special Operations still used it, and they considered real windows an unnecessary luxury. A hot breeze wafted through the shattered panes. Fat, droning flies kept the men awake as Max briefed them on the mission.

"Tonight and again tomorrow we run through the procedures we've been drilling. The mission begins in the evening in advance of the storm's arrival. It'll still be a ways off the coast, but it's going to be a rough ride to Cuba," he warned.

Hence the code name that the departing squad had invented for themselves—Rough Riders, a nod to local history and the group of men Teddy Roosevelt had commanded over a century earlier to seize San Juan. Brant, in his determination to follow his father's example in the rodeo circuit, had ridden rough throughout his youth. The thought of weathering a helicopter ride in a hurricane punched up his adrenaline only slightly.

What gave him a real jolt was Max's cold gaze, which seemed to go straight through him. He suffered the sudden certainty that the woman at the park had put a bug in Max's ear. That would account for the deadly glitter in the CO's eyes. Or maybe he'd learned that his laptop had been removed from the repair shop.

Not that it mattered either way. For the time being, they were still teammates with a common objective: Destroy the Cold-War era listening stations that the Russians had resurrected in Havana a year earlier, installing over three thousand soldiers and complex gadgetry to spy on the neighboring U.S.A. The hurricane bearing down on Cuba afforded the SEALs the perfect opportunity to disable the station while making it look like the storm had wrecked it.

Their mission took precedence over personal concerns. They were professionals. If Brant couldn't trust his own commander in a combat situation, who the hell could he trust?

Master Chief Kuzinsky's tenor voice wrested his attention as he took over the briefing. In spite of his slight build, the auburn-haired warrior struck fear into the hearts of junior SEALs because of his fearsome reputation. His dark brown, almost black, eyes reflected the horrors of the worst battles in SEAL history, which he alone had survived. He rarely smiled, more rarely cracked a joke, but when he addressed a group of SEALs, they hung on every word coming out of his mouth. Only the highest ranking SEALs ever called him by his first name, Rusty.

He brought up an aerial photo of a hurricane, three-hundred-miles wide and swirling toward the West Indies, then swiped the screen bringing Cuba into their line of sight. "Here's where you'll touch down, six miles from the target."

Toggling closer, he magnified their view of an uninhabited bit of swampy land on the edge of Havana Harbor. "You'll hunker here and wait for the storm to hit in earnest. Once the power's knocked out and the roads are flooded, you'll make your way along the shore and through this neighborhood called *Barrio de la Regla* to the listening station. You'll destroy the antenna boxes on the roof and disable the components exactly as we've drilled. When the job's done, you'll swim out through the harbor—" He toggled toward the north, "—passing over the Havana Tunnel. The sub will be waiting to pick you up three miles out. Halliday has the coordinates. Any questions? Sam?"

Officer in charge of the Rough Riders, Sam had thrust a hand into the air. "With all due respect, Master Chief, I think we need at least three contingency plans. I've weathered a category four before, and this is a five. Things aren't going to go down the way we're planning."

Sam's concern prompted a rumble from his platoon members.

"Plus our comms are bound to fail," Haiku added, implying that they'd have no way to communicate their back up plans.

"Look." Max pushed off the wall to pace before them. "You Rough Riders were chosen for your experience. You know as well as I do that there are too many unknowns in this assignment to plan for any fail-proof contingencies. Just use your combined savvy to surmount resistance. If you don't make it to the exfil in a reasonable amount of time, and if comms remain down, we'll find you by your infrared strobes, and we'll send in an extraction team. But let's hope it doesn't come to that. We have a critical goal here, and no one needs to know of our participation."

By no one, Max meant the Russians. If the SEALs were caught destroying the facility, that might well instigate a full-scale war.

Considering his fellow Rough Riders, Brant didn't suffer Sam's concerns. He had confidence in Sam, who would call the shots. Haiku would handle the radio. Tristan Halliday, a former NASCAR racer, would navigate. Carl Wolfe, their ordinance expert, would work with the dark-skinned Teddy "Bear" Brewbaker and with savvy Hack Stuart to destroy the antennas and the station's mainframe. Bullfrog, their corpsman, would patch up anyone who happened to get hurt. And Brant, a sniper with thirty-eight kills to his name, would dispose of unexpected human opposition.

Easy day.

"Enough talk." Max cut the briefing short by stalking to the door. "Let's get out there and run through this."

Joining the others in a resounding "Hooyah!", Brant pushed to his feet. It was hard to believe that in twenty-four hours he'd be slogging through a hurricane. His thoughts remained ensnared in Becca's circumstances and whether his intuition was right that Max had sold out to the mob.

But what if Sam's prediction of chaos proved correct, and the Rough Riders never made it back from Cuba?

The first seed of doubt rooted in Brant's mind. *Oh, hell, no.* He wasn't going to perish on this op and leave Rebecca to deal with Max all by herself. For the time being, he was still her friend. And friends didn't check out on you when you needed them most.

Max watched the Rough Riders flow flawlessly through the drill. The sun had dropped below the horizon, and their shadows drifted alongside them as they leapfrogged each other's positions up an alley lined with houses toward the mock-up of the listening station. The eight extras in the sixteen-man platoon hampered their approach, offering all manner of creative resistance, which the Rough Riders met without flinching. The one named Bullfrog harbored an uncanny ability to sense a trap before it happened.

Max narrowed his eyes on Chief Adam's silhouette as he raised a fist, bringing his squad to a halt. Through eyes that overlooked no details, the sniper scanned the three-story structure that was their target before giving the Rough Riders an all clear. Slinging his suppressed Stoner SR-225, a weapon with awesome range and accuracy, over one shoulder, he then shimmied up the pipe that ran vertically up the outside of the whitewashed building to the roof.

Max could see why Rebecca was drawn to him. Adams had the body of a hard-riding cowboy—broad shoulders, lean waist, muscular thighs. His reflexes were the fastest Max had ever encountered, and his aim was every bit as good as Max's. Plus, he was always smiling. Which was so fucking annoying. Even now, his white teeth flashed in the gloom, as he met each challenge with obvious enjoyment.

Jealousy burbled in Max's gut. Just how far had Adams gone with Rebecca? How close were they? Had she told him about his shortcomings in the bedroom? Was that before or after she mentioned Max's foreign account?

A moist spot formed between his shoulder blades. The rasp of Kuzinsky's voice, uttered practically in his ear, gave him a start.

"What do you make out their odds to be?" Kuzinsky's gloomy tone conveyed pessimism.

"They look good," Max retorted, watching as four of the eight men followed Brant up the metal pipes that fed water from the vestibule on the roof to the rooms below. Thank God for Havana's inferior plumbing system or the squad would have to get a rope up on the roof in hundred-mile-an-hour winds and then climb it. Once up there, they would dismantle the antenna boxes and pull wires, the storm masking their destruction. Meanwhile, Haiku, Bullfrog, and Halliday would guard the perimeter below.

"Ever experience a category five hurricane before?" Master Chief inquired.

A memory of torrential wind, slashing rain, and

falling trees flashed through his mind. "Once," he admitted, having helped his sister to weather Hurricane Katrina.

Kuzinsky's subsequent silence spoke volumes. The man had voiced opposition to Operation Rough Riders from the start. Taking out the listening station was tricky enough without adding Mother Nature's wrath into the mix. But Admiral Johansen, head of JSOTF, and the SEAL Team commander, Joe Montgomery, both believed the mission could be done.

Hell, the Commander-in-Chief himself had ordered it. So it wasn't Max's fault if the mission failed. And if some of the men lost their lives due to the storm or unforeseen resistance—then, oh well. They would have died protecting American interests, something every SEAL was prepared to do. It happened that way sometimes.

And, if it happened this time, all of Max's troubles would be over. A dark hope penetrated his bleak thoughts.

If Kuzinsky was right—and Max had never known him to be wrong—this mission was doomed from the outset. The Rough Riders never stood a chance. While Max couldn't afford to lose the best eight men in his task unit, how better to get Chief Adams out of his life for good than to let this mission proceed as planned?

"They'll be fine," he said, silencing Kuzinsky's implied protest.

For once, he hoped he was wrong.

Rebecca filled the boxes on her bed with her jewelry box, her favorite books, a photo album from her childhood, and her knitting bag. These boxes would contain the last of what she was taking with her. She'd decided to leave behind anything that didn't fit into her car. She would rather not bring any memories with her, and most of their furniture had been Max's before they married. Still, moving had taken the better part of two days. It was Sunday night. She had to get up at dawn for work the next day and meet with her lawyer in the afternoon, and she was already dead on her feet. Not a good way to start the workweek.

Coming across a framed photo of her wedding day, she studied it in the light of her bedside lamp. How naïve she had looked three years ago! She'd had no idea then who Max really was. It was the idea of him that had appealed to her more than anything else. Tipping the frame over, she left it face down on the dresser and turned to empty her nightstand.

Her gaze strayed to their bed. Thank God she hadn't had to share it with Max the night of their last awful encounter. He had spent that night at Spec Ops and left with his task unit early on Friday morning. The very next evening, she'd gone apartment hunting after work and found a sweet little garden apartment with immediate availability. Situated near the hospital, it offered every amenity she needed, plus an affordable lease.

Her new life was about to unfold. Not a single twinge of uncertainty had assailed her as she'd packed up her possessions, only a nervous tremor when she envisioned Max coming home to find her gone. The words he'd spoken in this very room echoed in her head like a death knell. *You'd better remember where your loyalty lies or, by God, you'll regret ever betraying me.* It sounded hauntingly similar to the other threat he'd made.

Of course, he would view her leaving as a betrayal. In Max's eyes, she belonged to him, the same way that his boat and his kit car did. Her leaving him wouldn't change the way he viewed her, she was certain.

With the boxes full, she taped them shut and took a final look around. The room she had so carefully decorated struck her as cold and empty. Carrying the boxes one at a time to the garage, she loaded them into her car.

As she wedged the last box into her trunk, her gaze went to the dark sky visible through the open garage door. Soon, she would arm the security system and close that door with her remote control—the same way she would close this short era of her life—never to return again.

But the lateness of the hour dismayed her. She had wanted to unload the last of her things before nightfall, where they would join the rest of her belongings and three suitcases in the unfurnished apartment. She had already gone grocery shopping to stock her kitchen cupboards and had even purchased a queen-sized airbed at the Exchange to carry her over until she could afford to buy herself a new mattress.

Closing her trunk with finality, she retrieved her purse from the hook inside and shut the laundry room door. Then she crossed to the black box on the garage wall and set the intrusion detection system to come on thirty seconds after the automatic door touched down.

Slipping behind the wheel of the car which she had backed in trunk first, she cranked the engine and pulled straight out. Lifting the visor to point the remote control in the right direction, she punched it one last time. The satisfying sound of the door rumbling shut reached her ears. *Good-bye house.* Then, from right behind her seat came a rustling that preceded a metallic click.

"Easy," crooned a familiar voice as she let out a startled scream.

A backward glance confirmed her first guess. The dark hair and eyes of the man who'd introduced himself as Tony caused the steering wheel to wobble in her grip. Knowing he had a gun pointed at her head, she nearly struck one of the oaks at the head of the driveway.

"Steady now," he ordered in his distinct inner-city dialect. "Take a right out of the driveway. I'll tell you where to go."

"Wh-what do you want?" Her voice came out high and frightened.

"Head toward the Boulevard and don't panic," he added ignoring her question. "I ain't gonna hurt you."

Max isn't around. She caught back the words in the nick of time. Tony might know that already, but why confess to her vulnerability?

Wrestling with her fear, she pointed her car in the direction indicated, driving without thinking as her mind raced. Was she being abducted? Shouldn't she do something immediately to prevent being taken?

She eyed a pickup truck on the side of the road, thinking she could swerve at the last instant and ram into the bed. Her airbag would deploy, keeping her safe while Tony would probably sail over the seat and hit his head. But what if the gun prodding the base of her skull discharged?

"Turn right at the next street," he instructed.

Right? They hadn't even left the neighborhood. There was nothing down this way but an empty, marshy lot where the road dead-ended.

In dread, having no other plan up her sleeve, she turned the wheel to the right, where the familiar black form of Tony's BMW sucked the remaining moisture from her mouth. Two men in ski masks rolled out of the rear doors, and she knew at once that they were going to put her in that car.

"No!" she cried, braking abruptly. She started to jam her gear shift into reverse.

"Ah-ah!" He rammed the snout of his gun hard against her skull. "Park the car," he grated in a sterner voice.

"Please don't take me anywhere," she begged. "Max isn't here. He can't negotiate with you right now." The words, whether wise to admit or not, tumbled out of her. The two other men descended on her vehicle. Her driver's door popped open.

"Out you go," Tony encouraged.

Certain that she would never be seen or heard from again, she resisted mightily, letting loose a cry for help. But the larger thug clapped a hand over her mouth and subdued her struggles with his superior strength. He dragged her to the BMW and tossed her onto the back seat. Then he got in beside her while his companion entered through the door on the other side, bookending her between them.

Terror held a vise-grip on Rebecca's vocal cords. She drew herself in tightly, hugged her chest and pressed her knees together to keep from touching either man. Her heartbeat crested against her eardrums as she waited for whatever came next.

Tony slipped into the front seat beside the wordless, masked driver. He turned sideways, his eyes glinting in the darkness as he assessed her defensive posture. "I had a feeling we would meet again." He chuckled when she failed to speak. "Don't be so standoffish," he scolded. "We ain't gonna hurt you, so long as Max cooperates. Tie her hands and feet and gag her," he said, contradicting his promise.

"No, please!" Tears of terror flooded Rebecca's eyes. Rough hands reached for her. In the next instant, plastic cuffs cinched her wrists and ankles together. A handkerchief went around her mouth, so tightly that her teeth cut her lips and she tasted blood.

"Good enough," Tony declared. He held up an

object that proved to be a phone. He used to take her picture, the bright flash blinding her briefly.

"Now," he said. "When my guy loosens the gag, I want you to tell me Max's cell phone number."

She started to shake her head, but then thought better of it. She wanted the gag loosened. And besides, why should she protect Max from receiving communications when he'd involved himself with these goons in the first place? She gave a slow nod of understanding.

The thug on her left untied the gag, and she licked her injured lips before relaying Max's number. The light of Tony's phone illuminated his smirk as he appeared to send Max the photo he'd just taken. She imagined what she looked like in it, bound and gagged and clearly terrified in the presence of two masked men.

At the risk of being gagged again, she asked the question burning inside her. "What do you want from Max?"

The two men in ski masks burst into guffaws, clearly amused by her ignorance.

Tony looked up from his cell phone. "Shut up," he barked at them, and they fell instantly silent. "What do you think I want?" he asked, regarding her intently.

"I have no idea," she answered honestly.

"You don't know what Max has done for us?"

She shook her head. "No." If only she did, she'd have no concerns about deserting him.

"Good," he said on a note of approval. "Max knows how to keep a secret, then. Let's see what he has to say about you keeping us company."

"You might not get through to him," she warned. "He's on a mission." Max's phone worked almost anywhere in the world, but sometimes he was too busy to notice his calls.

"For your sake, let's hope we do," he retorted. His words chilled her to the marrow while hollowing her heart with regret.

Why did this have to happen now, when she'd finally taken measures to live apart from Max? At this rate, she might never get to know Bronco the way she wanted to.

"Yee haw!" Brant sought to alleviate the tension in the rear bay of the Sikorsky UH-60 Black Hawk by pretending to ride a particularly ornery bronc. The blacked-out helicopter—the same aircraft used in the Osama bin Laden raid—bucked and shuddered as it clattered over the Caribbean ocean on its way to Havana, Cuba.

The operations officer must have underestimated the winds whipping over the water in advance of the approaching hurricane. It was all the Black Hawk could do to punch through the gale and to carry them toward their destination. Brant could see it in the faces of his teammates made barely visible by the muted striplighting—*doubt.* They weren't exactly certain they would make it.

Sam, more than anyone, sat still and stiff on the little seat that folded down, his mouth compressed in a resolute line. Haiku looked as if he were mouthing a prayer or one of his abstract sayings. Bullfrog had escaped into a deep meditative state. Only Halliday, a racecar driver in his former life, seemed totally at ease.

Brant felt compelled to reassure his platoon leader. "We're good, sir!" He had to shout to be heard over the rotors and the howling wind.

The welded pins that kept the Black Hawk in one piece strained and groaned as the hull flexed in the crosscurrents. They skidded through the sky—left, right, up, down.

"I think we're through the worst of it," he added. Stretching out a hand, he touched Sam's knee. It was easy to understand that he must be thinking of his wife and new baby, perhaps wondering if he'd ever see them again. "Remember the ride through Khyber Pass three years ago? This is a walk in the park compared to that."

On that particular mission, their helicopter had clipped a limestone overhang, causing it to spiral into a tailspin and crash-land in Taliban-controlled territory. Not a fun three days. Maybe he shouldn't have brought that up. "The point is we all survived. We'll get through this."

"Ten clicks to the LZ," the pilot reported, reinforcing Brant's assertion.

"See? We got this." No sooner had the words left his mouth than the Black Hawk pitched face down on an updraft. Brant's stomach vaulted into his mouth. The back end dropped just as suddenly, and he gritted his teeth to keep from losing his dinner. For the first time, doubt bloomed inside of him. Christ, they would be lucky if they made it ten more kilometers.

Under normal circumstances, he'd be sitting in the open doorway, manning the mounted M60 machine gun, fending off surface-to-air missiles. That was standard operating procedure in Afghanistan. But no one knew about their little vacation in the Caribbean, so defense wasn't necessary at this juncture. Besides, if the cargo door stood open, their helo would be blown around like a hot air balloon.

Turning to peer out the window, he sought any sign of land. Clouds surrounded them, and when he leaned close and looked straight down, all he could make out was the ocean, roiling fitfully below.

"Power on the mainland is down," the pilot

reported.

That was good for the SEALs. The inhabitants of Havana had battened down the hatches and were braced to weather the storm. Ideally, they'd never notice the muted clatter of the stealth helicopter as it swept over them.

Bam! The Black Hawk lurched sideways, nearly tipping over as a cross gale smashed into it.

Brant tightened his grip on the harness that kept him in his seat. "Hooyah," he managed, fighting to stay positive. He could sense the pilots scrambling to bring their aircraft under control. It plunged earthward, at the mercy of a hundred-mile-an-hour gust.

"Circling back to pass again."

They'd missed their opportunity to land. Brant surprised himself by sending up a quick prayer. *Please let me see Rebecca again.*

He glanced at Bullfrog, hoping his friend's visualization techniques were as effective as he claimed. Bullfrog once insisted that he could shape the outcome of events with only his thoughts.

Brant directed his gaze through the window again. This time he caught a glimpse of palm trees swaying in the dark, each one bowed under the onslaught of the wind. And Hurricane Ishmael hadn't even arrived in earnest yet.

Rooftops of the impoverished capital came into view next, and then they were skimming over a body of water that he guessed to be the Bay of Havana. The landing zone lay just beyond the head of the southernmost inlet.

Almost there. We're going to make it.

They dropped fifty feet, another twenty. Then the aircraft ceased its forward momentum. For a moment, it teetered uncertainly over what looked to be marshy terrain dotted by scrubby trees. With an ungainly clatter, they struck earth, first one wheel, then the other, nearly pitching over sideways. Then all movement ceased.

The rotors sang a descending scale that mirrored the exhalations of the operators and the crew. Brant didn't envy the pilots their return trip home. He would much rather swim out to a sub in deep, undisturbed waters than make a ride like that again.

"Let's go," Sam ordered in a tight voice.

It was Brant's job to pull open the bay door. Sultry, wet air billowed in.

Peering through his NVGs, he swept an assessing gaze around them. Not a soul in sight visible through his night vision goggles. Operation Rough Rider was still a go, and this was just the beginning of a near-impossible mission.

CHAPTER 8

———◆———

Max felt the cellphone in his breast pocket vibrate, but he ignored it. He, Kuzinsky, and the remaining eight members of Echo Platoon hovered around the radio in the TOC, eager for news of a successful insertion. The last report to reach them had come from the pilots several minutes ago, relaying that the LZ was ten kilometers away. But they hadn't heard anything since.

"Trust Buster to Rough Riders, do you copy?" Third-class Austin Collins, who manned the radio, repeated the hail for the fifth time. Everyone knew the Black Hawk ought to have landed by now. They ought to have heard something.

Max took note of the tiny beads of sweat glistening on Kuzinsky's upper lip as he leaned over Collin's shoulder. The possibility that the helo hadn't made it to Cuba didn't disturb Max the way it did the master chief. He would have one less problem in his life if Brant Adams perished that very night.

Their only answer was a steady hiss, rather like the roar of the wind and rain coming through the broken windows behind him. Hurricane Ishmael was skirting the southern coast of Puerto Rico on its way north to Cuba, but it was causing flooding and destruction, even in Vieques.

"Keep trying," Max instructed, and Kuzinsky nudged Collins to key the radio again.

Max's cell phone vibrated a second time.

With every eye in the room glued to the handset, he lifted his android out of his breast pocket and stole a quick glance at the screen. The only people who knew his private number were Rebecca, Kuzinsky, and a couple of paramours whom he trusted to be discreet.

We have your wife. The message, accompanied by a picture, hit him like a kick in the gut. At his stifled gasp, Kuzinsky glanced up.

Max swiveled away from the group to scan the rest of the message, his horror rising. *If you want her to stay alive, you'll take the job.*

The message came from a number he didn't recognize, but the New York area code leapt out at him. Tony was holding Rebecca hostage.

Ah, so they hadn't liked his refusal to kill the FBI agent. Now the fucking Scarpas were twisting his arm, threatening to harm his wife. The sons of bitches! Look at her!

Rage built within him like the winds whistling outside. She was sitting in the back of a car, wedged between two thugs, eyes glazed with panic and a gag over her mouth.

He swallowed the sour taste in his mouth. They had him over a barrel.

If he let them kill Rebecca, there would be a massive investigation. Law enforcement would probe into Max's business, possibly finding clues that linked him to the infamous Scarpas. Even if they didn't, people would gossip about him and speculate whether he had killed her. Besides, he was the only man with any right to determine her fate.

Damn it. He had to tell them what they wanted to hear. But he couldn't let them think he was easily intimidated or they'd continue to exploit him. He needed to be the one who called the shots. With thumbs that shook with rage, he typed a return message.

Double my deposit and let her go. Then you have my word.

Hitting send, he suffered the sense that he had crossed an invisible line and could never go back again. Stuffing his phone into his pocket, he turned toward the radio just as it crackled to life. The roar of a brutal wind muffled the voice of First Class Special Petty Officer Chuck Suzuki.

"Rough Riders to Trust Buster," Haiku shouted. The half- Japanese SEAL, who handled Echo Platoon's communications, displayed unflappable self-control at all times. "We're in position and waiting for go time."

Every man in the room aside from Max uttered an exclamation of relief.

"Copy that," Kuzinsky replied, his face cracking into a rare smile. "Doppler says you have about twelve hours until the storm reaches its peak."

"Roger. Any updates?"

Kuzinsky flicked an inquiring glance at Max, who shook his head. "Not on this end, Rough Riders. Stay the course, and we'll see you all in thirty-six hours or less."

Haiku said several words that the wind snatched away. "Over and out," he added, and then the line went quiet.

Max ordered Collins and his teammate to remain by the radio. "Get some sleep," he suggested to Kuzinsky. Sensing that man's dark gaze on him, he turned and exited the room.

Tomorrow night, with the storm unleashing havoc on the island, the Rough Riders would proceed with their mission. Meanwhile, back in Virginia Beach, Rebecca would require his reassurance, assuming that Tony had agreed to his demands. There'd been no answering text from him yet.

Resentment flared in Max when he realized she must have given Tony his number. What did he expect—that she would sacrifice herself to keep his number secret? Only a SEAL would be that noble.

Traversing a narrow hallway under lights that flickered, Max located the door to his self-appointed quarters. He shut himself inside, flipping on the bare lightbulb before drawing the curtains. Then he threw himself down on his neatly made cot and waited. Every muscle in his brawny body remained rigid until, at last, his phone vibrated.

Deal, Tony replied. *Screw with us again and your wife won't be so lucky next time.*

A surge of power curled Max's upper lip. Did Tony think his threat actually scared him? Hardly. He'd given in with laughable ease, which told Max he'd had no intention of harming Rebecca in the first place—that would cost him his new ace assassin. Max had more flexing power than he'd realized. He went suddenly lightheaded.

What if the sky was the limit and he could command whatever payment he desired? That home in Bermuda that he dreamed of didn't seem so out-of-reach anymore.

After he killed Special Agent Castle, making it look like an accident, the Scarpas would consider him indispensable. He would rise straight to the top of the pecking order, exactly as he had with his military career.

I am lord of my destiny, he marveled.

* * *

Rebecca sat unmoving in her driver's seat. Making use of her mirrors, she followed the taillights of the BMW with her eyes until they turned and disappeared from view. The flex cuffs had been cut from her wrists and ankles. They'd never put the gag back on. And now they'd let her go.

But Tony's parting words still echoed in her head, keeping her breaths shallow.

Next time you won't be so lucky. The lewd glint in his dark gaze as it trekked down her body had struck terror into her heart.

There won't be a next time, she vowed to herself. Groping for her purse, which still sat on the seat next to her, she located her new cell phone. Her first impulse was to call the police, to relay everything that had happened, including Max's involvement. But Tony's threat kept her from punching in 9-1-1.

Her thoughts went to Bronco. He would know what to do, except that he was on an op with Max, and his safety depended on him focusing and having no outside distraction, not to mention on his ability to trust his leader. She didn't dare upset their working relationship—not during a critical mission.

Who else? Maddy had a baby to care for and didn't want to hear about Rebecca's marital problems. Rebecca's mother would be sympathetic, of course, but *she* would insist Rebecca fly out to Hawaii, and her lawyer had advised her over the phone not to leave the state or it would *really* look like she'd deserted Max.

The only thing she could do right now was to drive straight to her new apartment and pray that Tony and his goons didn't follow her. He hadn't made mention of her moving. Perhaps he hadn't realized she'd been packing up with the intention of leaving.

Once at her new apartment, she would immediately make a sketch of Tony from her memory of the thug's face. The gift of drawing that had helped her pay her way through nursing school would come in handy when she worked up the courage to approach the Naval Criminal Investigative Service about Max's suspicious activities.

One thing she would not do was to call her husband and reassure him of her safety. It was his fault she'd been assaulted by those goons in the first place, even if his cooperation had resulted in her freedom. Not only that, but she didn't want Max knowing her new cell phone number. She'd surrendered her old phone when she'd gotten the new one.

If Max assumed, when he couldn't reach her, that the Scarpas had taken her, then that was his problem. He deserved to be shaken up after what he'd just put her through.

Searing pain exploded in Brant's cheek as a component flying out from the compromised antenna box smashed into his face as it went sailing off the building. *Damn it!* He peeled off his glove to assess the damage and came away with blood-soaked fingers. The cut was deep, and the blow had left his head ringing.

Sam skidded across the roof toward him, propelled by the steady hundred-mile-an-hour wind. He grabbed Brant to catch himself and peered with concern at his injury.

"You all right?" he shouted.

"It's only a cut," Brant bellowed back. Digging into his pack, he produced a square of gauze and tape, slapping the bandage over the laceration and holding it there with two large, sticky strips. But he could feel the blood welling up and soaking through the pad instantly.

Even a small cut at this juncture could have serious consequences. They'd slogged their way to the listening station, climbed to the top, and decimated the antenna boxes. Thus far, the mission was a rousing success. Sam's frown of concern told him he was thinking of the upcoming three-mile swim out to the submarine.

Sam gestured to the others. It was time to go, before someone came to look for the two guards Brant had shot in the head fifteen minutes earlier.

Still dazed by the blow and feeling more and more lightheaded, Brant began the perilous descent back down the pipes. An unexpected regret accompanied him as he slid down the rough cylinder and landed with a splash in four feet of water. He couldn't believe he'd never even kissed Rebecca. What if he didn't make it back? What if he never got the chance?

Don't think that way. Bullfrog had convinced him that negative thoughts resulted in negative outcomes. Their luck had held out thus far. He was going to make it back. And when he did, he would kiss Rebecca soundly, regardless of the consequences.

Agitation needled Max's skin, compelling him to pace the temporary operations command.

Blue skies filled the broken panes of the windows where a fresh ocean breeze and the calls of tropical birds conveyed the fact that the storm was long over. A hot sun beamed down from where the clouds had seethed and roiled just thirty-six hours earlier. The puddles of water Max had been stepping over in his circuit of the chamber were steadily shrinking.

Puerto Rico had weathered the storm with minimal destruction and casualties. But Cuba hadn't fared so well, and the fate of the Rough Riders remained a complete unknown.

Of the three other men in the room—Kuzinsky and two junior petty officers—only the master chief even dared to look at Max as he continued his orbit around the silent radio. No doubt he attributed his leader's seething tension to the fact that the submarine, waiting at the appointed coordinates, reported no contact with the Rough Riders as of yet. Whether they were living or dead, whether they'd succeeded or failed in their mission, no one knew.

Given Kuzinsky's grim expression, the Rough Riders were history. But optimism still shone in the faces of the younger SEALs who sat before the radio. As for Max, he wasn't even thinking about his men.

It was, in fact, the voiced recording that Rebecca's phone number was no longer in service that had him pacing like a caged lion.

He hadn't heard a word from her since Tony Scarpa had sought to blackmail him. Tony's last text had implied that they'd let Rebecca go, but if that was the case, then why wasn't her phone in service? Max had considered calling Tony directly, now that he had his number, but direct communication with a mob member wasn't smart. Plus, asking Tony about his own wife would weaken Max's image.

The uncertainty elevated his blood pressure. Growing hot in the warm room, he wrenched off his BDU jacket and cast it aside. The sub couldn't wait indefinitely for the Rough Riders to appear. If it didn't report contact in the next two hours, he was going to instigate a search and rescue mission.

The Joint Special Operations Task Force awaited an update. There'd been no word on the squad's status since they were dropped off in Havana forty-eight hours earlier. In retrospect, it seemed ludicrous to have dumped eight SEALs into the midst of such a storm and expect them to accomplish an already difficult task. But ludicrous was what they *did* and what they always succeeded at doing.

Max flicked a glance at his watch. "Collins, check the satellite images," he barked. The sooner he could proceed with a search and rescue, the sooner he could attend to his pressing business at home.

"Yes, sir." Collins swung away from the radio to download the latest satellite view of Havana Harbor.

Max and Kuzinsky stepped toward the monitor for a closer look.

"Holy hell," the master chief breathed. Only a few houses in *Barrio de la Regla* still had roofs. Those without a covering looked like rectangular swimming pools all filled with water and debris.

"The station is still standing," Max noted. "I want a close-up of the rooftop." He fully expected to see the antenna boxes lining the roof as before. When he didn't immediately see them, he frowned and leaned in closer.

"By God, they did it." Kuzinsky pointed to what was left—a few hunks of twisted metal. "They're completely destroyed."

"Could've been the storm," Max insisted. Conflicting emotions vied for preeminence. On one hand, if his men had accomplished their mission, then he could take the credit. On the other, if they'd managed to do that much, then they might just make it back to the sub alive—and he preferred Chief Adams out of the picture forever.

At that precise moment, the radio crackled. "Trust Buster, this is Low Rider. We have picked up eight hitchhikers. Repeat, eight Rough Riders have been recovered."

Max gave a start as Collins and his comrade vaulted out of their chairs with triumphant shouts. They threw their arms around each other, whooping and hollering.

Kuzinsky turned and eyed Max expectantly. Summoning his widest smile, he stuck out a hand for the master chief to pump with congratulatory zeal.

Damn it, Adams was harder to kill than Max had hoped.

CHAPTER 9

Brant craned his neck to peer out of the Globemaster's inset window in the hopes of glimpsing the U.S. coastline. He'd been gone a whopping five days, yet it felt more like five weeks. The C-17 cruised over wispy clouds that obscured his view and frustrated his desire to see land. Giving up, he faced forward again and flinched to find Bullfrog leaning close, inspecting the stitches on his face.

"I could have done a better job," his friend said, criticizing his own handiwork.

Brant fingered the cut. The sutures closed a gash about two inches long, running from just under his left eye and along his cheekbone at a diagonal angle. "You did great, considering how much I flinched."

"You're entitled to flinch when you don't get anesthetic," his friend said with a sympathetic smile. "Must suck to be allergic to Lidocaine."

"It sucked when I was riding broncs and needed to get stitched up every other week," Brant agreed. "But don't worry. It'll help me pick up chicks."

"Ever the optimist," Bullfrog drawled.

Brant had only mentioned picking up chicks

because it was expected of him. Getting laid might be a high priority after over two weeks of celibacy, but the truth was he wasn't thinking of chicks, in general. Only one particular female had occupied his thoughts with alarming frequency lately. Considering the message he'd found waiting on his cell phone, Rebecca had been thinking of him, too.

Please come over at your earliest convenience. I have something important to tell you.

Her new address had jumped out at him, making his head spin. She'd actually gone through with his suggestion and left Max! Now there was nothing to prevent him from spending time with her, even kissing her the way he'd regretted not kissing her while on top of the listening station. He could feel a kiss tingling on his lips, awaiting delivery.

Yet, while it thrilled him to imagine putting his lips to hers, kissing her the way he wanted was a bad idea. It would transform the nature of their relationship, changing it from friendship to something he had studiously avoided the whole of his adult life, especially with women he cared for.

You are so much like your father.

His mother had said that to him since he was a boy, usually with a poignant smile and heartbreak still evident in her eyes. Brant had been told who his father was. He'd watched him on television, developing a case of hero worship for the charismatic bull rider. As a teenager, he'd approached and even befriended the man, finding him warm-hearted and fun to be with. But he'd never forgiven Quinn Farley for breaking his mother's heart. And he absolutely refused to repeat his father's transgression, especially with a woman as special as Rebecca.

Yet she clearly had something important to tell him—something, he was certain, that had to do with

Max. He'd already involved himself in her effort to expose Max's questionable activities. He'd shared his suspicions with Bullfrog and enlisted Hack's help with the laptop. He couldn't just drop the ball now that she was living independently. He had to accept her invitation. To be honest, he really wanted to.

But he didn't dare drop by that night when he was as horny as a rabbit on steroids. "You want to go out tonight?" he asked his best friend.

Bullfrog grimaced. "Nah, I have to take a midterm."

"Again?" Brant stared at him incredulously. "Dude, how long are you going to be in school?" Bullfrog took two classes every semester through an online degree program.

"Until I finish my degree," he answered with a modest shrug.

"Or three," Brant retorted. "Did you even decide on your major yet?"

"Philosophy." Bullfrog gave a definitive nod. But then his hazel eyes glinted with zeal. "With a minor in British Lit and another in French," he tacked on.

Brant shook his head incredulously. "You are such a nerd, brother. But I admire your tenacity." He transferred his attention to the two men seated across the cargo bay. "Hey, guys." Haiku and Halliday broke off their conversation to regard him. "We're going out tonight, right?"

Halliday gave him a thumb's up and Haiku nodded.

Good, Brant thought, relieved to feel the plane's descent. He would go out that night, get laid at least twice, and maybe then he could visit Rebecca the next day and not be tempted to take their friendship to the next level.

"What the hell?" Max grumbled, tugging mail out of the overstuffed mailbox at the head of his driveway.

By the looks of it, Rebecca hadn't emptied the box since his departure five days earlier. Another sign that something wasn't right.

Tossing the mail onto the seat next to him, he sped up the driveway toward his dark house. Lights shone in the back yard where they'd been turned on by a timer. He thumbed the remote control and held his breath as his automatic door went up. Just as he feared—aside from his kit car, the garage stood empty. Rebecca wasn't there.

Where could she be? Having called the hospital directly, he knew she'd shown up to work the previous day and the day before that, but she'd been too busy to take his call. At least he knew for sure that Tony had let her go. And yet she hadn't bothered to contact Max to assure him that she was okay—a deliberate snub on her part, right up there with ending the service on her cell phone.

Anger burbled in his gut. She knew his expectations. Whether he was gone on a long mission or a short one, he expected to be greeted with a warm meal followed by sex, if he was up to it. This had to be her way of defying him—punishing him for failing to protect her from the likes of Tony.

He cut his engine, scooped up the unwieldy pile of mail, and grabbed his duffel bag, disarming the security system to let himself into the house. As he dumped the mail on the kitchen table and his bag on the floor, the dark stillness inside raised the hairs on his forearms. Flicking on the lights, he made his way through each room, gaining the impression as he went that Rebecca hadn't been there in days. Where could she be?

Everything stood in its proper place, offering no answers, until he came to their bedroom and turned on the light. Her nightstand and matching dresser stood bereft of all personal items, her books, and her jewelry box. His heart drummed out a heavy beat.

Crossing to her dresser, he righted the only object still sitting on it, a framed photograph of the two of them on their wedding day. The fact that it had been left face down slapped him awake to reality. *My God, she's left me!*

The empty dresser drawers confirmed his deduction.

He backed in shock toward the bed. The rumpled comforter recalled him to their last moments spent together and the words he'd snarled at her. *You're my wife!*

Apparently, that wasn't enough to keep her around.

His thick hands curled into fists. How dare she draw attention to their marital difficulties by leaving him? Soon everyone would know. The SEALs under his command would conjecture under their breaths about why she'd walked out after just three short years. Even his superiors would look at him differently. If a commander couldn't keep his household in order, how was he supposed to lead a team?

This ridiculous little game had to end at once. He would confront her at the hospital and demand that she return to him. An officer's wife didn't behave like a child running from her obligations.

Muttering darkly, Max returned to the kitchen to forage in the refrigerator. She hadn't even stocked it the way she usually did!

With nothing but eggs to eat, he pulled them out to make an omelet. As he turned to fetch a bowl from the cabinet, his gaze fell upon a fat envelope that had slipped from the pile of mail on the table and landed on the floor next to his bag. Postponing his cooking, he went to pick it up.

A portentous feeling ambushed him as he noted the

return address. It had been sent by the law offices of Kirby and Kirby. He slit it open, pulling out the packet inside, and slowly unfolded it. A high-pitched ringing filled his ears as he scanned the contents. She'd drawn up a contract for a separation agreement culminating in a no-fault divorce.

No fault? Hah. The fault was clearly hers for deserting him. He waded through the legalese once, twice, three times. With every reading, his resentment burned hotter. She wanted back the sum that she had put into the house two years ago, the first time he'd run into financial trouble. She wanted a thousand a month in spousal support. She wanted him to respect her privacy and to have no physical contact whatsoever outside of the courtroom.

The pages in his hands shook. What was she suggesting? That he was a danger to her? He was a Navy SEAL, by God—a hero! How dare she make him out to be the bad guy when she had been the one to desert him?

Hell if I will sign this shit!

Flinging the stapled pages onto the tabletop, he stomped back to the counter to prepare his omelet. She clearly hadn't taken him seriously when he'd informed her that she would rue the day that she tried to divorce him. She was *nothing* without him. Couldn't she see that?

He picked up an egg, pausing as he considered his next move. He would get her back, one way or another. But he had to do it soon, lest she mention his offshore account or her encounter with Tony to her lawyer. He crushed the egg with his fingers, letting the yolk drip all over the palm of his hand. What would her lawyer make of that?

My God, she had more ability to destroy him than he'd realized!

He had to fix this. Somehow, some way, he needed to maintain his foothold, but he could feel himself slipping, and he didn't like it one bit.

Rebecca shut her apartment door and leaned against it with a long exhalation. Was it her imagination, or was someone following her to and from work? She'd felt jumpy for days—probably a consequence of her scare at the hands of the mobsters. Or it could be the fact that Max was back.

Maddy, who knew that Rebecca had left her husband and gotten a new phone number, had forwarded the text message that all wives received just hours prior to the task unit's return. As grateful as Rebecca was to Maddy for thoughtfully warning her, she was equally grateful for the fact that her friend had asked no questions when she learned of Rebecca's decision to move out—merely offered her a shoulder to cry on should she need it.

Repressing a chill that made her scalp prickle, Rebecca flicked on the light switch. Her empty apartment might be devoid of furniture, but the cathedral ceiling and the high windows made the 994 square feet of space seem spacious and cheery, and her purchases tonight would contribute to a lived-in feeling.

I'm safe, she assured herself.

But Max's return was fraying her already taut nerves. If Tony and his thugs weren't stalking her, she had a feeling Max soon would be. The possibility had unsettled her so much that, instead of going straight to her apartment after work, she'd indulged in some shopping therapy.

Pushing off the door, she went to close her blinds before carrying her purchases to the mantle over her gas fireplace and setting them down one by one.

Three amber candleholders, each one taller than the last, supported the earth-toned pillar candles she had also bought. Their sandalwood scent had reminded her of Bronco—not that she had bought them for him. After all, he hadn't even replied to her text invitation, and he'd been stateside for several hours now. What was taking him so long? No doubt he was busy bedding his latest squeeze.

Stepping back to survey the effect of her impulsive purchase, she ignored the unexpected pinch of jealousy.

"Now all I need is a couch," she murmured, turning to regard the spot where it would go. She refused to envision her and Bronco curled up on it together.

She hadn't left Max in order to involve herself with the Team's resident playboy. Only a fool would do something as stupid as that. He might call himself a friend, might make her feel safe and cared about, but he wasn't remotely the type of stable man she needed.

So why was she waiting on pins and needles for him to text her back?

"Don't be stupid." She'd only invited him to drop by so she could tell him about her encounter with Tony. If and when he decided to pay her a visit, nothing more was going to happen.

Brant glanced at his Luminox tactical wristwatch and shook his head. He'd managed to put off visiting Rebecca for thirty-two endless hours.

Such willpower, Adams.

But he had a good reason, he assured himself, for parking his truck in front of Unit 3, Windsor Garden Way. Since their return, Hack had made strides in sifting through the information stored in Max's old Dell, and what he'd found had confirmed all of Brant's darkest suspicions. He couldn't go a day longer without warning Becca of Max's activity on the black market, suggesting his involvement with the mob.

You could just tell her over the phone, his conscience pointed out. After all, he'd promised himself he wouldn't venture near Rebecca until he'd gotten properly laid, and his attempts to do so the previous night had resulted in a big fat failure— though not for lack of trying.

He, Halliday, and Haiku had hit up a popular SEAL hang out called Chick's Oyster Bar, located at the north end of the beach. Finding a willing babe there was pretty much a guarantee. The weather had cooperated beautifully. They'd been seated on the outdoor deck, overlooking the ocean. Brant had ordered his usual shot of tequila and a beer. Within minutes, willing women dressed in scanty outfits had descended on their table. He'd smiled at them all, answered their questions, and waited for one of them to spark his interest.

But none of them had. First Halliday and then Haiku slipped away, each with a babe on his arm. They'd left Brant talking to a tenacious redhead committed to showing him all twenty-two of her tattoos. At midnight, Brant gave the redhead the slip and went home—still celibate, still hankering for something he couldn't put a name to.

Hey, I did my best.

Standard duty rotation had given him the next day off. He'd slept in, done his laundry, and washed his car. Thoughts of Rebecca continued to ambush him. And then Hack had called, all concerned and flustered, with information that had twisted Brant's intestines into knots. He'd tossed down the rag he was using to polish his fenders and decided that Becca needed to know what she was up against.

He would tell her that evening what they'd stumbled upon and get her permission to approach NCIS with the evidence. But he would not—should not!—make a move on Rebecca. The fantasies that had taken up residence in his mind were going to have to stay there, unrealized.

Rebecca searched her rearview mirror with an anxious eye. The sun was sinking fast, sending brilliant rays skimming over the tops of the cars behind her, and blinding her to whomever might be following.

Her premonition that Max was going to hunt her down that very day and demand she return to him had prompted her to leave the hospital right after work, skipping yoga. There'd been no sign of his Tahoe in the hospital parking lot. Still, she couldn't shake the feeling that he was out there, tailing her at a distance. Just in case he was, she took the circuitous route home, performing a number of detours meant to shake him. The last thing she wanted was for Max to know where she lived.

But just as she doubled back, heading for her apartment, she glimpsed a dark SUV weaving through the traffic behind her. That couldn't be Max.

Without using her turn signal, she veered into the turn lane, hoping to catch the green arrow and put distance between herself and a possible tail. An automatic glance in her rearview mirror prompted a double take as a Tahoe proceeded into the left lane behind her.

Oh, my God, that is Max!

The shape of his head was unmistakable, as was the base sticker—no longer required to get into the gate—but still mounted on one corner of the windshield.

She shifted her attention forward. "Go, go, go!" she

urged the cars in front of her as the arrow turned orange.

What did he want? Did he think he could make her change her mind about leaving? Would he even give her a choice? She had a vision of him dragging her by her wrist or worse, by her hair, right into his car and back into their house. She shuddered.

The cars before her sped up to beat the red. *I'm not going to make it.* But then she'd be stuck with Max only three cars behind her. He would follow her straight to her apartment. This was her best chance to shake him. The light blinked to red. Rebecca floored the accelerator and turned anyway.

A car blew its horn. She squealed in fright as she arced onto Bonnie Road. Arriving miraculously unharmed on the perpendicular street, she cast a wild glance over her shoulder, relieved to see Max glaring at her through the driver's side window.

Hurry!

She accelerated sharply, weaving around the car in front of her. Was it safe to head straight home? Did she have enough of a lead to get there without being seen?

Her heart hammered against her breast bone. Hoping the trees in the median and the deepening dusk would camouflage her movements, she turned into Windsor Gardens and raced toward the back of the parking lot, flying over speed bumps at a rate she would normally frown upon.

But Max wasn't stupid. If he didn't see her anywhere on Bonnie Road, he would likely double back to search the area. No need to lead him straight to her front door. She zipped into a space several units down. As she clambered from her car and hurried toward her apartment, she realized that the red and white truck parked in front of it was Bronco's. There he was getting out of it, causing her heart to race for an entirely different reason.

Forgetting her fear, she crossed the lot to meet him. They met by the fender of his truck, both of them grinning, uncertain whether to hug or not. The line of stitches on his cheek, visible even in the dusk, made her gasp.

"You were hurt!" She lifted a hand without thinking to catch his jaw and study the injury.

"It's only a scratch," Bronco insisted.

Of its own accord, her thumb stroked his bristled cheek, and a current of awareness arced between them.

"I'm so glad you're back," she admitted.

He searched her expression. "Is everything okay? You came in here like a bat out of hell."

Her fears came rushing back and she dropped her hand to peer behind her. "Max was following me. I lost him at the last intersection, but he might still come this way."

He sent a startled look toward the entrance to the apartments.

"Come on in," she invited, grabbing his sleeve and leaving him little choice as she pulled him toward her door. "How do you like the apartment complex?" she asked, releasing him to unlock it.

"It's nice." He sent an uncomfortable glance over his shoulder. "You might want to leave your light on when you go to work, though. It's getting darker earlier."

The tension in his voice was unmistakable. She could feel it within herself, as well—an unpredictable charge powering her impulses. Was it adrenaline caused by her close brush with Max? Did that make Brant nervous, as well? Or was he merely wary of being alone with her?

She flicked on the interior lights, and he followed her inside, studying the layout as she closed and locked the door behind them.

"Roomy," he said, with a wry look around the nearly empty space.

"I didn't want to take anything that Max could claim was his. I'll buy new furniture."

She got the impression he was more concerned about her safety, especially when he crossed to the nearest window and tabbed the blind to look outside.

Conscious of the medicinal odors rising off her scrubs she added, "Do you mind if I change real quick?"

His back seemed to stiffen. "Go ahead," he said without turning around.

"There are beverages in the fridge. Please, help yourself. I'll be right out," she added, edging into her room and shutting the door between them.

She stripped faster than she'd ever undressed in her life. Having waited for what felt like a lifetime for the chance to be alone with Bronco, she didn't want him getting cold feet and leaving. Finally, after all these months, they could talk freely without being interrupted by Max.

Talk? Is that really what you want to do?

Of course, she assured herself. She'd already been down that mental path. A fling with Bronco wasn't anything she wanted or needed.

Opting for a quick shower, she darted into her bathroom to turn on the water. As she waited for it to warm, she glanced critically at her reflection. The bright-eyed woman with her flushed cheeks and taut nipples seemed to have a mind of her own.

Max drove into an apartment complex named Windsor Gardens. Rebecca had to be there somewhere. By the time he'd turned onto Bonnie Road, her vehicle had disappeared, suggesting she had exited either into an office park or into an apartment complex. The very name of this place would have appealed to her, which convinced him she was here.

How naïve she was, how stupid, to think that she could live on her own when, truth was, she needed his protection now more than ever.

This game she had chosen to play would only put her into danger. She was a fool for not standing by her husband, especially when everything he had done was for her—to give her what she deserved. What good would it do her to walk away now—or worse, to undermine his hard-won reputation? In her foolishness, she didn't realize that if he went down, she would go with him. And now he was forced to protect her from herself.

Tall lamps lit the deep parking lot, revealing well-maintained walkways, flower beds filled with blooming chrysanthemums, and midsized, decent looking cars. Oh, yes, she had to be here; he could sense it. Driving slowly past the first few buildings, he searched for her vehicle.

Deeper and deeper into the complex he drove, rolling over speed bumps. He was just about to admit defeat when Chief Adams' one-of-a-kind classic Bronco had him jamming on the brakes.

Aghast, he searched his memory for Adams' address. Didn't the chief and the corpsman live in the same apartment building close to the oceanfront? Indeed, they did, in a complex called Sunrise Apartments. So what was Adams doing here?

Suspicion sliced him with a razor-sharp edge. He cast his gaze about again, and that was when he saw it—Rebecca's Jetta, peeking out from behind a larger Ford on the far side of the lot. They were both here—

together.

He idled, shock rippling through him, causing him to wring his steering wheel until his knuckles ached. The impulse to plow his vehicle into Adams' pride and joy rode him hard. The playboy chief hadn't wasted a minute reacquainting himself with his CO's wife, had he?

Which unit was hers? Adams had parked in front of one unit, she in front of another.

Max peered through the windows of each in hopes of catching a glimpse of her. The lights blinked off in one place, stayed lit in the other, but the drawn blinds hampered his view.

Even in his rage, he realized how unwise it was to confront her when he was angry. What's more, he would have Adams to contend with if he knocked down her door. Jealousy goaded him to unleash the beast inside him. But attacking Adams in front of his wife would only cast doubt onto his character, undermining his own interests.

But envy gnawed at him, keeping him from motionless. With a nickname like Bronco, Adams clearly didn't need a pill to get hard. He envisioned them in bed together, laughing at Max's impairment. His face burned with humiliation. Had Rebecca already told the chief about her husband's money sitting in a foreign account? Was Adams hoping he might end up getting some of it?

Damn it! If only the man had died on the last op. Alive, he posed a very serious threat to both Max's marriage and his reputation. On her own, Rebecca wouldn't dare to cast aspersions on her husband, but with Adams egging her on? That was a different story.

He needed to die.

The solution popped into Max's head like a clown out of a jack-in-the-box.

God damn it, he had enough on his plate planning the assassination of the FBI special agent. But what choice had Rebecca left him? The only way to safeguard his reputation was to eliminate Adams once and for all.

A sneer curled Max's upper lip as he made up his mind.

CHAPTER 10

Brant flicked the light switch, plummeting Becca's living room into darkness. *I should never have come over here.* Without a doubt, the vehicle idling in the parking lot and spotlighting his Bronco with its headlights was his CO's Tahoe.

Counting every beat of his heart, he waited for Max to make a move. One thing was certain; if the man got out of his truck, he'd be armed, and Brant had left his Sig Sauer pistol stowed under the seat of his Bronco, out of his immediate reach. He'd be at a serious disadvantage.

He tensed as the Tahoe's engine revved, but then it backed up, and Max drove away. Brant gave a long exhale, let go of the blind, and swiped a hand over his eyes.

That was close. The shit hadn't hit the fan tonight, but it was definitely coming.

Crossing toward the galley-style kitchen, he turned on the light there and looked around. The simple lock on the rear door prompted him to unlock it and take a peek outside. A small patio surrounded by flowerbeds gave way to a grassy alley and a privacy fence separating her apartment building from the office complex behind it. If anyone were going to break in, they'd do it through the back door, running out the same way.

Relocking the door, he turned toward the cabinets and hunted up an empty glass. Filling it with tap water, he chugged it down while pondering what Max would do next. He'd probably go straight to the repair shop to find and destroy his laptop.

The thought had him putting down his empty glass with a thud.

Given what Hack had told Brant about Max's activities recorded in his user profile, Max would freak when he realized that his Dell was gone.

The bedroom door gave a sudden squeak, and Rebecca emerged in a pair of jeans that hugged her trim figure and a lace blouse that highlighted her modest breasts. Combing her damp hair with her fingers, she struck him as fresh and clean and uncorrupted. The sweet smile that lit up her face immediately chased away his dark thoughts. She had no idea how close her evening had come to turning ugly.

"Sorry about that," she apologized. "Someone threw up on me today. I was afraid you'd smell it." As she walked his way, she glanced up at the light he'd extinguished. Stepping over to her mantle, she flicked a switch that caused flames to leap in her fireplace. Amber light licked over her walls finding reflection in the pretty candle holders on the mantle. "This is my favorite thing about the place," she added, keeping the overhead light off.

Brant found his tongue in knots. The fire's glow made her skin appear translucent. The romantic ambiance both unsettled and hypnotized him.

"Did you find something to drink?" she inquired,

her gaze falling to his empty glass.

"I had some water."

She clicked her tongue and eased past him to open the refrigerator. A clean, peppermint scent trailed in her wake, causing his awareness of the environment to shrink to the dimensions of the small kitchen.

"I can do better than that."

As she bent to peer into the refrigerator, his gaze slid to the small, firm contours of her heart-shaped bottom, and his mouth went dry. "This bottle of Chardonnay has been chilling for days. Share it with me?" She straightened to send him a guileless look.

Brant regarded the bottle in her hands. Drinking wine would rob him of his self-control. It might very well lead to what Max already assumed was going on between them.

"Sure," he heard himself reply.

Hey, if I'm going to be condemned for something I haven't done, what difference does it make? argued the devil inside him. But concern that he would hurt her in the end made him throttle back his eagerness.

"How about you open it while I throw some dinner together?" She set the bottle on the counter along with a corkscrew. Turning back to the refrigerator, she produced fresh fish fillets wrapped in plastic and a bag of green beans. "Are you hungry?"

"Starving." He popped out the cork, found two long-stemmed glasses, and poured them both a glass. It felt like the prelude to a long-awaited date.

This is not a date. He reminded himself that he had something to tell her.

"Thank you." Her chestnut gaze met his, keeping the words locked in his throat, as she took the glass he offered her. Then she turned her attention to preparing their meal. "I hope you like fish," she said, freeing tilapia fillets from their plastic wrapping.

"I like all seafood."

Her dimples flashed as she snapped on the oven.

Reluctant to sour her mood by sharing his discovery, he decided his announcement could wait until their dinner was over. He watched her pull out a colander and rinse the green beans. What subject was safe to touch upon? His recent mission was strictly off limits. He doubted she wanted to hear of his failed attempt to get laid last night, so he kept quiet and pondered the sensual yet comfortable undercurrent running between them. It felt good to be here in her home, just hanging out.

As he savored his first sips of wine, she set the fish in a shallow baking dish and drizzled it with olive oil. The wine—buttery with a perfect balance of sweet and tart—ran in a cool river down his throat, hit his empty stomach, and flooded him with warmth. He felt himself relaxing, enjoying her graceful competence.

"I'm making this too easy on you," she observed. "Here." She handed him a knife, handle end first. "Cut the ends off the green beans for me, please?"

"Sure." He'd never done that before, but he could wield a knife with lethal precision.

She made room at the sink for him. "Drop them into the disposal and put the good pieces in the steamer," she instructed helpfully.

He followed her directions carefully, pleased with himself when she praised his work.

"Do you always eat this healthy?" He already figured she did, but he had to say something.

"Well, I'm not a fanatic about it, but I prefer whole foods over processed ones and, of course, organic, if I can get it."

Hence her trim little figure, he thought, his sidelong gaze skimming over her curves to her bare feet. At the sight of her hot pink-painted toenails, his heart skipped a beat.

His elbow brushed hers unintentionally, and awareness licked over him, shortening his breath. As he continued his paring, she garnished the fish with salt and other spices.

It wasn't until she slipped the fish under the oven's broiler and placed the green beans on the stove to steam that she brought up the reason for her invitation.

"So," she said, putting her back against the counter and picking up her glass. A sudden frown muted her inner glow. "Something happened last weekend while the task unit was away."

He braced himself for what she might tell him. It couldn't be any worse than what he had to tell her.

"Remember that New Yorker I told you about, the one Max had thrown out of the house?"

A bad feeling rolled through him. "The guy named Tony who said you'd meet again someday," he recalled.

"Oh, we met again, all right."

His tension edged suddenly higher. Considering whom Max associated with online, what were the odds that Tony was exactly what he seemed—a mobster?

"He abducted me by hiding in the back of my car. With a gun to my head, he ordered me to drive to his BMW, which was parked at a dead end in my old neighborhood."

Brant slammed his glass down nearly breaking the stem. Alarm scorched his nervous system. "Are you okay? What the hell happened?"

She wrung her hands and kept quiet, causing him to fear the worst.

"Becca!" he exclaimed.

"They didn't hurt me. All they did was bind my

wrists and ankles and take a picture of me. I had to tell them Max's cell phone number. Then they sent him my picture along with their demands."

"What were their demands?"

She shrugged. "I don't know. But he must have agreed to them because they cut me free, put me back in my car, and drove off."

Oh, honey. He barely caught himself from blurting the endearment. "Did you call the cops?"

"No." Her head swung back and forth. "No, they said I wouldn't be so lucky next time, and I'd rather not find out what that means."

"Christ, Becca." He didn't plan on hugging her, but what else could he do? She looked so small and vulnerable that he closed the distance between them and pulled her to his chest. Her soft, scented warmth sank against him; her head fitted so neatly under his chin that he was struck by the thought that she was made for him. But then he felt her trembling.

Damn Max for mixing her up in his shady business! "You must have been scared to death."

"I was." She drew away reluctantly. "Here, I'll show you what Tony looks like." Crossing to a kitchen drawer, she withdrew a sheet of paper and handed it to Brant.

He found himself regarding a detailed portrait of a swarthy, broad-faced male in his thirties. "Wow, this is amazing. You can really draw," he marveled.

"Thanks."

"Is this a good likeness of him?"

"Pretty close," she said with a nod. She looked up at him with wide eyes. "So, what do you think? Max has money in a foreign account, and he knows people who used me to blackmail him for something. Do we have enough evidence to report him to NCIS?"

Brant drew a tight breath. She'd banished the

comfortable, uncomplicated atmosphere with her news. Now it was his turn to share what he'd learned. "Yeah, we have enough."

He dreaded even bringing it up. From here on out, everything was going to change. He and Rebecca could never go back to simply being friends. For one thing, Max probably already assumed that they were more. For another, it wasn't going to be pleasant trying to pull him off his high-and-mighty pedestal.

"Hack did find something on Max's laptop," he announced.

Her face reflected dread. "What was it?"

He took another fortifying gulp of wine and put the glass down more gently this time. "Max frequented a black market website that goes by the name Silk Road. You can get to it only by going through a dot onion, which is a kind of pseudo domain used by criminals to hide their traffic. Hack tried to explain it to me, but most of it was over my head. Basically, Max was looking for a way to make money."

Her lips parted in astonishment, but she didn't say a word.

"Hack says he came across a cached application form that Max had filled out. Someone was looking to hire a bodyguard to perform security detail." He put air quotes around the last two words, giving them emphasis.

"Oh my God. Then the sniper described in that newspaper clipping—that was Max! He's killed two people for the mob already?"

"We don't know that," Brant countered, tempering her conclusion. "But we can't discount the possibility."

"Well, if he did, then the FBI is looking for him. We could take our suspicions to them."

"We could. Or to NCIS."

Her eyes glazed over as she lapsed into thought. "That's where all the money came from," she considered out loud. "It wasn't an inheritance. He was paid by the mob, who deposited his payment in an offshore account so the government would never find out."

"According to Hack, Emile Victor DuPonte isn't considered a legitimate investment firm. The Swiss government doesn't recognize it."

Her expression hardened. "Because it's used by thugs," she guessed.

He scratched his healing stitches while thoughts rolled around in his mind. "But why did the mob have to grab *you* if Max willingly works for them?"

She shrugged. "I have no idea. Maybe they're asking too much from him. Maybe he's afraid the law is on to him and he wanted to quit. Whatever the reason, he must have agreed to their terms, or they wouldn't have let me go."

The urge to hug her again nearly overpowered Brant. Obviously the wine was going to his head already. And that kiss that had been tingling on his lips for days now demanded an imminent delivery. "Are you sure you want to pursue this?" he asked her.

The fish sizzled under the broiler as she fell thoughtfully quiet. Brant filled his empty wine glass, half regretting that the topic of Max had come up so quickly. Up to this point, he'd really been enjoying himself. At the rate things were unraveling, they might never get to share an evening together like this, ever again.

"Tell you what," he proposed, topping off her glass, as well. "Don't answer that yet. For the next thirty minutes, let's pretend Max doesn't exist." He met her startled, searching gaze. "Tomorrow, with your permission, I'll tell Master Chief Kuzinsky what we know. If we're going to take this information to the FBI or to NCIS, then we need his help."

She swallowed visibly at getting Max's right-hand man involved.

"Is that what you want?" he pressed. "Or do you want me to forget what Hack found on Max's laptop or what that creep, Tony, did to you?"

For a moment she appeared torn, but then resolve firmed her lips and she shook her head. "No, I don't want you to forget it. Max is breaking the law. If I want what's due to me, then I have to prove it. Besides, if he's getting paid to assassinate people, that makes him a murderer. I can't let him get away with that!"

He hoped he got the chance one day to deck Max for causing Rebecca the distress that tightened her sweet face. "Okay," he agreed, though not without a pang of concern. "I'll let you know what Master Chief has to say after Hack and I talk to him, hopefully tomorrow. In the meantime, let's finish every conversation we've ever started but had to cut short for obvious reasons. What do you say?"

He could see her putting aside the implications of their discovery and concentrating on the present. Summoning a smile that made her eyes sparkle, she said, "We can actually enjoy a full-length conversation. Imagine that!"

And talking is all you've got in mind, remember, Adams? "I'll set the table," he offered.

Under her guidance, he found placemats, silverware, and napkins and laid them on a small table that used to be in Max's gazebo, out by his pool. Rebecca, meantime, sliced up a loaf of wheat bread and placed it in a basket. Then she poked the fish with a fork and pulled it out from under the hot broiler. Taking the steaming green beans off the burner, she proceeded to transfer their dinner onto a platter, placing it in the center of the table.

They sat across from each other, and Rebecca bowed her head, saying a quick prayer. As Brant studied her, he could feel his contentment returning. "What's new at the hospital?" he began as they filled their plates with the fare before them.

A tired but contented smile teased her dimples into view. "Let's see. Today we had a record number of cardiac arrests—three in one afternoon. Two of them were splitting wood for the fall." She cut into her broiled fish with the side of her fork.

"That's hard work," he commiserated, having split plenty of wood in his youth. "So, I take it that even though the ER is stressful, you still like your job."

"I love it. Helping people when they need you most is truly rewarding."

Her words made him think about the unclaimed body. "Did anyone come for that dead guy who looks like me?"

She looked down at her plate and shook her head. "No, not yet."

"That really bothers you, doesn't it?"

She glanced up with wide eyes. "Am I that transparent?"

"To me, you are." *Watch it, Adams.* His tongue seemed to have a mind of its own tonight.

"His circumstances remind me of my father," she admitted, ignoring his remark.

"What was he like, your father?"

She rolled her eyes, but a fond smile came to her face. "Oh, he was something else—a dreamer, a visionary, an idealist. He was always searching for himself, never content with what he found." She forked up another morsel of her fillet. "Do you think your father was like that, too?" she asked, popping it into her mouth.

He considered his famous father with a frown. "Not at all. He seems perfectly content with himself."

She blinked at the bitterness that he couldn't conceal. "How well do you know him?"

He looked down at his half-empty plate. "I mother first introduced us when I was a kid. He didn't pay much attention to me at first. But I was so starstruck that I decided to follow in his footsteps, and we eventually became friends. My mom always said we were two peas in a pod."

"You did the rodeo thing to be like him," she guessed. "Except you rode broncos instead of bulls."

"Broncs," he corrected her.

"Sorry—broncs. Why did you ride them and not bulls?"

He shrugged. "Wanted to carve my own path, I guess. Plus, horses are less intimidating than bulls." He sent her a wry smile.

"But you still had your fair share of injuries as I recall," she pointed out. He had regaled her with stories of his bronc-riding days the first time they'd met, at the Team Twelve Christmas party. "Good thing, too, or you would never have become a SEAL."

He had told her at a different party how he'd broken his arm in three places and wound up sharing a hospital room with a former frogman. The retired SEAL had convinced him to quit the rodeo circuit and take on a beast called terrorism. Not long after, he had joined the Navy and gone straight from basic training in the Great Lakes to Basic Underwater Demolition/SEAL training in Coronado.

"You have an excellent memory," he pointed out, impressed by her recall.

"Not really." She smiled at him. "Your stories are memorable, that's all. Tell me more about your father," she pleaded.

He looked away, picturing his handsome but haggard father. "Fun to be with, great sense of humor. You can listen to him commentate on the Professional Bull-Riding Network any day of the week."

She searched his expression. "And yet, I get the feeling that he disappointed you," she guessed.

"No, he's a great human being," he protested, but since she'd glimpsed his true feelings, he told her something he didn't normally tell anyone, not even his teammates. "He just wasn't around for me when I was growing up. Other kids had dads, but all I had were my mom and my grandparents. I felt like I was missing out on something. Plus, my mom seemed lonely. I wanted her to fall in love again, but she said Quinn Farley had broken her heart, and she couldn't ever love like that again."

Rebecca's eyes turned limpid. "That's so sad." She heaved a sigh. "I'm starting to think there's no such thing as a perfect mate," she lamented.

She had to be thinking of her father and then Max, of course. "For you, there is," he insisted. "You're a good person. You deserve to be happy." Growing suddenly self-conscious, he lightly scratched the stitches on his face, itchy now that his cut was healing.

"Are you going to tell me how you got that?" she inquired.

He deliberated how much he could tell her. "I was hit by an electrical component, probably a circuit board."

"Probably?"

"It hit my face at over a hundred miles an hour, too fast to see and hard enough to concuss me."

She frowned and put her fork down. "You're lucky it didn't kill you."

"Yes, I am." He decided to add a few more details. "Right after that, we had a three-mile underwater swim, and I could barely stay awake." He left out the part about the great white shark accompanying the squad the whole way out to the sub.

Rebecca's gaze narrowed. "Why do I get the feeling you were operating near the hurricane?"

Wow, she was far too astute for him to say any more. He snapped a crispy bean between his teeth and simply looked at her.

She glanced down at his nearly empty plate. "More fish?"

"Sure, unless you want it. I like your cooking."

"Thanks." Her face took on a rosy hue as she dished the last fillet onto his plate. He dug into it with gusto.

"Who's your best friend on the team?" she asked him. "Is it Sam or Bullfrog?"

He reflected a moment. "Hard to choose," he answered. "Sam's a little busy these days, doesn't hang out with the guys as much, not that I blame him."

"Maddy's so lucky." She sent him a smile, but it struck him as terribly sad.

"You'll have a baby one day," he assured her.

His words seemed to startle her. "Are my thoughts written on my face or something?"

He contemplated her honest countenance. "I guess I have a knack for reading your mind."

His reply seemed to unsettle her. She got up again and crossed to the refrigerator. Opening the freezer, she studied the contents. "I wish I could offer you some dessert, but I can't keep ice cream around or I'll eat it all myself. Oh, I do have a bar of dark chocolate." She pulled it off the shelf in the freezer and showed it to him. "Ghirardelli. Would you like a piece?"

The thought of her indulging in occasional squares of chocolate made him like her so intensely that it hurt. "Sure, why not?"

She peeled back the wrapper and brought him several squares, resuming her seat across from him and nibbling on her own piece.

"Becca, I have to tell you something." He needed to give her an inkling of the challenges that lay ahead. The frozen bit of chocolate melted instantly in his mouth, filling it with delicious sweetness.

She visibly braced herself. "Go ahead."

"I really like you." *Wait, what*? He wasn't supposed to say that! But the pleasure that lit up her face kept him from denying it.

Her cheeks turned even pinker. Momentarily she lowered her gaze, then swept her lashes up and looked right at him with her chestnut-brown eyes. "I really like you, too." Her voice seemed to have gone a little husky.

To keep from lunging across the table to kiss her, he took another bite out of his chocolate. "But that's a problem," he pointed out.

"Is it?" She took a quick little breath and added. "Why?"

The real reason was because he didn't dare connect with a woman as wonderful as she was. But he heard himself blame his commander. "Because Max did follow you here tonight," he explained.

At her look of horror, he kicked himself for dropping the news like a bomb.

She clutched the edge of the table. "Are you certain?"

He tipped his head toward the window where he'd been standing. "I saw his Tahoe in the parking lot. He probably doesn't know which apartment is yours, but he sure as hell saw my Bronco parked right in front of your door."

All suggestion of color drained from her face. "Oh God."

"And if he suspects that you're telling me about what happened with Tony the other night, then we're both in over our heads."

"What have I done?" She stood up so suddenly that her chair skidded across the linoleum. Crossing the empty living area, she went straight to the window to look outside. "He's not supposed to come anywhere near me. I put that request in the separation agreement."

"Is that something that he has signed off on?"

She shook her head. "No, and he probably won't. More likely, he'll go to his own lawyer and file for a fault-grounds divorce, claiming I deserted him. Since I moved out first, I'll lose all the money that I put into that house, which was everything I had."

Brant trailed her to the window. "And now he knows approximately where you live. Plus he knows you've been talking to me."

She whirled to face him. Troubling thoughts flickered in her eyes the way the firelight flickered on her face. "Oh, Bronco, I'm so sorry."

Not any sorrier than he was. "It's not your fault, Becca." He fisted his hands to keep from reaching for her.

"Yes, it is!" She crossed her arms and hugged herself. "Max is going to go after you now, I just know it. He's going to ruin you, and it's my fault! I should never have involved you in our business."

"Hey." Despite his best intention, he reached out and clasped her shoulders, giving her a gentle shake. "I made you tell me what was bothering you, remember? Mad Max is the one who's doing something wrong, not us."

"Mad Max?" She'd clearly not heard the nickname before.

"Sorry," he said with a grimace. "That's what the team guys call him. Not to his face, of course, but..." he trailed off.

She pursed her lips and nodded. "I have a few nicknames for him myself."

He could imagine that she did.

She took a ragged breath. "I tried so hard to make my marriage work." Tears sparkled in her eyes. "I shouldn't have to lose everything."

It was all he could do not to reach for her. "Don't worry. We're going to take our evidence to NCIS. If Max is breaking the law, they'll expose him, and you'll get what's rightfully yours."

Her eyebrows flexed. "But in the meantime, Max is going to make your life a living hell," she predicted.

He had come to the same conclusion. "Don't worry about me. I know I can count on the master chief's support."

The time had come to say good-bye. If he stayed any longer, he was going to hate himself, sooner rather than later. "Maybe you should take a vacation, Becca," he suggested. "Doesn't your mother live in Hawaii? Why don't you fly out and visit her?"

She shook her head. "That would only validate Max's claim if he goes forward with a fault-grounds divorce."

"But there's Tony to think about," Brant insisted. "He's used you as a pawn once already. What's to stop him from doing it again? Maybe NCIS can offer you protection."

Thoughts shifted behind her wide eyes. "I wish you could protect me," she stated on a poignant note.

Her words both flattered and terrified him. There was nothing he would rather do. But then who would protect her from *him?*

"Honey, I can't." The endearment slipped out before he could halt it. He put his hands over hers, fighting to keep his touch platonic, but the effort backfired the instant their skin touched. Desire leapt between them as their fingers coiled together. He found himself wedging his digits between hers the same way he wanted to wedge himself between her thighs.

"Becca," he groaned her name in warning even as he tugged her close, covering her lips with his.

And then he was lost. Her soft, sweet mouth received him with such welcome that he couldn't have halted the kiss to save his life. She tasted like the chocolate they'd both consumed moments before. And when her tongue touched his, it sent such a shaft of need pulsing through him that he released her hands to pull her hips closer. The sound she made in her throat did nothing to restore his self-control.

"Tell me to stop," he begged against her lips.

She wrapped her arms tighter around him. "Please, don't stop," she demanded, and he dipped his head to blaze a trail of kisses down her sweet-smelling neck.

Lured by her candy scent, his nose dipped to her neckline and his hand slipped beneath her top to glide over the silken curves of her torso. She arched her back, lifting her breasts in invitation, her heavy-lidded eyes communicating desire.

Damn you, Adams.

In the face of her encouragement, he knew he'd never find the willpower now to walk away. It was exactly as he feared. He should never have sought her out in the state that he was in. Not that being celibate these last weeks had made it any worse. Even if he'd gotten laid last night, he'd still be this hot for Rebecca. The prospect of being with a woman so thoughtful, so classy, and whom he admired so much proved too tempting to deny himself.

Watching her expression, he brushed his thumb over the lace cup of her bra. Her gasp and the way her nipple stiffened aroused him instantly. He repeated the motion, his groin throbbing with anticipation as her tongue darted out to touch her upper lip.

Oh, hell. He was about to violate his own personal code of ethics by making love with a woman he both liked and respected. He'd have no one to blame but himself if he ended up hurting her.

CHAPTER 11

————◆————

Rebecca's senses gloried in the pleasure of Brant's touch. His confident and sensual caress awakened every cell in her body, causing them to clamor for more.

"I should leave," he muttered on a regretful note.

"Stay," she pleaded, clutching his broad shoulders for support. If he walked away now, her quaking knees wouldn't hold her up. "Please. It's okay," she added, wanting to dispel whatever doubts he harbored.

The conflict inside him registered on his face as he slowly lowered it to kiss her again. His restrained hunger warned her that there'd be no stopping if she let it go on much longer. With no intention of stopping, she sank her fingers into his golden mane, holding his clever mouth captive against hers, luxuriating in the softness of his hair, the warmth of his lips, and the certainty of his tongue.

He kissed exactly as she'd fantasized he would—not with Max's demanding force, but with such sensual consideration she was already damp with anticipation.

"God, Becca, you're so—" Seeming at a loss for words, he gazed down at her. "So beautiful," he finished, tucking a lock of hair behind her ear and searching her flushed face. "Come over here." He drew her closer to the fire, gathered the hem of her lace top in his hands, and pulled it over her head, leaving her standing in her bra.

Insecurity stabbed at her briefly, but the hunger blazing in his blue eyes immediately dispelled it.

"Nice," he said, pausing to appreciate the way the pretty lace bra cupped her modest breasts. Releasing the bra's single catch, he drew one strap over her shoulder, then the other, heightening her self-awareness. By the time the cups fell away, both pink nipples stood stiff and taut. "Exquisite," he declared, cupping her reverently.

His lean, tanned hands looked like a work of art against her fairer flesh. Ducking his head, he swirled his tongue over one peak, then the next, and her entire body trembled. She reached for his long sleeve T-shirt, tugging it up in a desperate need to expose the six-pack abs she'd beheld at the Labor Day party. He dragged it over his head, fueling her fantasy. With a gasp of wonder, she smoothed her palm over his lean, sculpted torso while his open mouth descended over her left breast and suckled gently. Her heart trotted at the decadence of the moment.

He straightened abruptly. "Lie down here with me," he suggested.

"Not the bedroom?"

"I want to see you in the firelight."

Happy to indulge his whimsy, she allowed him to lower her onto the expanse of cream-colored carpet in front of the fire—close enough to partake of its light, to feel a suggestion of its heat. He came down on all fours over her and stayed that way, pausing to examine her with appreciation in his blue eyes. Max had never looked at her like that. At last, he reached wordlessly for the front of her jeans, unbuttoning and unzipping them slowly.

Breathless with anticipation and incredulity, Rebecca watched him grasp the waistband of her jeans and peel them slowly down her thighs. She lifted her hips to aid him, noting how he intentionally kept her panties in place, how seductively he drew the denim down her legs.

He's had plenty of practice.

Squelching her prick of envy, she focused, instead, on the velvety sweep of his fingers as he started at the arches of her feet, caressing her up the length of her calves, to the sensitive insides of her knees.

She shivered, pleasure coiling in her belly like a spring. The worry that he would render her speechless before she had the chance to fulfill her own fantasies had her blurting, "Take your pants off."

He feigned shock at her demand. "You mean, get naked?"

"Now," she added, with a laugh. Coming up on her elbows, she locked her eager gaze on the front of his jeans. The bulge there left no doubt as to his arousal, a fact that thrilled her almost beyond bearing.

With a confident smile, he released the button first. Then he tugged at the zipper, putting on a show for her as the two halves parted, revealing several inches of his erection jutting through the gap in his boxers. A hot wave of anticipation rolled through her.

"Let me," she requested, sitting up the rest of the way.

Anticipation flashed in his eyes as she reached out and took hold of him.

"Becca," he groaned.

The smooth pillar of his sex slid like silk between her fingers, thrilling her as she imagined how completely he would fill her. Clasping him in both hands, she stroked him lovingly to presage what was still to come. But after a moment, he caught her hands and pulled them away.

"Easy, hon. I've got it bad for you right now."

She drew back, disappointed. "No women on your last mission?" she guessed, tamping down her jealousy.

His expression turned quizzical. "Not exactly. Actually, there haven't been any women since you made me that wager."

She thought back. "What wager?"

"You said I couldn't last a week without sex, remember? Well, it's been longer than that—almost three weeks, actually."

She searched his face in astonishment. "You've been celibate that long?"

"Yep. See, you should never challenge a SEAL, hon. We like to prove nothing is impossible for us."

The knowledge that he'd deprived himself for so long, by his standards, sent a thrill through her. Suddenly, she longed to push him over the edge and to reward him for his restraint. She reached for him again.

"Oh, no you don't." He rolled to his feet, standing just out of reach as he shucked off his remaining clothing. At last, he stood naked before her, all rippling muscles and smooth golden skin. The sight of him made her head spin and her heart expand. But then he lifted a shiny object to his mouth and tore into it, bringing her back to reality.

"Good thing you thought of that," she said. Here she was, a nurse, and she hadn't given any consideration to birth control.

He shot her a tolerant smile, while covering himself with ease of practice and no sign of being self-conscious. Then he dropped to his knees next to her, lowered his head, and kissed her until she melted back against the floor, delirious once again. And then he proceeded, at last, to peel away her panties, tossing them somewhere behind him and making her giggle, before he covered her body with his.

Easing between her legs, he gave her a moment to adjust to his weight. His erection lay hot and heavy against her inner thigh.

"You feel so good under me," he whispered. His eyes had never looked so blue. Then he ducked his head, delivering a kiss so intense that it caught her up in its vortex.

She could feel his heart pumping hard against his sternum. Tension strained the muscles of his back as the head of his sex nudged her opening.

Suddenly, he tore his mouth from hers and rested his cheek against hers, breathing hard.

"What's wrong?" she asked.

"I'm supposed to kiss you all over right now, but I can't bring myself to move," he admitted with a self-deprecating laugh.

She stroked the curls at his nape. Making love was supposed to be spontaneous, not a step-by-step process. "Then stay here." She rolled her hips in invitation.

"I'll make it up to you," he promised.

Clearly, his goal was to impress her, not to connect with her emotionally. Before she could say that there was nothing to make up, he surged into her with a helpless growl.

"Oh!" Her eyelids sank shut at the thick but delicious intrusion. He withdrew and thrust again, giving rise to a primal craving that demanded more of the same.

And then it was a mindless race to repletion. Without grace or style, Rebecca responded to his single-minded possession, driving her hips up to meet him. She dug her nails into the thick muscles of his upper back and pulled him closer. The carpet rubbed the base of her spine raw, but she scarcely felt it over the rapture that came from being filled and stretched.

His tongue, gliding along hers, mimicked his possession. The hair on his chest teased her pebbled nipples. The effect was too intense, too overwhelming for her to find release. He gave a groan, tore his lips from hers, and buried his face in her hair, shuddering violently.

Still poised on the edge of climax, Rebecca swallowed down her disappointment. Blinking back the tears that sprang to her eyes, she summoned a smile as he lifted his head, looking utterly dazed.

"What the hell was that?" he asked.

She hoped the question was rhetorical.

"Holy shit," he breathed. Withdrawing from her warmth, he rolled onto his back and stared up at the ceiling, panting like he'd sprinted to the finish line.

Rebecca cleared her throat. "Are you okay?"

Bronco turned his head to meet her bemused gaze. "Becca, I'm so sorry." Stretching out a hand he caressed her cheek with the pad of his thumb. "I haven't lost control like that since I was sixteen."

She didn't know whether to be flattered or embarrassed. All she knew was that her body wanted more and it was over. But that was okay. She wouldn't have traded the experience for anything in the world. If only it could have lasted longer. Feeling slightly self-conscious, all spread out on the rug with her nipples still pert and her body throbbing for release, she looked around for her clothes.

Chagrin kept a steady heat in Brant's face. If first impressions were as important as people said, he'd just blown his chance to impress Rebecca.

It was tempting to blame celibacy for his lack of control, but he had a hunch that was only half of the equation. The other half was Rebecca herself. He had never had sex with a woman whom he cared about so much. If he'd known what a difference it made, he might have tossed aside his rule to keep sex impersonal a long time ago.

She was trying to cover herself, for Christ's sake, grasping for her blouse that was just out of reach, but he could see by her carefully blank expression and her pebbled breasts that she was far from satisfied. *You selfish bastard,* he called himself, aching for the opportunity to try again. Fortunately, the sight of her creamy skin in the flickering firelight sent a fresh wave of lust through him.

"Can I use your bathroom?" He just needed to collect his poise first.

She paused in act of dragging her clothes closer. "Of course. It's through there, in my bedroom."

"Don't move," he ordered, glancing back at the soft pink flesh between her toned legs, and the sexy damp dark curls. "I want you exactly like that when I return. Okay?"

She eyed him curiously but then nodded her agreement.

In her bathroom, he disposed of the condom and cleaned himself up in record time before giving himself a stern glare in the mirror. *Ready to do better? Hooyah, Chief Adams.*

Returning to her living room, he was pleased to see she hadn't moved one inch in his absence. The surprise that widened her eyes when she saw him standing at full attention brought back his confidence. He searched his wallet for another condom and tore into it. "Let's try that again," he proposed, "in the bedroom, this time."

"You can do it more than once?"

The guileless question had him looking up at her. He knew that some men were one-and-done, but Mad Max seemed like he would be an overachiever, if anything. "Are you telling me that Max can't?" He held out a hand and pulled her up to stand before him.

She shook her head. "No. He...he can't."

She bit her bottom lip as if catching back details he had no desire to hear anyway. Suddenly he felt much better about his deplorable performance.

"Sorry about my hurried finish." Gathering her close, he nuzzled his lips against her ear. "I'm usually not that selfish. There's just something about you that makes me go a little crazy." He pulled back to send her a rueful smile. "I'm going to make it up to you, though. I promise," he added, assessing her reaction.

The lusty glitter in her eyes and the way she touched the tip of her tongue to her upper lip made him melt, especially when she nodded ever so slightly, offering him the smallest smile of desire. Christ, a man could fall in love so easily with this woman.

Not him, though. He'd hardened himself to women's wiles a long time ago, and it'd been easy to keep them at a distance because he didn't enjoy their company, outside of the bedroom, anyway. Rebecca fell into a whole different category. He liked her in every conceivable way, and it was starting to scare the hell out of him.

Rebecca's anticipation rose as Bronco led her by the hand to her bedroom, where he pulled back the covers and invited her to lie back on her crisp, white sheets across the queen-sized air mattress.

"I'm glad you didn't bring your mattress from home," he said, leading her to believe that he alone wanted to possess her on this bed.

Standing over her a moment, he studied her with a look that struck her as possessive, at least in the light that spilled from the bathroom. Coming down on one knee, he proceeded to kiss her from her mouth on down, just as he'd promised he would. Her neck, her breasts, and the smooth plane of her abdomen all benefited from the skill and warmth of his lips and tongue. She fought to contain a cry of anticipation as he outlined the triangular pattern of her neatly trimmed mound with his tongue.

"Please," she begged half hysterically.

"Do you want something?" he asked with laughter in his voice.

She squirmed, trying to get his mouth onto the apex of her sex, where the throbbing nubbin clamored for his attention.

"Yes." The mere thought of him teasing her *there* with his tongue nearly sent her over the edge.

Burying his nose against the strip of hair that crowned her pubic bone, he inhaled the scent of her arousal. "You are unbelievably sexy," he rumbled.

A self-conscious heat glowed in her cheeks, as did a flash of anticipation. *So close.*

He stroked the pad of his thumb over the slick swollen center of her desire, and her eyelids fought to stay open. And then—at last—he replaced his hand with his mouth and her self-consciousness fled as wave after wave of bliss rolled over her. Of their own accord, her hips bucked against him as his name was pulled from her lips.

"Bronco!"

To say that he had developed unparalleled skills in the amorous department was clearly an understatement. Yet she was the one benefitting now, as his clever tongue sent her catapulting toward a climax.

"Wait, wait!" She didn't want it done and over with so quickly. "I want you to be with me when I—" she faltered, suddenly too modest to articulate her desires.

He sent her a wicked grin. "Just enjoy the ride, sweet Becca. Don't worry, you'll come again."

The promise of still another climax was all it took to make her shatter. It had taken him less than five minutes to launch her off the pinnacle into a sea of bliss.

"You're really good at that," she said when she could speak again.

"Spoken with such reproach," he mocked, stretching himself over her. "You ready for more?"

"I think so," she said, feeling a little lightheaded. It had been ages since she'd climaxed, and never like that.

He eased into her slickness, moving with slow measured strokes that awakened her senses and brought her right back to the brink of ecstasy. He didn't kiss her this time, but studied every nuance of her expression, perhaps to determine what pleased her most.

With a desultory rhythm that kept her in a sensual stupor, he took her to the summit of ecstasy and kept her there, eliciting sounds of primal pleasure that she had never made before. Suddenly, he rolled over, taking her with him. She found herself straddling him, deeply united but free to move any way she liked.

"It's all you, Becca," he invited.

Having lost all inhibition, she resumed the rhythm he'd begun earlier while rolling her hips to receive every inch of him.

His hands sought her breasts, lifting and rolling and plucking. His right thumb slipped between their bodies to stroke the cradle of her pleasure. She promptly started to unravel.

"Bronco!" There was no way to stem the rapturous tide that swamped her without warning.

He joined her in it, pulling her to him and growling his repletion. Her pleasure peaked and ebbed, and she spilled across his chest, utterly fulfilled and deeply content.

All this time, she'd had no idea what making love really meant. Until now.

A peaceful quiet fell over them, interrupted only by the sound of their breaths coming in tandem, slowing to a peaceful ebb and flow. Bronco stroked her hair with a tenderness that curled her toes. At last, she lifted her head and looked at him in the light coming from her bathroom.

"Is it always like that for you?" she heard herself ask, only to regret the question. She didn't want his mind going to other women he'd had sex with, not while holding her.

For an inordinately long time, he gazed back at her. "Actually, it's never been like that," he admitted on a gruff, uncertain note.

Her heart glowed at the confession, but did he have to sound so wary about it? It was obvious he had his doubts about being involved with his commander's estranged wife. Who wouldn't?

Kissing the corner of his mouth, she separated their bodies thinking he might want to get up as he had the last time. But, instead, he pulled her snugly against him. Wriggling closer, she settled her head comfortably on his shoulder and sighed. A huge yawn seized her. With a sense of completion unlike anything she'd ever experienced, she closed her eyes and promptly fell asleep.

Brant lurched awake, his heart hammering, a

clammy sweat on his skin.

Just a dream, he realized, lowering his head back down on the pillow and reorienting himself. Rebecca lay with an arm and a leg thrown over him. Her steady exhalations calmed his racing pulse.

Closing his eyes again, he pondered the realism of his dream. He and his teammates had been drilling close-quarters hostage rescue techniques in the sturdy outdoor structure they called The Pen. Brant had volunteered to play the hostage, while Tristan Halliday acted as one of the terrorists. Brant had been tied to a chair, a bandana secured over his eyes keeping him from seeing anything but shadows. Listening to Halliday pace before him, issuing mock threats, he awaited rescue.

Something metal rolled across the floor. A flashbang exploded, lighting the room with enough brilliance to penetrate his blindfold. Booted feet scurried toward him. Rubber bullets peppered the wall, and Halliday hit the floor with an oath. One of the rescuers bumped into Brant and whipped the blindfold off his face.

Even in the dark, he recognized Max's blunt features. What was the CO doing participating in the training? Before he even could answer his own question, the snout of a pistol gouged his temple. The soft *click-click* of a round being advanced into the chamber provided his only warning before the gun discharged and sprayed his brains across the wall next to him.

He'd startled awake at the unexpected violence. And now the gritty realism of the hallucination kept his heart beating unevenly. Max had fucking shot him in the head!

He peeked at the digital clock on the other side of Rebecca. Not yet zero five hundred hours. Common sense dictated that he forget the dream and try to fall back to sleep, but the condom he was still wearing was leaking. More than that, the dream seemed to be warning him to get up.

Brant had seen the chilling calculation in his CO's gray eyes several times already. Now that he was cognizant of what the man was up to in his spare time—killing for a price—he had to consider the possibility that he might become Max's next target.

Rebecca stirred. Smoothing a hand down her naked back, Brant memorized the texture of her skin. He kissed her temple, inhaling the scent of peppermint sticks and woman's musk one last time.

This is good-bye, he realized, and his throat closed up with unexpected loss.

It wasn't as if he hadn't anticipated this moment. One way or another, he'd known he was going to have to bow out of her life. He just hadn't realized it would be this soon or this hard, but things had escalated between them at a record pace.

He eased out of the bed, taking pains not to wake her. Crossing to the bathroom, he shut the door and washed up with the lights off. Then he passed through her room on his way to her door, fighting not to glance in her direction. In the living area, he dressed in his cast-off clothing, jammed his feet into his tennis shoes, and retrieved her sketch of Tony.

Autumn-crisp air brought him more sharply awake as he peeked outside, half-expecting to see Max's Tahoe idling where it had been last night. A mockingbird twittered at the first suggestion of light to pearl the sky. Patting his pocket for his car keys, he took one last look back at Rebecca's apartment.

Regret held his heart in a painful vise. If he didn't like her so much, this wouldn't be so damn hard, but he did. He liked her more than he wanted to admit.

And he needed to get to the bottom of this mystery before something awful happened to either one of them.

"Take care, Becca."

Locking the knob, he pulled the door firmly shut behind him. Then he headed for his truck, searching the shadows for any sign of Max.

Once inside of his Bronco, he fished his cell phone and his pistol out from under the seat. A portion of his confidence returned. He had Hack, Bullfrog, and Master Chief to help take on Max. It was good to know his teammates had his back, even if his own commander didn't.

CHAPTER 12

———◆———

Bullfrog slipped into Brant's passenger seat, bearing a gym bag and a bagel slathered in cream cheese. He handed the bagel to Brant, shutting the truck door behind him.

"Oh, you read my mind." Brant accepted the offering and took a huge bite out of it. "Anyone follow you?" he asked around a mouthful. The area around the dojo had begun to attract its most dedicated patrons, even this early on a Saturday.

"No one." Bullfrog ran an assessing gaze over his rumpled attire. "You stayed with Rebecca all night?"

"Yep," Brant admitted, ignoring his friend's unspoken disapproval. Starting up his truck, he drove cautiously around the building, on the lookout for Max's Tahoe. Maybe it was his conscience dogging him, but he already felt as though he was wearing a big, fat bull's-eye on his back.

"Sure hope she was worth it," Bullfrog said, looking away.

Memories of the night before stirred in Brant like a bed of leaves under a soft wind. "Best night of my life," he admitted, hearing his own amazement.

His friend flicked a frown at him. "Hack says he'll meet us at Kuzinsky's at seven."

Grateful for Bullfrog's lack of commentary, Brant nodded and pointed his Bronco south. Leery of running into Max, who might have been staked out at his apartment, he had waited at the dojo for Bullfrog to join him. Now they had only ten minutes to get to Kuzinsky's new place, a fixer-upper situated in rural Pungo, ten minutes down the road.

They drove in silence, passing fewer and fewer buildings until nothing but flat farmland surrounded them. Brant found himself reconsidering his future. If he followed through with exposing Max's actions, he could probably kiss his career as a SEAL good-bye. Did he really want to go through with this?

Rebecca's sweet smile came to mind, and the answer was unquestionable: *For her? Yes.*

Ten minutes later, they arrived at Kuzinsky's mailbox, situated at the start of a long dirt driveway. Brant swung down it, and a dilapidated farmhouse came into view. Granted, it was backdropped by a picturesque creek framed in marsh grass and cattails. Not a single building other than a newer detached garage stood within sight, just water snaking through the marsh, a lot of trees, and blue sky. But the old house was covered in clapboard that had weathered to a dull gray. Yellow caution tape ran the perimeter of the sagging front porch, and several of the windows were boarded up.

"What the hell?" Brant marveled.

Spying Hack's motorcycle parked at the rear of the house, he drew alongside it. As they stepped out of his truck, Kuzinsky poked his auburn head out of the back door and waved them both in.

The smells of bacon and coffee beckoned them into a warm kitchen. In spite of the home's rough exterior, the kitchen had undergone a full remodel, with handsome white cabinetry that complemented the shiny hardwood floors. Hack looked up from a long table where he sat in front of Max's laptop.

"Morning," he said, booting it up.

"Coffee?" Kuzinsky asked.

Brant and Bullfrog both said yes and pulled out seats. Kuzinsky brought them two steaming mugs as they all sat down.

He nodded at the equipment in front of Hack. "That's the CO's laptop?"

"Rebecca gave it to us," Brant explained. He drew a measured breath and let it out slowly, the way he did whenever he settled behind his Stoner SR-225. "She thinks Commander McDougal is up to something he shouldn't be."

As usual, Kuzinsky's expression gave nothing away. "What makes her think that?" he asked, taking a sip from his mug.

"She saw something she wasn't supposed to see," Brant continued, "a foreign account in Max's name with fifty thousand dollars in it. He told her it was the task unit's money. Prior to that, according to her, they had maxed out their home equity line and were in danger of foreclosure. Next thing she knew, the loan was paid in full. She asked Max where the money had come from, and he said some great uncle had died, leaving him an inheritance."

Kuzinsky's freckled face could have been set in stone. He took another slow sip of his coffee. "Go on," he said.

Brant gestured to Hack. "I figured Hack could find out more if he had the CO's laptop, which was in the shop because it caught a virus."

"A boot-sector virus, actually," Hack inserted, "which kept it from turning on. But I was able to boot to a CD in a pre-executable environment, which gained me access to the hard drive. Using specialized tools, I removed the virus and took a look into his user profile."

A tense silence fell over the table as Hack prepared to share what he'd found.

"For a period of three months last spring, the CO visited a black market website called Silk Road. He also logged in to a Swiss financial firm called Emile Victor DuPonte. On the surface, it looks like a regular institution, but the Swiss government doesn't recognize it, which means it has some shady investors."

"Did you get his login information?" Kuzinsky asked.

"As a matter of fact, I did. But the account is gone. He must have closed it after he realized that his wife saw it. Maybe he opened a new one with the same company. Who knows?"

"There's more," Brant warned, reclaiming the master chief's attention. "A couple weeks back, Rebecca came home from work and Max was tossing some guy out of the house. Speaking with a New York City accent, he introduced himself as Tony." He turned over the sketch he had laid face-side down on the table and slid it toward the master chief. "This is what he looks like."

Kuzinsky's russet eyebrows came together. "Who drew this?"

"She did. It's good, right? Around that same time, she found out Max was using her old post office box. She got into it herself and found this." He handed Kuzinsky his copy of the newspaper article mentioning the mob-related assassinations. "I re-sent the original in an identical envelope in the hopes that Max would never know the difference. Go ahead." He nodded at Kuzinsky. "Read it."

The coffee machine dripped quietly in the background as Kuzinsky waded through the article. At last, he looked up, his dark eyes as inscrutable as ever. "What are you getting at?" he demanded.

"We think the CO's working for the mob," Brant stated. Even to his own ears, it sounded ludicrous.

"Oh, come on," the master chief scoffed.

Brant looked over at Hack. "Show him what you found on Silk Road," he invited.

Hack turned the screen toward their leader. "This is what the website looks like. Trust me, it's not easy to find. Only way in is through a pseudo domain." He displayed a handsome website with a black background and blood-red font. "On April 1, the CO responded to an anonymous advertisement posted by—and I quote—'a powerful family seeking a security expert for all their security needs.' He even submitted his resume, which he deleted but I found in his recycle bin." He expanded a minimized document and let Kuzinsky take a look.

A crease bisected Kuzinsky's freckled forehead. "He listed his sniper qualifications. Why would he do that?"

"Think about it," Brant answered for Hack. "What kinds of security issues do mobsters have?" He waited a beat and answered his own question. "They wanted someone who could eliminate their problems—an assassin, basically." He stretched out a hand and tapped the copy of the news article. "I think he's the sniper working for the Scarpa family. The timeline matches up perfectly. He applied for the position in April. The two murders described here took place in May and July. Both men were shot in the head at a distance of half a mile from the vantage of a boat. We all know Max owns a boat."

Kuzinsky pushed his chair back. "There's a lot of speculation going on here," he stated. But an odd light glimmered in his dark eyes as he lifted them to gaze out the window at the marsh in his back yard.

"That's not all," Brant said, reclaiming his attention. "Did you know Rebecca left Max last weekend?"

Kuzinsky blinked, refocusing his attention on Brant. "No, I didn't."

"Of course not. Max would never admit to having marriage problems. But get this. The night she moved out, Tony was hiding in the back seat of her car. He made her drive at gunpoint to another vehicle." In as much detail as he could recall from Rebecca's rendition, he relayed how Tony had sent a photo of her, bound and gagged, to Max and threatened her life if Max didn't agree to Tony's terms.

Kuzinsky broke eye contact and stared at his empty mug. "I remember he got a message on his phone while we were in the TOC." He looked up suddenly. "Who else knows about all this?"

"Just the three of us," Brant said. "And Rebecca, of course."

The master chief considered the laptop for a moment. "Okay," he said, reluctance dripping off the two syllables. "You've convinced me that there's something going on. I'll take your suspicions to NCIS as soon as they can see me."

Relief loosened the knots in Brant's shoulders. "Thank you."

"In the meantime, I suggest you keep a low profile and keep your distance from Rebecca," his leader added sternly.

A wave of heat rose up his neck. "Yes, Master Chief." He determined that he'd heaped enough onto Kuzinsky's plate without bringing up his fears that Max might try to kill him. That was something he was going to have to deal with on his own.

Hack and Bullfrog would, of course, help to cover his six. But no one had held a gun to his head forcing him to sleep with the CO's estranged wife. That had been his decision alone and, in spite of the shit storm that was about to break loose, he couldn't bring himself to regret it.

Rebecca stirred and stretched. Her heightened senses catalogued the smooth glide of the sheets, the tenderness of her satiated body, and then the empty space beside her. She lifted her head with a stab of concern at finding herself alone.

"Bronco?" she called, not expecting an answer. Not a trace of his body heat remained, suggesting that he had left some time ago.

Disappointment pinned her back against the mattress, and her heart gave a throb of loneliness. What had she expected—that because it was a Saturday, he would spend the day with her? Yet, after last night, it had seemed nothing had the power to keep them apart, so why hadn't he stayed?

Because of Max, of course. Max had seen the one-of-a-kind Bronco parked near her apartment. If the evidence Hack had found on his laptop were true, then Max had announced his credentials as an experienced terminator to the mob. He probably had no compunction about killing Bronco, as he'd hinted at more than once now.

"Oh God." She rolled out of bed, stripped of her happiness.

Regarding her pale reflection in the bathroom mirror, she asked herself what, if anything, she could do to protect him. As she brushed the tangles from her hair, a suggestion skated into her thoughts. She recoiled from it, slamming her brush down on the marble sink top. *Never.*

She left her room and crossed the living area, where her gaze strayed to the spot in front of the fireplace where they'd first made love. Her clothes still lay in a heap on the floor where Bronco had dropped them. Longing rolled over her in a powerful wave.

She went into the kitchen to fix herself a cup of tea. There, she encountered the dishes left over from their dinner. With a troubled heart, she washed them, replaying every special moment of their conversation, cherishing every spoken word, every subtle nuance. He'd told her that he really liked her. The words warmed her heart anew.

Then the awful idea that had occurred to her earlier lodged itself in her mind a second time. She was certain Brant could convince Master Chief Kuzinsky to approach NCIS with the evidence against Max. But then Bronco would be the first person Max suspected of betraying him—unless Rebecca rushed in and doused the flames of his suspicion.

She drew a troubled breath and let it out. Her heart beat unpleasantly hard.

A detestable plan, but it just might work.

Bronco, of course, would abhor it. She could practically hear him insist that he was a big boy, fully capable of defending himself.

But Bronco didn't know Max quite as well as she did.

I should do it. Grim resolve slowed the tempo of her heartbeat. If it kept Bronco safe, then it was worth the humiliation and even the danger and punishment that could potentially arise.

Like a person being led to the gallows, she walked slowly toward her charging cell phone. Every fiber of her being rebelled at the prospect of talking to Max. And the last thing she wanted to do was to give him her new number, but if she called from a payphone, he would have reason to doubt her sincerity, and she had to be convincing—for Bronco's sake. She needed to make it look like she still trusted her husband.

Wetting her dry lips, she picked up her phone and tapped out Max's number. So long as progress was being made to investigate his wrongful actions, she could pretend to consider reconciliation. It was the only solution she could think of to keep him from going off the deep end.

Standing in a short line at the computer repair shop, Max willed the woman in front of him to hurry the hell up. He hated running errands on a Saturday. A dozen items needed to be struck off his to-do list that day. Amazingly, he had checked his new account and discovered that his advance had indeed been doubled. Now he was committed to killing Special Agent Doug Castle. But first he had to advance his plan to strike Brant Adams off the face of the earth.

It all came down to strategy. Luckily, Max had twenty-plus-years of experience at tactical planning. He was still the puppeteer, pulling the strings to make others dance at his command. Even the Scarpas had proven malleable to his will. The only person still making him look weak was his wife, who had left him to cavort with another man.

But not for long, Max vowed. All too soon, Adams would succumb to a drug overdose. His death would reveal his unhealthy habit, and a disillusioned Rebecca would realize what a mistake she had made in turning her back on her upstanding husband. If he had to coerce her to make her return to him, he would. But he would not, *could not,* let her go. What was once his would remain his forever.

The buzzing of his cell phone pulled him from his

dark thoughts. He eyed the unfamiliar number before answering, "Commander McDougal."

"Max?"

Rebecca's familiar voice kept him mute.

"Can you talk?" Her hesitant tone was counterbalanced by a warmth that kept him intrigued.

He considered the customer in front of him, too engrossed in discussing her wireless connectivity issue to pay any heed to his conversation. "What do you want?" *Besides a divorce?* he added in his mind.

"I…I wanted to apologize."

He slit his eyes with immediate suspicion.

"I know that my leaving must have caught you off guard."

"Is this your new phone number?" he asked, ignoring her observation. He eyed the number again, glad to have it.

"Yes. I didn't think it was fair to you to stay on your phone plan."

What was she up to, trying to play nice when she'd deserted him? Oh, of course. She wanted him to agree to a no-fault divorce. Like *that* was going to happen.

"Anyway," she continued, plowing ahead in spite of his silence, "Chief Adams dropped by my place last night and suggested that I call you to try to patch things up."

Intrigued, he turned his back on the woman in front of him and marched to the front of the store to stare at the busy parking lot. "Did he, now?" He highly doubted it.

"Yes. I'm sorry I left the way I did. It must have jolted you to find me gone like that. It's just…I was traumatized by what happened to me."

He cupped a hand over his mouthpiece, hissing words that were meant for her alone. "That should never have happened. I told you the man was trouble.

You should've called me to say you were okay. I was worried sick for days!"

"I'm sorry," she repeated. "I was so upset by what those thugs did to me. But you're not like them, Max. I should have trusted you to explain what's going on. Why would you even know people like them, anyway?"

Was this an olive branch she was extending? Why now, when she and Adams were surely conspiring against him?

"It's complicated," he hedged.

"I guess so." Her pitch conveyed disappointment. "Well, I wouldn't be talking to you right now if Chief Adams hadn't convinced me to try again. He reminded me what a skilled and capable commander you are," she insisted.

Christ, she was trying to protect her lover! To keep her husband from adding infidelity on top of desertion, as his reasons for declining her no-fault divorce. Not that he intended to pursue a fault-grounds divorce. She would be his again before any kind of divorce took place between them.

"Have dinner with me," he demanded. If he could look into her eyes, he could begin to work his will on her, while finding out how much, if anything, she'd already told the chief.

"Oh. I'll need to check with my lawyer to see if that's a good idea."

"You're referring to that line in the separation agreement about respecting your privacy and having no contact with you outside of the courtroom." He let her know by his mocking tone what he thought of the stipulation. "I haven't signed the agreement," he informed her. "Nor will I, ever."

"Oh." She fell quiet for a moment. "That-that line was my lawyer's idea," she stammered. "He thinks

Tony sounds dangerous, and since he associates with you, it's better if you and I aren't seen together."

Christ, she knew Tony's first name. Did she know his last, too? Was she fishing for more information about him in order to taint Max's reputation? A cold sweat swept across his brow. "He's not an associate. Listen, I'm busy. I'll talk to you later," he told her, hanging up.

It made little difference whether her apology was sincere or not. She was threatening his hard-won prestige with her show of independence, and he wouldn't stand for it.

"Sir, can I help you?"

Marching back to the counter, he told the technician that he wanted his laptop back. The man had had it for a month, and he obviously hadn't fixed it yet.

At his hostile tone, the employee's eyes glazed over. "I'm so sorry. What's the name?"

"McDougal. Max McDougal."

"I'll be right back with it."

Five long minutes ticked by. The woman with the wireless issue departed, and two more customers ambled in. Max glanced at his watch, his jaw muscles jumping as he clenched and unclenched his molars.

Finally, the technician emerged from the back. His wispy hair stood on end. "Sir, I'm sorry, but my associate says your wife picked up the laptop almost two weeks ago. She didn't tell you?"

Shock reverberated down Max's spine. "You released it to her?" he growled.

"I-I didn't think that would be a problem. Can't you just ask her for it?"

Max curled his right hand into a fist. It was all he could do not to reach across the counter and crush the man's windpipe.

"Of course," he replied, tamping down his temper

and summoning a tight smile. "Why didn't I think of that? I'll just ask her for it."

He wheeled away from the counter and stormed out of the store, nearly shattering the glass door as he tossed it open.

Rebecca had taken possession of his laptop. What did this mean? His heart flung itself against his ribs. What could she possibly think to gain when the virus that infected it kept it from powering up?

He forced himself to breathe as he crossed the parking lot. He could think of only one reason she would take it. She wanted to pry into its memory to search for the account she had glimpsed. Or perhaps she sought answers to the questions she'd asked him—who was Tony and what were Max's dealings with him?

Having minimal computer skills herself, she would have to enlist someone's help in her quest for answers. And who would that be? Someone her lawyer would hire? Or a friend of Chief Adams—someone like Hack, the new computer genius?

Horror broke Max's stride.

"No." His lungs convulsed. That couldn't be the case. She would have to have guessed that the laptop's memory held secrets he didn't want exposed—which it very well might. Until he got the Dell back and wiped its memory clean, he would live in fear that she might ruin him before he reeled her in again.

His thoughts in turmoil, he climbed slowly into his Tahoe and sat there.

He knew which apartment was hers. All it had taken to find that out was to call to the leasing office and tell few white lies. But breaking in to look for the laptop himself was far too risky.

The best way to get it was to hire some of the thugs

who advertised their services on the Silk Road website. As long as total strangers broke into her apartment, Rebecca would have no cause to connect Max to the laptop's disappearance. What's more, Silk Road offered potential employers complete anonymity, if that was their preference. That would prevent the thugs he hired from fingering Max if something went wrong.

If the hoodlums-for-hire frightened Rebecca in the process, then so be it. Maybe she'd realize just how vulnerable she was, living all alone—especially after Adams was out of the picture.

Max rubbed his hands in anticipation then started up his engine. Not too long from now, Rebecca would beg for him to take her back.

Mark my words, he assured himself.

Rusty Kuzinsky took the stairs to the second floor of the NCIS building on Oceana Naval Air Station in lieu of the elevator. Situated next to the air field, the steel-and-cement structure reverberated with the frequent roars of fighter jets and other military aircraft, taking off and landing.

At the height of the steps, he consulted the directional plaque mounted on the stark wall and turned left to course the long hallway. As he walked with stealth by habit, his boots scarcely made a sound on the marble floor. The number he sought jumped out at him from above a door up ahead. Special Investigator Maya Schultz was expecting his arrival.

He glanced at his watch and quickened his step to arrive precisely on time. She'd accommodated his last-minute request for an appointment by giving up her lunch hour. That was perfect for Rusty, who'd told Max he needed to meet with a contractor back at his house.

Approaching the cracked door, he transferred his briefcase—heavy with Max's bulky Dell tucked inside—to his left hand and pushed the door open wider. The reception area stood empty; the receptionist was probably out to lunch. Nonetheless, a pleasant voice called out from the inner office, "Come right in, Master Chief."

He crossed to the next door and stopped dead.

Ms. Schultz wasn't a day over thirty five. Her dark blond hair was curly and cut in short layers to frame her heart-shaped face. Light green eyes assessed him through plastic framed glasses that lent her an intelligent demeanor. She wore a black pantsuit over her slight frame. And when she stood up, she was still shorter than he was, even in heels, which he glimpsed as she came around the desk to greet him with her hand outstretched.

"Welcome," she declared, confirming his identity with a glance at the name stitched above his breast pocket. "I'm Maya."

Her handshake was a contradiction—firm yet dainty. "Call me Rusty," he said, impressed with her professional demeanor but suddenly doubting she was the right person for the job.

"My late husband fought with you on Gilman's Ridge," she announced, keeping his gaze captive. "Major Ian Schultz, 4th Marine Battalion. Perhaps you remember him?" Her casual tone could not disguise how important his answer was to her.

Gilman's Ridge. The very name conjured up memories that gnawed at his heart like a parasitic worm. Eight years ago, every brave warrior on that rugged peak had died in their effort to hold off the insurgents. He had been the only man to make it out alive. The vision of a handsome, robust Marine who had taken over the M240 machine gun after his gunner blew up panned through his mind.

"I remember him well." He especially remembered how the man looked with his guts strewn across the rocks, but she didn't need to know that. Poor woman would have been a newlywed, still, when her husband died. "He gave everything he had and more. You should be proud," he added.

She sent him a tight smile. "It's a miracle that you survived."

Miracle was not the word he would have used. "Thanks for working me in," he said, eager to change the subject and get down to business.

"Please, have a seat." To his relief, she went and closed the door behind him. The kinds of things he had to tell her didn't need to be overheard. Returning to her desk, she sat down at it gracefully, laced her hands together, and set them on the glossy, mahogany surface. "If I understood you correctly, you said you had some concerns about your commander's actions outside of the office?"

In lieu of answering, he toggled the locks on his briefcase, flicked it open, and pulled out Max's laptop, which Hack had fixed to run again. "May I?"

At her nod, he set it on the edge of her desk then handed her the detailed print out providing login information and what to look for within Max's user profile. "This laptop was given to me by Commander McDougal's estranged wife," he said, bending the truth for simplicity's sake. "There is history on here that bears some scrutiny, including evidence of a foreign account and activity on a black market website called Silk Road."

She eyed the laptop and the paperwork with interest as she took it from him, along with the power cord.

"Will you be working on this alone?" He couldn't stop himself from asking.

She regarded him for a moment. "Are you concerned that I can't get the job done?" Her polite tone held an edge to it that made him reevaluate her.

"I just hope you're tougher than you look," he admitted ruefully.

Her finely drawn lips curved into a smile. "Oh, I assure you, I am. But if it diminishes your worries, I do have a male partner who is currently out to lunch. You'll see him at our next encounter," she informed him sweetly.

Her feistiness tickled him. His mouth twitched toward a smile. He sent her a nod instead, gathered his thoughts, and presented the evidence that Brant Adams had brought to his attention, including the newspaper article found in Max's secret mailbox and Rebecca's portrait of the thug who'd briefly abducted her. He left nothing out that he could think of, not even Rebecca McDougal's marital discontentment and her possible affair with Chief Adams.

All the while, Ms. Schultz scribbled cryptic notes onto her yellow notepad. She broke off to examine the sketch more closely. "She drew this?"

"Yes."

"It's very detailed." Laying down the drawing, she perused the article next, her dark blonde eyebrows pulling together as she waded through it. "Someone sent this to him?"

"Yes. Mrs. McDougal believes her husband might be the sniper that the FBI is looking for."

The dubious glance Maya Schultz shot him over the top of the sheet brought unaccustomed heat to Rusty's face. "That's interesting," she said in a tone so skeptical he could tell she didn't believe it for a moment. She put the article back down. "Thank you for explaining all this so succinctly. I'll need to take a look into the user profile of this laptop, plus I'd like to speak with the parties involved, minus Commander McDougal, of course. Do you think you could provide me their contact information?"

He reached inside his briefcase one more time. Chief Adams had shared Rebecca McDougal's new address and phone number, simplifying the task. "Here you go."

"Well!" she exclaimed, clearly impressed by his foresight. "You do come prepared. But, then again, you can't anticipate every event, can you?"

Her words seemed to carry a veiled accusation. If he had planned better in anticipating the magnitude and firing power of the insurgent force on Gilman's Ridge, her husband would still be alive today. "Not every event," he admitted, pained by his shortcomings.

Her celadon gaze, paired with her pert nose and elegant mouth, made him want to sit there and stare at her forever.

She stood up, breaking the spell. "Give me a day or two to consider what you've brought me. I'll talk to each of these individuals either by phone or in person, and then I'll let you know whether we'll be investigating further."

"Thank you," he said, snapping his briefcase shut and rising to his feet.

"It was a pleasure to meet you, Master Chief," she said, extending her hand a second time.

Guilt gnawed at him as he squeezed her slender fingers and pictured her struggling through life without her strapping husband. *I'm sorry.* He swallowed down the apology. "Likewise, Ms. Schultz."

"I'll be in touch," she promised, opening the door and freeing him to leave.

CHAPTER 13

In his peripheral vision, Brant watched his platoon leader run a critical gaze up his rumpled battle-dress uniform to the bristles growing on his jaw. They stood on the edge of the obstacle course which was situated behind the Spec Ops building with the sun blinding them as it rose over the nearby Atlantic, awaiting their turn to put the junior SEALs to shame.

"You look like hell, Bronco," Sam finally declared, rubbing his hands together to warm them against the crisp autumn breeze that blew in off the crashing surf.

"Thanks, Sam. I feel like hell." He pretended to watch his teammates scramble up the unwieldy rope ladder to throw a leg over a thirty-foot bulkhead. But thoughts of how and when Max was going to ambush him kept him scanning the open area for suspicious activity. Thanks to his inability to sleep that week, his reaction time was seriously impaired. Max now had the edge he needed to catch him unawares.

"Does your present condition have something to do with Rebecca?"

Hearing her name on Sam's lips brought his head around. He met his friend's sympathetic gaze and looked away again. The desire to confide in him vied with the certainty that doing so would further undermine the cohesiveness of the task unit. They were still a fully operational unit that could go wheels up at any time. As platoon leader, Sam couldn't afford to view Max as anything but absolutely trustworthy.

"Can't tell you," he apologized, clapping Sam on the back. "Maybe one day." It all depended on whether NCIS thought Max was guilty of a wrongful act.

"Is Rebecca okay?" Sam pressed. "I hear she left the CO."

Brant blew out a breath. The rumors had begun already—Max wouldn't like that. "Yeah, I think so."

The desire to speak to her, to make love to her again, to hold her as she slept rode him so hard and relentlessly that he felt like he was one of the ornery broncs that used to try to toss him to the ground. He had never experienced a hankering this persistent. It made him numb to the chill that had Sam turning up the collar of his BDU jacket.

"I've noticed the chemistry between you two," Sam added, unsettling him further. "Always wondered what she saw in Max. Maybe you'd make a better couple. I'm sure you would."

The comment both gratified and terrified him. "No way." Brant stared straight ahead, ignoring Sam's puzzled frown.

"Why not?"

He gave a humorless laugh. "Dude, I'm not like you. I'm not the domestic type."

Sam rounded on him. "Christ, you make relationships sound like a disease. You're obviously crazy about her."

Brant refused to comment.

"And she obviously likes you. Enough to leave her

husband."

"Whoa." He held up a hand to stem Sam's words. "She didn't leave him for me. Let's get that straight right now."

"Monogamy is not a disease," Sam continued, ignoring his protest. "Have you ever even tried it?"

Of course he hadn't. If anything, he deliberately sabotaged potential relationships by dating multiple women at once and not spending quality time with any one of them.

"I know you haven't," Sam said, answering his own question. "You've gone your whole life keeping women at a distance. If Rebecca's the right one for you, then pull her close, man. Otherwise, I'm telling you now—you're going to regret it. One day, you may realize she meant more to you than you knew, and it'll be too late."

Brant swallowed hard. Sam's advice only sent him into deeper confusion. Even if he trusted himself not to hurt her, Rebecca still had a jealous husband with nearly unlimited power on the base and also over Brant's life and career. The ease with which Max could set up a training situation that resulted in his getting fatally injured kept him on edge.

In war zones, he had gone for days and weeks in this state of hyper-awareness. At least back then, he'd known he could count on his fellow SEALs to look out for him, the CO included. Everything was different now. The CO was out to get him, and only Kuzinsky, Hack, and Bullfrog even knew about the situation. He would rather face a hundred enemy combatants than live with this kind of internal threat.

"Our turn," he announced, forestalling further counsel as he dashed toward the obstacle course.

With a curse, Sam sprinted after him. The man had nothing to worry about; he was still going to trounce him. Brant's mixed–up mental state and his serious sleep deficit would ensure Sam's victory, in spite of his own hefty head start.

How long can I keep this up? he wondered. Something had to give.

Hope spurred Rebecca's pulse at the feel of her cell phone vibrating in the pocket of her scrubs. *Please be Bronco!*

She wasn't supposed to keep her phone powered in the ER, since any electronics had the potential to hinder the operation of the many life-saving machines. But desperation had driven her to flout the rules. She didn't want to miss Bronco's call—if and when he finally decided to call her back.

"You'll feel the anesthesia kicking in any minute now," she assured the patient with a fractured tibia. She had recently added a dilution of Dilaudid to a port in his IV. If only pain relief were so easy to come by for herself.

Days had passed since Bronco had left her apartment, Saturday morning. His silence was eviscerating. Hadn't he felt the perfect connection she had experienced the night he'd stayed over? The sex had been phenomenal—yes—but it was the sense of completion she'd experienced afterwards that had convinced her that they belonged together, that he would want to stay with her.

But, perhaps with his much more extensive experience, he had felt the same post-coital glow a hundred times before, and she was naïve to think she was anything special to him. Hearing nothing from him day after day left her questioning her perceptions, her reasons for leaving Max—everything.

Had she been played for a fool? She couldn't bring herself to believe that the warmhearted human being she knew Bronco to be would treat her so callously.

As the young man's grip on the gurney's rail slowly relaxed, Rebecca edged toward the curtain. "The orthopedist is on his way," she promised, slipping through the door.

Hurrying to the break room, she stepped inside and sneaked a peek at her phone. Her hopes plummeted. Not Bronco. Nor did she even recognize the number that had left her a voicemail.

At least it wasn't Max calling to pressure her for that dinner date he'd suggested the other day. In spite of his stating, emphatically, that he would *never* sign off on her separation agreement, he seemed to be honoring her request for privacy and no contact. Or was that just wishful thinking on her part? It wasn't at all like Max to remain complacent and let circumstances take their course. He had to be planning something awful—she just didn't know what, yet.

Accessing her voicemail, she listened to the message.

"Hello, Rebecca. This is Special Investigator Maya Schultz with NCIS. I was wondering if you would be free to visit my office on Oceana NAS, tomorrow at 4 P.M. Sorry for the last-minute notice, but I had a cancellation. You can text me your response, if you like, or call me back at your convenience."

Rebecca's heart trotted. *This is really happening.* Master Chief Kuzinsky had initiated the investigation of his own commander.

Her stomach churned with sudden doubts. What if Max hadn't done anything wrong and she'd instigated a pointless witch hunt? *Nonsense.* What kind of honest man associated with the likes of Tony, who'd pressed a pistol to her head and bound and gagged her? All that money that had gotten them out of debt and the other money that she'd glimpsed in a foreign account under Max's name hadn't come from his fairy godmother any more than it had come from a great uncle.

With a tremor in her fingers, she texted the investigator back. *I can make it tomorrow at four. Thank you.* Within seconds, she received a reply text with an address and a room number.

Phone in hand, Rebecca battled the impulse to reach out once more to Bronco. She had called him the morning she'd awakened to find him gone. She had called two more times after that and left heartfelt messages. What made her think another call would make any difference? Clearly, he had no wish to communicate. But how could that be?

Closing her eyes, she puzzled it out. If only she could be angry with him. He'd taken advantage of her vulnerability—used her to satisfy himself and then left her without so much as a thank you, the way he treated all those other women who meant nothing to him!

Just as she succeeded in whipping herself into a rage, her conscience spoke up in his defense. *She* was the one who'd begged him to stay. He'd given her multiple chances to rein in their runaway passion. And he had told her point blank that he couldn't protect her. What he had meant, evidently, was that he wasn't the man for her. He was a love-'em and leave-'em kind of guy. She'd known that all along, hadn't she, so how could she possibly blame him now?

I can't, she decided, powering her phone off and sliding it back into her pocket.

Thank God for her job, which kept her too busy to dwell on her loneliness and confusion, at least while she was at work. And now she had an appointment the following afternoon to look forward to. That sure beat returning to her quiet and empty apartment, where the memories of her night with Bronco lingered like a haunting perfume.

The following afternoon, Max threw open his office window to bellow across the Spec Ops parking lot.

"Adams, where the hell are you going? We have shooting quals at sixteen hundred hours today."

The handsome chief drew up short, tension in his spine as he slowly turned around. "Yes, sir," he called back, shading his eyes against the glare of the late afternoon sun. "Master Chief needs me to pick up some paperwork from supply before they close. Their fax machine's not working."

The depot that stored most of their equipment was located at Oceana NAS, ten minutes up the road from Dam Neck.

"He should've run that by me first," Max grumbled. Adams would miss the mandated testing, which took place every Thursday. Not that there was any need for him to prove himself when he was already the sharpest shooter in the task unit, possibly in all of Team 12, with the exception of Max himself.

"Go ahead," he barked, slamming the window shut and watching the chief climb nimbly into his truck.

Just wait, Max thought, anticipating the moment that he would slip enough OxyContin into the chief's veins to stop his heart. The fact that Adams hadn't ventured anywhere near Rebecca since the night he'd parked his Bronco in front of her apartment didn't change Max's mind about killing him. The way the chief looked at him these days made him suspect he knew more than he should. If Rebecca had told him about Max's offshore account and they'd decided together to dig into the memory on Max's laptop, then the situation was more severe than he'd guessed.

Luckily, he wouldn't have to wait long before the

laptop ceased to be an issue. Members of a local street gang had agreed to pillage Rebecca's apartment and retrieve the laptop in exchange for four thousand dollars. Their fee amounted to highway robbery, but getting that laptop back meant all the difference to Max's future, so he'd agreed to two thousand up front and two thousand later.

Hopefully, the Scarpas never caught wind of his dealings. If they knew how careless he'd been in leaving information out where his wife could get a look at it, they'd probably take him out themselves before he proved a liability. As it was, they had to be less than happy with him for arousing the suspicions of the FBI special agent.

Out in the parking lot, Adams' old truck pulled away, scattering the seagulls taking refuge in the parking lot. Max turned back to his desk, where his cell phone gave a muted chime, alerting him to the chief's movements. The transponder he had affixed to the old Bronco had sent him a signal, providing the man's exact location on a map. In a matter of minutes, he would know if Adams was lying to him about his destination or not.

Riveted to his phone, Max counted his heartbeats as he watched the tiny dot progress toward the gate and up Dam Neck Road. If he continued straight past General Booth, then he had probably made plans to rendezvous with Rebecca, either at the hospital park where they'd met before or—worse yet—at her new place, where she might even hand off Max's laptop.

For five full minutes Max's temples throbbed as he waited for an answer. But then the dot turned right onto General Booth and then left at Oceana, suggesting that Adams was bound for the supply depot, exactly like he'd said.

Max still didn't trust him. Chances were the chief

had already impressed Rebecca in the bedroom, giving her something with which to compare her husband's performance. He could think of no better reason to get rid of the man. But, even in concentrated form, OxyContin dissolved in water wasn't enough to stop a man's heart. Alcohol provided the other half of the equation. Luckily, Adams was known to go out drinking every Friday night with his friends. Catching him without around them would be the hardest part.

Once Rebecca's lover lay dead from an overdose, her eyes would be opened to his true character. She would realize that her influential and well-respected husband was the better choice, and she would come back to him.

If that didn't do the trick, then the street gang breaking into her apartment and giving her the scare of her life would make her long for the security of their well-protected home.

"Does this Tony look exactly like your sketch?" Special Investigator Maya Schultz's celery-green eyes conveyed skepticism as she regarded Rebecca from the other side of her large desk. Beyond the walls of the woman's third-floor office, the NCIS building thrummed with activity.

Ms. Schultz's partner, an older gentleman introduced as Ben Metier, occupied the chair adjacent to Rebecca's. Given his benign expression and the manner in which he inclined his robust frame close to her, Rebecca guessed that he had elected to play "good cop" while Ms. Schultz asked the tough questions. To her dismay, the female inspector didn't seem to fully believe that a man calling himself Tony had abducted her in order to procure Max's phone number.

"Yes, it's a close resemblance." She wished her tone

didn't sound so prickly, but she resented the implication that she would make up such a story. "I used to earn money drawing portraits at the waterfront."

Ms. Schultz laid the picture back down and consulted her notes. "Tell me more about the foreign account you saw in your husband's name."

Rebecca described what she had seen—an account held by a company called Emile Victor DuPonte with a balance of fifty thousand dollars in it.

The roar of a departing fighter jet delayed the investigator's next question. "Has he held any other jobs outside of the Navy while you've known him?"

"Only one. A security firm paid him to be a consultant, once. But that was three years ago, and they paid him hardly anything."

"I see." The woman put her pen down and laid her interlaced hands on the surface of her desk. "Well, the account you mentioned has been closed," she announced, articulating her words carefully. "If he has a new account, we don't know where it is, how much is in it, or where any money in it could have come from. And it's beyond our powers to find out."

Rebecca stared at her. "You think I'm making this up." She sat up straighter. "Do you think I'd pursue this matter if I weren't absolutely convinced that Max is doing something illegal?"

"We can see that he paid off his home equity line of credit," Ms. Schultz allowed, "with cash," she added, her eyebrows flexing, "which makes the source of the money untraceable but isn't, in itself, illegal. Nor does it constitute proof that he made any money by illegal means." She sent Rebecca a helpless shrug.

"Why would he pay cash unless he's covering his tracks?" Rebecca challenged.

"Listen." The investigator met her gaze with an

intent expression. "In order for your husband to be charged with illegally obtaining funds in a foreign account, we would have to initiate an Article 32 hearing. Once your husband was apprised of the hearing, he would also learn that you were planning to testify against him for actions that occurred when you lived together. His best tactic would be to discredit your testimony. It is therefore critical that you be a credible witness."

"Of course," Rebecca agreed. Why would the investigator think her anything but a credible witness?

"I have to ask you a very personal question, Mrs. McDougal," the woman warned her.

Rebecca braced herself. "Go ahead."

"Are you and Chief Adams having an affair?"

Rebecca's blood flashed cold then hot. It took her a moment to find her tongue. "I wouldn't call it an affair, exactly," she muttered. Heat won out, rising up the column of her neck like mercury in an old thermometer. "We haven't spoken in six days."

The older woman sat back, her fingers interlaced. "But you're lovers?"

Ben Metier sent her an encouraging nod, as if to say that it was safe to answer.

Rebecca drew a tight breath. "Chief Adams has been a friend of mine for years. I never cheated on my husband while I lived with him, if that's what you're asking me."

Silence filled the spacious office. Behind her lenses, the investigator's eyes softened slightly. "You're not lovers, then," she paraphrased.

A fresh wave of heat flooded Rebecca's cheeks. "Not currently," she said between clenched teeth.

Ms. Schultz's finely drawn lips quirked. "I'm glad to hear it," she said, in a firm but not unfriendly voice. "If you were having an affair with Chief Adams, it might look like you were trying to discredit your husband in order to justify your infidelity—not because he was doing anything illegal."

In other words, she and Bronco needed to keep rumors about their relationship from reaching the ears of the military judge. Good thing Bronco had been keeping his distance since their one night together. Perhaps that was the reason? she wondered hopefully.

"I understand," she murmured, thoroughly humiliated.

Mrs. Shultz studied her notes a moment then looked up at her again and nodded. "Well, I think that's all I need for now. Thank you for coming in on such short notice."

"Wait." Rebecca gripped the arms of her chair and sat forward. "You *are* going to initiate an Article 32, aren't you?" She suffered the suspicion that, for lack of evidence, NCIS might just wash their hands of the matter.

Ben Metier laid a reassuring hand over hers. "Under normal circumstances, it would have taken place already," he explained. "But then Commander McDougal would be well aware that he was being investigated and, due to the nature of these allegations, we think it best that he remain unapprised while we review the evidence."

They don't believe me. Her hopes for a future resolution sank, along with her heart.

As if sensing her dismay, Metier added, "I'm sure you're not aware of this, but the military judge doesn't make a final decision whether to dismiss the case or refer it to General Court-Martial. He writes up a recommendation and gives it to your husband's senior commanding officer—Admiral Johansen, leaving the disposition of the case up to him."

Understanding dawned, making Rebecca suddenly

queasy. "Max is good friends with the admiral," she whispered. "They play golf together every other week."

Metier sent her a tight smile. "Indeed." He squeezed her hand and let go. "All the more reason to strengthen our case before the hearing."

Rebecca put a hand to her forehead. How long would that take—weeks? Months? Could she survive all that time without Bronco speaking to her?

Maya Schultz stood up, reached across her desk and offered her a brief but firm handshake. "We'll be in touch," she promised, letting her partner usher Rebecca to the door.

Moving down the hall on leaden feet, Rebecca considered the matter from the investigators' standpoint. Max was more than just a Navy SEAL commander. He was a Bronze Star recipient with an impeachable service record, who counted untold members of the upper brass—men like Admiral Johansen—as his friends. With his off shore account gone, it was impossible to prove that she had ever seen it in the first place. Without proof of that account, Maya Schulz had no way of showing to a military judge that Max had been paid by the mob— let alone that he had killed for them. From the outside looking in, the allegations seemed ridiculous.

The nonslip tread on her nurse's shoes squeaked noisily as she made her way to the elevator, her eyes downcast. A figure springing out of the central staircase startled her into looking up. The unexpected sight of Bronco striding toward her in his BDUs sent her heart winging toward the stratosphere, only to falter like a bird with a broken wing.

He had already recognized her, his stride slowing. The mix of longing and regret, so apparent in his face, kept her heart from hitting the earth and breaking into pieces. With a firming of his mouth, he continued doggedly in her direction. She saw right away that the cut on his face was healing nicely, the stitches gone. As soon as they were close enough, he grabbed her with both hands and hauled her into a crushing embrace.

"Becca," he exclaimed on a tortured whisper.

The hurt she had carried around for days evaporated in the face of his warmth. She let it go, encircling his lean waist, dropping her head onto his shoulder, and muffling a whimper of relief against the fabric of his jacket.

Home again, she thought—at least for as long as he allowed it.

Brant buried his nose in Rebecca's shiny hair. His voice had gotten stuck somewhere between his fast-beating heart and his dry mouth. He breathed in her peppermint scent until his head spun. In spite of all reason, he couldn't bring himself to loosen his grip. He kept her locked against him, grateful that she was hugging him back and not kicking him in the groin.

"I've missed you so much," he heard himself confess, ignoring the voice that raged, *No, no, no! You are not supposed to say that.*

But the pleasure that lit up her face as she tipped back her head and looked him in the eye kept him from regretting his words.

"I've missed you, too," she said. Tears of happiness and hurt commingled, sparkling on her lower lashes.

He sought some glib excuse for ignoring her since their blissful night together. Nothing came to mind. "I'm so sorry," he ground out.

She blinked to keep her tears from falling. "You don't have to apologize."

"The hell I don't." Her acceptance made him

inexplicably furious. "The hell I *don't*," he repeated, hating himself more with every passing second. "You deserve so much better than what I can give you," he managed, hoping she could read between the lines and glean what he really meant—that he wasn't even *boyfriend* material, let alone the steady kind of man she deserved.

"Why do you say that?" she asked earnestly.

"Because it's true."

He longed to explain that he'd spent his entire adult life trying to do the right thing by keeping his distance, only with her it didn't feel like the right thing. But giving her any reason to hope for a future for them would be heartless because from everything he'd learned about himself he was, in fact, the spitting image of his father.

But all of that was way too complicated to explain, and kissing her was so much easier.

Crushing his mouth to hers, he groaned out loud at the bliss that the simple connection of their lips engendered. Her kiss was like the first day of spring after an endless Montana winter, warming and thawing him.

Pulling her soft curves closer, he expected her to resist him, but she didn't. She offered herself up like a flower opening its petals to the sun. Out the corner of his eye, he spotted a petite blonde exiting an office door at the end of the hallway. She took one look at them, turned on her heels, and disappeared back into her office.

Brant didn't care. He drowned in Rebecca's kiss while telling himself, *I'll stop soon.*

The sweet glide of her tongue sparked the memory of their lovemaking. Immediately and forcefully, the blood rushed from his head through his heart to his groin. If they'd been standing by a closet or a private room, he wouldn't have the willpower not to pull her into it and lose himself in her sweetness.

Luckily, she came to her senses before he lost complete control. Breaking off the kiss, she pulled back to regard him. Bright bands of color streaked across her cheeks. Her breasts rose and fell as if she'd run a race, and a light of discovery shone in her wide, chestnut eyes.

"I love you," she declared.

The world went utterly quiet. There were only her words and nothing else, floating into his ears and around his head like doves looking for somewhere to roost.

"No matter what you do or don't do," she continued in a husky but earnest voice, "nothing is going to change that fact. I expect nothing in return." She shook her head. "I just love you. It's that simple, Bronco."

"Okay." His paralyzed brain seemed incapable of firing.

Is that all you have to say to her, shit bird?

Not a single, coherent response leaped to his tongue. It took the roar of a fighter jet taking off in the field out back to recall him to where he was and what he was doing.

Rebecca sent him a slow, poignant smile, went on tiptoe, and pressed a lingering kiss to the cut healing on his cheek. "I'll see you soon," she promised.

Slipping out of his grasp, she walked away, her shoulders back, her head held high. She didn't even sneak a backward glance as she stepped into the elevator, disappearing from his view as the doors closed behind her.

He listened to the pulleys hum as the elevator delivered her to the lower level. And still, he didn't move, could barely remember how to breathe.

I just love you. It's that simple, Bronco.

One summer, when he was nine, he had climbed to the top of Tweedy Mountain all by himself. The sun was shining, and a warm breeze buffeted his face. He'd felt something cold touch his cheek. Looking up, he'd realized it was snowing, in July! Of course, he'd seen it snow in the higher altitudes plenty of times after that, but the amazement he had felt then was the closest thing that came to what he was feeling right now.

I expect nothing in return.

Her addendum drew his eyebrows together. That couldn't be true. All women had expectations—as they very well ought to, especially Rebecca, whose father had taken off when she was a young teen. Of all the women in the world, she deserved to have a man she could rely on, who could promise to love her for the rest of her life. Not a guy like him.

He reached for the wall, needing it to steady himself.

Never once had he envisioned making eternal promises to any woman. What had kept him uninvolved was the certainty that he would break his word and in the process break a woman's heart. But he was too involved now to backpedal. And he had only himself to blame, having spent as much time with her as he had, causing their affections to deepen, and her to conclude that she loved him.

And yet, he could think of nothing more amazing than sweet, giving Rebecca loving a silver-tongued cowboy like himself. Astonishment kept him in a trance. He didn't deserve her kind of love, no more than his father had deserved his mother's. Closing his eyes, he expelled a harsh breath.

You cannot let her down.

CHAPTER 14

Rebecca stared at the kaleidoscope of light and shadow shifting across the wall closest to her bed. Even though she had volunteered to work over the weekend—anything to keep her mind off her present misery—sleep eluded her again tonight.

Reliving her encounter with Bronco two days earlier, she wondered as she had the previous sleepless night if it had been a mistake to admit her feelings for him. Her confession had so obviously astounded him. He certainly hadn't rushed to reciprocate her feelings, nor had he called or texted her in the hours and days that followed. And, still, her stubborn heart refused to believe he didn't love her in return, not when his feverish kiss had told her that he did. He simply didn't *want* to love her. Or was she only fooling herself into believing that?

With a whimper of longing, she rolled onto her back. The fierceness with which he'd held her, the heat of his kiss, and the unmistakable hardening of his sex had all suggested that he wanted to be with her. Yet he still kept his distance. Granted, there were valid reasons why he ought to, not the least of which was the fact that his commander could destroy his career or even arrange for some terrible accident to befall him.

Fear sliced through her. She sat up abruptly in bed, her heart pounding as the thought crossed her mind again that Max was behaving too passively these days. Aside from the one night he had loitered briefly in the parking lot in front of her apartment, he'd respected her expressed wish for no contact. He'd stayed away from the hospital. He hadn't called her on her cell phone even though he knew her new number. It wasn't like him to be so complacent.

Had she actually succeeded in persuading him that Bronco *wasn't* her lover?

Not likely. Max was suspicious by nature, not gullible. It was far more likely that he'd contrived a plan of his own which consoled him for the time being. He didn't mind giving Rebecca time and space because he was confident that he was going to get her back in the end...by eliminating the competition.

"Oh God." The seemingly paranoid fear which she'd harbored for some time now morphed into a certainty.

Lunging for her cell phone, she noted the time. Bronco was likely asleep at just after midnight. After all, SEALs worked half a day on Saturday, and he wouldn't want to exhaust himself. She dialed his number hoping he would answer regardless of the time.

"Please pick up, please pick up," she canted, but his phone went right to voice mail, letting her know that he'd turned it off. But—wait—that made no sense. Frogmen were on call 24/7. They weren't allowed to turn off their phones.

"Hey, it's me," she said, following the instructions to leave a message. "Is everything okay?" She paused to collect her thoughts. "I can't shake this feeling that Max is going to target you, like he threatened to do once before, remember? Please, tell me he hasn't done it already. Why aren't you answering? If you need to transfer to a different team to get away from him, then do it. Do it before he hurts you." She paused to catch her breath. "I guess that's it. What I told you the other day—it's true, Bronco, and it always will be."

She ended the call before bursting into tears. Moisture rolled down her cheeks. It was scary enough that she'd fallen in love with a man who avoided intimacy in his relationships. Intuiting that Max might well kill Bronco before he had a chance to work out his own demons—that terrified her.

She needed to talk to someone about her fears, or she'd go quietly out of her mind. Her friend Maddy lost enough sleep looking after her baby. Her friends at work all thought her foolish for leaving Max in the first place. Only her mother, whose newfound happiness she'd been reluctant to disturb until now, would provide her the support she needed. Luckily, the night was still young in Hawaii.

With trembling fingers and a fresh wave of tears, Rebecca speed-dialed her mother's number.

"It's closing time, hon." Maura, who tended bar at Brant's favorite watering hole, stretched a veined hand, five fingers encrusted with rings from her admirers, across the counter to retrieve Brant's empty glass. "Make sure you walk home. No driving for you." She always looked out for "her boys" as she called the SEALs.

Brant slapped a twenty on the bar by way of a tip. Good old Maura had kept his mug brimming with a tasty lager that had the highest alcoholic content of any of the beers on the menu. Putting away his wallet, he rolled off of his barstool and nearly pitched face first onto the floor as it lurched like a ship on a stormy sea. Clearly, he *did* need to walk home—if he could make it that far.

It was not until he pushed into a windy September night that the full extent of his idiocy revealed itself to him. Here it was, zero two hundred hours on a Saturday morning and he was facing muster in four hours, followed by half a day's work.

Atlantic Avenue had teemed with activity only a few hours earlier. But now it stood practically deserted. Hotels loomed against a dark sky, just a few lights still shining in the glittering windows. A taxi cruised by him, the driver eyeing him hopefully.

Brant waved him on. He'd left Maura with his last bit of cash, and he needed to walk if he was going to sober up.

What a night. It had started out with a small group of SEALs sharing drinks in the basement bar at the Shifting Sands Club on Dam Neck. But then Bullfrog had gone home to study, and the rest had taken off to go dancing at Peabody's. Brant's run-in with Rebecca the previous day had turned him into a morose companion—a real kill-joy. He hadn't wanted to ruin their fun, so he'd given them the slip, driving toward the oceanfront and winding up at O'Malley's Irish Pub.

The ocean, only one block away, kept a steady roar in his left ear as he headed toward his Bronco in the public parking lot. A crescent moon skated behind a thick layer of clouds, leaving it up to the intermittent street lamps to light his way. The cool, salty air sobered him sufficiently that he remembered Max was out to get him.

He cast a wary eye around, but the only suspicious activity was what looked to be a drug deal taking place up an alley across the street. He walked faster, spying his old Bronco up ahead, one of only three cars left in the lot. Not that he could even drive it home in his present state. He had drunk way more than usual tonight.

You're an idiot, his conscience pointed out.

The two-mile walk to his apartment would comprise his punishment.

Weaving down the narrow sidewalk, he teased his cell phone from his pocket to see why Bullfrog hadn't called him. The answer became apparent when his phone refused to light up. It was as dead as a doornail. Under normal circumstances, it would be charging at this time, just as he would be sleeping. But these weren't normal circumstances because the world had turned on its axis—Rebecca fucking loved him.

Bullfrog had a quote that he said from time to time that fit the situation perfectly. *It was the best of times. It was the worst of times.* The quote came from some famous English book, but Brant couldn't have said which one.

"You're such an idiot," he said out loud this time, shoving his phone back in his pocket.

Given his luck lately, the task unit was responding to a crisis half a world away, and he was now officially AWOL. He would be court-martialed and held accountable. And what would his excuse be? That he'd drunk himself into a stupor because the wife of his CO loved him but she had no expectations— probably because she knew what a loser he was.

He stumbled over a crack in the sidewalk. *Watch it!* The warrior within him ordered him to stop for a moment, expand his awareness, and sense his environment. A rash of goose bumps skated up his forearms.

Was someone watching him? He put his back

against the building next to him and searched the dark street, hunting for the source of his sudden disquiet.

"You're an idiot," he whispered, only to wish he hadn't said it three times. Now he was committed to it, like Bullfrog once said.

The purr of a motor reached his ears along with the corresponding whisper of tires over asphalt, but that was one block over. This block remained quiet.

Repressing a shiver, he resumed his walk, picking up his pace, while keeping a sharp lookout. But soon his intoxicated brain started listing all the things that came in threes.

"Three little pigs. Goldilocks and the Three Bears. Three Stooges. Three Musketeers. Three-ring circus."

Recalling his tenuous situation, he glanced around again, saw no sign of pursuit, and went right back to amusing himself.

"Three primary colors."

He nodded, proud of himself for that one.

"Three French hens." He chuckled. "Three blind mice—see how they run. Oopsie."

He bumped into a bicycle that was leaning on a street sign and caught it as it toppled over. Propping it back up, he noticed that the bike wasn't secured. It was sitting there like a gift from the gods, waiting for a rider. Made for a teenager, it wasn't the biggest or the best-looking bike on the planet, but the tires weren't flat and the chain was still attached.

He swiveled his head left and right. The bike appeared to have been abandoned. With a shrug, he helped himself to it.

Gripping the rust-speckled handlebars, he focused on the monumental task of riding a two-wheeler down a narrow sidewalk. The little ramp that swooped down onto the road nearly got the better of him.

God, I am so drunk. "Three sheets to the wind."

He laughed out loud at his brilliance. Peddling faster, he came to the street that led to Sunrise Apartments. He could make out his building now, still about a hundred yards away.

"Three feet in a yard."

Thinking of the meager sleep he'd get before wake-up, he increased his speed. He was peddling furiously past the rental office of his apartment complex when a hulking figure leapt out from behind a bush to intercept his path. Brant locked up his brakes to avoid a collision. Rough hands seized his shirt. He tried jumping off the far side of the bike, caught a toe on the crossbar, and crashed face-first to the sidewalk, splitting open the cut on his cheek that had nearly healed.

An immense weight pounced on him, crushing him onto the pavement. He tried to squirm free. But the man proved heavier, more agile. The all-too familiar rasp of Mad Max's breath sent a shard of horror straight into Brant's muddled brain.

Told you, said the voice of reason. Now Max was going to slit his throat or put a bullet in his head. He'd left himself wide open.

A knee gouged his spine. Brant sucked in a painful breath. "Get off me, motherfucker."

A sharp sting in his upper arm drew his gaze to the syringe in Max's grip. It had gone straight through the fabric of his shirt into his deltoid to pollute his bloodstream. With a glint, the syringe disappeared, and the crushing weight abated as Max climbed off him.

Too befuddled to move, Brant listened to Max's stealthy footfalls retreating. A car door slammed and the same purring engine he had heard earlier revved to life. He ordered himself to get up, but he couldn't move. His body seemed to be floating. He couldn't see. Darkness filled his vision. And now he could hear nothing except the drum of his decelerating heartbeat.

Hear no evil; see no evil; speak no evil.

The drunken reveler inside him declared victory with this last set of threes.

Jeremiah rolled over and groaned. The last time his intuition had whispered for him to wake up, he'd been sleeping under a fallen tree in the jungle in Chiapas, Mexico. Heeding the inner voice, he had rolled out of his hiding spot three seconds before the tree splintered under a hailstorm of gunfire. Since then, he'd put his full faith in it.

Tossing back the blanket, he put his long, narrow feet to the floor and reached for his cell phone. The absence of a return message from Bronco made his stomach drop. He stood up, grabbed his plush, black robe with the yin/yang symbol embroidered on the back, and tied it around his hips as he crossed to his bedroom window to check the parking lot.

The sun wouldn't rise for another hour, but the moon shining behind a bank of clouds cast enough of a glow for him to see that Bronco's parking space stood empty. He hadn't come home last night, which meant that he was probably with Rebecca.

So no need to fret. Except Bronco had said he was going to steer clear of her, at least until the investigation was over. And Bronco was a man of his word.

Anxiety kept Jeremiah from crawling back into bed. He showered and dressed in his BDUs. Then, with a longing glance at his cappuccino machine, he headed for the door. He would splurge on coffee at Starbucks *after* he found his friend.

An uneasy feeling ambushed him as he trotted down the staircase in the breezeway. Chilly, damp air increased his foreboding as he hurried toward his Jeep. Widening his peripheral field the way he taught his martial art's students, he spotted two unusual lumps on the sidewalk in front of the leasing office.

As he headed toward them, he made out the handlebars of a bicycle first. The realization that the second lump was human had him sprinting toward it, dropping to his knees, his worst fears confirmed.

"Bronco!" he croaked, getting no response.

His friend lay half on his stomach, half on his side, like he'd taken a spill, tried to get up, and promptly passed out. Jeremiah reached for his wrist and sought a pulse.

Nothing. Where was it? *There.* Under the cold flesh, a faint and feeble pulse leaped against Jeremiah's fingertips. He bent over, putting his ear by Brant's nose and flinching at the odor of beer coming off him. His breaths were slow and shallow. Had he passed out from drinking too much?

"Bronco." Even in the feeble light, the blue cast of his friend's lips was unmistakable. He looked half dead already.

Jeremiah shook his shoulder. Not so much as a groan emerged. Noting the pool of blood under his cheek, he gently rolled him over. The cut that he had stitched over a week ago had been torn clean open, and now the wound bled copiously. At least there were no apparent lumps or lacerations on his skull.

He reached for his wrist again, counting heartbeats as he consulted his watch.

Forty-three beats per minute. *Way too slow.* Pulling out the pen light he kept handy in his breast pocket, he thumbed an eyelid open. The pinpoint pupil staring back at him almost stopped his own heart. This was looking serious.

Get help. With a sense of unreality, he pulled his

phone from his pocket.

"9-1-1. Do you have an emergency?"

"I need an ambulance fast," he heard himself say. His training as a corpsman enabled him to function in spite of his shock. He provided the operator with Brant's heart rate and listed his symptoms. He heard himself suggest that the paramedics come supplied with Narcan, an opiate reversal drug.

Brant would never do drugs. What the hell had happened?

With the promise that help was on the way, the operator let him go. He shucked his jacket, tossing it over Brant's prone form to keep him warm.

"Stay with me, brother," he ordered, in a voice gruff with fear. Closing his eyes, he laid both hands on Brant's head, cleared his thoughts and concentrated on sending him the energy he needed to survive.

Rebecca was hanging her jacket on one of the hooks in the break room when a voice came over the intercom.

"EMS report. Patient is a Caucasian male, twenty-eight years old, probable opiate overdose. Bed assignment on arrival."

The urgent situation coming so early on a day she didn't normally work jump-started her adrenaline. Delaying the cup of tea she'd been about to pour herself, she quickly washed her hands and left the break room to relieve the night-shift nurse.

Sandy greeted her with a smile of relief and a list of the patients under her care. The previous night had been a quiet one, but Rebecca sensed that was about to change as the doors at the ambulance entry swished open. The tramping of boots and the clatter of a gurney heralded the arrival of the opiate overdose patient.

Dr. Edmonds joined her in the hall as the paramedics burst through the swinging doors into the ER. Rebecca summoned them toward the closest available room, keeping out of the way as they transferred the patient from the gurney to the bed. When the lead paramedic began to list the victim's symptoms, Rebecca jotted herself notes.

"He's got something toxic in his system, and it's not just alcohol, though he's definitely been drinking. The cut on his face is an older wound, torn open." Whisking the crinkly metallic blanket off the man, the paramedic revealed a pair of blue jeans and a long-sleeved polo.

Dr. Edmonds leaned over the patient, giving Rebecca the barest glimpse of a face covered in blood. "Fixed and constricted," he announced, examining the man's pupils. "I think you're right about the overdose."

"We administered .4 mgs of Narcan already, but his BP keeps dropping and he's barely breathing." He shook his head at the grim outlook.

Dr. Edmonds glanced up at him. "Thank you, Thompson. We've got it from here."

The paramedics withdrew, and Rebecca clipped a pulse oximeter on the man's index finger. Dexterous-looking fingers and a powerful wrist suggested a healthy physique. At least he had that much going for him.

Watching the clock, she counted the sluggish beats. "Only forty-one beats per minute. Oxygen is eighty-eight percent."

"Blood pressure is seventy over thirty-eight," announced the nurse on the other side.

"He needs more oxygen. Sandy, help me with the endotracheal tube so we can ventilate with an ambu bag. April, cut away his shirt and get him hooked up to the EKG. Rebecca, draw his labs. I want to know what's in him within five minutes flat," the doctor stated.

"Yes, sir." She stepped toward the cabinet to raid it for the necessary supplies.

The emergency tech peeked through the curtain, holding out a chart. "His friend is here. I got as much information as I could."

April, the nurse's aide, took the clipboard from her and scanned it. She turned toward the doctor. "His name is Adams."

The catheter in Rebecca's hands clattered onto the countertop as fear shrink-wrapped her heart.

"Can you hear me, Mr. Adams?" the doctor asked.

Adams is a common name, Rebecca told herself. But she knew in her heart that it was Brant. Very slowly, she turned to look at him.

He lay with his face and hair caked the blood still oozing from the gash on his cheek. April had cut his shirt up both sleeves and down the torso, peeling back the two halves to reveal the muscle-plated chest that had been Rebecca's playground.

With no response from Brant and with Sandy's help, the doctor proceeded to insert the endotracheal tube through the laryngoscope into his mouth, tipping back Brant's head to get the tube down his throat. His chin stubble glinted under the bright lights. Rebecca rocked back on her heels, and the room went into a slow spin.

"There's a bruise here with a tiny puncture mark," Dr. Edmonds noted, frowning at a welt on his right anterior deltoid. "I wonder if he injected the drugs or swallowed them."

"He's not a junkie." Rebecca's voice sounded alien to her own ears. "He's a Navy SEAL. Someone did this to him."

Both the doctor and the aide looked over at her. "You know him?" the doctor guessed.

"Yes." Icy pinpricks stabbed the tips of her fingers and the top of her scalp. *Max. Max had gone after Bronco already!*

He eyed her with concern. "I need another nurse in here!" he called through the door. "Have a seat, Rebecca, before you faint."

"I'm not going to faint." She clung to the counter behind her as shock drove the strength from her legs.

"Sandy, get that catheter in him and draw his labs for her," he said to the other nurse. "You can take them down the hall as soon as she's done," he added to Rebecca.

Relinquishing the paraphernalia to Sandy, Rebecca watched with a sense of surrealism as Sandy first catheterized Bronco then moved to his side to draw his blood.

"April, give him a saline bolus," the doctor instructed the aide on Brant's other side. Adjusting the pads on the electrocardiograph, he frowned at the intermittent hills that represented his slow heartbeats. "He'll need .5 mgs of Atropine every five minutes until his heart rate comes up to sixty."

Sandy filled two vials of blood. Stoppering them, she sealed a cup of urine next and handed them all to Rebecca to rush to the laboratory.

This has to be a nightmare. I'll wake up soon.

Rushing out the door to deliver the warm fluids to the lab, she collided with a tall figure in BDUs hovering just outside.

"Bullfrog," she exclaimed, startled to see him. "What happened?"

He shook his head. "He never came home last night. I found him outside of our apartment building. Someone must have attacked him."

"There's a puncture wound on his arm," she relayed.

His widening gaze locked onto hers. Neither one of them spoke aloud what they were thinking.

"I'm taking his labs down the hall," she added, with a quick glance over her shoulder. "Walk with me." Visitors weren't allowed in the ER, let alone back in the laboratory.

They moved down the hall in stunned silence. Bullfrog's hand, placed against the small of her back, helped to steady her. She left the blood and urine with the technician telling him to run a toxicology screen immediately. "Dr. Edmonds said five minutes," she told him. "I'll be right back for the results." Turning to Bullfrog, she added, "I need you to do something for me."

"Sure."

She led him to the break room. Retrieving Maya Schultz's business card from her purse, she pressed it into his palm. "Call this woman." Her shock abruptly gave way to helplessness. Tears swarmed her eyes. "Tell her what's happened to Bronco. Tell her we know who did this," she added, her composure eroding.

Bullfrog looked up from the card. He sent her a pained nod, lifted a hand briefly to her cheek, and turned away, heading for the lobby.

Rebecca raced back to the lab, running the last few yards to get there quickly.

"Please hurry," she begged the technician. She fought to keep herself together. A crushing weight pressured her chest. *How could Max do this to one of his own men?* Tremors began to wrack her spine. Her legs wobbled. *How could I have married such a monster and brought this upon Bronco?*

In the back of the workroom, the printer spat out a

sheet of paper. The technician quickly scanned it then passed it through the window to her. "Opioids," he stated. "They're interacting with the alcohol sugars in his bloodstream."

Rebecca hurried back to the room with her report. Handing it to the doctor, she noted that Bronco was still being ventilated. His vitals hadn't improved. If anything, they looked worse.

"I'll need another .4 mgs of Narcan," the doctor barked, adding the lab report to the clipboard. "Sandy, call ICU and give them a heads-up. We're transferring him upstairs before he goes into cardiac arrest on me."

Rebecca's thoughts flew to the homeless man who'd died only two rooms over, a couple of weeks ago. A cry of denial tore from her throat. *Not Bronco!*

Reaching for his limp hand, she squeezed his ice-cold fingers and willed him to respond. But he lay as still as death, his heart beating so slowly that it was painful to listen to the telltale bleeps coming from the EKG.

White-hot rage rose from her chest to brand her consciousness. Through eyes that burned with banked tears, she watched Sandy administer the injection of Narcan via the IV. Seconds ticked by. Brant's blood pressure dropped to sixty-three over thirty-five.

Dr. Edmond's shook his head. "Another dose of Atropine. Once he's stabilized, we'll transfer him to ICU."

CHAPTER 15

The door separating ICU from its private lobby swung open. Rebecca's heart jumped up her throat as a gaunt doctor stepped through it, followed by a plump nurse. Dread ran in a cold river through her veins as the doctor took in the size of the throng awaiting word on Bronco's situation. She pushed to the edge of her seat, hopeful of news.

They'd been waiting four hours for word of Bronco's fate. Excused from her work, Rebecca had been the first to join Bullfrog up in ICU. Then several SEALs from the task unit had trickled in, including Sam Sasseville and Master Chief Kuzinsky. Later Haiku, Halliday, Hack, Teddy, Carl Wolfe, and Austin Collins arrived to keep vigil. Even Maddy had put in a brief appearance, bringing her baby, who'd provided a badly needed distraction.

Max, however, remained notably absent. It was all Rebecca could do to keep her accusations in check when Kuzinsky had passed on Max's regrets. As soon as Maya Schultz and her partner arrived, however, Rebecca had pulled them into the hall to share her suspicions. To her profound relief, they'd taken her more seriously than at their last encounter.

"You're all here for Brantley Adams?" the doctor asked to the room in general. He moved into their midst, clearing his throat before making his announcement. "The patient is presently stable. While we remain optimistic, his condition could deteriorate. It all depends on the strength of his heart and the extent of the damage to his brain."

Rebecca's lungs ached as she continued to hold her breath.

"We're monitoring him closely, but there's not likely to be any change soon. If you'd like to leave, simply relay your name and number to Nurse Kelly here—" He nodded at the middle-aged nurse—"and she'll call you in four hours with an update."

Four more hours! Relief congealed into despair. Rebecca dropped her face into her hands and exhaled painfully. If only the prognosis were more encouraging. Bullfrog laid a hand on her shoulder and she turned toward him wordlessly, receiving the comfort she so badly needed.

"He'll pull through," he promised, not for the first time.

The sound of high heels crossing the linoleum had her glancing up. Investigator Maya Schultz had beckoned the doctor off to one side, where she flashed her badge and introduced herself. The doctor's blue gaze sharpened. Ben Metier joined them also, blocking Rebecca's view of the exchange.

"Would you like to go?" Bullfrog inquired.

"Wait one second."

She strained to hear Maya Schultz's words, but the other conversations taking place muddled her reception. Was Maya asking whether Rebecca's suspicions might be founded—that Bronco could have been intentionally drugged? The doctor opened the door behind them and invited the investigators to join him in ICU.

Encouraged, she left her name and number with Nurse Kelly and let Bronco's best friend take her to lunch.

Dr. Peterson divided an intrigued gaze between the two investigators sitting on the other side of his office desk. Ms. Schultz's pointed question had stirred his imagination.

Is there anything about the patient's condition that suggests he might have been attacked and deliberately drugged?

On the one hand, if he replied that there was, these two investigators would be up his butt wanting copies of all the related paperwork. On the other hand, HIPPA laws did not protect patient medical records from law enforcement. He was required to hand them over, even without a warrant. The thought of defending it in court dismayed him. However, he owed his medical degree to the Navy, and he'd watched every episode of NCIS that had ever aired on television. There was nothing like a good mystery to enliven his humdrum existence.

"Honestly," he said, measuring his answer with care, "there are several indications that he was forcibly subdued and drugged. First, he bears a number of cuts and bruises consistent with a struggle—but then he is a Navy SEAL. An older wound that had been close to healing on his face was torn wide open—we'll wait for his vitals to strengthen before we sew him up. Given the concentration of the opiate in his bloodstream, it's my opinion that he was injected with OxyContin dissolved in water, which concentrates it while making it easy to deliver in one powerful dose. It's downright lethal when mixed with alcohol."

The woman cocked her head at him. "What makes you think he was injected?"

"There's a bruise on his right anterior deltoid where his skin was punctured by what might have been a large hypodermic needle. Even if the patent were left handed, he wouldn't have injected his right deltoid so close to the bone. One, that would have hurt like hell. Two, he's got plenty of available muscle elsewhere on his arm."

"Tell me more about OxyContin and what it does," she requested.

"Once in the body, it breaks down, releasing a steady supply of oxycodone. Mixing oxycodone with alcohol depresses the central nervous system. Considering that his blood-alcohol level was .21, he should be dead right now. But he's in remarkable shape. His heart is strong, and that's what has kept him alive."

The woman touched her fingertips to her lips. "We may need you to make this assertion in a court of law," she warned.

Intrigued, he gave a nod.

"It is imperative that we speak with the patient the minute he regains consciousness."

"*If* he regains consciousness," he corrected her. "I must caution you, too, that he may have suffered brain damage. He may not make a very good witness."

Her mouth firmed. "I understand. Still, we absolutely must speak to him the instant he awakens."

"I'll see to it that Nurse Kelly calls you first," he agreed.

"Thank you," she said, rising in advance of her companion. It was clear that, between the two of them, she was the one who called the shots. "We'll be in touch, doctor."

* * *

Max looked up from his desk at the Spec Ops building. It was all he could do to keep his mind on matters involving the task unit when he had yet to hear whether his effort to eliminate Chief Adams had succeeded. Then, too, the Scarpas were pressuring him via Google chat to hurry up and eliminate his next target.

For the tenth time that day, he checked his silent cell phone, hoping for a message. Chief Adams should be dead already. Nearly five hours had passed since First Class Winters had left a message on his commander's voicemail explaining that Adams had been rushed to the hospital.

Desirous of an update, Max dialed his master chief directly.

Kuzinsky answered right away. "I'm on my way back to Spec Ops now, sir."

Max's heart hammered. "What's the news?"

After a split second's hesitation, the master chief responded, "He's hanging in there."

Trepidation skidded through Max. Adams should be long dead by now. How the hell was he hanging in there considering the concentrated dose he'd been given?

"Has he regained consciousness?" The fear that he'd wake up spewing accusations bathed him in a cold sweat.

"No, sir. Doctor says he's still critical. I'll get a call if anything changes."

"I see. You'll keep me informed?"

"Of course, sir." Kuzinsky hung up on him.

Max lowered his phone with a frown. Were the vibes he'd been getting lately from his right-hand man real or just a product of his imagination? Kuzinsky had no reason to suspect he had anything to do with

Adams' overdose. They'd worked together tirelessly for going on two years. But what if Adams had conveyed Rebecca's suspicions to his master chief? Surely her suspicions alone wouldn't sway Kuzinsky's opinion of him.

I'm imagining things, he assured himself.

Swiping a hand over his clammy brow, he put his phone away. Adams was dead or as good as dead. It had to be that way. Max had bigger fish to fry, but he couldn't even begin working on a plan to off the FBI agent until he knew for certain that his efforts to clean house had succeeded.

Plus, it was hard to strategize while Rebecca had possession of his laptop.

"Not for long," he muttered to himself. The gangsters he had hired on Silk Road had promised to leave the laptop at the drop by midnight, where they'd collect the remainder of their payment.

Clearing his mind, he sought to finish up his work related to the task unit. Retaining his reputation as a top-notch commander meant everything to him—yet, that was becoming increasingly difficult with all these loose ends that needed tying up.

"You sure you'll be okay? Maybe you should try to sleep."

Bullfrog's concerned expression caused the tears Rebecca had repressed all day to surface suddenly. They'd gone out to a late lunch—early supper, really. Neither of them had eaten much. As weary as she felt, she doubted she'd nap at all, knowing that her *husband* had attempted to murder Bronco.

If he died in ICU—she couldn't stand to even think about it—she would never forgive herself for involving him in Max's secret. Turning toward her kitchen, she forced herself to nod, even as her face crumpled and the tears started to flow.

The door of her apartment closed softly. Sniffing first, she looked over to find Bullfrog locking her door from the inside. He hadn't left, after all. "Bronco would never forgive me if I left you alone right now," he explained. "Do you have any books or a board game?"

Sending him a wan smile, she wiped her face on a dishtowel and went to retrieve a handful of thrillers she had brought with her when she'd left Max.

For the next two hours, they lay on her living room floor, alternately dozing and staring sightlessly at pages that failed to engage them. The sky in the windows went from gold to mauve to black. Rebecca made them both a cup of tea, while stealing a glance at the time on her microwave. In half an hour or so, Nurse Kelly would call them with an update on Bronco's condition.

A knocking at her door had her lowering the mugs onto her kitchen counter and shooting Bullfrog a puzzled glance.

"Expecting someone?" he asked, rolling to his feet. "You want me to answer it?"

The fear that Max had decided to pay her a visit prompted her to nod. "Yes, please."

She edged around the counter as Bullfrog approached the door. He had to stoop in order to peer through the peep hole. "Looks like a woman delivering pizza."

"She must have the wrong unit."

He unlocked the door, pulling it halfway open. Rebecca glimpsed a young, dusky-skinned woman with cornrows in her hair standing beyond him.

"Sorry, we didn't order any pizza," Bullfrog said.

The young woman flung aside the pizza box to point a wicked-looking pistol in Bullfrog's face. "I know that, motherfucker. Back the hell up."

With lightning-quick reflexes, he grasped the weapon, twisting her arm up and back. But then two more men sprang into view—both of them brandishing firearms.

"Let her go!" one of them commanded. "Back inside."

Bullfrog released the weapon and put his hands up. Barrels trained on him, they forced him to retreat into the apartment, and they made their way inside, shutting the door behind them.

Too shocked to move, Rebecca gaped at them.

"How can we help you?" Bullfrog asked them calmly. His taut expression betrayed not a drop of fear.

"You can help us by holdin' still. Don't move." The man with a sawed off shotgun kept it aimed at Bullfrog's chest while his two cronies fanned out searching her apartment.

The woman sauntered up to Rebecca with a sneer of contempt. "Where's all your furniture?" she demanded. "Don't you even got a TV?"

Unable to find her voice, Rebecca shook her head. Her stomach tightened to see the other male stalk into her bedroom.

"Where's your purse?" the woman demanded. Her dark eyes scanned the kitchen. She crossed to a closet and grubbed inside it, coming out with Rebecca's hand bag. Dumping the contents onto the carpet, she dropped to one knee to paw through it.

The man in Rebecca's bedroom leaned out of the door with her jewelry box tucked under one arm. "Where's your computer, bitch?" he demanded.

Bullfrog stood deceptively still, his hands still raised, his gaze focused on no one in particular yet seemingly aware of everything at once. The woman on the floor laid the pistol down as she tore into Rebecca's wallet.

"I…I don't have one." Rebecca's voice quavered, as the woman pocketed her cash.

"Come on, not even a laptop?" the thug scoffed.

"Man, hurry up and find it!" urged the man, holding Bullfrog at bay with his sawed off shotgun.

"No, I don't have a laptop either," Rebecca insisted.

"She's lying," the leader snarled. "Look under the bed, beneath the mattress, in the closet. You got ten seconds!" He shot a wary glance at Bullfrog, whose utter calm clearly disconcerted him.

"I got a cell phone," the woman announced, holding it up with a triumphant smirk.

"No, please!" Rebecca took an involuntary step in her direction. "I need that. I'm waiting for an important phone call."

The ringleader looked her way, and that was all it took. In a flurry of movement too fast for her to make out, Bullfrog kicked the shotgun out of the man's grasp. As it landed at Rebecca's feet, Bullfrog drove the man to his knees, gripping a pressure point on his shoulder. Caught off guard, the woman grabbed for her pistol, but Rebecca had already snatched up the shotgun. She brought it up, adrenaline juggernauting through her veins as she bore down on the woman with a feral growl. "Leave it!" she yelled, before kicking the pistol out of the woman's reach.

By then, the third thief had barreled out of her bedroom holding the jewelry box in one arm, his revolver in the other. As the first man swooned to a faint, Bullfrog seized on the second man's astonishment to deliver a roundhouse kick to his shoulder.

The revolver discharged as it fell to the floor, along with her jewels. *Crack!* A hole appeared in Rebecca's wall where the bullet had imbedded. The second man put up a valiant struggle but, in short order, he joined the first man in the heap on the floor, except that he remained conscious and groaning in agony.

Bullfrog swiped up the fallen weapon. As he patted down the men, collecting another pistol and a switchblade, he looked over at Rebecca, whose death grip on the sawed-off shotgun made her a liability.

"Easy, there," he crooned.

Keeping the revolver trained on the second man, he went to pick up the pistol that Rebecca had kicked to one side. He brought it to her, trading it for the shotgun, which he laid on the kitchen counter. He gestured to the wide-eyed woman still kneeling on the floor.

"Shoot her if she moves," he said to Rebecca. "I'll take that," he added to the woman, who surrendered the cell phone without protest.

Her knees knocking, Rebecca listened to Bullfrog dial 9-1-1 and relay the bizarre episode to the dispatcher. A chilling suspicion splintered her thoughts as she recalled the intruders' determination to find her laptop.

Her gaze strayed over mulish faces. They might seem like ordinary thieves, going after her jewelry, her wallet, and her phone, but finding the laptop had clearly been their chief objective. Was that because electronics were so easy to pawn? Or was it possible that Max had found out that she'd retrieved his Dell from the repair shop, and he had arranged for this robbery to take place?

As they waited for the police to arrive, Rebecca hugged herself to quell her tremors. She sidled up to Bullfrog who stood threateningly over the thugs and whispered, "Why do I think Max was behind this?"

He cut her a speculative glance before considering

the thugs at his feet. The one he'd rendered unconscious was just starting to come to. "You want me to find out?" he asked her.

Why not? All SEALs were versed in interrogation techniques. "Go ahead," she invited.

At that instant, her cell phone rang and her heart stopped at the realization that this was the call she'd been waiting for. She took it, withdrawing into the kitchen as Bullfrog began his earnest discussion with the thieves.

"Hi, this is Kelly from ICU at Princess Ann Hospital. Is this Rebecca?"

"Yes." She swallowed against her sudden nausea.

"I'm calling with an update on Mr. Adams. I'm sorry, but there's been no change in his condition. He is still critical but stable."

"No change," Rebecca repeated. She didn't know whether to faint with relief or curse in her frustration.

"I'll call again in four hours," Kelly promised.

Another four torturous hours. "Thank you."

Emerging from the kitchen, Rebecca found Bullfrog straightening away from the thugs with a grim but satisfied expression. He backed to the center of the room, where she joined him to share her news. "Bronco is still the same."

He shook his head, his brow knitting with concern.

"What did they say?" she asked, gesturing at the thieves.

He inclined his mouth to her ear. "Your hunch was right." He nodded at the thug who'd searched her bedroom. "According to him, they picked up the job from an advertisement on a website."

"Silk Road?" she guessed, her fury with Max rekindling.

"He wouldn't say. But he did admit that they were paid to break in and rob you, and if they'd managed to recover a Dell laptop, their pay would be doubled."

"We need to tell Maya Schultz about this," Rebecca determined. Considering what had happened to Bronco, the woman had damn well better believe her story now. She turned away to make her call.

Maya's phone shrilled, pulling her attention from the documents displayed on her laptop. They'd been sent to her by the renowned FBI Special Agent Doug Castle, to whom she had taken her suspicions and who was now sharing the details of his ongoing investigation.

As she plucked her phone off her bedside table, the late hour on her digital clock caught her by surprise. She'd been studying the special agent's notes for hours. She should have gone to bed ages ago. "Special Investigator Schultz."

"Hi, this is Kelly again with another update."

As she had with the last two calls, Maya braced herself for bad news. "Go ahead."

"The patient has regained consciousness."

The words had her sitting forward and setting her laptop aside. "He's awake? He's responsive?"

"Yes, ma'am. Dr. Peterson said I was to call you first. According to the nurse on duty, Mr. Adams is asking to speak with you."

"Right now?" She glanced back at her clock.

"Now would be preferable. Since his vitals have stabilized, we're going to be re-stitching his cheek soon. He may not feel like talking after that."

It was midnight on a Saturday. Her thirteen-year-old son had probably just fallen asleep, having stayed up playing video games. Curtis would be dead to the world until late the next morning. "I'll meet you at the doors in half an hour," Maya promised.

Exactly half an hour later, Nurse Kelly admitted her

into a quiet ICU. "Almost everyone is asleep."

For that very reason, Maya hadn't bothered to involve her partner. She would update Ben and the FBI special agent later. After perusing Doug Castle's files, she could see why he was intrigued with Rebecca McDougal's allegations. Her own skepticism had morphed into a chilling certainty that the commander was, in fact, mixed up in the notorious organized crime family, the Scarpas. Rebecca's sketch of Tony Scarpa resembled him right down to the bags beneath his eyes. That would come in handy during the Article 32 hearing, but was it enough to persuade a military judge, let alone the final arbitrator who played golf with McDougal?

The soles of their shoes scuffed the floor as they coursed a silent hallway. All but one of the glassed-in rooms on either side stood dark and still. Kelly swiped her hand over a sensor, and the door to that room swished open.

The broad-shouldered figure illumined by soft strip lighting inspired Maya's immediate sympathy. Brant Adams lay reclined in a wide hospital bed, the covers pulled to his waist. The gash on his face ruined the perfect symmetry of his wickedly handsome features. Tabs connecting him to the EKG dotted his tanned warrior's chest. Oxygen tubes snaked into his nostrils. He studied her approach through bleary blue eyes.

The last time they had met, which had been minutes after catching him kissing his CO's wife, he'd struck her as being so virile, so brimming with vitality, that it was obvious why Rebecca McDougal was smitten with him. At present, he looked decidedly less vital. Dark hollows gave testimony to how ill he was. But, even with his sallow complexion and red-rimmed eyes, he struck her as a force to be reckoned with.

Cautious of the array of medical paraphernalia

attached to him, Maya drew carefully near to one side of the bed. "You made it," she stated, meeting his sardonic gaze.

His mouth quirked into a challenging smile. "Do you believe me yet?"

She appreciated his candor. After all, he had insisted at their meeting on Thursday that his CO was going to try to do him in. At the time, she had scoffed at the assertion. But now foreboding kept a tight grip on her scalp.

"I believe you," she admitted.

His eyes glinted before they swung toward the nurse. "Ma'am, could you give us a second alone?" He sent her a slow smile that visibly flustered her.

Nurse Kelly backed reluctantly out of the room. "Oh, all right. But we need to get you stitched up soon."

The moment the door closed behind her, Brant announced, "Max attacked me on my way home from the pub. He's not going to rest until I'm dead."

Maya glanced at the nurse standing in the hallway, regarding them through the glass. "You were legally intoxicated," she felt obliged to point out. "How can you be certain? Did you see him? Hear him?"

A humorless laugh grated in his throat. "Trust me. We work so closely in the Teams that I know how each man breathes and moves. It was Max."

The spiking on the EKG machine behind him made her nervous. "You don't need to convince me," she assured him. "I've been communicating with Doug Castle, the FBI special agent who's been investigating the Scarpas for years. According to him, Commander McDougal fits the profile of the assassin. But we still need a lot more evidence if we're going to convince Admiral Johansen of that. If you claim he tried to kill you, then we have to arrest him, with or without solid evidence. He could then take measures to block our evidence-gathering. I'd rather he remain ignorant of his impending charges until we're ready for the Article 32."

His mouth curved into a bitter-looking smile. "Maybe I should just die, and then you won't feel so rushed," he suggested.

She wagged a finger at him. "You're catching on, but that doesn't mean I want you to actually die."

His eyes narrowed. "Witness protection?"

"Something like that," she agreed, "except that I'd like McDougal to believe he got away with killing you."

His head fell back as understanding dawned. "We fake my death," he concluded.

She couldn't tell whether the suggestion appalled or relieved him. "Think about it. It would get your CO off your back. And it would give us a few more days to build our argument before the hearing."

A faraway look entered his eyes as he gazed down at his feet tenting the covers.

"The problem is finding a body to use in your stead," Maya added, mostly to herself.

"I know of one," he said absently.

"I'm sorry?"

He grimaced as if regretting what he was about to say. "There's an unidentified male in the morgue in the basement. Rebecca told me that he died in the ER two or three weeks ago. Supposedly, he even resembles me."

Her pulse quickened. "Well, let's hope he's still there." She started to turn toward the door.

"Wait. Who else is going to know about this?"

She swung back around. "I've already thought it through. Only one man on your team needs to know, and that's Master Chief Kuzinsky. He's got enough clout that he can sign the paperwork and retrieve the body."

"Max will want to see it, too."

"Then we'll have to cremate it."

Suddenly, she could sense regret emanating off him.

"Everyone else will think I'm dead," he stated. By everyone, she could tell he meant his teammates and, most especially, Rebecca.

"I'm afraid so. We need to convince your commander. It's the only way."

"How do you know he won't try to kill Rebecca, too?"

The terse question dropped a new seed of worry in her mind. "Has he ever threatened her?"

His jaw hardened. "Not that I know of, but that Tony creep has."

"Don't worry. We'll keep an eye on her," Maya assured him. "Now that the FBI is working with us, we have more manpower. She'll be safe, I promise."

His eyes sank shut. "How long?" he asked.

She knew what he was asking. How long before he could have his life back? "It's hard to say. Our evidence is good, but it's not complete. We need to work hard if we're going to convict someone of his stature."

The equipment blipped in the silence as she waited for his agreement. She couldn't force him to disappear. Frankly, she'd be astonished if he agreed to such a plan.

"Okay," he said at last, proving himself completely unpredictable. "Where are you going to send me?"

"How does a ranch in Idaho sound?" Having looked into his background, she knew he'd feel at home on a dude ranch out west.

"Fine," he muttered.

Her intuition told her that his outward calm disguised an inward battle, one he didn't want her to witness. She backed toward the door. "I'll let the nurse stitch you up while I go check on that body in the basement."

He sent her a faint, dismissive nod. She could practically see the thundercloud forming over him, and who could blame him? It wasn't in the makeup of a SEAL to walk away from a fight, to leave his arch nemesis gloating over his seeming victory. Worse than that, he'd be letting his teammates and the woman he loved believe he was dead.

Joining Nurse Kelly in the hall, she explained that she would need to speak to her and Dr. Peterson in his office, at the doctor's earliest convenience.

Brant paid scant attention to the nurse and her aid as they puttered around him, preparing to re-sew the gash on his face. His heart, still sluggish, contracted in slow painful beats that reflected the funeral march taking place in his mind.

Letting Rebecca and his teammates believe that he'd died when he hadn't went against every instinct he possessed. Still, Maya Schultz's rationale could not be argued. Max had to think his death was real, and for that to happen, his teammates needed to believe he was gone, too.

What other choice did he have? If he stuck around, Max would redouble his efforts to kill him. Plus, having had narcotics in his bloodstream, Brant would be removed immediately from active duty. People who didn't know him would automatically assume he'd taken recreational drugs and overdosed. A Navy SEAL from SEAL Team 4 had been caught just last June dealing heroin.

Agitation prickled his skin, making him claw his

neck.

Rebecca, he assured himself, would know better. She would know that Max was behind his attack. Not only would she defend his reputation, but she might well verbalize her accusations, putting Max on the defensive. Alarm bells tolled in Brant's mind. How far would the CO go to protect his reputation? He would never consider harming her, would he?

I wish you could protect me. The memory of her words caused him to gasp for the air that seemed suddenly harder to take in.

"Easy, hon," the nurse crooned, mistaking the reason for his gasp. He realized she'd been sticking a needle into his face, prepping him for the repair.

"The lidocaine will kick in soon. You won't feel a thing."

Lidocaine. "What? Wait! You can't...I'm allergic."

He didn't get the chance to say anything more as his lungs suddenly seized. The room began to twirl, and one of the machines behind him gave a warning beep.

"His blood pressure is plummeting!"

"Did he say he's allergic to lidocaine?"

Past the roaring in his ears, he heard Nurse Kelly put two and two together. "Oh, dear God, he's going into anaphylactic shock! Get the epinephrine!"

Brant wheezed for breath. His vision clouded. He heard the nurses scrambling to save him, felt a needle jab his biceps. The noises in the room grew fainter. The world went gray and then black.

I'm dying for real! was his last astonished thought.

CHAPTER 16

Sunday afforded Max the time he needed to plot Doug Castle's demise. Drawing the blinds in his office to keep the worker draining the pool out back from observing him, he sat at his desk researching his next mark on his home computer. A mug of black coffee and a cinnamon bun provided the fuel he needed to concentrate.

As he'd suspected, Special Agent Doug Castle laid claim to an impressive service record. He'd been a New York City cop for fifteen years before transferring to the federal side of law enforcement. At fifty-six years of age, he looked fit and formidable in his bio photo, which Max had found on a secured website. His clearance had given him access to all of Castle's personal information, including his permanent address and the names of his family members. The Scarpas would be pleased that Max had found out as much as he had, but they wouldn't pay him another dime until he dispatched Castle for good.

Where and how he did that were both up to him. It went without saying that he had to change his *modus operandi*. But with his pool man thumping around out back and so many loose ends snaking around in Max's thoughts, inspiration was slow to come. First off, incredibly, Adams was still alive. Secondly, the gangsters whom he had hired to steal back his laptop had not only failed in their attempt, but they'd been thrashed by one of Max's own SEALs and had wound up in custody.

A growl of frustration rumbled in Max's chest. At least law enforcement couldn't trace the gangsters back to him, thanks to the anonymity offered by Silk Road, but his laptop remained at large. It was still out there somewhere, a potential threat to his reputation.

The possibility that his own wife—a woman who had pledged to remain in his corner forever—had turned the laptop over to the authorities was a pill that Max refused to swallow. But why else would she have taken it from the shop? Perhaps she'd told Adams about his foreign account, and they'd put together a plot to run off with Max's money. Since he'd closed his old account, that couldn't happen. And now Adams was as good as dead. It wouldn't take much to send him on his way. If push came to shove, he'd pay his chief a visit in the hospital and speed him to hell himself.

Without Adams' corrupting influence, Rebecca would certainly see the error of her ways. She would soon come back to Max. He would entertain no other outcome.

His cell phone, skipping on the glass desktop, pulled him from his dark thoughts. He snatched it up, his hopes soaring as he recognized the number. "Yes, Master Chief?"

"Sir, I have…disheartening news."

He held his breath, anticipating the words he longed to hear. "Go ahead."

"Chief Adams succumbed to heart failure at zero

eight hundred hours this morning."

Max drove a fist into the air in silent triumph. *Yes!* "My God, that's terrible," he said out loud. He breathed once, twice, three times into the phone as if fighting his shock. "I guess I'm needed at the hospital to sign forms and claim the body?"

"No, sir. I've taken care of that. But you could call the mortuary affairs office so they can notify his family. According to his reenlistment papers, Adams wanted to be cremated. I'll arrange for that. If you could call the base chapel and fix a date for a memorial service, I'll follow up with the details."

"Absolutely," Max replied, grateful to Kuzinsky for doing so much legwork—though he would have liked to have seen the corpse for himself. "You think maybe a midweek service?" The mob was pressuring him to kill Castle by Friday.

"Midweek sounds perfect, sir. Sorry to be the harbinger of bad news."

"It happens. Adams was a solid sniper." He forced himself to say a kind word or two. "It'll be hard to replace him."

"Yes, sir, it will."

Max hung up, pushed his chair back, and surged to his feet with renewed optimism. He hoped Rebecca would be open to his consolation. If she let him, he could be her pillar of strength the way he'd been at the start of their relationship. Just as he picked up his phone again, the doorbell chimed.

Who could that be? With a mutter of annoyance, he stalked through his great room to the foyer and peeked through the little window next to the door.

The lean, weathered face of the man standing on his front stoop stripped the air from his lungs. Christ Almighty, what was Special Agent Doug Castle doing here?

Recovering his poise as quickly as possible, he opened the door with what he hoped was an inquiring smile. "Yes?"

Bright blue eyes—that oddly enough reminded him of Adams'—searched Max's face. "Commander McDougal?"

"That's me."

"Sorry to bother you." The man displayed the badge clipped to his belt loop. "Special Agent Castle, FBI. I require your cooperation in an ongoing investigation. Do you have a minute?"

"Uh…" Panic put a momentary vise on Max's tongue. "Sure." Pulling himself together, he invited the man inside.

The FBI agent joined him in the foyer while looking around. "Nice place," he said. "I noticed your lot is on the water. Do you get out boating much?"

Max reeled. That had to be a leading question. "From time to time," he hedged.

"You're on Rudee Inlet, right? So you've got access to the ocean?"

"Yes." A cold sweat bathed his pores.

"So you have your own boat." It wasn't a question. The man would have seen his boathouse from the driveway. "I'm an avid fisherman myself," Castle continued, "Maybe you'll take me out one day." He flashed Max a friendly smile, diminishing his concern that the man was toying with him.

Max managed a careless shrug. "How can I help you?" he prodded.

"Oh, yes. I'm investigating a couple of homicides that took place this past year. I hope you're not offended, but you fit the description of the perp."

Max forced a smile. "How's that?"

"It's simple. You're one of the ninety-six Special Forces snipers who can hit a mark from a distance of half a mile, from the water no less." He drew an index card and pen from his left breast pocket.

Max gave a snort of derision. "Sounds like you're looking for a needle in a haystack."

"No doubt I am, so I'll keep my questions brief. What kind of boat do you own?"

Max refused to let the question rattle him. He had blacked out all identifying stickers both nights before taking his boat out. "It's a 32-foot Carver with a cabin."

The man scribbled on his index card. "Old school," he said, mocking himself. "I can't make myself use an iPad." He looked Max straight in the eye. "Can you vouch for your whereabouts on the nights of May 23 and July 6 of this past year?"

Max snorted. "I'm supposed to remember those dates?"

Castle shrugged. "Check your calendar," he suggested.

"Who were the victims?" Max asked as he pulled his phone from his pocket and accessed his calendar. "Where did these murders take place?"

"I'm afraid that's classified."

Max frowned up at him. "I have a top-security clearance."

"With the Department of the Navy." Castle smiled sympathetically. "That's not the same as DOJ."

With a grunt, Max accessed the calendar on his phone and scrolled to May 23. "I was stateside on the first date." He moved to July 6. "And also on the second. I would have been working on Dam Neck at the Spec Ops building by day and home at night."

"Could your wife attest to that?" Castle peered down the hallway as if looking for a woman.

The man had to be mocking him, but how could he know that Rebecca had moved out? "She could if she were here," he said shortly. "But I can prove I was home even without her statement. Follow me." He swiveled toward the garage, gesturing for Castle to trail him through the great room.

On their way through the kitchen and the laundry room, it occurred to Max that he could kill his mark, right here, right now, and get it over with. Adrenaline stormed his bloodstream. There'd be no witnesses. His cameras weren't running.

But there was a chance that his pool man might overhear something. Plus, his nosey neighbor might have seen Castle enter Max's house. No, there was simply too much left to chance, and impulsive kills went against Max's grain.

"Watch your step," he said, opening the door to the garage and inviting Castle to precede him into the shadowy chamber.

"What's in there?" Castle asked, putting his hands on his hips. The gleaming butt of a Magnum peeked out from the holster under his arm.

Max took due note. "My security system." Flicking on the lights, he crossed to the black box mounted on the wall. Opening the panel, he stepped back to show Special Agent Castle the fancy components. "Every night, I arm this baby. If any door or window opens, an alarm sounds, the police are notified, plus I get an alert on my cell phone. If that's not enough of a deterrent, I've got motion sensing cameras that send videos to my phone. The system keeps a log. Let's see what happens when I look up those dates you mentioned."

He'd saved every bit of data since the date of installation. "May 23 was it?"

"Yes." Castle eyed him curiously as he opened the app on his phone and sifted through the data.

"On that date, the alarm was armed at 8:36 PM. No

exterior doors were opened. I went to the kitchen for a snack at zero three thirty hours, then went straight back to bed. The pattern is similar on July 6."

The special agent glanced from his phone to his face. "What about your wife? She doesn't get up at night?"

"Not to leave the room. We have an *en suite*." He didn't add that Rebecca took melatonin at night and consequently slept like a log.

"Is there much crime in the area?" the man inquired, looking around him.

"Not too much. I merely like to secure my possessions." Max sent him a tight smile. "Same way I keep my country secure," he added, with innuendo.

"Your service is much appreciated," Castle assured him. To Max's bemusement, he closed the panel on the security box, his gaze resting on the company logo. "Well, I've wasted enough of your time." He stuck out a hand and Max automatically shook it, wishing his palm wasn't so moist. "Thank you for your cooperation, Commander. I'll check you off my list."

"You do that," Max encouraged.

Castle took note of the side door. "Might as well go out this way," he suggested. "Oh, take my card." He drew a business card from his breast pocket and handed it to Max. "If you can think of a Special Forces sniper who would sell his soul to the devil, be sure to call me," he added, edging around Max's Tahoe.

The words were like barbs sliding under Max's skin. He trailed the man wordlessly toward the exit.

"Whoa, is this a Ferrari?" Castle had run into the kit car.

"No, it's called a Roy Kelly. The components are all Porsche," Max boasted.

"You've got some nice toys, Commander. Don't blame you for wanting to protect them." With those parting words, Doug Castle unlocked the garage from the inside and let himself out.

Max trailed him outside and watched him climb into his unremarkable pickup truck. The man lifted a hand in farewell, backed carefully out of the driveway, and drove away.

What the hell was that about?

For a long while, Max stood staring up the road where the pickup disappeared. How could the FBI possibly suspect his involvement? The angle of the shots and the muzzle flashes could have given away his location, but no one had been close enough to see him. Someone might have had a camera and taken a picture, but what details could have been captured on a night so dark and from such a distance? The only evidence out there was on the laptop he couldn't seem to lay hold of.

It had to be as the special agent had said—he was one of ninety-six men capable of making either kill. That fact, alone, wasn't nearly enough to implicate him.

Rebecca stared sightlessly at the two small pills Bullfrog pressed into her palm.

"Take these," he urged. "They'll help you sleep while I'm gone."

Her distraught mind scarcely registered the fact that they were her own melatonin tablets, extremely mild compared to what she longed for—something that would put her in an unconscious state, indefinitely. Uncurling from the ball in which she'd lain for God-knew-how long, she accepted the cup of water to her mouth and swallowed both tablets obediently.

"Where are you going?" she asked.

He sat on the edge of the bed next to her. "The platoon is having a bonfire," he reminded her, sorrowfully.

"That's right." He had told her about the bonfire a couple of hours earlier, only she'd forgotten. Nothing seemed to matter anymore. With Bronco dead, the entire world could go up in a bonfire and then crumble into cinder, and she wouldn't lift a finger to stop it.

"I'd invite you to come with me, but it's a sort of team ritual. We honor our fallen brother…" His voice cracked, and he averted his face to keep her from witnessing his grief.

In the back of her mind, Rebecca knew he needed comforting as much as she did. But despair had sucked all the strength from her body, leaving her, for once in her life, too apathetic to see to someone else's needs. All she could do was raise a hand slightly toward his shoulder, barely making contact with him, before she let it fall again.

"I need you to lock the door behind me," he reminded her.

She let him pull her to her feet and trailed him to the door on spongy knees.

"If the doorbell rings, don't answer it," he advised as he stepped outside.

She blinked in surprise at the brilliant sunset—a burnished color similar to the highlight in Bronco's hair. It took her aback that the sky could look so glorious after such a hideous occurrence.

"I'll check on you tomorrow." Bullfrog grimaced. "Unfortunately, I have to report to work, but you should call in sick."

She hadn't given a thought to her job. He was probably right. In her distraught state, she'd be no good to anyone at the hospital and could be a downright risk.

"I'll stop by as soon as I get off, all right? Make sure you eat something."

She sent him a faint nod, her stomach rebelling at the thought of food.

As he turned and climbed into his Jeep, Rebecca shut the door, locking both the deadbolt and the handle. Feeling like an alien in someone else's body, she turned and plodded to her room, where a fresh wave of grief crashed over her.

The racking sobs that shook her gave proof that she wasn't as dead as she felt. Only Bronco was dead, and Max had killed him—all because she'd naively involved him in Max's illicit activities.

I will never, ever forgive myself.

"Here is some money."

Brant looked over at Maya Schultz, who was holding out a folded wad of cash. Her voice, scratchy with fatigue, echoed off the metal walls of the dome-shaped hangar they'd just entered. Creeds Naval Outer Landing Field in Pungo had been decommissioned after WWII, but it was still apparently used by the Virginia Beach police and their affiliated pilots, as evidenced by the two fixed-wing aircraft standing behind them. Special Agent Doug Castle had enlisted one such pilot to fly Brant out of the area that night.

"Take it," Maya insisted, as he continued to ignore her offering. "We cover all the costs associated with witness protection. Plus, it's going to be a long trip home. You'll need it."

Brant pocketed the money in the jeans she'd supplied him. Like the button-up shirt he wore, they hung loosely around his frame, suggesting that the previous owner had been a burly man. He hadn't asked whom the clothes belonged to, and she hadn't explained.

"Plus, I figured you could use an overnight kit."

She pulled a plastic baggie from her purse and handed it to him. He took a peek inside, catching a glimpse of a comb, razor, and toothbrush. He shoved it into his back pocket. "Thank you."

"And here's your cell phone." The familiar object glinted under the halogen lights buzzing high overhead, inspiring his first emotion of the day—relief that he had something connecting him to his past to carry with him.

She pulled it back before he could pluck it from her hand. "Remember, no contact with anyone but me until we call you back for the Article 32." A smirk touched her elegant lips. "I can't wait to see your CO's face when you walk into the courtroom."

Allowing himself a small smile as well, Brant took the phone and stuck it in his other back pocket. His military ID, his driver's license, and his old truck would remain in Master Chief's possession until the glorious day that Maya Schultz had just described, when Max would find himself facing court-martial on charges of multiple homicides, as well as attempted murder.

That day wasn't long in coming, he assured himself. Soon enough, Rebecca would realize that he'd been alive all along. Yet how would she ever forgive him for letting her believe he was dead, even for as short a time as a week? How could he bring himself to disappear on her, as abruptly as her father had—especially now, when she needed him more than ever? His thoughts in turmoil, he widened his stance to keep from keeling over.

Maya glanced at her watch. "The pilot ought to be here any minute."

"You don't have to stay," he told her shortly. The gamut of emotions and confused thoughts twisting through him demanded his attention, and he couldn't sift through them all with her present. Besides, she looked like she hadn't slept in forty-eight hours.

She searched his face through red-rimmed eyes. "I shouldn't leave you. You really should be sitting down," she insisted.

"I'm fine." Yes, he was weak, but considering how close he'd come to death—first at the hands of Max and then from his reaction to Lidocaine—he could tell that he would recover eventually. His anaphylactic attack had come at the perfect time. Maya Schultz had returned while they were reviving him. Pulling Dr. Peterson and Nurse Kelly into her scheme, she'd suggested that they pronounced him "dead" a short while later. And everyone else in ICU fell for it.

Master Chief Kuzinsky, who'd been let in on their secret, had been promptly called to sign the paperwork and claim the body. Brant had been covered with a sheet and wheeled to the morgue, where his clipboard had been transferred to the corpse named John Doe. While Metier ran interference at the hospital, Maya provided Brant with his present wardrobe and spirited him out of the morgue and into her van. They'd driven straight to a nondescript office building where Special Agent Doug Castle, an astute and determined man, had grilled him for hours about Max. After catching a bite at a drive-thru, Maya had then brought him here to await his flight.

"Seriously," he said. "You go ahead. You look beat."

"I am exhausted," she admitted. "My son is probably eating Cheetos for dinner."

The vision evoked a chuckle. "You'd better rescue him." He nudged her toward the exit. "I'll wait for the pilot right here."

She ordered him to text her when he got to Idaho. Then, looking like she couldn't decide whether to hug him or shake his hand, she sent him a curt nod and marched to her car. He watched her cross the tall grass, get into her car, and leave.

As her minivan disappeared around a bend, he tried and failed to accept the fact that, to the world, he was dead. He pictured his fellow platoon members all gathered around a bonfire on the beach—a custom they would enact tonight—grieving his death. He envisioned Rebecca's devastation. Knowing how sensitive she was, his death would make her physically ill. Yes, it made sense to let Max think he'd succeeded in killing him. But toying with the emotions of the people closest to him? It made him want to puke.

Besides, he wasn't the only one threatened by Max's existence. Max might not have verbalized any threats toward Rebecca, but the mere fact that he worked for the mob put her in imminent danger, as witnessed by the night she'd been abducted. Tony and his goons had demonstrated that they were willing to use her as a pawn to get what they wanted. What prevented them from doing so again? And wouldn't Max be tempted to snuff out her life if she accused him publicly of murdering Brant? Sure, Maya had promised NCIS would keep an eye on her, and Castle had reiterated that promise, but was it enough?

I wish you could protect me.

The memory of her words and of the faith shining in her brown eyes impaled him. He sucked in a breath, dropped his face into his hands, and dragged his fingers over his eyes. How could he leave her here to defend herself? That would make him a selfish bastard, thinking of his own safety over hers.

His heart slowed to a trot as he realized he could *not* simply get on a plane and leave her behind. "Forget this." It went against his code of honor, his very essence.

Making up his mind, he headed for the door right as a dark sedan turned the corner. The pilot had arrived in a police cruiser.

"Sonofabitch." Brant ducked back into the hangar, spotted a door on the far side of the building, and made his way swiftly toward it.

Without being spotted, he slipped out the back, hurrying as fast as his weak legs allowed toward the cover of nearby woods. Not a sound followed him into the forest of stunted evergreens. Pine needles crackled under his tennis shoes as he threaded his way through the trees. Feeble rays of sunlight showed him where to go, but it would soon be dark. He teased his phone from his pocket and accessed his map application, pinpointing his whereabouts in relation to Master Chief Kuzinsky's fixer-upper.

Brant might be as helpless as a kitten and perilously lightheaded at the moment, but for Rebecca's sake, he could walk as far as it took to find asylum. Luckily that was only three miles or so. Kuzinsky would probably chew him up one side and down the other, but he would respect Brant's decision to stay and, more importantly, he would help him protect Rebecca.

The second layer of silvery green paint provided the coverage that Rusty was looking for. He didn't want to have to paint all these rooms again, anytime soon. If everything went according to plan, he'd be too busy in his retirement to do any more home improvements.

Applying the roller in smooth up-and-down strokes, he paused to slide the spotlight over on the floor so he could see what he was doing. The light fixture overhead hadn't been updated and provided only a pale glow, and the windows in the room were still covered with clapboard, the new windows due any day.

As he worked his way along the wall, he thought of the men in Echo Platoon, presently gathered around a bonfire, lamenting Brant Adams' passing, and probably wondering why their master chief hadn't put in his usual appearance.

He didn't want to see his boys suffering for no reason. He'd only agreed to this charade because if Mad Max was as crooked as NCIS and the FBI believed, then Bronco was better off dead, or at least safely hidden on a ranch in Idaho. He ought to be halfway there by now.

A furtive tapping at Rusty's front door suspended his rolling. Why would anyone approach that door when it stood behind a partition of yellow caution tape? The porch could crumble at any moment. It had to be one of the birds nesting under the eaves pecking at the rotten wood in search of termites. He drew the roller the rest of the way down the wall.

The tapping came again, and this time there was no mistaking its human source. Or was it possibly one of the ghosts that haunted Rusty's dreams?

He eyed the boarded window as he lowered the roller into the tray of paint. Having no way to see outside, his imagination ran amuck. Why stop at one ghost? Why not a horde of disfigured operators standing in his front yard like zombies demanding to know why he hadn't managed to save any of them?

He thrust aside the ludicrous image and approached the door with his senses heightened. He put his mouth to the crack and asked, "Who is it?"

Someone panted out an answer in the form of a whisper. The sound of ragged breathing reached

Rusty's ears. He reached slowly for the blade strapped to his calf. Unlike so many of his teammates who preferred to carry a pistol, Rusty opted for the versatility of a Gerber blade. The weapon complemented his short stature, giving him an instant advantage in any hand-to-hand encounter. Gripping it expertly in his right hand, he slowly unbolted the door with his left.

The knob turned on its own, and the panel swung abruptly open. Alarmed, Rusty went to block it, but the brilliant blue gaze of the intruder made him instantly recognizable, and he let him in. Chief Adams staggered over the threshold, nearly impaling himself on Rusty's weapon as he threw an arm around his master chief's neck to keep from hitting his knees.

"Bronco, what the hell are you doing here?"

Rusty staggered. Adams, who outweighed him by fifty pounds, held onto him like a man drowning at sea. They both went down. The Gerber blade skidded across the hardwood as they landed in a heap in the entryway.

Rusty stretched out a foot and kicked the door shut.

CHAPTER 17

Brant awoke to the smell of bacon and the first suggestion of daylight shining through a bare but pristine window. Jerking to one elbow, it took him several seconds to realize where he was—in one of the upper bedrooms in Kuzinsky's farmhouse. The bed he lay in might have been original to the early twentieth-century home. Springs squeaked as he sat up and put his bare feet to the floor. He was still wearing the clothes Maya had given him, though the contents from his pockets were now on the bedside table.

Snatching up his phone, he was not surprised to see four missed calls from Maya Schultz, along with a text that made him wince. She had vowed to flay him alive the next time they met. Stowing it in his back pocket, along with the wad of money, he headed for the stairs.

Master Chief stood at the sink in his kitchen, washing the pan he'd recently used. Dressed in his work BDUs, he turned at Brant's entrance, ran an assessing gaze over him, and turned the water off. "Help yourself," he said, gesturing to the plate of bacon and toast on the table.

The gnawing in Brant's belly urged him to accept the offer. He dropped into a chair and dug in. Kuzinsky brought him a glass of orange juice. "Thank you," he said between bites.

The master chief then occupied the seat across from him and watched him eat. "Ready to talk?" he asked, when Brant polished off the last strip of bacon, licking his fingers for good measure.

"Yeah. Sorry, I was wiped out last night."

"Obviously. Why are you here?"

The terse question conveyed aggravation, yes, but also a tinge of respect. Brant cast around for the best way to explain himself. "Would you leave if it was you?" he finally asked.

Kuzinsky blinked. "Probably not," he admitted.

"I need your help. The mob went after Rebecca once already. I have a really bad feeling that they'll come after her again."

"Then you came back to protect her?"

"Right," Brant affirmed.

"How are you going to do that when you're supposed to be dead?"

Brant shrugged. "I was hoping you could help me figure that out. Is my Bronco in your garage?"

"You can't drive that. You'd be recognized in a heartbeat."

"Not if I sell it."

Surprise registered widened the master chief's dark eyes. "Holy Christ," he exclaimed.

Brant wasn't used to seeing emotion on the man's face. "What?"

"Let me get this straight. You'd sell your truck for a *woman*?"

Brant's own surprise rose before he dismissed it

with a shrug. "Well, yeah. But Rebecca's not just any woman, and I need a van. Something I can hide inside."

Kuzinsky considered him a moment longer. "You can borrow my dad's old delivery truck. It's in the garage along with your Bronco."

"You sure? Does it run?"

"Runs okay, if you don't drive too fast." Kuzinsky got up from his chair, crossed to a drawer, and pulled out a set of keys, which he tossed across the room.

Brant caught them. Touched that Kuzinsky would trust him with something of his father's, he said, "Thanks. I'll be careful with it."

The master chief cut a critical look at his attire. "You'll need to change your appearance." He nodded at the orange juice. "Drink that, then follow me."

Intrigued, Brant downed the contents of his glass before standing to follow his leader up the creaking stairs to another of what seemed to be countless bedrooms. Kuzinsky flipped on the light, revealing a hodgepodge of mismatched furniture. He crossed to an old maple chest and lifted the lid. "These clothes were my father's."

Recalling that Kuzinsky, Sr. had died the previous winter and his son had taken a week of leave to close his estate in Orange, New Jersey, Brant peered into the chest, seeing several pairs of neatly folded, brown coveralls.

"*Tata* delivered produce," Kuzinsky explained, using what Brant assumed was the Polish word for father. "He worked from dawn to dusk, every day of his life, until he dropped dead."

Brant didn't know what to say. Maybe that explained the rumor that the master chief was planning to retire soon. He didn't want to do what his father had done and work up to the day he died. He reached into the chest and pulled out a brown hat with a large bill that read *Garden Grown* on the logo.

The master chief handed him a pair of silver-framed glasses. "The prescription's not too strong. Try them on," he invited.

Brant put on the hat and glasses together. Kuzinsky's father had been slightly nearsighted, but the lenses didn't distort his vision too badly.

Kuzinsky nodded his approval. "Good. Now trim your hair, don't shave, and no one will recognize you. That's all I can do for you today. I'm late for work."

"This is plenty. Thanks, Master Chief." As the other man turned away, Brant studied his reflection in an old mirror and marveled at how different he looked.

Kuzinsky paused at the door. "You need anything else?"

Brant remembered his pistol. "Is my Sig Sauer still under the seat in my truck?"

"I haven't moved it." Kuzinsky headed for the door. "Help yourself to whatever you need, and try to stay out of trouble."

His tone implied that trouble was pretty much inevitable.

Brant listened to him walk downstairs and exit his home via the back of the house. Seconds later, he glimpsed a familiar Toyota Camry disappearing up the dirt driveway. Sliding a hand into his pocket, he pulled out his phone.

Becca. The urge to call her rode him like a determined rodeo rider. Maya had warned him that Max needed to believe he was dead. Rebecca's knowing the truth might possibly jeopardize their game of cat and mouse. For now, Brant would respect Maya's wishes.

He regretfully set his phone down. Dropping the baggy pair of jeans he wore, he reached into the chest and pulled out a pair of brown coveralls. Fortunately, Kuzinsky, Sr. hadn't been as vertically challenged as his son. Tossing the uniform over his shoulder, he went hunting for a bathroom and a pair of scissors with which to cut his hair.

Rebecca eased into her Jetta and sat for a minute, her hand on her car keys, trying to remember where she was headed. Oh, yes, to discuss what had happened to Bronco with Maya Schultz. Compressing her lips into a determined line, she started up her engine. Bronco's death would not go unatoned, she vowed. She would make certain Max paid for his hideous crimes.

The sound of her own ragged breathing brought her out of her churning thoughts. *Focus.* She was a danger to herself and others driving in her present condition. Her sleep had been intermittent at best and filled with horrific dreams. She'd spent her waking hours unable to work, unable to eat, and ignoring her mother's worried phone calls.

With a sharp exhale, she depressed the clutch, toggled her shifter into reverse, and peered over her shoulder. The jangling of her cell phone halted her progress, even as it startled her overly taut nerves. She glanced down at her purse and decided to answer the call, in case it was Maya, canceling their appointment.

"Hello?"

"Is this Rebecca?"

The voice sounded vaguely familiar. "Yes, it is."

"Hey, this is TJ from the morgue at the hospital. Sandy gave me your number. I hope that's okay."

"Yeah, sure."

"So, you wanted me to tell you when John Doe's body was claimed? I came in this morning, and it's gone. Some family member came in yesterday while

Fritz was working and took him home."

"Oh, that's good," she said, trying to muster some enthusiasm, but all she could think of was that Bronco's body would have been down in that morgue, too, where someone from the team must have come to collect him. Bullfrog had told her his body would be cremated, and sent home to Montana following a memorial here. He'd wanted his ashes scattered on a mountaintop. "Thanks for letting me know."

"No problem." TJ hesitated. "Hey, is everything okay?"

"Not really. I'm sorry, but I have to go." She hung up quietly and put her phone back in her purse, before backing up.

A sense of vulnerability assailed her as she exited her apartment complex. The worry that Tony and his henchmen were keeping a close eye on her had grown into an abiding certainty. Since the break-in the other day, she hadn't felt safe inside of her apartment, let alone driving around by herself. With Bronco now dead, she might well be the next one to die, especially if the mob realized what Max was probably starting to suspect: that she had turned his laptop over to the authorities.

Surprisingly, even though life held very little appeal for her at that moment, she refused to become Max or the mob's next target. They were not going to win this fight, she vowed, gripping her steering wheel with white-knuckled hands.

The memory of Bronco's infectious smile tore a sob from her chest. She caught it back, struggling to keep tears from blurring her vision as she drove along the busy streets toward Oceana Naval Air Station. The heavy traffic required her concentration. She edged into the right lane, letting a pushy red Volvo race around her. In her rearview mirror, a shiny black

BMW mirrored her adjustment.

Her pulse ticked upward as she stared back at it. Were her fears manifesting, or was Tony and his posse following her? There was one sure way to find out. Checking her blind spot first, she shot out of the right lane and accelerated as quickly as her 2.5 liter engine allowed.

Forty-five. Fifty-five. Sixty-five. If she were pulled over now, she'd be cited for reckless driving.

To her horror, sunlight glanced off the sunroof of the BMW as it moved into the center lane, increasing speed to close the gap between them.

"Oh God." *Not again.*

It *was* Tony. She was sure of it. The Scarpa family was stalking her, which meant they knew she was on to Max's dealings with them. Her days were numbered.

Suddenly, a third vehicle, a brown delivery van, caught her attention as it cut off another car to keep pace with the sedan. Now three vehicles were flying up Oceana Boulevard at well over the speed limit. Did the van belong to the mob, too? Rebecca wondered. Maybe they were planning to box her in somewhere, toss her in the van, and drive off with her.

Relief shuddered through her at the sight of Oceana Naval Air Station coming up on her left. She edged her speed even higher, waiting until the last instant to whip into the turn lane. She took advantage of a break in the oncoming traffic to peel into the entrance. The driver of the BMW started to follow her, realized she was heading into a military installation, and made a correction. The van showed no sign of turning in either.

Glancing over her shoulder, Rebecca sought a glimpse of the van's driver. The air surged back into her lungs. Even wearing a hat and glasses, he looked just like Bronco!

Tears swarmed her eyes at the cruel circumstances. Letting her foot off the gas, she slowed to a stop at the guard house, lowered her window, and handed the MP her dependent ID.

He glowered down at her over the tops of his sunglasses. "Ma'am, you need to decrease your speed."

"Yes, I know." She sent him a distracted nod. "I'm sorry. I'm safe now."

He frowned in puzzlement, glancing into her back seat as he handed her back her ID. "Is everything okay?"

Everyone seemed to be asking her that lately.

"Not really." Offering up the same answer she'd given TJ, she put her car into gear and proceded toward the NCIS building, her speed far more subdued.

Brant used his cell phone to video record the BMW as he drove past it. Icy incredulity had ambushed him when he'd caught sight of it peeling out of a parking lot to follow Rebecca up Bonnie Road ten minutes earlier. Before that, he had thought himself the only one keeping an eye on her. The fact that the mob was tailing her confirmed his worst fears.

He'd hung back a healthy distance, letting the driver of the BMW think he was the only one in pursuit. After Rebecca turned in to the air base, Brant decided he could overtake the sedan without endangering her.

As he'd intended, the driver took note of his aggressive driving. Through the tinted glass, a broad-faced man shot him a dirty look. Brant gave him ample time to notice the cell phone pointed in his direction. A figure in the back seat lurched forward and gestured to the driver. Brant dropped his phone in his lap and flipped them both the bird before speeding past. The driver predictably accelerated, pursuing him, just as he'd hoped he would.

"Come and pick on someone your own size," he invited.

There'd been only two men in the car. Following a good night's sleep, he was confident he could handle two opponents, regardless of how much firepower they had, regardless of their tactics. After all, Rebecca's well-being hung in the balance.

Brant frustrated the driver's intent to pass him. Without warning, the BMW crossed the double yellow line, breaking into the oncoming lane and unsettling an approaching driver so badly that she veered off the road and smashed into a ditch.

Crash!

"You crazy fuck!" Brant exclaimed, moving immediately into the right lane before the mobster killed somebody.

The sedan slid along next to him, its fender mere inches from Brant's driver's-side door. Glancing over, Brant made out a face pressed against the back window, sending him a hard stare. Confident that the hat and spectacles concealed his features, he stared back. There wasn't any question that the man glaring at him resembled Rebecca's sketch of Tony Scarpa, identified by NCIS as the oldest son and heir to the notorious crime family.

"Come and get me, asshole," he invited, mouthing the words clearly.

Several seconds elapsed as he waited for the mobsters to try to force him off the road. His vehicle was bigger, but theirs was better built, and they couldn't ask for a more convenient place to do it. He'd get stuck in the grassy ditch and be forced to stop. And then the real fun would begin. But the man in the rear seat sat back, and the sedan sailed right past him. With a puff of exhaust, it pulled away so swiftly that Brant didn't even bother trying to keep up.

Frustration burned the backs of his eyeballs as he watched the vehicle put more and more distance between them. Looking for the first safe place to pull over, he swerved onto a utility road and came to a stop. As his overheated engine cooled, he forwarded the video he'd taken of the mobsters to Maya's cell phone. With proof that the Scarpas were tailing Rebecca, she would have to take Rebecca's safety as seriously as she'd taken his.

Rebecca McDougal's pale face reflected abhorrence at Maya's proposition that she pretend to reconcile with Max. Ben Metier cleared his throat uncomfortably, while Doug Castle waited for Rebecca to process the request. Like Maya, he was certain she would come around.

"Why would you even ask that of me?" the young woman demanded, her voice quavering. "Max *murdered* Bronco like a cold-blooded serial killer. How am I supposed to even look at him, let alone pretend to want to reconcile?"

Maya bit her bottom lip. "I understand your reluctance—I do." She nodded. "But this could be the only way to convince both the military judge and Admiral Johansen of your husband's culpability. Look, just start out by giving him back the laptop. We've installed spyware on it. If he uses it again, we can capture his keystrokes, his passwords, that kind of thing. If he accesses an offshore account, we'll know it, and we'll be able to view it. If he was paid by a mysterious source to *do* something, that'll clinch our case."

Rebecca's brown gaze dropped to the laptop sitting on Maya's desk. "What do I say when I give it to him?" she asked, with audible reluctance.

"Tell him that you've had it in the trunk of your car for a while. You took it to a friend of a friend who fixed it, and you forgot to give it back, until now."

Rubbing her forehead with a hand that visibly trembled, the commander's wife mumbled, "I'm sorry. I don't think I can bring myself to even speak to him."

Frustration got the better of Maya's tongue. "Stop thinking with your heart and start thinking with your head," she implored. "Honestly, we could arrest him so easily if you would cooperate with us."

Her words startled Rebecca's head up. At last, she had her attention. "How?" she asked.

"Max's security company, HomeWatch, sends the FBI live audio and video feed of his security footage. Doug Castle has agreed to share the footage with us."

As Rebecca's gaze swung toward the FBI special agent, Maya could see her comprehension dawning, and she pressed her advantage. "Max knows that you're aware of his relationship with the Scarpas—after all, they held you at gunpoint to procure his cell phone number. If you could get him to discuss what he's done for them under any one of the cameras in his house, his own words will implicate him. The military judge will recommend a court-martial. Admiral Johansen will realize he has no choice but to concur with the judge's recommendation. McDougal will be court-martialed, convicted, and find himself serving a life sentence."

In the profound silence that followed, Maya's phone gave a muted chime signaling the arrival of a new text message.

"You do want Max to go to jail, don't you?" she

added on a gentler note.

"Of course," the vacant-eyed woman whispered.

"Then help us put him there," Maya implored. "At least give him the laptop. I can't force you to pretend to reconcile with him if you don't want to."

As the two men in the room, Doug Castle and Ben Metier, waited patiently for Rebecca's answer, Maya stole a peek at her phone and realized Brant had just sent her a video clip. *Well, look who the cat dragged in.* After ignoring her calls, he sends her a video recording? What was this about?

"I'm going to use the ladies room while you think about it," she said to Rebecca. Glancing at the men, she added, "I'll be right back."

In the women's restroom, situated just down the hall from her office, she peered under the stalls, ensuring that the room was empty before playing the recording. After a few puzzled seconds of watching a car chase, it dawned on her that this was the episode Rebecca had related upon her arrival. Looking shaken and pale, Rebecca had sworn she'd been followed from her apartment to the Navy base by none other than Tony Scarpa. Maya, perceiving her to be out of her mind with grief, had doubted her story, given how dramatic it had sounded. Why hadn't the MPs gotten involved if there'd been a high speed chase right up to the gate?

But there was no mistaking the scene depicted in the video for anything other than a show of intimidation on the part of a black BMW. The chase had been filmed from the perspective of a brown delivery truck, only the hood of which was visible, driven by none other than Brant Adams.

Maya scowled. The SEAL had some nerve undermining her efforts to conceal him. Here he was insinuating himself into the middle of her investigation, adding a whole new variable to an already complex equation, although he may very well have just saved Rebecca's life.

Had the mobsters recognized him? Did they even know who he was? How could they?

Besides, he'd pointed out something she hadn't fully acknowledged—that Rebecca McDougal was in serious danger. From now on, Maya would do well to take her at her word. The poor woman wasn't any safer in this harrowing situation than Brant Adams had been—except it was the Scarpas and not Max who apparently wanted her out of the picture before she ratted on either one of them.

Damn it! If Rebecca stuck around here pretending to reconcile with her ex, she could very well end up with a bullet in her head. Maya gave a low growl. So much for her plan to get incriminating evidence the quick and easy way.

Dialing Brant's number, she glowered at her reflection in the mirror as she willed him to pick up.

"Did you get my video?" he asked in lieu of hello.

She counted to five before answering. "Yes. What the hell do you think you're doing?" she demanded.

"Your job, I think."

Guilt pinched the tops of Maya's shoulders. "I'm sorry. You're absolutely right," she admitted. "We should have had people watching her already. I didn't realize the Scarpas were so suspicious of her."

"You need to send her away. Make her disappear like you did me."

"If you'd disappeared, I wouldn't be talking to you right now," she said on a sarcastic note. "Besides, I can't just send her off. I need her to testify at the Article 32 hearing."

"Have you filed for it yet?"

"Not yet." She wanted to procure Max McDougal's unwitting confession before he was made aware of the charges being brought against him. "Maybe in a week or so."

"Plenty of time for the mob to do her in," Brant pointed out. "Just put her on a plane to Honolulu. Her mother lives on the Coast Guard base there. You can fly her back for the hearing, but she's safer there than she is around here."

Maya pondered the logistics of flying Rebecca back and forth between Virginia and Hawaii. "I'll look into it," she promised. "Listen, while I appreciate you protecting our witness this morning, might I suggest that you fly a little lower under the radar? It will completely undermine my surprise tactic if your CO suspects that you're alive before you walk into the court room."

"Yes, ma'am." He chuckled at her vehemence.

A sudden suspicion skewered her. "Wait, who gave you that van, anyway? Is Kuzinsky harboring you?"

"Fugitives get harbored," Brant retorted. "I'm a dead man, remember?" Severing the call abruptly, he left her fuming and furious, her anger directed at a man whom she hadn't stopped thinking about since meeting him in the flesh a couple of weeks prior.

Master Chief Kuzinsky might be considered the biggest badass in the Spec Ops community, but she wasn't the least bit awed by his reputation. In fact, she'd like to give him a piece of her mind, in person, at the earliest opportunity.

But that would have to wait. Right now she had a depressed, exhausted, and very frightened woman in her office, whose life was imperiled by mobsters. Maya's hopes had hinged on Rebecca getting her husband to implicate himself, but she wouldn't be doing her job if she allowed her to get killed in the process. Plus, she needed her alive to testify.

She would have to rely on the evidence they had

procured so far. But was it enough to convince Admiral Johansen that his favorite commander had sacrificed his integrity for the chance to pay off his mountain of debts? The odds of that happening, Maya figured, were only about fifty percent.

Rebecca's jaw slackened in amazement at Maya Schultz's one-hundred-and-eighty-degree turnaround. Suddenly, the woman was hell-bent on putting her on a plane to Hawaii.

"Hawaii?" she repeated with surprise. "My mother lives in Honolulu."

"Yes, I know." The investigator sent her a tight smile. "You'll need to stay with her until Tony Scarpa no longer poses a threat to you. I'll fly you out this afternoon, if I can get you a seat."

"But Bronco's memorial is tomorrow," Rebecca protested. "I have to go."

Maya thrust her glasses higher up her nose. "What time tomorrow?"

"Two o'clock in the afternoon."

The blonde investigator sent a harried look at the FBI special agent. "Can you spare a couple of agents? I want round-the-clock-security on her until she's out of the area."

It dawned on Rebecca that something had happened to convince the investigator that her life was truly in danger.

"Sure," agreed the FBI agent. His concerned blue gaze reminded her of Bronco's.

Picking up the laptop on her desk, Maya held it out to her. "Please give this to your husband at the memorial tomorrow," she pleaded. "If you can convince him that it's safe to use, it would help us so much."

Picturing Max being apprehended and hauled off in

a police car, Rebecca managed a slight nod. She would have to overcome her abhorrence long enough to talk to him.

"Thank you." Maya slipped the hardware into a protective carrier. Handing it to Rebecca, she sent her an encouraging smile. "This will all be over eventually—I promise you, it will."

Eventually. That made the waiting sound endless. Would it take months or even years for Max to be found guilty of the mob-related murders? And what about facing charges for Bronco's murder? Maya had said they had scant proof of that.

Then there was Tony Scarpa to consider. Mobsters were historically adept at avoiding jail sentences. Rebecca might never get to return to her old life. But then, without Bronco alive to share it with her, what difference did it make?

"Is there anything else?" she asked wearily.

"Give me a minute to scramble up some men," Doug Castle requested.

As he got on his cell phone, Rebecca envisioned how awful it was going to be to face Max at the memorial. Her stomach roiled at the task before her.

Castle put his phone away. "Hobbs and Meyer will be here in twenty minutes. You can wait for them in the lobby, if you prefer."

Leaving the investigators and the special agent to brainstorm a new approach, Rebecca left the office, headed for the lobby. Approaching the part of the hall where Bronco had held her in his arms and kissed her, her steps slowed.

Was it only half a week ago? Tears she was reluctant to shed in public stung the backs of her eyes. Directing her hopeless gaze to the empty stairwell, she wished futilely that he would reappear.

At least he knew that you loved him, her logic

consoled.

That was true. She'd never had the chance to tell her father that, and she'd always regretted it. But Bronco had died knowing that he meant everything to her. That was something, wasn't it? With a sob rising up in her throat, she crossed quickly to the elevator and pushed the down arrow.

Max stared at the message from Tony on Google chat. In the dark of his home office, he could see his own dumbfounded expression reflected on the screen.

Your wife is in cahoots with the Feds.

Denial sat on Max's shoulders. *No way in hell,* he thought. But he could not ignore the many signs that indicated that was possible. After all, Rebecca had taken his laptop from the shop. What for, if not to use it against him? The thugs hadn't been able to find it, suggesting that it was now in someone else's hands. Still, he had trouble envisioning his docile wife undermining his reputation—she simply wasn't cunning enough. Chief Adams might have emboldened her to defy him, but now Adams was dead. And it was just a matter of time before Rebecca came back to him.

You're wrong, he typed back. *She doesn't know anything.* In the back of his mind, however, he questioned the truth of that assertion. She'd seen his foreign account with her own two eyes. Her testimony alone could be damning.

We followed her to the air base this afternoon. Some guy in a delivery truck tried to pick a fight with us. He even took pictures. Who the hell was that?

Max's fingers hovered over the keys. For once, he lacked an explanation. *No idea*, he finally typed as his mind sifted through the possibilities.

Was it possible that Rebecca had already betrayed

him? It wasn't like her to take that kind of initiative. It was Tony whom she feared, not him. After all, the man had abducted her once before and was now following her.

Don't you lay a hand on her, Max warned. *She obviously hired a bodyguard because she knows you're following her. Back off. I've got this.*

In the silence that ensued, Max ground his teeth together as he waited to see how Tony would reply. The last time he'd played hardball, the man had caved in to him.

The Feds are on to you, Max, Tony finally replied. *We're cutting all ties. Don't think you can finger us if you're caught,* Tony added. *You'll never get the chance.*

Max's laptop gave a bleep, and Tony's avatar disappeared from the upper corner of the screen, indicating that he'd left the chat.

Max licked the sweat off his upper lip. Holy hell, Tony Scarpa had just threatened him! Alarm scorched his nervous system, forcing him to suck in a several breaths.

But then another thought occurred that calmed his racing heart. By cutting ties, the mob had just freed him of future obligations. He didn't need to kill Special Agent Castle. But what about the money he'd already been paid? Would they take it back? They didn't have the capability to withdraw money from his account—did they?

He decided that it didn't matter. He could do without a house in Bermuda, as long as his reputation remained untarnished. The Feds couldn't possibly be on to him. It was Tony's menacing behavior that was drawing unwanted attention.

I'm still good, he reassured himself. But what if he wasn't? What if Rebecca had taken her suspicions to

NCIS and they were now investigating him?

If they possessed his laptop and could delve into his profile on the hard drive, then maybe they had reason to arrest him. God forbid that it ever came to that. Not only would the humiliation be unbearable, but Tony Scarpa would never let Max face prosecution—not when he could cop a plea in exchange for all the dirt he'd picked up on the Scarpa family. Tony would kill Max himself before he let that happen.

Max swallowed hard. Had the hunter now become the hunted? Did the Scarpas consider him so dispensable? Where was the respect that they'd shown him only a short while ago?

And what about Rebecca? Now that Tony had cut ties with Max, would they leave her alone, or would Tony seek try to silence her because she'd become a wild card, one that could identify him?

Max drew a hand down his cold cheek. He couldn't let anything happen to her. He would protect her. But first he had to convince her to come back to him.

The ringing of his doorbell cut through his tortured thoughts. The last time his doorbell had rung, the FBI special agent had been paying him a call. Who could it be this time?

Fearing the worst, he withdrew his Glock from the strong box inside his desk drawer and tucked it into the waistband of his khaki slacks, against the small of his back.

A peek through the window by the door lowered his tension a notch as he recognized the uniform worn by the HomeWatch people who'd installed his security system and came out every couple of months to make sure it was working perfectly.

"Yes?"

The young man pinned a smile on his face. "How are you, Mr. McDougal? Ron from HomeWatch." He gestured at his name tag.

"*Commander* McDougal," Max corrected him. "I thought Ron had blond hair."

"That's the other Ron," said the tech with a dismissive shrug. "Had any problems with your system lately?"

"No, it's working fine."

Ron checked the clipboard in his hand. "That's odd. We've been getting an error message back at the call center telling us that one of your circuit boards in the mainframe is defective. I'll need to open up your unit, test it, and if it's burnt, replace it. It'll take me half an hour at most."

Suspicion tickled Max's nape. "Where's your partner? You guys always work in pairs."

"Home sick," Ron said with a grimace. "I'm on my own today."

Max hesitated. Was it coincidence that HomeWatch wanted to work on his system so soon after he'd mentioned his alibi to the FBI special agent? Was Doug Castle looking for a loophole? If this tech looked long and hard enough, he'd realize Max's security system wasn't complete—that the window in the master bath had never been wired, leaving him free to enter and exit at his whim. But could he discover that much in only half an hour? Not likely.

"You should have called first," Max groused. "I have to leave the house soon."

"I'll be done in a jiffy," Ron promised him.

"Fine. I'll let you in through the garage."

CHAPTER 18

Brant wedged his driver's license deeper into the crack between the rear door of Rebecca's apartment and the frame, working to depress the simple latch. Annoyance simmered in him that he had made it this far without being waylaid. He didn't bother keeping his movements stealthy. Apparently, he had to announce his presence to the special agents if he wanted to face their resistance.

Granted, he was a Navy SEAL sniper, and he'd slithered behind her apartment building on his elbows, six inches at a time over the course of the last two hours. But these men, working for Doug Castle, most likely, were supposed to be experts in the area of security. If they hadn't noticed Brant yet, how could he trust them to protect Rebecca from ruthless mobsters who would let nothing get in their way?

Obviously he couldn't. And it was up to him to point out their shortcomings in the hopes that they'd make the changes necessary to keep their witness safe.

As he'd noted before, Rebecca's back door was the obvious entry point for an intruder. The flimsy lock was already yielding to the stiffness of his plastic coated driver's license. The patio offered profuse cover in the form of bushes and low walls. All he had to do to disappear completely was to jump the privacy fence at the back of the complex into the maze of office buildings behind it.

Of course, keeping the FBI on their toes wasn't the only reason he was here. He'd kept his distance from Rebecca for as long as he could stand. The thought of her believing him dead all this time had worn him down. Now that she was heading to Hawaii, what harm was there in her knowing the truth?

Of course, Maya Schultz wouldn't see it that way, but Brant didn't particularly care whether he pissed her off or not.

The lock yielded suddenly, and the door clicked loudly open. Brant flinched. If that didn't bring an agent running, nothing would.

He put his back to the exterior of the building and waited. A beetle or a mole scuttled through the mulch under his feet. The noise of someone's television floated out of an adjacent apartment building. What was taking the man so long? He ought to have apprised his partner of an intruder by now. If the men played it out right, they would come at Brant from different directions and box him in.

At last, he detected a soft thud, followed by the cautious opening of the door. The snout of a pistol penetrated the widening crack followed by a pair of hands.

Oh, please. Did they have to make this so easy for him?

Brant lunged forward, smashing the door against the gun and the hands holding it before jerking the agent forward and tearing the weapon from his grasp. Then he rammed his elbow into the agent's nose. With a grunt of agony, he sagged to his knees. As he pitched forward, Brant struck the base of his skull with his own weapon, rendering him immediately unconscious. As the agent collapsed facedown onto the patio, Brant stuck the second gun into his waistband.

Sorry, buddy. Crouching down next to the unconscious agent, he checked his pulse before prying the earpiece from his ear and sticking it into his own to listen.

"Hobbs, you there? What just happened?"

Brant hadn't heard a car door or any footsteps approaching the building, so he assumed that the second agent was still sitting complacently in his car. Christ, what did it take to get these guys to react with any urgency?

Lifting Hobbs's wrist, Brant spoke into the microphone he knew was hidden there, connected to the earpiece by a wire running down the agent's sleeve. "Hobbs is going to be fine," he reported, matter-of-factly. "You, on the other hand, are going to get your balls blown off if you open any door or window on your vehicle. Don't worry. I'm not one of the Scarpas, and I'm not going to hurt the girl. Hobbs will come around soon enough. Consider this a drill. Your security sucks."

Dropping both communication pieces, he stood up and stepped over Hobbs, entering Rebecca's kitchen. There, he locked himself inside and the unconscious agent out on the back porch.

The familiar scent of her apartment licked over him like a warm tongue. His adrenaline rush gave way to a soaring of his testosterone. Crossing her dark living room to the front windows, he peeked through the blinds at the stymied agent. The man sat frozen in his vehicle, no doubt deliberating whether he should risk being ridiculed by calling for back up or whether he should wait for Hobbs to come to and rescue him. Brant figured he had fifteen minutes, tops, to complete this mission before at least one FBI agent came bursting through the door.

Rebecca lunged for her cell phone, only to knock it off the bed stand she'd bought from Walmart.

No! It tumbled to the floor, rolling out of sight in her dark bedroom.

The sound of a brief scuffle outside had wakened her a minute earlier. Fear that the Scarpas had come to finish her off kept her heart hammering, which drowned out every other sound as she strained to hear.

For a long minute, there was nothing but silence. Then the stealthiest of footfalls moved across her living room. Impelled by fear, she rolled off the far side of her inflatable bed, dragging her blankets with her.

How could someone have broken in so easily with two special agents protecting her?

Her doorknob gave a jiggle. Envisioning Tony standing outside her door, she made her body as small as possible, covering herself from head to toe with the blanket. If only she hadn't dropped her phone, she could be dialing 9-1-1.

Too late now. The lock gave way with a *snick*. She froze, holding her breath to keep from being discovered.

"Becca?" called a voice she thought she'd never hear again.

It couldn't be Bronco. Her sleep-deprived mind was playing tricks on her.

Someone walked around the end of her bed.

"Honey, it's me. Is that you under there?"

His amused voice couldn't be mistaken for anyone else's. The covers slid off her abruptly, and a pair of eyes shining blue in the moonlight peered down at her.

Her heart forgot to beat as she stared up into his smiling face. "I'm dreaming," she declared.

"No, you're not." He stretched out a hand, reaching for her.

Terrified that he would evaporate when she touched him, she slowly put her hand in his. His warm fingers closed around it. With every cell of her body singing, she let him pull her to her feet and reach for him.

"Becca," he exclaimed. His arms encircled her, pulling her against the solid wall of his body.

"How can you be here?" she breathed against his chest, her voice as thin as a thread. "You're dead."

He pulled back to look down at her, and she saw that he was well on his way to boasting a full beard. "I'm not dead, honey. I never was. NCIS used that unclaimed body to make Max think that I was finished."

In light of TJ's call yesterday, his words made perfect sense, but she still didn't dare to believe it. "Why?"

"Why keep the truth from you?" he interpreted. "NCIS needed Max to believe I was no longer a threat to him. Everyone's grief had to be real, or he might not have bought it. Plus Ms. Schultz wanted to send me far away so I wouldn't be tempted to see you again. She doesn't want rumors of our affair discrediting your testimony. She tried sending me off to some ranch in Idaho, but I couldn't leave you, Becca." He pulled her close again, holding her tenderly, inviting her to rest her head against his shoulder.

Surrounded by his scent, his gentle strength, reality fully penetrated her consciousness. She gripped the fabric of his BDU jacket, pressed her face into the soft canvas weave, and gave a sob of abject relief.

Alive! Alive! He wasn't dead. That *was* him driving the brown van yesterday! She wasn't losing her mind, after all.

"Oh my God," she murmured, over and over, unable to comprehend that the past days of suffering were really over. He was here, in the flesh. *Thank you, God.* But she couldn't stop the tears that came gushing out to roll down her cheeks. Her shattered heart contracted as the shards came cautiously together.

He rocked her as he would an inconsolable baby. "It's been killing me to let you think that I was dead." His gruff voice conveyed powerful emotion. His palm swept up and down her spine. "I used to think that I was like my father and I'd walk out on the best thing that ever happened to me. But I'm not." She felt him shake his head. "I could never let you think I was dead, let alone leave you here fending for yourself. I'll be so relieved when you get on that plane tomorrow."

She pulled back a little to look up at him. "I'm going to your memorial first."

"No, you don't need to do that," he assured her. "I'm not dead."

"But I have to. I'm giving Max's laptop back to him. NCIS put spyware on it. Did you know he hired some thugs to break into my apartment looking for it?"

A look of horror seized his face. "What? When was this?"

"While you were in ICU, before you...died. Bullfrog was here. He overpowered them, and they admitted they were hired for the job."

"Jesus."

"Anyway, Max never got his laptop back, but now he will. I'm going to give it to him."

He scrubbed a hand over his forehead, betraying

agitation. "*Damn* it. I told Ms. Schultz to put you on plane to Honolulu as soon as possible. You're not safe here, Becca."

She gave a rueful laugh. "Was that your idea to send me to Hawaii? I should have known."

He gripped both her hands. "I swear if something happens to you, I'll never forgive her."

"It was my idea to stay," she assured him. "Besides, what's one more day? I'm leaving on the first flight out on Friday."

"Friday is two days away, not one."

Spying the neat line of stitches just above his new beard, she reached up and gently traced it. "They sewed you back up," she noted, changing the subject deftly.

"Yeah." He gave a short laugh. "They didn't know I was allergic to lidocaine."

She gasped. "What?"

"I went into anaphylactic shock. Almost died for real because of it."

She couldn't even begin to process that there'd been another threat to his life. "You looked so terrible when you came into the ER. I've never felt so helpless in my life."

"It's okay." He squeezed her hands. "I'm not that easy to kill." Lifting her fingers to his lips, he erased the awful memories by kissing her knuckles tenderly and then her palms. "Besides, I would never die on you like that."

The words sounded so much like a promise, but no one knew ahead of time when they would die. Life, so fleeting, so precious, could be snuffed out in an instant.

A car beeped in the parking lot, and he seemed to recollect himself. "Listen, we don't have much time." He reached behind his back, pulled out a pistol and laid it casually on her bedside table. Then he reached for her again. "I'm sure you've realized by now that the Scarpas consider you Max's weak link. They'd like to stop you from exposing him and, by association, them."

"You mean, they are going to kill me," she interpreted, with a brittle nod.

"Don't say that," he ordered gently. "No one is going to kill you, Becca. I won't let it happen. I'll be watching, protecting you every minute of every hour until you're safely gone. You may not see me, but I'll be there."

The thought of not seeing him before she left, and certainly not after, had her pulling his head down for a kiss. At the first touch of their lips, heat ignited. Their tongues twined in a sultry dance. Desire that demanded nothing short of complete surcease exploded between them.

Rebecca whimpered. Bronco responded by grasping the hem of her nightie and drawing it in one smooth motion over her head.

She drew his mouth down to her breasts, rising on tiptoe to guide a taut nipple between his parted lips. Sinking her fingers into his hair, she realized he had cut it shorter. Her head fell back as he lapped first one peak, then the other, into stiffness.

"Make love to me," she begged, heedless of the special agents who were out there somewhere.

He turned her toward the inflatable mattress and lowered her across it, all the while lavishing her with his lips and tongue.

She reached for the buttons of his jacket, undoing them with hands shaky with desire. Sliding them inside his jacket, she encountered yet another weapon, holstered under his left arm. Afraid to touch it, she slid her fingers lower to his fly, where she worked with single-minded purpose to free him. At last, he filled her hands with his tumescence, straining against her grasp as she lovingly cradled him.

"God, Becca," he groaned, pausing to enjoy her sensual caress.

Their breaths rasped in the quiet room. With a rumble in his throat that was half regret for his necessary haste, half eagerness to sink into her sweet warmth, he hauled off her panties, wedged his thighs between hers and sank into her snug slickness.

Tears of joy and repletion streamed from Rebecca's eyes as they surged together, mouths locked, tongues seeking. Pleasure saturated her senses as they strained closer, harder, deeper.

To think that she'd believed him dead a mere ten minutes ago! The joy that had been stripped from her then was resurrected now. In the wake of her supposed loss, her love for him had tripled.

If time would just suspend its relentless march, she would cling to this moment forever. But the bliss scorching her body brought her ever closer to incineration. The magic of their union proved too powerful for either of them to command. It ran its course, burning hotter and brighter, until it spent itself in rapturous paroxysms that ended all too quickly, leaving her bereft and frightened for the future.

"Bronco?"

He was gazing down at her, suddenly alert, almost tense.

Belatedly she overheard what he was listening to—the sound of someone banging at the back door.

"You have to go?" she guessed with regret. A hundred scenarios could happen before she saw him again—*if* she ever saw him again. Getting him back, only to lose him again, was unthinkable.

He rolled away and pulled up his jeans in one

continuous motion. "This gun belongs to one of the agents," he whispered, gesturing to the pistol he had left on her bedside table. "Be safe, Becca," he added, dropping a kiss on her lips before crossing to her window. "I'll be looking out for you."

"I love you," she called, watching him release the latch and open the window.

He paused, turning his head to regard her intently. For a breathless second, it seemed to her that he might acknowledge her words with a confession of his own.

But then from her kitchen came the sound of her back door crashing open. Someone had broken through the lock.

Bronco popped the screen and put one knee up on the sill. She heard him utter, "We'll be together soon. I promise." And in the next moment, he disappeared, jumping feetfirst into the darkness. She heard a bush rustle as he tripped over it, but the sound of him running away assured her that he was okay.

She had barely snatched the comforter off the floor and covered her naked body before the special agent named Hobbs burst into her room. Blood seeped from his nose. His wide eyes went straight to the curtains fluttering at the open window.

"You okay?" he demanded with gunfire urgency.

"Fine," she said, fighting an urge to laugh and weep simultaneously. "Is this your pistol?" she asked, pointing out the one beside her bed while noting that he wasn't carrying a gun.

"Who was in here?" he demanded, crossing toward her to snatch it up before stepping to the window to peer cautiously outside.

"A friend," she answered. Why bother lying? "I think he wanted to see how well you could protect me," she added pointedly.

He sent her a surly scowl, put his gun away, and

lifted his wrist to his mouth. "The witness is unharmed," he reported to his partner. "I'll be right out to check out your situation."

Rebecca wondered what Meyers' situation could possibly be.

Hobbs pointed a warning finger at her. "Don't you leave this room," he ordered.

Rebecca waited for him to exit her bedroom before tunneling back into her nightie. The moisture seeping from inside her made her realize that, in their haste, neither she nor Bronco had spared a thought for birth control. With the mob determined to kill her and no guarantee of tomorrow, an unplanned pregnancy was the least of her worries.

But then she remembered his promise that they would be together one day, and hope fluttered momentarily, only to grow still and cold.

Until Max faced the consequences of consorting with the mob, Bronco would remain dead to those who knew him, and Rebecca would be sent to Hawaii for her safety's sake. How long she would remain there was anyone's guess. First Max would have to be jailed, the mob subdued. But, even then, what prevented them from keeping a hit out on her forever?

Existing five thousand miles away from Bronco while they waited for justice to run its course struck her as intolerable.

There had to be another way.

There *was* another way.

Maya had said if she could just think with her head instead of her heart, she could help NCIS secure what amounted to a confession from Max. All she had to do was to get him to talk about his affiliation with the mob under one of the security cameras in his house. HomeWatch would then send live feed of their conversation to the FBI, and they could promptly arrest him. Tony Scarpa would be picked up shortly thereafter, and, after testifying, Rebecca and Brant would be free to spend their lives together—perhaps transferring to the west coast as a precautionary measure against reprisal. But at least they'd be together.

You can do it, her heart insisted.

Rolling out of bed, she dropped to her knees to search for her fallen cell phone.

CHAPTER 19

Rising from his seat on the front pew at the Chapel by the Sea, Max McDougal climbed the platform at the front of the church and approached the lectern to deliver the eulogy. Wearing his dress white uniform, the same one that he had worn on his wedding day three years ago, he wondered if Rebecca was remembering that occasion in this very sanctuary. As he moved behind the podium, he searched the packed church for a glimpse of her.

With all thirty-five members of his task unit present, plus a slew of other SEALs from Team 12, including Commander Montgomery and *his* boss, Admiral Johansen, it was no wonder he hadn't been able to find her. But *there* she was, seated on the last pew, behind the broad shoulders of the dozens of men in attendance.

Catching her eye, he sent her a faint nod of acknowledgment and was pleased when she returned it. The sunlight streaming through the tall windows of the contemporary chapel seemed to wash all color out of her face, or perhaps it was the black dress she wore—not her best color.

What thoughts lay behind her fixed regard? he wondered, as he smoothed his speech on the lectern. Was she remembering her wedding vows to love and to cherish him for better or for worse?

Clearing his throat, he projected his robust voice for all to hear what an outstanding SEAL chief Adams had been. Despite the possible addiction that had brought his life to a premature end, his unflagging optimism would always be an inspiration. His skill with a long-range rifle was the stuff of legends. He had served his country and his fellow frogmen tirelessly, and he would be sorely missed.

It was all so easy to say, now that the man wasn't here to steal his wife.

Confident of his eloquence, and under the approving gazes of his superior officers, Max abandoned the lectern to approach the life-sized poster of Adams' smiling face propped on an easel near the altar. Next to it, atop a wooden pedestal, there stood the white urn containing the man's ashes.

Fixing his gaze on a point just above and behind Adams' photo, Max rendered a lengthy salute as the bugler standing by the flag played *Taps*. Over the haunting notes, he could hear people in the congregation sniffling. It was a touching moment, the highlight of his day. Yet, oddly, there would be no three-volley salute, no pounding of SEAL tridents onto the lid of the coffin.

A belated suspicion tickled Max's nape as he cut his glance to the pristine white urn.

Why would any SEAL forsake the honor of taking his teammates' tridents with him into the next world?

What if he's not dead?

Goosebumps crawled over him as he lowered his arm. For that to be true, Kuzinsky would have had to deliberately deceive him. Turning his head, Max sent the master chief a piercing glare, only to receive a blank stare in return.

He gave himself a mental shake. It couldn't be. Of course Adams was dead. Just because the Scarpas questioned his housekeeping skills, that didn't mean he had no idea what was going on around him. He was still fully in command, still the puppet master.

Stepping aside to let the admiral and team commander pay their respects next, Max lost sight of Rebecca as SEALs stood up to make their way forward. He waited impatiently for her to do the same, but as the chapel slowly emptied, it became apparent that she had slipped out.

Discouraged, he reminded himself about the reception at The Galley at the Dunes, where he'd arranged for a light repast, giving his men the rest of the day off. Surely she would be there, and he could begin the challenging but achievable feat of winning her back.

"Max," Rebecca called. The ocean breeze, wafting across the parking lot, carried her voice in the wrong direction, but his head turned, proving he had heard her. At the point of stepping through the double-glass doors into The Galley, his gaze fastened on her, and her stomach immediately roiled.

Oh, God, help me do this.

She tentatively waved him over, holding her breath as his eyes narrowed with suspicion. He made his apologies to Admiral Johansen and crossed the parking lot to join her by her car, casting a surreptitious glance over his shoulder to see who might be observing them.

"Hello, Rebecca," he said, drawing to a stop before her. He tugged the bill of his white cap lower so that it cast a shadow over his eyes.

"Hi, Max." It took every ounce of her concentration to speak to him without betraying her disgust and contempt. Tucking a loose strand of hair behind one ear, she turned toward the trunk of her car. "I've been meaning to give you something."

He took a precautionary backward step as she pulled it open.

"It's your laptop," she explained, scooping up the bag Maya Schultz had given her and holding it out to him. "It's been in the trunk of my car for weeks," she added at his gathering frown. "My friend Sandy's husband fixed it. He's an IT guy. This way you don't have to wait for the repair shop to fix it." Her heart raced as she waited for him to accept or reject her olive branch.

He plucked it from her grasp, freeing her to release her held breath.

"You've had it all this time?"

"Yes. Sorry. I've been meaning to get it back to you," she said.

His shuttered expression could not quite disguise the relief blazing in his eyes as he peered into the bag. "Thank you," he said. He raised his gaze to study her face.

"Sandy's husband said it had a boot sector virus, whatever that is. It didn't take him long to fix it."

"I see." His dark gaze seemed to take in every detail of her tense expression. "How are you doing?" he asked, with credible concern.

Fury and disgust strangled her vocal cords. "I've been better," she admitted. Here was her chance to set up what Maya Schultz wanted from her. "Lonely." She choked out the single word.

"Missing Chief Adams?" His upper lip curled into his mustache.

Her arms stole across her chest in a purely defensive

gesture. "Do you think we could talk sometime?" she asked, instead of answering his question. The offer tumbled off her lips in her haste to get their conversation over with.

His ran a possessive gaze over her shivering frame. "You're cold," he noted. "Why don't you come inside?"

"No, I'm not staying. I only came here to give you back the laptop." She couldn't ask him the questions in The Galley that Maya wanted answers to—not in front of everyone else. It was clear to her he simply wanted to be seen with her to allay the rumors about their separation.

"Dinner then," he suggested smoothly. "What are you doing tonight?"

While marveling at his nerve, she was nonetheless grateful that he hadn't suggested a later date. "Tonight?" She pretended to think about it. "Nothing, as far as I know."

"We could go to The Pelican, like we used to do."

She envisioned the upscale restaurant they used to frequent, mostly so that Max could be seen by the upper brass there. "Too many windows," she said with a shudder. "I'd feel safer at the house with the security system armed. If that's okay with you," she added.

He looked pleased and mildly surprised by her suggestion. He shrugged. "Of course. But there's nothing in the refrigerator since I don't have time to shop."

"Take out would be fine," she suggested.

"The Vietnamese place up at the shopping center?"

"Sure. What time?"

"Let's say nineteen-hundred hours. I'll have to work late to make up for this time I'm taking off. You'll have to excuse the shape that the house is in."

Oh, poor Max. It had to be so hard for him to look after himself with his domestic servant no longer there to help.

The sudden, clawing need to get away from him had her shutting the trunk of her car abruptly. "I'll see you at seven," she murmured, edging toward her car door only to jerk to a halt as Max flashed out a hand to stop her.

His thick fingers bit into the flesh of her forearm.

She suppressed the urge to snatch her arm free. "What?" He couldn't suspect her motives, could he?

He glanced around at the full parking lot. "Is there someone looking out for you?"

There was no way to stop the blood from draining from her face as her thoughts flew immediately to Bronco. "Wh-what do you mean?"

Max's eyes turned to slits. "I heard a rumor that you hired a bodyguard."

Then she remembered the FBI special agents. "Two of them, actually," she admitted. "I told you, Max. I'm afraid of that guy, Tony. He's been following me."

A muscle in Max's square face twitched. She could see him searching his peripheral vision. "Are they here?" he asked. "Are they watching you now?"

Her heart thudded uncertainly. She had no wish to admit to her vulnerability but no desire to point out her protectors, either. "They're civilians. They couldn't get on base," she answered.

His grip on her arm tightened. *No!* she protested inwardly as he hauled her closer, holding her prisoner against his brilliant white jacket. An array of service pins and medals swam before her eyes. His scent, intolerable to her now, had her holding her breath.

"You don't need to hire bodyguards, Rebecca," he whispered fervently in her ear. "Move back in with me. I can protect you."

The sudden wail of a car alarm startled both of them and gave her the excuse she needed to wriggle free of his embrace. Master Chief Kuzinsky's Camry, parked immediately across from her Jetta, blared its horn at steady intervals while one of the hazard lights flashed. The other appeared to be broken.

Max stepped back and glared with annoyance at the offending car.

"I'd better go." Rebecca wrenched open her car door at the same instant that Kuzinsky burst out of The Galley to check on his vehicle.

"Be safe," Max called as she settled behind the wheel.

Casting him a weak smile, she shut her car door with relief, revved the engine, and backed out of her parking space. *Be safe.* What horrible irony, coming from his lips.

A clammy sweat coated her. Belated chills ran down her spine. At least, that was done. Max had taken the laptop without seeming overly suspicious of her story. Now she just had to get through dinner with him that night.

What was it Bronco would say to encourage her— not that he would agree to the plan if he found out. *Easy Day*, he would say.

Yeah, right.

Racing toward the gate, she broke the speed limit in her haste to get away. In her rear view mirror, she saw the special agents squeal out of their hiding place in their nondescript sedan. While their protection clearly wasn't foolproof, it was still a comfort to have them on her bumper now.

As the base exit came into view, her cell phone rang. It was probably Maya Schultz wondering how the transfer of the laptop had gone. Glimpsing

Bronco's number on her caller ID, she gave a strangled cry of joy. He wouldn't want to hear what she'd decided to do for both their sakes. Taking advantage of her car's Bluetooth capability, she took the call with the push of a button.

"Hello?"

"He put his fucking hands on you!" came the explosive observation. "Baby, tell me you're okay. Did he hurt you?"

She nearly drove off the road searching her mirrors for him. "You saw that? Where are you?"

"Yes, I saw that. I was in the trunk of Kuzinsky's car. You didn't say if you're okay," he pointed out, still audibly fuming.

The realization that Bronco had been responsible for the car alarm going off drew a half-hysterical laugh out of her. "I'm fine," she assured him. "And no, he didn't hurt me. Thank you, though," she tacked on, letting him hear how shaken the encounter had left her. "That was really hard to do. I'm such a terrible liar."

"But it's over," he assured her. "You gave him the laptop, and he fell for your story?"

"I think he did," she marveled.

"Then you're done with your part," he cheered her. "All packed and ready to leave town tomorrow?"

"Um..." Now that the moment had come, she didn't know how to tell him.

"I need to be with you before you go," he added, without giving her the chance to answer. "I'll meet you at the airport. We can have coffee, maybe slip into a family restroom for a few minutes alone. You might not recognize me right away. I'll be wearing my disguise."

"Bronco, I'm not leaving." The sudden silence in her car had her checking her hands-free connection.

"Are you there?"

"What do you mean, you're not leaving?" His flat tone conveyed a myriad of emotions, not the least of which was dread, which served to undermine her self-confidence.

"Listen to me," she begged, as she drove toward her apartment. "I don't want to fly five thousand miles away from you right now. I only agreed to that in first place because I thought you were dead."

"My being dead or alive isn't the issue," he countered, with restrained heat. "The issue is your safety. The fucking Scarpas have you on their hit list!"

"Yes, I know. And the only way to stop them is to arrest Max, who will throw them under the bus in order to save his own hide."

"How are you supposed to help?" Bronco demanded.

"I'm having dinner with Max at the house tonight."

"God damn it!" The expletive rattled her speakers.

She explained what Maya had told her about getting Max to discuss his work for the Scarpas while his security cameras were running. "She says that's all they need to ensure that the Article-32 hearing leads to a court-martial. He'll convict himself with his own words."

"Becca, don't do this." Bronco's dismay tugged at her heartstrings.

She wrung the steering wheel in her clenched hands. "I have to," she choked out. "I don't want to leave you here for God-knows-how-long, when I can help NCIS implicate Max. It could be over tomorrow."

"You really think it'll be that easy? Come on, Becca. Max isn't going to discuss the Scarpas. He won't admit that he's done anything wrong. What he's going to do is punish you for leaving him, then try to get you into bed."

She didn't want to hear what Max might do. "Maya's going to coach me on what to say. I have to try!"

"I don't like it," he muttered. "I don't like it one fucking bit."

This was Bronco in a rage, Rebecca realized, only he couldn't yell because he was hiding in the trunk of his master chief's car. "Sounds like you might be jealous," she suggested, praying he would just tell her that he loved her.

"Hell, yes, I am jealous!" he bit out.

Happiness blended with pain in an exquisite montage of emotion. He hadn't said he loved her yet, but his behavior suggested he did.

"I'll be okay, Bronco," she promised him.

She listened to him breathing—a beautiful sound that reminded her that he was alive, part of her life, and hopefully part of her future.

"I'll be close by the entire time," he told her gruffly. "Just don't be afraid. Max is a predator. If he smells your fear, he'll become suspicious."

A frisson of terror crackled through her. Her heart beat heavy in her chest as she waited for him to say the words she longed to hear. But the only thing to reach her ears was a *click* as he brought their conversation to a close.

Brant's vibrating cell phone made him jump. Until that moment, he hadn't realized just how tense he was, sitting in the brown delivery truck at the front of Rebecca's apartment complex, waiting for her to drive by on her way over to Mad Max's house for a dinner date.

A fucking dinner date with a homicidal psycho! It didn't help that the hours had crawled by at an agonizing pace since he'd first heard about her and Maya's crazy plan. He had immediately called Maya Schultz to grill her on the security measures she planned to put into place. Her refusal to answer his calls only increased his agitation. Obviously, she didn't want him anywhere near Max's house, where motion-detecting floodlights and hidden cameras threatened to expose Brant as being very much alive.

Well, that was too damn bad for Ms. Schultz because Brant wasn't going to leave Rebecca's well-being in the hands of NCIS or the FBI. He had meant what he'd promised her—that he would be close by, as close as he could get without being spotted.

This had to be Maya calling him now. Or maybe Rebecca was calling to say that she'd changed her mind. But it wasn't either of them. The name on the caller ID had him shaking his head.

Should he answer it, or go on letting Bullfrog believe that he was dead, even though the man had obviously intuited that he wasn't?

"Hey," he said, opting to put his friend out of his torment.

A prolonged sigh on the other end. "Did you end up in heaven or in hell?" his friend asked in a voice choked with relief.

"Oh, this is definitely hell," Brant assured him.

"Things are hellish in the task unit, too," Bullfrog divulged. "Mad Max has been living up to his reputation."

A fresh concern fizzed in Brant's belly. "Why? He doesn't suspect I'm still alive, does he?"

"N-no," but Bullfrog dragged the word out, conveying that he wasn't positive. "I think Rebecca leaving him has stressed him out. That or his business with the mob has him on edge."

Brant didn't like the sound of Max on the edge. Not

when Rebecca was having dinner with him.

"When did you guess that I was still alive?" Brant asked, lifting the scope he'd removed from his Stoner SR-225 to his left eye and peering across a distance of two hundred yards and through the shadows of large trees at Rebecca's front door. Kuzinsky had retrieved his sniper rifle from his old locker at Spec Ops. It lay across the seat beside him. She still hadn't come out.

"I don't know," Bullfrog answered. "I wasn't completely sure until you answered the phone just now. Things just didn't feel right. That white urn at your memorial? It didn't have your aura."

Brant gave a grunt as he panned the area around her apartment keeping a sharp eye out for the black BMW. Hopefully, Max wasn't as astute as Bullfrog.

"So, what circle of hell are you in, exactly?" his friend inquired.

There wasn't a single BMW in the parking lot. "I'm sorry, but you lost me there," Brant admitted.

"*Dante's Inferno*," Bullfrog explained. "The second circle of hell is for sins of lust. Maybe you found a place there? The seventh circle is for sins of violence. Given our profession, we might end up there together one day."

"I think I'm just in limbo," Brant muttered. The crosshairs of his scope ran across a black cat skulking from one building to another, but nothing more suspicious than that. "Rebecca's having dinner with Max tonight, at his place."

"What?" It was Bullfrog's turn to be mystified.

"The Feds have tapped into Max's security cameras. They want Rebecca to ask him some pointed questions while his security is up and running. Depending on his answers, they might go ahead and arrest him."

"You'll be keeping an eye on her," his friend

guessed.

"Goes without saying."

"Can I help?"

More than anything, Brant wanted to say yes. SEALs worked in pairs. That was the way he'd always operated. But with Max's security system turned on, it would be hard enough for him not to trip it accidentally, and he was a trained tracker. If Bullfrog were caught peeking through Max's windows, it could ruin his career, especially if their commander never went to jail.

"Not this time, buddy," he replied. "But maybe you could do your visualizing trick and bring about a positive resolution. If something happens to Rebecca—" His voice failed him suddenly.

"You got it, my friend," Bullfrog assured him. "I'm a phone call away if you change your mind."

"Sudden movement at Rebecca's door had him peering through his scope again. "Hey, I gotta go," he said. A special agent preceded her out of her apartment. Rebecca followed, wearing a pair of dark slacks and a purple top. Even with the distance between them and under the cover of twilight, he could tell that she was terrified.

"I'm right here, honey," he whispered.

Her head came up. As if sensing his scrutiny, she paused and looked around her. Squaring her shoulders, she continued to her car and slipped behind the wheel, while the agents quickly got into their own vehicle.

CHAPTER 20

—◆—

"Okay. He's home."

Maya Schultz's hushed voice came through the hands-free system in Rebecca's car, and her heart leaped like a racehorse out of the gate.

"He just pulled into his garage," Maya added from her hiding place in a mid-sized RV. It was parked on Max's street, several houses down, where he wasn't likely to notice it. "Give him a few minutes to prepare for your arrival."

Parked on the same dead-end road where Tony and his thugs had bound and gagged her, Rebecca hugged herself both for warmth and to subdue her shivers. Darkness surrounded her. It was just past seven o'clock, the time when Max had invited her to arrive.

Half an hour earlier, Maya had prepped her for the dreaded date. She'd been invited into the FBI-owned RV, where state-of-the-art surveillance equipment lining three interior walls offered immediate reassurance—that was, until the techs failed to bring up the feed from Max's cameras.

"What's happening?" Maya had demanded. "Why can't we see inside the house?"

The tech had shaken his head. "Apparently, he forgot to arm the system when he went to work this morning."

Maya had shared an incredulous look with Doug Castle. "And we're just now realizing this?"

"He never forgets." Rebecca's assertion had wrought a tense silence in the RV's dim interior.

"But he turns the system off whenever he's home," Maya had insisted, "at least during the day. That's what we've observed."

"Right, but he never forgets to arm it when he leaves the house. At least not when I lived there," Rebecca had amended. "Perhaps he was preoccupied today." He certainly ought to have been, heading to a memorial for a man he had tried to kill.

Maya had crossed her arms and gnawed on a thumbnail. "I don't like this," she'd admitted. She surprised Rebecca by reaching out to touch her arm with concern. "You really don't have to do this if you don't want to."

Rebecca's knees had knocked together. Having dinner with Max was the last thing in the world she wanted to do, but if it led to Max being court-martialed and to her and Bronco getting to see each other, then she had to do it.

"I'm fine," she'd assured the investigator. "I'll just make sure that he arms the system as soon as I get inside. I'll tell him I don't feel safe without it."

Maya had given her arm a squeeze. "Okay. But if, at any time, you feel overwhelmed and you want to leave, just slip away into a restroom and text me the word *Out*. We have a contingency plan in place to get you out of there."

Rebecca had agreed. And after receiving a few more instructions about what sort of incriminating language they needed Max to use, she'd been told to wait on this dead-end street for word on when to approach the house.

"Okay, Rebecca." Maya's soft voice held an edge to it that betrayed her uneasiness. "You can start for the house now. We'll be able to see you enter the front door from here, but until he arms his security system, you'll be out of our sight and hearing."

Sliding her gear shift into drive, Rebecca drove slowly out of the dead-end street. Behind her, her two FBI watchdogs in their sedan crawled along in her wake. Keeping their lights off, they would follow her to within a hundred yards of Max's property, get out of their vehicle, and approach the house—near enough to see into the windows, but not close enough to activate Max's motion-sensing floodlights.

Fear dropped like a cold rock into Rebecca's stomach as she turned onto her old street, her gaze going at once to the familiar outline of her former home. Lights shone brightly in the front windows, making the home look as hospitable as it did when Max hosted his enormous parties.

The closer she drew to the long driveway, the more ragged her breathing became.

"We're right here, Rebecca," Maya reminded her.

The disembodied voice provided momentary comfort, but soon she would be entirely on her own.

Just don't be afraid. Bronco's words of caution returned to her as she slowed to a stop before the closed garage. *Max is a predator. If he smells your fear, he'll start to suspect.*

Oh God. Her fear was so palpable right now, Max would suspect a ruse right away.

Get yourself together, she ordered herself. You can't afford to be afraid.

Implementing a technique she practiced in yoga, she managed to slow her breathing, steady her frantic pulse. Then she settled the mantle of self-imposed calm around her like an invisible cape. That same calmness had seen her through hundreds of life-and-death situations in the ER, and it would see her through this one last evening with her husband. She prepared to turn her car off.

"Okay," she said to the listening occupants of the RV. "I'm going in now."

"Good luck, Rebecca," came Maya's final words.

The hands-free connection ended as she turned off the motor. She swallowed hard and pushed her door open.

Max's silhouette drifted past the window. He'd sensed her arrival. Clutching her purse to her chest, she stepped out of her car. A sense of surrealism accompanied her across the paving stones to the front stoop. When she'd fled the house, just before Tony had abducted her, she had thought she would never again walk up this particular path and enter this house. As she climbed the steps, her gaze fell to the potted plants illumined by the porch light. In her absence, Max had let the geraniums wither and die. The brown blossoms and shriveled stalks struck her as a bad omen.

But then a sound like the twitter of a bird reached her from the periphery of the front yard. It was all she could do not to turn her head toward the cheerful sound. *Bronco.* It had to be him, offering whatever encouragement he could. Straightening her spine, Rebecca reached for the chime just as the broad black door swung open.

There stood Max, filling the threshold with his larger-than-life presence. Just the sight of him inspired another wave of panic, but by sheer force of will, she beat it back, fixed a smile on her face, and approached him with outward confidence.

"Hello, again," she said.

His glittering gaze went from the mulberry colored blouse to her black slacks and matching black boots, back up to her face. "I was hoping you would wear a dress," he said on a sulky note.

"Next time," she promised, leading him to believe that there would be one.

His gaze shot past her toward the dark street. "Where are your bodyguards?"

"They have the night off." He wouldn't mention his relationship with the Scarpas if he thought anyone was skulking about his property. "You said you could protect me," she reminded him.

His expression brightened. "Of course. Come on in." Stepping back, he invited her into her former home.

There was nothing the least bit welcoming about the prison she had spent so many hours redecorating. The familiar smells of leather and lemon wax turned her stomach, even though they were masked by the distinct aroma of Vietnamese food. Max had remembered to pick up dinner on his way home.

"You'll have to forgive my own attire," he said, gesturing to his work khakis. "I didn't want to sully my dress whites by leaving them on at work, and I just got home a minute ago, so I haven't had time to change." He gestured for her to follow him through the great room, where a peek into his office gave her a glimpse of the laptop she'd given back to him, charged up and sitting on the corner of his desk.

Through the wall of windows at the back of the room, she noticed that the swimming pool had been covered by a tarp for the off-season. Without the submerged pool lights glimmering in its depths, she could clearly see the boathouse and the pier, jutting out into the glinting inlet.

"What a lovely night," she said, for lack of anything better to say.

"Perhaps we'll walk out to the water later," he suggested.

His words offered the perfect opportunity to bring up his security system. "Oh, I wouldn't feel safe doing that." She shook her head and shuddered simultaneously. "Not with your friend Tony stalking me constantly."

"He's not a friend," Max retorted shortly. "You should never have spoken to him in the first place. Do me a favor," he added, storming into the kitchen, where she could see the take-out boxes on the granite island and the dinette table set with plates and silverware. "Don't bring him up again."

Dismayed, she trailed him into the kitchen, glancing up by force of habit to see if the camera was on. The absence of the telltale light turned her mouth dry. Maya was still waiting for the security system to be activated.

"Could you at least turn on the alarm?" she requested, pretending to cast a nervous glance out the window. "I really don't feel safe without it."

Max shot her a penetrating look.

Fighting to keep her expression as neutral as possible, she returned it.

"If it makes you feel safer," he agreed. "Help yourself to a drink." Gesturing to the pair of tumblers he had set out below the liquor cabinet, he strode out of view through the laundry room and into the garage.

Rebecca opened the liquor cabinet to assess its contents. They could both use a stiff drink. Alcohol would keep her panic at bay and hopefully loosen Max's tongue. Selecting a bottle of top-line whisky, she filled their tumblers with ice from the fridge dispenser, then added whisky to the halfway mark.

What was taking Max so long? Cocking an ear toward the garage, she could hear him muttering obscenities. *What now?* she wondered, taking a sip of her drink. It scalded her throat and pooled warmly in her stomach.

Max stormed out of the laundry room, startling her. As he glared up at the camera on the kitchen ceiling, she followed his gaze, noticing with a sinking sensation that the light was still off.

"That inept motherfucker," Max exclaimed.

A shard of fear imbedded itself between her shoulder blades. "What's wrong?"

Casting her a distracted glance, he helped himself to his own tumbler and tossed the whisky down in one swallow. "Oh, those HomeWatch people were out the other day, supposedly fixing the system when it was working just fine. Now I can't get the damned thing to turn on." Tugging his phone out of his back pocket, he accessed the HomeWatch application, all the while shaking his head in puzzled exacerbation.

Rebecca's blood abruptly thinned. The realization that Maya and her crew could neither see nor hear her ripped the mantle of self-imposed calm right off her shoulders. She was alone with the monster who'd tried to murder Bronco, a man who'd kept her under his cruel thumb for three tortuous years, who would certainly turn violent if she suddenly decided to leave.

"Well," he declared, oblivious to her sudden distress and putting his phone away. "I just sent them an emergency repair request, but you know how those things go. I'll be lucky if they come out before noon tomorrow."

All she could do was stare at him, the breath in her lungs petrified, completely mute.

Max took a step in her direction, and she couldn't stop herself from retreating.

He eyed her suspiciously. "What the hell's your problem?"

"This just…isn't a good time for your security system to break down." Her thin voice was scarcely audible. If she told him she needed to leave, he would first accuse her of overreacting, then suspect her motives for coming in the first place.

Max sent her an insolent smile. "Don't trust me to protect you?" he mocked. Snatching the tumbler from her hand he turned to the whisky bottle to refill it. "Here, drink some liquid courage," he invited, handing it back to her. "And have a little more faith in me," he added. His eyes glinted with dark promise.

With a stab of regret, she realized Bronco was right. Max was planning to get her into his bed tonight. *Never.* She would rather die than endure his insufferable touch ever again. She needed to leave—now. And yet, putting an abrupt end to their plans would certainly infuriate him, not to mention spark his suspicions. She needed to extricate herself carefully. Recalling Maya's contingency plan, she laid her glass on the table.

"The food smells delicious." She pretended to savor the aroma. "I'd like to use the restroom first, if you don't mind," she said airily.

The roll of his eyes communicated that he did mind; however, he waved her toward the front of the house, where the guest bath was situated at the head of the hallway. Purse tucked under her arm, Rebecca hurried toward it, conscious of Max's observant gaze as he watched her retreat.

She had just stepped into the L-shaped hallway and was reaching for the bathroom door when a soft sound drew her gaze down the dark, angled corridor. To her horror, a figure turned the corner, coming into the light. His aspect was so familiar and so unexpected that her throat closed up, keeping her startled scream locked inside.

Tony Scarpa, followed immediately by two of his goons, neither of whom wore hoods over their heads tonight, bore down on her. Each carried a wicked-looking gun and wore a grin of delight. Rebecca froze in shock.

"Well, look who we got here," Tony murmured, seizing her arm in a brutal grip. The point of his pistol jabbed her ribs as he jerked her closer. "Not a sound," he warned, thrusting her into the arms of his similarly stocky but bearded sidekick who covered her mouth with a beefy hand. "Don't shoot her yet," he added. "We'll make it look like the husband did."

Fear coiled around Rebecca's body, squeezing her like an anaconda. Thinking she could outwit Max, the king of cunning, in the first place was naïve. Now she'd put herself squarely into Max's embroilment with the mob. Maya couldn't see inside to know how dire her situation had suddenly become. And even if Bronco, who had promised to watch over her, *could* see inside, how could he possibly prevent the bloodbath that she could sense was about to take place?

"What is going on in there?"

Maya paced the narrow space between the walls of computers and monitors, waiting for anyone of them to blink on with an inside view into Commander McDougal's house. They'd waited ten minutes and nothing had happened yet. The worry that she had sent Rebecca like a lamb into a wolf's den kept her from drawing a deep breath.

Doug Castle conferred with his agents via radio. "Hobbs, Meyer, we need eyes on our witness, *right now*. Cut the wire on the floodlight on the southwest side of the house so you can move in closer. I want a situational report in one minute."

A sudden idea freed Maya's stymied thoughts. Snatching her phone from the nearest console, she accessed Brant Adam's number. "Come on, I know you're here," she muttered as it started ringing.

"Adams." The terse syllable uttered in a low growl evoked an image of him sprawled on his stomach on some raised platform peering through the scope of a rifle into Max's house.

"I need to know what you're seeing. The security system isn't working. What's going on in there?" she demanded.

"Well," he drawled. "They talked a little. Poured drinks. Looks like they're about to eat, but Rebecca just headed toward the front of the house. I've lost sight of her. Max is dishing out their dinner."

"Maybe she's about to text me. I told her to slip away and text me if she needed to get out. Something must be wrong with the security system. She was going to make him turn it on, but it wasn't armed earlier. What if it's broken? I should never have let her go in there."

"Well, I agree with that statement. Oh, *shit!*"

The expletive dropped on her head like a missile from a stealth bomber. "What happened?" she dared ask.

"Scarpa scum. Three of them, at least. Fuck, they were in the house all this time! Must have been hiding in the back bedrooms." Disbelief laced the syllables rolling off his tongue. "Fuck!" he repeated.

She could tell that his training alone kept his thoughts from shutting down completely.

"Describe what you see," she begged.

"They're all in the family room at the back of the house. I recognize Tony from her drawing—he's armed. One of his men is holding onto Rebecca—he's armed. So is the third man. Looks like they caught Max by surprise. He's got his hands in the air. They're talking."

Maya clung to the console to keep herself together. "Stay on the phone with me, Brant."

"I'll put you on speaker. I need two hands."

"Wait, don't shoot anyone yet."

Doug Castle had heard enough to catch the gist of what was going on. "Hobbs, Meyer, we have a hostage situation in the house with three additional hostiles inside," he said into his radio. "Try to get eyes on them, but don't be seen."

"They're all in the back of the house, the family room," Maya relayed.

He repeated the information to his men then turned to one of the techs. "Ringo, you come with me. Maya, stay here with Blake. Blake, call SWAT. I want them here ASAP."

She had been the one in charge until the Scarpas made an appearance. Frustrated, Maya watched the RV door close quietly as Castle and Ringo slipped out to help Hobbs and Meyer. Listening to the agent named Blake relay the situation to FBI SWAT, she wondered how her plan to implicate Max McDougal could have gone so terribly off track.

"Well, hello, Max," Tony purred, grinning at the look of stunned dismay that Max wasn't able to conceal.

Having heard voices, he had rushed toward the front hall to investigate, only to realize that he'd underestimated the Scarpas.

"What a nice surprise," the mobster added, advancing cautiously into the great room, his pistol trained on Max's heart. "We came here to chat with you, and who should we run into but your two-faced wife?" His dark eyes trekked to the kitchen where Max had just laid out the food on porcelain plates. "Oh, I'm so sorry." He affected remorse. "Did we interrupt your romantic dinner together?"

"What do you want?" Max demanded. "You said you were cutting ties."

Thanks to his training, he was able to keep calm, to catalogue as many details as possible, including how many weapons they had and the ashen hue of Rebecca's face. Caught in the arms of a bearded man whose resemblance to Tony suggested blood kinship, she knew full well the Scarpas weren't going to let her go this time. And, until he got a weapon in his own hands, Max didn't stand much chance of stopping them.

Tony swaggered close enough to lean a hip against the leather love seat across from where Max stood. "You think we'd leave without getting our deposit back? You let us down, Max. We want our money."

"Of course you do." Max hid a smile. Without meaning to, Tony had just evened the playing field. "Let me get onto my PC, and I'll transfer it back to you. All I need is your account information." He started edging toward his study.

Tony tsked his tongue and waved him toward the couch. "Sit," he ordered, gesturing with the point of his semiautomatic.

Max sank reluctantly on the edge of his Italian leather sofa.

"You won't find what you're looking for in there." Smirking, Tony produced a second semiautomatic from behind his back and waved it at Max tauntingly. "I already have your Glock."

At Max's smoldering stare, Tony chuckled, reveling in his cleverness. He tucked the Glock out of sight again.

"I'll give you back your deposit, plus another ten thousand if you let her leave now," Max promised.

"Oh." Tony clapped his free hand over his heart, as if moved by the gesture. "Did you hear that, boys? He'll pay us ten thousand dollars to spare his wife's life. Hard to believe he would be so generous considering his wife has Feds watching her back." He cut a scathing look over at Rebecca, still in the clutches of the dark-haired goon. "She reported you to the authorities, Max. Can't you see the truth? Or are you too besotted with your bride to realize what a backstabbing bitch she really is?"

The words expanded Max's thoughts. Cutting his gaze to Rebecca's stricken face, he considered whether Tony might be right. What if she'd duped him into thinking she was open to reconciliation when, in fact, she was after information that would help the Feds?

"She's neither mean enough nor smart enough to play me like that," he insisted.

"Oh, yeah? Well, we'll see, Max. We'll see. Nick, go get that laptop off his desk and bring it to him. Easy in the handoff. Remember, he's a Navy SEAL. No funny business, Max, or I'll shoot you in the foot. Ever been shot in the foot before? It hurts like a sonofabitch, but the thing is, you can still use your brain and your fingers."

The chilling threat made Max wonder if they were going to kill him after getting their money back. He'd thought he could play with the big boys of the underworld and come out on top. He'd always won at everything before—when his task unit took on various scumbags all over the world. But terrorists and drug lords had nothing on these soulless bastards.

As Nick extended the laptop to him cautiously, Max

glanced up and did a double take. "You," he accused, as the reality of the situation dawned on him. He knew immediately why his security system wasn't working.

"So, you remember me." The blond man grinned. "Thanks for letting me steal your HomeWatch password." He shrugged unapologetically. "You really shouldn't be so trusting."

Relief mingled with fury. At least it wasn't Doug Castle who'd ordered HomeWatch to scrutinize his security system. At the same time, he longed to punch the smirk off Nick's pug-nosed face. The unexpected appearance of a luminous red dot on the man's forehead prompted a surge of adrenaline as it drew his gaze up briefly. He forced himself to look down at the laptop.

Holy shit! Someone—friend or foe?—was holed up in his back yard, probably over by the gazebo, aiming a rifle with a high-powered infrared scope into Max's great room.

He glanced over at Tony to see if the mobster had noticed, but Tony's gaze was fixed on the laptop Max now held in his hands.

"Come on, Max," Tony urged on a tense note. "We don't got all night. You need me to shoot your wife in the foot to make you work faster?" He aimed his pistol at Rebecca's left foot.

She cringed, visibly expecting to be maimed.

"I'm working on it!" Max raged. With stiff, uncoordinated fingers, he finished logging in to the online banking page for Emile Victor DuPonte. His browser speed was better than ever now that the laptop was fixed. If only his mind could work so quickly at identifying the shooter out back. Maybe Tony had set up his own sniper in case Max managed to turn the tables and get the upper hand.

The alternative made his heart stop.

Or maybe Tony was right, and the Feds were out there watching everything that was happening. Maybe they hadn't bugged his security system, but if Rebecca was the backstabber Tony insisted she was, then the laptop he was using right then might be loaded with spyware that allowed them to track his online activity.

If that was the case, he'd just revealed the contents of his offshore banking account.

"I'm in," he stated, lifting his gaze up at Tony and finding the infrared dot now fixed on the mobster's right shoulder. "Where do I send the money?" he asked, swallowing hard.

Tony never got the chance to answer. The glass window behind Max exploded into a million shards, and Tony flew backward, landing with a thud on the carpet, dropping his pistol and reaching for his bloody shoulder with his other hand.

One down.

Max shoved the laptop aside, sprang out of his chair, and tackled Nick to the ground. Within seconds, he controlled the blond man's weapon. Turning it against him, he shot him in the chest.

Two down.

The bearded thug was backing toward the foyer, dragging Rebecca with him and shrieking his boss's name. "Tony! Tony!"

But all Tony could do was writhe on the floor and moan.

Max watched the telltale dot settle ominously over the bearded man's forehead. Six inches lower and Rebecca would become the target. *Thunk! Phoof.* A dark red circle the size of a quarter appeared over the thug's unibrow while a pink cloud of brain matter billowed out the back of his skull. He dropped where he stood, leaving Rebecca hunched over, her hands over her mouth, stifling a scream of pure terror.

That made three.

Max rolled across the carpet, sprang up, and ran to her. Snatching her against him, he concealed as much of himself as possible behind her petite, quaking body as he started to retreat toward the hall. But then he froze, staring spellbound out the shattered window at the familiar form of a man he thought he would never see again.

Chief Brant Adams was rounding the swimming pool, stiff-arming his Sig Sauer in lieu of the deadly sniper rifle he had wielded moments earlier, and it was pointed directly at Max.

Max's ears rang in the aftermath of gunfire. How was it possible that the man he had poisoned could be back from the dead and looking fully intent on getting revenge?

"Stay back!" Max yelled. For the first time in his life, he heard his own voice crack with fear. "You'll *never* have her," he vowed, forcing her chin up with the barrel of Nick's pistol. He knew if he fired it and killed her that Adams would take him out in the next instant. At this point, that was looking like his only exit strategy. "She is *my* wife—all mine. I'll take her to hell with me if I have to!"

This is it, Rebecca thought. The muzzle of the gun gouging her chin was still hot from the shot that had killed the thug named Nick. Tony Scarpa lay only feet away, sobbing in agony. The third man was also dead. She'd heard his skull explode right before he released her. And now Max, who had promised he would never let her go, was going to keep his word and take her to the grave with him.

"Max, please," she begged, so weak with fear and dread and regret that Bronco would have to watch her get killed that she could scarcely stand. Max kept her upright as he hugged her from behind. "Don't do this."

At Max's threat, Bronco had gone perfectly still, a torn expression on his face. "Becca, remember what you told me when I was leaving your apartment last night?" His gruff voice betrayed the certainty that she was about to be taken from him. "I should have said the same thing back to you."

He loves me! Rebecca realized, as Max pressed the muzzle of his gun harder into her chin. How sad that she could neither revel in Bronco's confession now nor lament the loss of what they could have had. Max was going to enact her darkest presentiment and take her life before she'd barely begun to live again.

Suddenly, with a terrific crash, the front door burst open, suspending her dark thoughts. A stream of masked specters swarmed into the house, their assault rifles aimed at her, Tony, and Max. Caught between two armed parties, Max swiveled back and forth, his breath rasping in her ear, the muzzle of his gun bruising her tender flesh.

Then Doug Castle walked calmly into the house. Rebecca blinked at him in desperation as he surveyed the carnage in the great room. Crossing to the writhing Tony, he plucked up the man's fallen weapon and dropped it into the pocket of his trench coat. Tony stopped sobbing and stared up at him in astonishment.

"Well, Commander," Castle said, turning his attention to Max and looking not the least bit harried by Rebecca's predicament. "It looks like your money-making scheme with the mob backfired on you tonight," he observed, taking a step toward them.

"Get back!" Max's shrill command caused Doug Castle to raise his eyebrows. "I'll kill her," Max swore in a voice that made it horrifyingly apparent that he wasn't bluffing. "I'll kill us both. You are *not* going to take me in," he insisted, "as if I'm some low-life piece of shit like that bastard there!" He glanced at Tony, who'd gone back to moaning.

Doug Castle tipped his head to one side. "Of course not. You're a Navy SEAL commander, and you'll be shown due respect," he promised. His gaze met Rebecca's briefly then looked away. "All you need to do is step away from your wife. She's not a threat to you, is she?"

But Max's grip only tightened. "She betrayed me," he insisted in a tortured voice. "She's the reason you're here, isn't she?"

"Oh, no. I've had my eyes on you for a while, Max," Castle replied, rocking on his heels.

"I *won't* be taken! SEALs don't surrender. And they don't let their enemies live either."

The thick arm shackling her to Max's chest became a shackle. She could no longer draw air into her lungs. He expelled a shuddering breath, and she just knew that in the next instant her life would be over.

Crack! Crack! Crack! Crack!

Cringing, Rebecca welcomed the darkness, only it never came. Max's arms went slack as he keeled away from her. Her eyes flew open. The scream she'd stifled earlier erupted from her throat as she fell to her knees and found Tony dead, his chest riddled with bullet wounds. Max's Glock, which Tony must have just pulled out from behind his back, was still in his hand. He'd obviously intended to shoot her and Max simultaneously, only SWAT had taken him out before he could.

Rebecca sucked in a grateful breath. *I'm alive! I made it! But what about Max?*

Very slowly, she turned her head to see what had become of him, only to wish she hadn't. He lay sprawled across the Italian leather loveseat with the top of his head blown off.

"Rebecca!" Bronco hurtled the window frame, skidding over broken shards of glass in his haste to get to her.

Too weak even to lift her arms in welcome, she let herself be hauled into his embrace as he dropped to his knees and gathered her tenderly to him. "You're okay. You're okay," he canted.

She could feel him trembling when he rocked her, his heart hammering against her breasts. "I love you, Becca." He pulled back far enough to gaze into her eyes. "I was so afraid I wouldn't get the chance to tell you that. God, I love you so much!"

"I love you, too," she whispered.

"Come on, baby. Let's get you out of here." He helped her climb unsteadily to her feet. Out of the corner of her eye, she saw Agent Castle bending over Tony to check his pulse. As the agent yelled for an ambulance, Bronco led her past the phalanx of SWAT team members through the open door.

Maya Schultz stood on the front stoop pacing back and forth. Grabbing Rebecca's arm, she said, "I am so sorry." Tears shone in her eyes as she fought for her composure. "But you did it, Rebecca. We captured Max's account number, thanks to you—not that we'll need it to charge him, obviously, but it will explain these crazy circumstances." She lifted her gaze to Bronco. "And you," she added. "You saved her life—again."

Bronco shrugged. "I'd say it was a team effort. If you don't mind, I'm going to take her home."

Maya shook her head. "Not yet. I'm sorry, but we'll need to get statements from both of you first."

"We'll be out back then, if that's okay," he suggested.

"Sure. I'll come get you when we're ready."

Keeping one arm securely around her shoulders, Bronco escorted her around the side of the house and into the back yard, past the pool and the gazebo and across the lawn that Max had insisted on mowing himself because the gardener never got it right.

Rudee Inlet glimmered like a black sapphire under the thumb-nail moon hanging over it. The tang of brackish water filled her nostrils, eradicating the nauseating odors of gun oil and gore. Together they stepped out onto the pier, moving slowly over the wooden planks, past the dry dock that housed Max's boat, to the bench positioned at the point that jutted over deep water.

There, they sat down, side by side, thighs and shoulders touching. The wind that caressed her hair cut tiny rippling patterns across the water's glistening surface. On the opposite shore, lights twinkled in the many well-appointed houses.

When she thought about the past few months of her unraveling marriage and her growing friendship with Bronco, she could never have imagined that it would work out this way.

"I'm so lucky," she marveled, turning her head to take in Bronco's beloved profile. "I should be dead right now."

"No," he refuted. "I would never have let that happen." He lifted her hand to his mouth and kissed her knuckles tenderly. "You've been through so much, Becca." He lowered his head to look her in the eye. "Are you okay?"

His question had her raising one of her own. "Did you shoot Max when the SWAT team fired at Tony?" She searched his shadowed gaze. "Or did they kill him, too?"

He visibly swallowed. "Would you love me any less

if I said yes?"

Did it make any difference? she wondered. Max was gone. SWAT would have killed him with or without Bronco's assistance. "No," she decided.

"I meant what I said when I told you I would protect you." His reply seemed to confirm that he'd participated in sending Max out of this world and into the next.

She gave a slow nod. "Then you meant it when you said you loved me, too?" she prompted.

"Hell, yeah, I meant it." His grin put the moon to shame with its luminescence.

Happiness chased away the horror still fresh in her mind. "Well," she declared, "in that case, I'm fine. I'm fine with everything," she added, letting him know that it made no difference whether his bullet had been the one to end Max's life or not. "In fact, I'm terrific."

He squeezed her to him. "I've always known that," he affirmed. "You're way too good for a shallow jerk like me."

She gave his arm a playful slap. "Stop it. You have proven through all of this that you are *nothing* like your father."

He laid his cheek against her temple and sighed with acceptance. "You're right," he admitted on a note of self-acceptance. "Turns out I'm the type to stick around. Bet you'll get sick of me one day," he predicted.

In spite of the horror that was still so fresh in her mind, a droll laugh tickled her throat. "Right," she replied, knowing she would never tire of loving him. "Like *that* is going to happen."

EPILOGUE

Rebecca brushed the hair out of her eyes as they headed into the wind, walking toward the beach from her mother's on-base home in Schofield Barracks, Honolulu. They'd arrived only two hours earlier to a warm Hawaiian welcome from her mother and her husband, complete with *leis* made of plumerias and tuberose. The sun sat warmly on her shoulders. The smells of seafood and suntan oil mingling on the breeze made her smile. In spite of the nightmares that still plagued her, life was good.

"Do you think she likes me?" Bronco's uncertain question drew her gaze to his worried countenance.

"Are you serious?" She squeezed his hand reassuringly. "You had her hook, line, and sinker when you asked her permission to date me. Her husband, too."

"But what if they think it's too soon?" he continued. "Max has been gone less than a month. Seems kind of tactless of us to show up acting like honeymooners."

"Which is why she hinted about you sleeping on the couch in the den."

"No problem," he earnestly agreed. "Whatever

makes her happy."

His eagerness to please brought a laugh out of her. It felt so good to laugh again. "You would do that for me, wouldn't you?"

"Becca, I'd do anything to keep you in my life," he insisted, rubbing his thumb across her knuckles, a gesture that both soothed and aroused her. "If that means sleeping on the couch while I'm here, even though it'll drive me crazy not to hold you at night, I'll do it."

"Don't worry. Mom's pretty progressive. She'll come around when she sees how happy you make me."

To herself, Rebecca admitted that, even though her mother was open-minded, it was a relief not to have to tell her she was pregnant—although disappointment had been Rebecca's first reaction when her period had started a week late. But, since Bronco had hinted that they would have a gaggle of children one day, she hadn't dwelled on her loss for long.

Glancing up at the horizon, she gasped with delight. "Look," she cried, pointing at the panorama that had come suddenly into view. "The ocean looks so much bigger here! It takes up the entire horizon! And it's so much bluer than the Atlantic."

"Looks a little like Puerto Rico," he agreed. He walked faster, pulling her along with him as they hastened toward the picture-perfect vista of palm trees and turquoise water, and the siren sound of waves rolling onto the sand. The public beach was only a short stroll from where her mother and stepfather lived.

"You know, NCIS could have sent us to Idaho instead of Honolulu," Rebecca reflected as they started down a flight of wooden stairs. "We should buy Maya Schultz a gift as a token of our appreciation."

"I was thinking the same thing. Maybe something she and her son would both enjoy."

Sand crunched beneath their sandals as they neared the last step. "Will a month be long enough, do you think?" she asked.

He drew to a stop at her uncertain tone. "Hey." Catching her against him, he raised his hands to cup her face. "This is all just a precaution," he reminded her. "Tony Scarpa was killed by the FBI SWAT team. I killed his cousin," he admitted without a trace of remorse. "Doug Castle says Scarpa senior is old and suffering from Alzheimer's. Even though the FBI proved that Max killed two former mobsters on behalf of the Scarpas, there's no one left in the Scarpa family for the FBI to prosecute, so you're not a threat to them. No one's coming after you."

"I guess not," she agreed. But it was hard to believe that the terror was all behind them.

"Do you honestly think some distant cousin of Tony's is going to go to the trouble of hunting you down? Trust me, once they find out that you've married another Navy SEAL, they'll keep their distance."

Gazing into his frank blue eyes, she felt the last claw of fear loosen its grip on her heart. "Even if someone tried, you would protect me," she pointed out.

"Damn right, I would," he assured her. "I'll protect you and I will never, ever leave you."

Fortunately, he didn't seem to get tired of telling her that, and she never got tired of hearing it. "Wait, did you just propose to me?" Though he'd often sworn that he would be with her forever, this was the first time he'd brought up the actual m-word. She raised her eyebrows at him and waited.

He sent her a slow grin. "I think we should wait six months before I officially propose—don't want to shock your friends and family."

Half-disappointed, half-relieved, she bit her lower lip and nodded her agreement.

"But while we're on the subject, what do you think of a Hawaiian wedding?" He turned and gestured at the beach. "We could get married right here."

"Here?" Following his gaze, she imagined herself in a simple white dress, barefoot, standing next to him with all of his SEAL team buddies in attendance. Recalling their mixed hurt and euphoria when they'd found out that he wasn't dead, she didn't find it hard to believe that they'd fly all the way to Hawaii to attend Bronco's wedding.

"That does sound amazing," she allowed, "but that's asking a bit much of your friends, isn't it? Hawaii is a long way from Virginia."

His forehead creased as he considered her reservations. "True. And some of them haven't forgiven me for keeping them in the dark."

"They understand though," she insisted. Another possible setting came to mind. "What about Montana? Your family is already there, and a flight to the Midwest has got to be cheaper than airfare to Hawaii."

His face lit up with a new idea. "Oh, I know where we're getting married."

She could tell by the exultant look in his eyes that he'd thought of the perfect place.

"Tweedy Mountain," he elaborated.

She nodded. "The place where they were going to spread your ashes—only they weren't yours."

"Trust me, John Doe likes it there," he assured her. "This place is perfect! The first time I climbed to the top, I was nine. I thought I'd climbed all the way to heaven. It was that stunning—paradise on top of the world. Picture a meadow full of wildflowers and snow-capped peaks in every direction."

Imagining it in her mind's eye, she found herself smiling. "I can't wait to see it."

He blinked and looked back down at her. "Wait! We're in freaking Honolulu," he recalled. "What are we doing dreaming of Montana?"

Shucking off his sandals, he issued a whoop of joy and lifted her off her feet. Locking her hips against his shoulder in a fireman's hold, he ignored her shriek of surprise and ran for the surf at full speed.

Dangling upside down, Rebecca clung to him for dear life. "Wait, we're going in now? I still have my clothes on! What about my sandals?"

"Kick them off," he advised.

"What about sharks?" she shrieked, as she shook off her sandals.

"Sharks are afraid of SEALs," he boasted, without any sign of slowing down. Holding her aloft, he charged straight into the crashing waves.

She screamed with laughter which ended on a gasp as he tipped her thigh-deep into the warm, water.

His grin was a picture of devilish delight. "Don't worry," he assured her, swinging her around so that the swells rushing toward them broke against his back instead of over her head. She already knew what his next words would be before he said them.

"I'll protect you," he promised, pulling her deeper and deeper into the ocean. "We're going under on the next one. Get ready," he said, and she peered with trepidation over his shoulder at the next massive swell rolling toward them.

Pinching her nose and catching her breath, Rebecca reflected that as long as she was by his side, she would be ready for anything.

Turn the page for an

excerpt from

FRIENDLY FIRE

The Echo Platoon Series
Book Three

Marliss Melton

An air of festivity accompanied the motley crowd of cruise ship passengers as they shuffled in an unruly line up the gangplank and onto the *Norwegian Pearl*. Even in early April, the noonday sun had begun to infuse the spring air with the kind of humidity expected in the port city of New Orleans. Crew musicians played upbeat jazz on the receiving deck, welcoming the passengers as they stepped off the gangplank onto the floating city that would be their home for the next seven days.

At six feet, three inches, Navy SEAL First Class Jeremiah Winters took advantage of his height to observe what was happening up ahead as he took his first step onto the ship. Crew members had formed a line on either side of the passengers moving down the receiving deck. They hurled confetti, shook hands, and called out words of welcome over the happy music. The tolerant smile on Jeremiah's lean face faded slowly as an unexpected premonition skittered over him, causing his scalp to prickle.

He cut a sidelong glance at his teammate and fellow passenger, Justin Halliday, and wondered if the former NASCAR racer had picked up on the dark energy. Of course, Justin hadn't noticed. Grinning and grooving his way along the deck, the golden haired navigator's thoughts were entirely optimistic as he anticipated their voyage to the Western Caribbean. He had intended to travel with his girlfriend of several years, but their recent break up had necessitated Jeremiah coming in her stead.

I'm imagining the dark energy, he assured himself. After all, he worked day in and day out with a small group of the most highly skilled warriors on the planet protecting innocent people just like this boatload of vacationers. He and Justin kept the populace safe; they didn't mingle with them. But it was hard to dismiss his premonition out of hand, having invested so much time and energy in learning to harness his sixth sense—especially when it whispered that something bad was going to happen.

He dragged his feet. "Wait," he said, putting a hand on Justin's musclebound arm as he hunted for the source of his disquiet.

"What?" Justin's blue-green gaze touched briefly on his profile, and then he, too, started looking around.

Ahead of them, passengers were being pulled aside for their boarding photos, which they could purchase later. The cameraman called out instructions. "You, little one, turn to the right. Mother, shift to the left. Now, everyone smile!" Holding his camera to his eye, he peered through it.

Click, click, click. In Jeremiah's mind, he saw a rifle scope instead of a camera, heard bullets explode from it and punch into the family members, spraying blood and gore over the canvas backdrop. He blinked and the vision disappeared.

"Damn it!"

Justin elbowed him. "Dude, what's wrong?"

Jeremiah looked over his shoulder at the line of passengers behind him. What could he possibly say? *I've got a really bad feeling about this?* His teammates had learned to take his intuitions seriously, but he had no desire to burst Justin's bubble right now, not when this was the happiest he'd seen him since his girlfriend left him. Nor did he wish to ruin their vacation before it even got started. "Nothing. I'm good."

The cameraman waved off the family and called up the next party to stand before the screen. The long auburn tresses of a thirty-something woman captured Jeremiah's attention as he faced forward again. Watching her move into position with her teenage daughter, along with another mother-daughter pair, the breath tangled in his throat as she turned her face in his direction, per the photographer's instructions.

Professor Albright? It couldn't be.

He blinked, doubting his eyes. The college professor who had so utterly captivated him, who had altered the course of his life forever and remained the ideal of womanly perfection in his psyche, had scarcely aged in the five years since he'd left George Mason University. She might be thinner, almost willowy now, her cheekbones more sculpted, but the lips that curved into a smile as she made bunny ears behind her unsuspecting daughter's head, were the same rosy lips that had brought Wordsworth and Coleridge to life for him. They'd shared something intense and illicit and so confusing to his impressionable heart that he had dropped out of school midsemester to become a knight errant, taking on such giants as drug cartels and ISIS extremists in her name.

What were the odds that he would drive all the way from Virginia to New Orleans to board a cruise ship and run into her here?

Click, click, click. The camera's digital sounds summoned the same horrific vision of bullets puncturing flesh, blood spraying, and bodies falling. *Jesus, no! Not her.*

As if drawn to his horrified stare, her gaze shifted past the photographer to make eye contact with Jeremiah. His heart suspended its beat as he waited for a sign of recognition in her soft blue eyes. Her brow knit as if she were struggling to place him, but then she turned away, throwing an arm around her daughter's shoulders. With a prick of hurt, he watched her move away, chatting amiably with her friend.

Picturing himself from her point of view, it wasn't any wonder that she hadn't recognized him. Five years ago, he'd been a lanky twenty-three-year old with thick-lensed glasses. The Navy hadn't just corrected his vision with laser surgery; they'd packed fifty pounds of raw muscle on his frame. Even if she had recognized him, there would be two-thousand-four-hundred passengers sailing to the Western Caribbean on this ship. They could travel for the next seven days and never cross paths again.

But that wasn't what he hoped would happen, was it?

———————◆———————

FRIENDLY FIRE

Marliss Melton is the author of twelve gripping romantic suspense novels, including a seven-book Navy SEALs series, a three-book Taskforce Series, and continuing with the Echo Platoon series. She relies on her experience as a military spouse and on her many contacts in the Spec Ops and Intelligence communities to pen heartfelt stories about America's elite warriors and fearless agency heroes.

Daughter of a U.S. foreign officer, Melton grew up in various countries overseas. She has taught English, Spanish, ESL, and Linguistics at the College of William and Mary, her alma mater. She lives near Virginia Beach with her husband, tween daughter, and four young adult children.

You can find Marliss on Facebook, Twitter and Pinterest. Visit www.MarlissMelton.com for more information.